The McClane Apocalypse
Book Four

Kate Morris

Ranger Publishing
Copyright © 2015 by Ranger Publishing

Note to Readers: This publication contains the opinions and ideas of its author. It is not intended to provide helpful or informative material on the subjects addressed in the publication. The author and publisher specifically disclaim all responsibility for any liability, loss or risk personal or otherwise.

All rights reserved; including the right to reproduce this book or portions of thereof in any form whatsoever. For information, email: Ranger Publishing @gmail.com.
First Ranger Publishing softcover edition, March 2015
Ranger Publishing and design thereof are registered trademarks of Ranger Publishing.
For information about special discounts for bulk purchases, please contact, Ranger Publishing @gmail.com.

Ranger Publishing can bring authors to your live event. For more information or to book an event, contact Ranger Publishing @gmail.com or contact the author directly through KateMorrisauthor.com or authorkatemorris@gmail.com

Cover design by Ebook Launch.com

Manufactured in the United States of America
Library of Congress Cataloging-in-Publication Data is on file
ISBN 13: 978-1507855218
ISBN 10: 1507855214

For my fans: I've included a character sheet at the end of this book for reference purposes. Just a hint, though try not to peek at the list until after Chapter 7. There will be new characters introduced and the same McClanes who we've come to love.

Hope you enjoy the direction the McClane saga is taking. Connect with me through email at authorkatemorris@gmail.com or on Facebook at the McClane Apocalypse fan page or through my website at www.katemorrisauthor.com.

Best Regards,

Kate

Chapter One
Simon

He's been to Clarksville and Nashville for supply runs many times, as well as to the smaller, nearby towns and neighborhoods during the past three years, and it never feels safer, the trip never any easier. A woodpecker sounds off his signature tapping against a tree high above him in the dense forest. It reminds him of automatic machine gun fire. A bitter, late winter wind whips through the surrounding trees and blasts him in the face, causing a sudden chill to run the length of his entire body. His riding companion seems oblivious, however, much the same as he always is.

"We'll make the cabin by nightfall if we keep up at this pace," Cory calls over his shoulder.

Simon would like to tell him to stow it because he could care less how soon they get there. This trip sucks and there is no denying it. Making the pilgrimage in the summer season is considerably easier. Winter weather can be bitterly cold. It's nothing like where he grew up in Arizona.

"Cool," Simon answers because he knows Cory doesn't want to hear him lament about being homesick.

He'd much rather be back at the McClane farm in their shared log home and in front of the wood-burning stove or even in the big house with the calamity and noise of the kids. A few years ago they'd built another small ramshackle hunting cabin closer to Nashville that mimics the one near Clarksville. They have only once seen evidence that anyone had found either, but nothing was stolen. Perhaps someone had only used the cabin for a one night stay to get out of the weather like they do. Cory had been so angry about it that he and John had spent three days patrolling the woods searching out the "creeps" who had squatted in their cabin. It had been a fruitless pursuit. That had happened about a year and a half ago and hadn't been repeated, which left Simon to believe that it was a single, harmless incident and probably just a desperate person or group of persons who had needed to take shelter.

Sometimes John or Kelly goes with them, but they are both busy at the farm and likely relieved that they can pass this duty on to the younger generation of McClanes. They both have their own set of responsibilities to take care of back at the farm. It's understandable that they'd want him and Cory to take on the job of supply runs.

His favorite gelding prances beneath him as if he, too, would rather be back at the farm munching hay or flirting with one of the mares who would likely kick his butt since he's a worthless gelding and not capable of getting the job done, though Simon often thinks he'd like the chance nonetheless.

"I want to go in this time at night, and then we'll sack out at the cabin," Cory says. "We can go back in tomorrow morning again and then be on the trail for home by the end of the day."

Simon calls back his agreement. The 'going in' part that Cory is referring to is the city of Nashville for which they are in route.

Cory has slowed his stallion down to a more manageable pace in an open pasture so that Simon can bring his gelding in beside him. Though his stallion is still young, only four years old, Cory manages him with ease. Even though her grandfather advised it, Reagan had not allowed the stud colt to be gelded. It had turned out to be a wise decision since their other stallion had passed away a year later from colic. Now they have a way of breeding the mares at the farm to keep the stock producing and thriving. The horses are nearly the only source of transportation that they have anymore, the only source of transportation that most people have. Gasoline is reserved for their trips to the clinic in town. Every once in a while when they are in one of the cities or towns, they catch sight of someone on a motorcycle, ATV or even more rare are the people traveling in a car or truck. There aren't exactly any oil refineries still delivering gas to the local 7-Eleven. The family traded two older horses that were dead broke and safe for riding to the Reynolds family for two new dairy cows about three and a half years ago. Trading is about all that anybody does anymore.

"I hope we can find another carburetor for the tractor," Cory says as he peers into the distant tree line.

"Yeah, me, too. Gonna suck if we can't get both planters going this coming spring," Simon replies as he spies a hawk circling overhead, likely searching for a late day meal of mouse, rat or some other undesirable rodent.

"No kidding," Cory companionably agrees.

He's easy to get along with and they have become like brothers instead of what they really are, which are orphans of the new world. Simon had liked Cory, his brother and young sister and all of the McClane family from the start. They were honest, hard-working and loyal people, and their sense of family was like none that Simon had ever seen before. It made the ache of losing his own mother, father and sister just a little easier to cope with.

"Did you hear that?" Simon asks and reins in his horse.

Cory spins sharply, pivoting his horse on just its rear legs and faces backward toward the woods they've just left.

"Yeah, I heard it," he answers with agitation.

The sounds of twigs breaking and dried leaves crunching can be heard above the wind and the birds and the sounds of nature all around them. Someone is either following them or moving through these desolate woods, as well. The lush camouflage of thick underbrush and the wide, flat leaves are gone from the trees, leaving them more exposed to being seen. All of the summer foliage is dead, snow-covered or wilted and covering the ground instead.

Simon swings his horse and the pack horse about, and they trot over to seek cover at the edge of the forest to await their would-be stalker. Cory takes his rifle from its scabbard while simultaneously flinging his reins over a long, spindly branch to stay his stallion. He slides fluidly and near silently to the ground. Simon removes his revolver from his hip holster but does not dismount. It is imperative that should Cory be shot and killed, then Simon will still make it home to the farm, especially with the two remaining horses. Unfortunately, the depletion of ammunition in the country hasn't completely run its course. People are still shooting and killing one another on a daily basis for food, for supplies, for women and for survival.

"Easy, bud," Simon shushes his horse who is starting to feel that familiar tension of its rider whenever something bad is about to happen. Simon hates this. He hates the dread that comes with the violence this world has bred. He hates the apprehension. And most of all, he hates the idea of any harm coming to Cory or that his best friend could be killed.

Cory signals to him and they both nod in understanding that Simon will stay put while Cory hunts down the predator. He disappears into the forest, going wide and to their south so that he can come up behind whoever is following them. It only takes but a few minutes for him to return and he's looking about as pissed off as one person could be.

"Damn it, Em!" he is shouting as he stomps from the woods in a rage of two hundred pounds of pure muscle and righteous anger. "What the hell were you thinking?"

A second later, Em plods along looking sullen and thoroughly reprimanded on her chestnut mare. She is Cory's little sister and only fifteen years old, way too young to be going on a dangerous supply run with them. Unfortunately, she also knows this because she'd vehemently argued with them the previous evening at the farm over this very point. Apparently she didn't take to Cory and his side of the argument about being too young to tag along because here she is. They are simply too far along to turn back now to return her.

"I was thinking for myself for once, Cory," Em grumbles in an outburst of petulant teen anger as Cory reaches his mount again.

"Bullshit!" Cory shouts as he jerks his stallion's head too roughly, garnering him a snort. "You're just a kid. You don't belong out here with us. Kelly's gonna be pissed. Did you even think of anyone back at the farm? They're probably freaking out that you're missing."

"Cory, I left them a note," she tries to explain. "They'll know I'm with you guys. I'm not a complete idiot. It's cool."

"It's *not* cool, Em," Cory rants.

He is quite the adversary when he wants to be, which Simon has seen too many times for his taste. They've both had to do things that are unmentionable to stay alive during these runs for supplies.

"I'll be fine, Cory. Tell him, Simon!" she pushes.

This is one family battle that Simon really doesn't want to get involved in. Also, he doesn't want Cory to haul off and deck him. He can be kind of volatile sometimes. Luckily for Simon, though, Cory's anger is usually pointed toward dangerous people who would mean them harm.

"Um… well," is all he manages before Cory is right back on her.

"You do something stupid like this again, young lady, and you'll be grounded for a month!" Cory reprimands with loud authority.

"So? What are you going to do? Ground me from chores?" Em asks in a more hushed tone.

"No, but I can lump onto your chores and you can stop going over to hang out with the Johnson kids," Cory threatens in a father-like tone.

She goes back to sulking and follows in their wake. Simon tries to placate her with a conciliatory smile, but it doesn't work. She stares off to the side, snubbing him for not defending her.

"We should radio home," Simon tells Cory as he pulls his gelding in next to his friend's horse in the open pasture right before they cross into deeper woods again. Cory just nods with unresolved irritation.

"Tango Three to Bravo One," his friend says into the walkie-talkie.

Almost a full minute goes by before Kelly's voice comes through loud and clear.

"Gotcha, Tango, go ahead," Kelly returns.

"Got a stowaway," Cory retorts angrily.

"Yeah, we just figured that out about five minutes ago," his brother answers.

"Should we bring her back to base?" Cory asks.

He is clearly having mixed feelings as to whether or not they should scrap this trip to return Em to the safety of the farm.

"Negative, Tango," Kelly replies. "You're too far out now for a return anyways."

"Right," Cory says.

"Just be careful. Watch your asses out there."

"Roger that, Bravo. Over and out," Cory tells him with a sigh of frustration.

Cory stashes the radio in his bag again and leads them through the rough, dense forestry of Tennessee. They ride in silence for another few hours or so until the hunting cabin comes into view. The small structure is nestled at the bottom of a ravine and covered in thick foliage, sticks and forest debris strategically placed there to conceal it better.

"Let's leave Em here with the extra horse, and we'll head into the city," Cory calls over to him. "It'll be safer for her, and we can move faster without her."

"Sure, Cory," Simon agrees and also dismounts as they come to a stop in front of the rustic cabin.

Em whines, "I want to go, too, Cory!"

"Don't even start, Em," Cory berates her. "I'm already pissed that you're even here. You aren't going with us."

His friend lugs heavy bags into the cabin that contain their food and supplies for the two to three day trip as Simon dismounts and slings his reins over the cabin's hitching post, installed there by John and Reagan two years ago.

"It would be safer if I went with you," she pleads her case when Cory returns. "I could stay somewhere with the horses till you guys get back to them."

"No way, Em," Cory lectures as he re-tightens his stallion's girth. "It's not safe there. It's sometimes a damn war zone. You're safer here."

Simon is keeping pace and has placed the pack horse in the timber frame, three-sided shed they built last spring. It isn't exactly a fancy show barn with individual stalls, rubber mats, hooks for bridles, or gold-framed nameplates, but it keeps them dry and warm which is preferable to standing outdoors in the rain, snow or cold all night. As he's taking off the saddle, Em comes up to him, and he frowns because he knows what's coming.

"Simon, can't you talk to him? I want to go with you and help, not sit here and babysit the horses and an empty cabin," she implores with big puppy eyes.

She has hit a growth spurt recently, but she sure as heck isn't going to get as tall as her brothers anytime soon. She's maybe five eight or so, but her two older brothers are bulls. They each look like they could've played for Simon's home state's Arizona Cardinals football team. Cory topped out a few years ago at around six-three, which is still a few inches shorter than Kelly. However, Simon's only five-ten, the same height his father had been. His red hair and his height are the only things he will ever know for sure that he inherited from his deceased father. Even though Simon's almost twenty, he's not thinking he's going to get any taller and neither does Doc, whose opinion is more important. Cory had stopped growing after his nineteenth birthday, something Reagan said she was glad for because she'd joked that if he kept hitting growth spurts, they'd need to butcher an extra steer.

"Em, come on. Don't make me get in the middle of this," he says gently. "If Cory says no, then it's a no, kid."

He's trying to placate her, but he knows she's not about to relent so easily. Cory calls over to them that he's going inside and will be ready to leave in a moment.

"But if I go with you, then I can stay with the horses so nobody gets to them, right?"

She is using her flirty wiles and her swingy, chestnut hair to try to sway him. Normally it works, but never if he has to go against his best friend. Simon is well aware of the fact that Em has a crush on him, but he'd never act on it. She's like a little sister to him. It's the same way that Cory looks at Samantha.

"Yeah, I guess. But that argument isn't going to work on your brother, Em. He's pretty peeved at you right now," Simon tells her the obvious.

She smiles broadly and takes the saddle blanket from him to hang over a board to dry. Cory joins them a moment later.

"You ready, Simon?"

"Yeah, just a minute. Gotta hang this bridle and then we can get moving," he replies.

"I'm ready, too!" Em declares so slyly as if her brother had not told her ten minutes ago that she wasn't going.

"Em, seriously. Grow up. You aren't going," Cory tells her and turns to leave.

Her next argument stops him, though.

"Simon agrees that I could be helpful by looking after the horses for you while you guys do the raid, ok?"

Simon's eyes about pop out of his head. What the heck is she doing?

7

"Really?" his friend asks. "You're encouraging this crap, Simon?"

Cory runs a hand through his shoulder length black hair.

"Well, she could keep an eye on the horses," Simon states but gets a deadly glare from Cory. "Remember that one time a couple years ago in Clarksville when those two men tried to take our horses and we caught them at the last second before they took off with them? That could always happen again. Besides, we'll tuck her away somewhere safe with the horses where she's not in danger."

He is aiding Em, although he's not sure why he is doing so. She literally beams at him. She's so pretty and youthful and positive and everything that her brother is not. Cory's only twenty-two years old, but he has enough negative mileage on him to be ninety. He's seen and done too much to carry the flair of youthfulness or naïve hopefulness with him.

"Fine, damn it!"

Cory curses with a fury that is now mostly aimed at Simon. Great. He doesn't like it when there is strife between them. Even if it is rare that it happens.

He continues on with the same anger, "She can go with us, but she stays with the horses. We'll leave her at the one place near that car dealership that we stowed the horses before."

"Ok, Cory. That'll work," Simon answers cautiously.

They ditch the rest of the bags and remount to move out to the city that lies only about four miles further east. The sun is just setting when the skyline of Nashville breaks over the tree-lined horizon. Soon it will be dark, but they have their night vision gear. Unlike Simon, Cory prefers to move around in the dark and feels safest when they are doing so. They are mindful of danger as they approach the rear of the permanently closed car dealership where what few vehicles still remain have been torched. They will leave Em about ten yards behind the building still well within the cover of the surrounding forest where she will be safe.

"If we aren't back in one hour, leave for the cabin and wait there," Cory explains as he dismounts.

Em hops down, too, and mostly huffs and stomps dramatically because she wants to go with them.

Cory glares at her and continues, "I brought you this far and should've left your ass back at the cabin. Stay here. I'll be back, ok?"

"Fine," Em complains. "But tomorrow I'm going with you guys. This sucks! I'm not a baby, Cory."

"Then don't act like one and wait here," her big brother orders.

Simon takes his rifle from its scabbard, checks his pistol at his hip and pulls his night vision goggles from the sack on his horse. Cory is mimicking his movements and getting ready to move out, as well.

"Stay put, Em," Simon says with a smile. "We'll be back quicker than this." He snaps his fingers and gets a smile from her. However, she goes right back to frowning at her brother, who just shakes his head impatiently at her.

"I'll stay and babysit the horses," she laments. "Great! This is so exciting."

Her sarcasm makes Cory chuckle and tap the tip of her upturned nose affectionately. He also snatches her into a bear hug and then releases her.

"We'll be right back, kid," Cory tells her. "Then we can all go back to the cabin and you can make us dinner!"

"Hey!" Em says on a pucker, trying to hide a grin.

They move quickly through the city, jogging here, sprinting there, collecting items as they go and stuffing them into their backpacks. There are a few areas where fires are visible in the distance that people have likely lit to stay warm. Usually these people are harmless or just indigent persons trying to stick together for support and sharing fires for warmth or cooking. Mostly they are newly appointed victims of the modern apocalypse. Some could be lawyers or professionals, former doctors or even the mayor of this city. Many people have taken to living on the streets of America, their homes likely raided or burned to the ground or destroyed by natural disasters. One time a few years ago when they were doing a neighborhood raid near Clarksville with John and Kelly, they'd spied a small group of people who had barricaded off their short street in the suburbs. They'd used abandoned vehicles and tall fencing to cordon off and secure the street. None of these people have the luxury of living somewhere like the remote, flourishing McClane farm, however.

It doesn't take long to find a small, mom-and-pop auto parts store on an obscure, side road in the city where they locate and take the last two carburetors on one of the back shelves in the storage overflow. Cory also grabs a few other parts and hoses that he says may come in handy. Simon leads the way out the back door, and they take a knee in the alley. The pack on Simon's back is heavy and full with contraband items. Pretty much all of the food items in stores are gone now, but sometimes other, more obscure things like rope, buckets, tools, books, car and tractor parts, and building supplies are still there. His pack probably weighs a good sixty pounds.

"We'd better head back to Em. Saw a band moving to our west," he tells his friend. His stomach grumbles in protest of keeping such late dinner hours, and Cory smirks at him.

"Should I have brought you a croissant, good sir?" Cory teases with good humor.

Simon punches his shoulder. It's a massive thing, Cory's shoulder.

"Yeah, I saw them, too," Cory relays. "You're right, bro. We should move."

They double time it back to the site where they left Cory's sister of whom he is so protective. They are both protective of Em and Samantha, as well. They are orphaned young women who need all the protection they can get in this cruel new world.

They carefully make their way down the steep hill behind the dealership and move through the dense woods behind it to where Em awaits them. Her eyes are wide and frightened when they get to her.

"What is it, Em?" Simon inquires and touches her arm lightly.

"I saw some people a little while ago over there," she tells them in a rush and points to their south.

Her small hands shake, so Simon squeezes her right one to give her courage.

Cory immediately scans the area and then does so again with the night vision scope on his rifle to get a better gauge of their outlying surroundings. Simon does the same.

"I've got nothin'," Cory says.

Simon agrees with him, "Yeah, me either. We should move."

"Em, mount up. Let's get out of here," Cory orders and they all jump into action.

They are twenty yards into their return trip to the cabin when a shot rings out in the moonlit night, causing both men to jerk their heads to their left where the sound originated. Cory spins his stallion in a tight circle and trots to the rear of their caravan.

"Go!" Cory shouts. "Take her to safety, Simon. Go!"

Two more shots are fired. Cory takes off at a canter to hunt down their enemy as Simon takes lead and rushes with Em in the direction of the cabin. He's taking a different route, lest they are followed. John and Kelly had taught them when they were still just teen boys how to take evasive maneuvers, avoid the enemy and get out of a tight spot. Within minutes, Cory is back with them, and they're all riding at a fast pace.

"What happened?" Simon asks him as they climb a short hill.

"Shot two. Think there were more, but they got away," Cory answers. "Let's just keep moving."

They certainly don't want to engage the enemy in a firefight since Em is with them.

When they come to flat ground again, another shot rings out, this time from ahead of them. It whizzes past Simon, and another follows in lightning succession. They had not anticipated the enemy circling around and flanking them. This is the type of move they'd do. It doesn't generally happen to them. It pisses Simon off that they were able to do this, and he unsheathes his pistol and quickly fires directly at two men on foot at the crest of the hill. He hits the one in center mass, and Cory strikes the other to the head with a round from his rifle.

They ease over behind a copse of trees and dense foliage to obtain better cover and to observe. Holding as still as concrete statues, the horses also picking up on the nerves of the situation, their group waits for more gunfire or movement. Nothing happens, though. Apparently the threat has been neutralized. They wait like this for another full minute before turning back toward their trail. They start out at a slow trot. Time to get back to camp and lock down for the night.

A dull thud behind him alerts Simon, and he swings around in his saddle just in time to see Em hit the ground. She lands hard on the forest floor. He and Cory rein in tight, skidding to stops. Em's horse trots a few feet away from them.

"Em!" Cory screams.

He swings his leg over the thick neck of his stallion and rushes to his sister, falling to his knees beside her. Cory rolls her onto her back as Simon jumps down and whips off his goggles. He clicks on the flashlight from his cargo pocket. They hadn't even realized she'd been shot. Under the harsh glare of the grayish white light from the flashlight's beam, Simon can see a lot of blood.

Rushing to his saddle, he unhooks his medical bag and then drops to his knees beside Cory, who is cradling his sister's upper torso and head in his lap. It looks like she's been hit in the shoulder, but the bullet does not appear to have gone all the way through as he examines her more closely. That's not good. It will need to be extracted.

"We gotta get her home to the farm," Cory says in a panic.

Simon can read the fear in his friend's eyes. They've been through bad situations together but nothing like this.

"I don't think that's a good idea, Cor," Simon counters. "It's too far to ride. Let's get her back to the cabin where I can work on her and get her stabilized for the trip. We'll have to radio the farm. Have Doc or Reagan come out to the cabin with supplies and a truck to transport her."

As he is relaying this, Simon has taken strips of cloth from his satchel and is pressing them to her shoulder. Cory also pushes another rag tightly against it to squelch the blood flow. Simon uses a piece of long, thin material to tie the cloths tightly against her shoulder, wrapping it under her armpit and knotting it. Em's lovely hazel eyes are wide with fear, and she's clearly in shock because she says nothing but stares up at them with blind faith.

"Let's move," Cory demands as he quickly collects his horse and mounts with a wide swing into the saddle.

Simon carefully, gently lifts Em and then passes her with extra care up into Cory's lap where he balances her in front of him.

"Just go!" Simon tells him with new urgency. "I'll get her horse and be right behind you. Cory, just go."

Cory wastes no time in spurring his stallion into motion and literally races over the hill, disappearing from Simon's line of sight. Simon chases down Em's frightened mare and remounts his gelding. He gallops after Cory, not bothering to look overly long at the two dead men on the hill who are prone and awkwardly twisted in puddles of their own blood. Clenching the reins of both horses in one hand, he yanks the satellite radio from his saddlebag so that he can call the family.

"Tango Three to Bravo One, come in," Simon pleads desperately. His impatience at not getting an immediate response erupts from him a guttural and urgent groan.

"Bravo One here. We gotcha'," John says after another minute.

"Em's been shot, John," Simon responds. "We're headed to camp two right now."

"Shot?"

John's voice is disbelieving. Of course, he's incredulous. Nobody in their family has been injured like this during any of their city raids. John had been stabbed during the raid on their neighbor's farm, but none of them have been wounded like this.

"Repeat sit rep. Repeat," John demands.

"Em's been shot! We're going to camp two so I can look at her. Shoulder shot. We need Reagan or Doc."

"Got it. We'll be there within the hour. We'll meet you on OWR7," John responds.

Their code names for the oil well roads that run like veins and arteries throughout their county and the surrounding, rural counties tell Simon exactly where they'll meet. They have used these roads for the past three years to move about, which is considerably safer than using the main roads or freeways.

"I'll get her stabilized and you can take her to the...," he doesn't finish. Talking about the farm on the radio is off limits, to say the least.

"Over and out," John replies in a serious, austere tone.

Simon repeats the mantra and spurs his horse harder, pushing him even though the gelding has already been ridden so many hours today. When he gets to the cabin, Cory is already there, his horse standing near the stables and recklessly abandoned which is not something he would do under normal circumstances. Cory is very conscientious and caring toward the animals on the farm. Simon ditches both horses in the same fashion, however, and sprints for the cabin.

"Easy, Em," Cory says softly, placating his sister.

13

He's also holding her down by pressing her shoulder into the mattress.

"Everything's gonna be ok. Simon's here now. Everything's cool, Em," his friend avowals.

Simon is hoping that Cory's prediction is correct. He lights the two oil lamps and takes his medical bag to the bedside. Cory has already removed her coat and sweater, leaving her in a simple blue t-shirt that exposes a bloody mess.

"The family will be here in less than an hour," Simon imparts to his friend, who looks nearly out of his mind with worry. "We need to meet them on the oil well road so that they can transfer her back home."

"Ok, that's good. That's good," Cory says quickly.

"Let's get her stabilized before we get you back on the horse with her. I'm gonna tie this all off," Simon explains.

Cory holds a flashlight for him as Simon ties a tight strip of cloth around Em's shoulder wound and adds more padding underneath. A dark red droplet splatters onto the toe of his distressed leather work boot, causing him to look down. Simon grabs the flashlight out of Cory's hand and scans the bed, the side of it and Em's torso and hip. The mattress under her is soaking with blood, but it's not near her shoulder at all. It's under her bottom.

"She's been hit somewhere else, too, Cory. Look," he says in a rush of panic.

Em says, "My leg hurts."

Cory's eyes grow even wider with fear. As they move her gently, easing her onto her side, Simon has a pang of terror punch to his stomach. Em moans loudly from the pain of being moved.

"Easy, Em," Cory coos to her. "We're just checking you out, honey."

The mattress and bedding are soaking through with her blood, and Simon sticks the flashlight right into the wound area so that he can better see what the hell they're up against. She's been shot through her hip area somewhere, and blood is literally pumping out.

"I'm sorry, Cory," she says weakly. "I should've listened to you."

"It's ok, kid. It's gonna be ok, Em," Cory tells her softly. "Just be easy. Be still, Em."

When Simon regards his friend, there are tears streaming down Cory's face, but he's not even sure if Cory realizes it. Simon frantically pushes another clean towel against her wound, but when he pulls it back to see what he's dealing with, it starts streaming blood again. He yanks the material of her pants away so that he can find the source to stop the bleeding.

"I'm really cold, Cor. Is that normal?" she asks.

Simon is working as rapidly as his fingers can move. He's found the entrance and is glad to see that there is an exit, as well. Unfortunately, it seems as if an artery has been hit because he doesn't think veins would be pumping blood this fast or hard. He cuts the material away with scissors and presses hard again to get the bleeding to stop.

"Yeah, it's normal, Em," Cory lies. "It's cold outside tonight. You're just cold from that, ok? You'll be fine. You'll be just fine, honey. Simon's got you covered. We're here, and Simon's gonna get you fixed right up and then we're taking you to meet Doc and Reagan."

Cory is soothingly stroking her forehead and holding the flashlight again for him. Simon doesn't dare look up at him. There is blood on both of their hands, though his friend doesn't seem to care.

He pushes more cloths against her side. It isn't working, but he can hardly do surgery on her in this cabin. He just needs to stifle the bleeding and get her stabilized. He rips another piece of cotton from his sack and ties it as tightly as he can around her slim thigh. She is no doubt going to need a blood donor. He's afraid he might be hurting her by tying it so tightly, but there's no choice.

"We gotta get her to that road," he says to Cory, who nods. "We need to move. We have to get her to Doc as quick as we can. I've got this tied good, but I can't see to do anything more."

Simon ties off more rags around Em's slim hip as tightly as he can get them so that the bleeding stops.

"Cory?" Em asks as they roll her onto her back again.

Simon rushes to the cabinet and pulls down a wool blanket that will keep her warm for the ride. Thank God they aren't too far from that oil well road.

"Yeah, Em? What is it, honey?" Cory asks his beloved sister.

"I love you, you know," she confides without guile.

He is the only person with whom she is so openly affectionate. Losing her parents, having those parents replaced with Cory had changed her, made her guarded with most people. She's not even as close with Kelly or any of the women on the farm as she is with Cory. She's been his constant shadow since Simon had come to live with the McClanes almost four years ago.

"I know, kid. I love you, too," Cory says unashamedly. "Come on. We gotta move, honey. I'll try to be gentle, honey."

"Lift her torso and I'll slip this blanket under her, Cory," Simon commands easily.

Cory does as he says, and Simon slides the heavy blanket under and around Em's slight body. She tries to whisper something to Simon, but her voice is too quiet to hear.

"Easy now, Em," Simon instructs. "Cory, lay her back and I'll hit her with morph before we move her to the horses. I don't want her to be in pain."

Cory makes brief eye contact, his dark eyes sick with worry, but he nods anyway. When they gently lay her back again, Simon fishes the morphine vial out of his bag and pops off the cap, squirts a tad out the end of the hypodermic.

"Em?" Cory says in a rushed panic. "Em?"

His voice is so strained and urgent that Simon looks up. Cory shakes his sister as Simon catches a glimpse of her. Her eyes are open and unblinking.

Simon jumps into action. He performs CPR as Cory looks on helplessly.

"Cory!" Simon shouts and snaps his friend out of his frozen state. It's enough to get Cory to start blowing puffs of air into his sister's mouth.

Simon works for longer than he can calculate. Seconds turn to minutes. He pumps her chest, and Cory blows again into her mouth. Again and again they repeat the process. Simon takes out the emergency stash of adrenaline and plunges the needle into her chest. There is no hesitation in his movement. He's been working in the field as a medic for almost four years and at the clinic in town for as long. There is no choice in the matter. She's dying. He's seen Reagan do this once on a patient who'd been crushed by debris in a crumbling building. They'd brought their family member to the only clinic that was around, Doc McClane's old practice. It hadn't worked then. It isn't working now. He resumes his chest compressions. Cory resumes breathing the essence of life into Em's small body.

There's just no bringing her back. Her blood loss has taken her life, stopped her heart. The second gunshot must have hit her femoral artery to have bled her out so quickly, leading to cardiac arrest. Without a proper surgical room, equipment and a blood transfusion, this type of wound in the field is hopeless.

"I'm sorry, Cory," he says as he stumbles back from her many minutes later. Simon hits the wall behind him and stops. "Jesus, Cor. I'm so sorry."

The look on Cory's face is one of pure horror. He emits a broken sob of sadness and heartbreak mixed into one frightening, God awful sound as he pulls her limp, frail figure to his chest. Simon flinches from Cory, afraid his friend may hurt him. He doesn't, though. Cory is shaking from head to toe.

Finally, he simply stands, lays her gently down, turns away a moment, then turns back to her. He takes a deep breath and kneels beside her again. He bows his head as if in prayer and remains there for a few long moments with his eyes closed and his hand on hers. Then he turns her small hand over, unclasps the gold bracelet she and the other women at the farm all wear and removes it. He stows it away in the cargo pocket on his coat. Cory slowly wraps her in the blanket on which she's lying but not before he closes her lifeless eyes. Then he takes a length of rope from the cabinet and ties her blanket around her.

"Give me your ammo," Cory demands hoarsely, stoically.

Simon notices that his hands no longer shake. He is back to being himself, cool and hard.

"What?" Simon asks with a certain amount of confusion. He blinks hard at his friend, whose look is so wild and feral.

"Give me your extra ammo," he demands again with an extended hand.

His tone is so firm that Simon does as he says and hands over his three extra magazines for his rifle and the one extra mag for his pistol. Cory sets them on the bed. He then lifts his dead sister carefully, cradling her as if she is still alive. He exits the cabin which forces Simon to follow him. Does he wish to bury her?

With impatient anger, Cory snatches the reins of the pack

horse, causing the animal to back up a step and toss its head. He carefully lays Em across the saddle on her stomach. He ties her body down so that she won't fall off the other side. Next, he catches Simon's horse and hands him both sets of reins.

"Take my sister home," Cory mandates.

"Ok, Cory," Simon agrees as he takes the reins. "Get your horse. We'll just leave the gear here and…"

"No," Cory interrupts him. "I'm not coming."

"What do you mean, Cory? You have to…"

"Take my sister home," Cory interrupts again and just continues. "Take her home to the farm. I want her buried at the farm. Bury her next to Grams on the hill."

"Cory…" Simon tries to say more, but his voice cracks.

"Take her and go, Simon," Cory responds with flint. "Take her home. Please take her home for me."

This time he does make eye contact, but Simon wishes that he wouldn't have. The look in Cory's eyes is haunting. Simon knows with certainty that he'll never forget this look in his best friend's eyes. There is something so intensely horrifying there that Simon does not argue again. He's too afraid to.

Simon takes the reins, mounts his gelding and leaves for the oil well road where the family will be waiting for them to deliver Em safely. They will not be expecting her dead body to be greeting them there. When he is less than a mile away, Simon hears a scream of rage and anguish like he's never heard in all his nineteen years on this earth. It sends a chill down his spine that he is sure will never fully fade.

Chapter Two
Paige

The sun has set, which means that the temperature will be falling fast. She wraps a blanket around Maddie and tucks it tightly down into the space between the wall and the bed so she doesn't kick it off in the middle of the night. Paige pushes the little girl's hair back from her forehead and presses a kiss there.

"She out?" Talia questions from the open doorway.

"Like a log," Paige returns as she retrieves the oil lamp she'd only just placed on the dresser.

"Good," Talia whispers. "We need to have a meeting."

Paige nods and adjusts the small kerosene heater. They will all four sleep in this room later for safety reasons. She steps around the queen size mattress they'd dragged into this room yesterday and follows her friend from the once nicely appointed kid's room in this broken down mansion. There weren't any dead bodies in this one, which is why they'd chosen it to crash in for a few days. They walk carefully down the stairs, avoid tripping and falling or twisting an ankle on the debris scattered everywhere. Paige doesn't know where the occupants of this home have gone, but apparently they left in a hurry because some of their belongings have been dropped and discarded or forgotten.

"Gavin back yet?" she asks of her friend.

"No, not yet, but he should be soon."

Talia sets her own lamp down on the granite counter-top in the expensive kitchen as Paige places hers on the round, bird's eye maple table with the intricate wrought iron base. Their simple meal awaits them there, as well. Tonight it's canned tuna, some cooked squirrel meat from yesterday, some greens picked from the field behind the house and a can of black beans all to be split equally among them. For a special dessert tonight, Paige has been saving a can of apple pie filling that she found a week ago in a desolate corner of a burned-out grocery store. It had likely been accidentally kicked and had skidded across the floor to that forgotten corner.

She'd fed Maddie about an hour ago, and Paige had made her promise not to tell their secret about the apple pie filling dessert while Talia was busy going through the upstairs closet searching for some clean clothing to pilfer. Maddie had eaten two helpings of the pie filling, and Paige made sure to give her a big portion of the greens and beans, too. She's only four years old. She needs the nutrients and proteins more than they do.

Talia takes plates from the custom made maple cupboards and silverware from the drawers, placing them on the table that Paige had wiped clean of three years' worth of dust earlier today. The upstairs bedding they'd taken out to the back yard and had shaken out dust and dirt. Luckily this home still has bedding. It's rare. They've already made plans to take some of it with them when they leave. Last fall while camping in the forest in their two tents, some of their supplies had been stolen while they were fetching water and Gavin was hunting for squirrels or rabbits. They'd immediately packed up what was left and took off. They've had shoddy, threadbare blankets and one sleeping bag since then. This home has apparently not been raided for much because it's still stock full of supplies, minus food, of course.

"Found some clothing upstairs. Think there's some stuff that you can use, too, Paige," Talia offers.

"Awesome," she declares happily. "These clothes could damn near stand up without me."

Talia laughs and agrees. "Yeah, mine, too! We are some nasty, skanky chics, huh?"

"Ya' got that right," Paige jokes. It's rare that they joke, laugh or smile about anything. Their days are simply about staying alive, and there's usually no room for anything else. "Haven't washed my hair in over a week. Maybe I'll do that tonight. Gonna suck as usual."

"Yeah, that's going to be one cold wash, girl," Talia concurs with a smile.

They have no hot water. They almost never do. Sometimes they'll heat water on an open campfire so that Maddie doesn't have to wash with cold water, especially not now with winter still hanging around. Paige pines for the warm weather of Georgia where she'd been attending college when the first tsunamis hit. Her home state's weather was even warmer, milder and super hot in the summer. She misses Arizona. But as much as she misses her home, she misses her family so much that the pain from it is hard to even think clearly sometimes.

"No kidding," Paige says. "But I'm starting to smell like a grizzly bear."

There is a soft tapping on the door that connects the home to the attached garage. It's Gavin. This is his signal that it's him and not some creep predator.

Talia crosses quickly to the door, unlocks it and ushers their companion inside. He has a dusting of snowflakes clinging to the nylon material of his winter coat.

"Snowing again, huh?" Paige asks. She hates this snow shit.

When she was seventeen, she'd gone with her brother and mother with a small group of their family friends to Aspen to ski. Their father was detained in D.C. for a special vote that he needed to be present for. She'd hated the snow then, too. Also, she'd fallen and broken her wrist on the first hill. Yeah, snow sucks. Talia's from New Orleans, though, so she's not at all used to it. Gavin's a former South Carolina native, so he basically feels the same as Paige about the cold, miserable Tennessee weather.

"Yes, and I'm froze," he complains and stomps a few times to clear the snow from his boots and clothing.

"Find anything?" Talia asks as he sets his sack on the counter.

"Sure did," he declares with a big smile. "Went a little farther than me and Paige did yesterday and hit six homes in the next neighborhood over."

"Gavin, that's kind of far," Paige points out. "You shouldn't be going that far without one of us."

"Yeah, Gav. We've only got a few rounds of ammo left. That's dangerous," Talia also gangs up on him.

He just smiles again and tosses his knitted hat onto the counter, followed by his holey gloves. His sandy blonde hair is damp from the snow where it hangs below the line of his hat. Talia needs to cut it for him again. It's getting too long.

"Relax, girls," he chastises. "It's all good. I got a box of macaroni and cheese."

"Oooh," Paige says with awe. They haven't had anything like that for months. Mostly it ends up being wild meat and edible picked greens.

"Yeah, there's more," he adds with genuine enthusiasm.

He starts removing the items from his bag and stacks them on the counter. There is a bar of soap, a tapered candle, two lighters, a stuffed doll for Maddie, a can of creamed corn, a half full bottle of shampoo, three pairs of socks, a small bag of oatmeal, a new pair of used gloves for Maddie and two cans of salmon.

"Wow, Gavin, this is a lot," Paige exclaims.

"Told ya' it was worth it," he says.

They'd argued earlier today when he said he was going on a run by himself. He says it's because he can move faster without her or Talia with him, but Paige knows it's really only because he wants them to be safe.

Paige smiles at him and then the three of them embrace in a warm hug. They'll make it another week with this much food, along with the wild game they catch. They've become quite talented with setting snares and hunting with the bow and arrow that Gavin uses.

"You did good, Gav," Talia praises. "Now let's eat!"

They all agree and take a seat at the luxurious table with the pricey table settings. The floral pattern on the dinnerware reminds Paige of her mother's dishes. She chokes down her tuna and squirrel meat and tries not to think of her mother. She knows that her mom is dead. During their last, sketchy conversation, her brother had broken the news of it to her.

Now she travels with this ragtag group of survivors and just focuses on staying alive another day. They'd met at a FEMA disaster center that wasn't much more than a couple hundred tents, cots and draped off areas in the former Atlanta Braves stadium. It was there that she and Talia had become fast friends. They had made friends with another woman named Jenny, but she'd passed away from a bad strain of flu and left them with baby Maddie. The FEMA workers had wanted to take Maddie from them and send her to another camp for orphans, but Talia had jumped in and claimed her as her own. The fact that they are both light-skinned African American had helped. The fact that the FEMA workers hadn't wanted to pry a crying baby from its supposed mother had also helped. The fact that Gavin, a complete stranger to them at the time, had come over and claimed to be the father had sealed the deal. And they've been a band of misfit survivors ever since.

When they are finished, they do the best they can with cleaning the dishes and utensils, using as little water as they can from the buckets they'd filled from a nearby stream. Water conservation is one of their daily struggles and something they are constantly working to improve upon. They've learned how to collect water in cisterns, store water in sanitized jugs and even how to find it when they are traveling in the forest.

There are so many things that Paige is thankful for every day, but there is a truckload of regret that she also carries with her. She regrets arguing with her mother about going to Georgia Tech instead of a college closer to home. She regrets being rebellious with her father, who worked as a senator for their state. She regrets not leaving college and going home when the situation overseas had started escalating. And most of all she regrets not being there for her brother and that he was all alone in Arizona when their mother was killed, and he was forced to leave the state with their aunt, who their mother had disliked so intensely.

"I think we're getting close," Gavin states when they are finished eating and sitting around the table again.

Even though it's only seven o'clock in the evening, the sun set almost two hours ago, which usually leaves them in near darkness. Sometimes if they find extra oil for their lanterns, they'll play a hand or two of cards. But most nights they turn in immediately after dinner and get moving again, weather permitting, at first light.

"Me, too, Gavin," Paige returns.

Talia pulls out the wrinkled, tattered map of Tennessee that they found almost a year ago and opens it, spreading it out on the smooth surface of the table.

"Look here," she states as she points to a section near the west. "We passed through Franklin last week. We're getting close. This looks like we're almost to Springfield."

"Right," Paige agrees. "Maybe another ten miles or so to Springfield and then another twenty or less to Pleasant View."

"We could maybe be there in a few weeks," Gavin offers with hope.

"I think so, too," Talia states.

Moving with a four-year-old child on foot isn't exactly the fastest mode of travel. They haven't had a vehicle for almost a year.

"Let's stay here another night till this bad weather passes through, and then we'll move," Paige suggests.

"Right. Sounds good, Paige," Gavin agrees. "This weather's horrible. I don't want Maddie to get sick or catch pneumonia or something."

"Well, now that that's settled, wanna' play a round of poker?" Talia asks with a grin.

"Only if you don't cheat this time, ya' sneak," Gavin jokes with her.

Paige offers her friends a soft smile that belies her underlying state of edgy apprehension. This is a last ditch effort they are making to find someone, anyone that they'd known before the fall. Paige's brother is literally the only person left on their list of relatives who might still be alive. They've already exhausted searches trying to find Talia's parents, and Gavin's family was simply gone. His entire neighborhood was destroyed when they'd arrived there three years ago. Some of it was flooded; some simply destroyed by intense fires that had resulted from the earthquake aftershocks of the tsunami, which had struck over eighty miles south. The aftershocks had taken down electrical lines, causing sparks that didn't mix well with the broken natural gas lines. Paige has seen enormous cracks in streets and freeways big enough to swallow semi-trucks. Massive fires had swept through the coastal states of the U.S. within days of the initial tsunami. Whole towns had burned to charred rubble. Large metropolitan areas had followed suit. Fire and rescue crews had not been able to slow the fires down. Paige remembered studying in high school the great San Francisco earthquake that had caused similar, devastating catastrophes, but she'd never imagined witnessing anything like it for herself. And little did she know at the time, that was only the beginning.

She rummages for the deck of worn out cards from her backpack. Tonight she'll enjoy a hand of dirty poker with her friends, and they'll use pilfered jewelry and money they've found here and there over the years.

"I'll start the first bid with this diamond tennis bracelet," Talia states with a smile.

Her friend tosses it into the center of the table after the first hand is dealt.

"I'll match that with this Rolex and raise you by two ruby earrings," Gavin says lightheartedly.

"I'll see your earrings and match them with this 10k stack," Paige replies and tosses a bank-wrapped, wrinkled stack of hundred dollar bills onto the pile.

Their poker games can become rather high roller status, but it doesn't really matter. Money has no value anymore. If they were going to bet on something that had actual value, they'd be using a can of peas or a tube of toothpaste.

Chapter Three
Reagan

"Is the truck gassed up?" John asks of Kelly.

Her husband is stressed out but trying not to show it. They'd buried Em yesterday, and ever since, they've all been running on nerves and adrenaline alone. Reagan knows John well enough to recognize the signs and signals he puts off when he's under duress.

"Yeah, it's ready. Let's go," Kelly returns impatiently.

Reagan is also ready. She's packed them enough food for today and has her medical bag in hand.

"Be careful," Grandpa says.

"Yes, sir," John tells him and shakes his hand.

Reagan hugs her grandfather and kisses his whiskered cheek. Sue hugs her next, but Hannah has not come out of the house. She's still sitting in the music room on Grams's favorite sofa. It's all right because it's what she does most days now.

Derek says, "Radio if you need more help."

Her beloved brother-in-law will stay on the farm with Simon and Grandpa to protect it while they are gone. Reagan is going with the men should Cory be injured or shot by the time they get to him.

"Will do," John answers his brother.

"Bring him home, Kelly," Grandpa orders gravely.

"Yes, sir," Kelly returns but doesn't meet his eyes.

The sun has just risen, the children are still in bed, and they are headed to hunting cabin number two to retrieve Cory home. She rides in the middle of the bench seat between Kelly and John. Reagan takes John's hand into her own, and he gives it a gentle, reassuring squeeze. She's thankful for his size and strength. He leans over and kisses the top of her head. Reagan tries not to let the tears loose again. The loss of Em has shattered her family. Nobody even went to bed last night. They've all been up since yesterday because sleep wasn't going to come to any of them, not after burying one of their own.

Kelly is speeding along the county road, not something they'd normally do. However, the circumstances this time merit the use of public roads. Somehow they have to get to Cory before he does something reckless that could get him killed. When Simon had met them on the oil well road without Cory but with Em's dead body, Kelly had immediately wanted to go after him. Grandpa had convinced him to do the honorable thing and bury their sister first. Today, though, is a different situation altogether. Today, nothing could stop Kelly from this mission.

They drive for nearly forty minutes until their secret, overgrown oil well road comes into view. They've never encountered anyone else on these abandoned service roads which makes them ideal for covert travel. Kelly slows to a more reasonable pace since the gravel and mostly dirt road is bouncy, rutted and full of potholes. They even stop once so that the men can clear away a long fallen branch from the road. They drive as far as they can on the snow-covered road and come to a stop at the end of the trail where a forest begins. They'll go in on foot from here. It's not far, less than a mile.

Within twenty minutes, the cabin comes into view. There isn't a fire burning within, and no smoke comes out of the chimney. Reagan tromps through the snow, which had fallen last night and dropped a good four additional inches on them. She finds the horse shelter empty.

"I don't think he's here," she calls over to John as he comes out of the cabin also shaking his head.

"We'll have to wait it out here for him," John says as he adjusts the rifle sling on his shoulder.

"To hell with that. I'm going to look for him," Kelly says angrily. "I'm not sitting around here waiting for him to come back."

"Kelly, we have no idea where he might be," Reagan argues as she joins the men under the overhang of the cabin's roof line. It's starting to flurry again, and she has no wish to soak herself through with wet, cold snow.

She wishes she could offer her big friend some small semblance of comfort, but what could she possibly say that would bring back his baby sister? In the middle of the night, she'd found him on the back porch sobbing brokenly. Kelly had obviously gone out there to be alone and fall apart away from Hannah. Her friend is shredded to pieces from this but is clearly trying to hold it together, hold onto what is left of his little family. She'd left him uninterrupted and sought out the comfort of her grandfather's arms in his study where he sleeps most nights.

"Bravo One to Tango Three, come in Cor," John says into his radio.

Her husband is holding it together better than anyone else, which is nothing more than what she'd expect from John. He's as strong as one of the thick, oak support beams in the cattle barn in situations like this.

Static from the cabin alerts them, and they go inside only to discover Cory's radio sitting atop the small table.

"Damn it," Reagan swears under her breath.

"I'm gonna light a fire," John offers.

"Thanks, babe," Reagan says as she rubs her gloved hands together. "I'm freezing."

Her husband, as usual, has a low burning, crackling fire going in the fireplace within a few minutes.

"Why the hell didn't he take his radio?" Kelly growls and paces the floor restlessly.

"Don't know," John mutters as he pokes at the fire to keep it going.

"Shit! I don't want to wait here for him. He could be hurt," Kelly stresses, his bloodshot brown eyes frantic.

"He's smarter than that, Kelly," John tries at appeasing his friend. "We wouldn't even know where to start."

"No, but I could take a run into the city and start looking," he says with frustration.

"Just stay here, Kelly," Reagan says. "He'll show up. His gear's all here. Literally the only things that are missing are the guns. Look, even his backpack's here."

"What if those men came back and found him here? Maybe they took his horse. Maybe they…"

"No way, bro," John stops him. "Simon said they killed the last two. There's no way they could've tracked Cory and Simon here at night even if there were others that got away. There aren't any tracks in the snow outside, either."

"Right. You're right," Kelly says.

Reagan has to look away from her brother-in-law, this man who has become so important to her family. Despite their rough beginning, Reagan has come to love and care for Kelly like a brother. She's also come to love Cory and poor little Em, who has now been taken away from them. Fuck! She was just a kid. Reagan can't think about it or she'll lose her shit... again.

"We'll wait for him here," John asserts. "He'll come back here. He has to."

"Right," Kelly agrees. "He'll come here."

Kelly may be agreeing with her husband, but he's still pacing. He's still worried sick about his kid brother. They've already been through so much together and now for Cory to lose Em on his watch must be an enormous amount of guilty burden. Last summer they'd lost Grams to cancer though she'd fought for nearly three long years to win her battle. Grandpa had been ripped apart by this loss. And Hannie hasn't been the same since. She's lost so much of her joy and spirit. Many days she just sits in the music room by herself or with her and Kelly's daughter, Mary. They'd named their baby girl after Grams before any of them had even known she was sick. Reagan's glad that Grams was still alive to see Mary born. It would've made it even more difficult on Hannah not having their grandmother be a part of her first child's life. Mary is two already, which reminds Reagan of how fast time moves forward, even when they don't want it to.

They sit or pace or check out the windows at least a hundred times each over the course of two long hours before they finally hear the familiar nickering of Cory's stallion. Kelly rushes out the front door, followed by John and then Reagan. When Reagan sees Cory, it's almost like looking at a stranger.

"Cory," Kelly says in a rush and nearly yanks him from his horse.

Reagan and John stand back, holding hands and giving them some space.

"God, I was worried about you," Kelly exclaims and hugs his brother so tightly Reagan is afraid he'll hurt him.

Reagan quietly observes Cory's appearance and demeanor. He's not returning the embrace but standing perfectly still and unmoving. When Kelly pulls back, she can see that Cory has spots of dried blood on his face, some splattered on his coat, and his hands are covered with it. His eyes seem vacant and empty.

"I'm sorry, Kel," he finally says.

"It's not your fault, little brother," Kelly says and grasps his brother by both shoulders.

Cory won't look at his brother. Instead, he stares at the ground or off to his left.

"It was my fault. I let her go with us to watch the horses. I should've made her stay here at the cabin," Cory analyzes in monotone syllables.

"No!" Kelly says vehemently. "It's not. It was *their* fault, the bad-guys. Not you and not Simon. Don't ever say that."

Reagan has to look away when Kelly's voice cracks. Tears spill onto her cheeks again, and she wipes them quickly so as not to spread that emotion throughout their group. Everyone's trying to process this, to deal with it on any level.

"Cory?" Kelly speaks softly.

His brother's semi-catatonic state is obviously starting to worry Kelly. Reagan's also concerned about Cory. His brown eyes flit around but won't make direct contact with anyone.

"We're here to help," John says and steps forward. "We're going after this group that did this. Reagan will stay here, and me and you and Kelly are gonna go clean house on these bastards."

"It's already done," Cory replies.

This time he does look up, but Reagan isn't so sure she's glad that he did so. His eyes are so hard and cold that it sends a chill creeping up the back of her neck. There is no warmth in his brown eyes anymore.

"What do you mean, Cor?" John asks.

Reagan steps forward and sidles in against her husband's side.

"They're all dead," Cory answers.

"Who's dead? The men who killed her or..." Kelly asks.

"Yeah," Cory says. "They were with a bigger group that I located in an old warehouse. Thirteen of them. I took care of it."

Reagan, John and Kelly regard each other with even more concern. That would've been very dangerous. He could've been killed. How the hell had he killed thirteen people on his own?

"Cory? Are you serious, little brother?" Kelly inquires nervously.

"There's bound to be others out there like them," Cory relates in an empty tone.

"We'll head back to the farm and reinforce. We can go after anyone you want to, brother," Kelly offers.

"You can go now," Cory dismisses them and tugs his horse along to the barn.

They follow him, but Reagan and John hang back while Kelly talks again. Cory begins untacking his stallion by placing the saddle, blanket, pad and bridle on the hooks and railing surrounding the makeshift stall.

"You need to come home now, Cory," Kelly says and places a large hand on his young brother's wide shoulder.

"I'm not coming home," Cory answers in haste and steps away to brush down his sweat-covered horse.

Reagan is fairly sure that this is the first time his stallion has rested since he left the farm two days ago. His chest and flanks are covered in white lather, and the stallion shivers from the cold air hitting him when the last of his padding is removed.

"What do you mean you're not coming back?" Kelly asks. "You need to come with us and go back to the farm."

Cory momentarily stops brushing his horse and turns to face Kelly straight on.

"I'm not coming back. I have work to do," Cory states emphatically and turns away again.

Kelly blows up.

"You are coming home!" he shouts. "Get your shit packed up. You're coming home with me, or I'll drag you. You're not staying out here by yourself. Do you hear me?"

"I'll only be here a few days and then I'm moving on," Cory tells them as if he has a plan.

"Moving on to where exactly?" Kelly asks angrily. "The only place you're moving on to is back to the damn farm, Cory."

"I'm not coming back. You need to leave. Go home. Go home to Hannah and your daughter. They need you. I don't need you anymore, and I'm not coming home," Cory declares calmly.

"Cory, this isn't safe," Reagan tries. "Honey, come home. Please."

"Sorry, Reagan," Cory answers her.

"You need to be with us, not out here in the middle of nowhere by yourself," Reagan implores.

"You all need to get back before dark," Cory suggests. "You know the roads are more dangerous at night."

"You have a long ride, too," Kelly tells him. "It's going to get dark for you, too, and I don't want you making the ride home in the middle of the night."

"I'm not coming," Cory says with remarkable clarity.

Kelly is about to step toward his brother, and Reagan believes that he is literally going to drag Cory physically out from under the barn shelter. But John grabs Kelly's jacket and jerks him slightly back. Her husband nods over his shoulder to indicate that they should talk in private. Kelly frowns hard but follows. The three of them walk toward the cabin. When Reagan glances back, she notices that Cory just continues to brush the horse.

"You gotta let him be, Kelly," John tells his friend.

"What?" Kelly asks with a mixture of hard anger and anguish and helpless misery in his tired eyes.

"Let him go, Kelly," John repeats.

"What the hell, John?" Reagan questions her husband and looks into his blue eyes. "That's insane. He needs to come home. This shit isn't safe out here. It's not safe anywhere alone anymore."

"He's not staying here by himself," Kelly affirms.

"You can't stop him. If you force him to come home to the farm, he'll only leave again," John explains. "You gotta let him go, man."

"To hell with that. I'll stay with him then," Kelly reasons.

"Kel, he's not staying because he wants to," John says.

Her husband removes his stocking cap and rakes a hand through his blonde hair. He is haunted by his own bad memories, and Reagan can tell that he's trying to impart a wisdom to Kelly that she can't comprehend.

"No," Kelly retorts.

"He can't come back, not yet," John says and lays a hand gently on Kelly's shoulder. "Let him go."

"No way," Kelly repeats.

"You have to let him deal with this on his own. He's not coming home, man," John says.

"I can't," Kelly says and his voice cracks again. "I can't lose him, too."

"You won't, bro," John says with confidence. "He has to do this. He'll come home someday, but if you make him do it now when he's not ready, it'll break him. He'll never reconcile this. He needs to do what he has to do. You know this. We've *seen* this before, brother. Kelly, we've seen men like this before."

Kelly hangs his head and nods. When he raises it again, there are tears in his eyes. He leaves them to go to Cory again. John takes her to the porch where they've left their packs, a crate and bags full of supplies. Together they unload the provisions inside the cabin. John gets into the burlap sack he'd lugged along and stacks cans of vegetables, home canned jars of soup, potatoes, beans and meat. She didn't pack these things. She'd only brought enough for them to eat one meal at the cabin with Cory. He must've packed these provisions. Had he known this would happen? They leave everything on the table and bed and go back outside. It's probably enough food for a week or maybe two if Cory is conservative. She just hopes that by then Cory has settled this demon within him and has returned to the farm where he belongs.

Kelly joins them near the cabin. Cory has followed.

"There are some supplies in there for you, Cory. Food and stuff," Reagan says awkwardly.

"Thanks, Reagan," he returns.

Kelly walks forward and embraces his young brother again, although it is not returned. He pats Cory on the back three times and steps away. Kelly nods and his brother does so, as well. Kelly turns and walks swiftly toward their path, leaving her and John to stand there with Cory.

Reagan doesn't hug him, not because she doesn't want to. She's done so many times in the last three years. But it seems like he doesn't want anyone to. She can relate.

33

"You should wash that... off," she indicates toward his bloody hands and he nods.

"I will, Reagan," he says.

Reagan walks a few feet away so that John can say his good-bye with some privacy.

"Take however much time you need, bro," John says.

Her loving husband, who is so openly and easily affectionate with most everyone, takes Cory's hand in his. Reagan thinks he is about to pull Cory in for an embrace, but he doesn't. Instead, John slaps an extra mag for Cory's rifle into it with a resounding crack.

"You do what you have to do, Cory," John says very intensely. "You come home, but only when you can. Do you understand me?"

"Yes, sir," Cory answers.

"Only when you can," John reiterates firmly.

Cory says nothing but nods with a new fierceness in his brown eyes. John nods a few times and turns from Cory.

He takes her hand and pulls Reagan along the path that will take them to their truck. It's not until they are a distance far enough away from the cabin that Cory won't hear that she loses her shit... again. Her knees buckle. John holds her until she's all cried out as Kelly continues to pull ahead of them on the path. He holds her close and imprints his strength into her. It gives her enough gumption to get her emotions in check and continue on until they reach the truck again.

She wants to be home so badly, back at the farm and within the safe confines of it. She wants Em to be waiting there, not just the family, which is so down. She wants Cory to come home with them. She wants everything to go back to normal and her grandmother to still be alive. These are useless, childish thoughts, she knows, but Reagan also can't help them from taking root.

They swing onto the county road eventually, and Reagan has to have Kelly pull over. She climbs quickly over John and jumps out. She vomits the contents of her stomach, which is mostly just liquid and acids because they haven't eaten since breakfast, onto the berm of the road. John is right behind her and rubbing her back soothingly. Then she has a hard time catching her breath. Just breathing in and out is laborious. It hurts. She wants Em back. She wants Cory home.

"It's ok, babe," he consoles.

"I'm fine," Reagan replies when she stands straight again. "I just got to dwelling on everything and that damn oil well road was too bouncy. Sorry."

"That's no problem," he tells her. "It's just been a bad few days. It's understandable. Let's get you back to the farm."

"Yeah," Reagan says and leans into him for support.

She climbs into the truck again and lays her head against John's chest where she likes to rest. His arm wraps around her shoulders, and he tugs her even closer. She likes the slow, steady beat of his heart in her ear. It always brings her comfort, just like everything about John. She'd been thinking about Em and became overwhelmed with sadness. She'd been thinking about the look of haunted desolation in Cory's eyes, too. Reagan prays that it is gone when he returns to the farm. She never wants to see that in him again.

Chapter Four
Sam

It's been almost three weeks since they've buried her friend, Em. Sam's heart is broken, crumbled into pieces by this tragic new loss. They'd grown so close over the last three and a half years. They'd shared secrets and dreams and hopes for the future. Even though she's almost nineteen and Em was only fifteen, they were good friends. Her friend was a kindred spirit to her and likewise. Sometimes she was the only person Sam felt like she could talk to about things because Em had been through so many of the same horrible situations as her.

Sam's lost so many people of whom she's loved so deeply. Em is just one more loss in the long list of tragedies in her life. Her parents, her older brother and her twin, baby siblings were all killed, murdered in the horse barn behind their home by the types of low-life degenerates that her father had always lectured her and her older brother about staying away from when they grew up and moved out on their own.

She's standing in her horse's stall, giving him a good brushing and reminiscing some of the good times she's had on this farm with the McClane family and with Em, in particular. She and Em used to enjoy riding together, galloping across the high meadow and racing. She was such a happy, free spirit. Sam sketched portraits of her friend that she'll put behind glass if she can find some picture frames somewhere. She knows that Kelly has a small photograph of her with Cory and their parents that he keeps in his wallet. It must be from about a year before the apocalypse. Em still had braces on her teeth in the picture. Her light chestnut hair was shorter then, too. But she still had that promise of beauty which she was growing into while living on the McClane farm.

Sam only wishes that Em had told her she was going to sneak off to join up with Simon and Cory that morning. She would've talked her out of it, or at the very least Sam would've told Cory. Em had been nagging them for days before they left. Sam should've known her friend would do something impulsive. Em was that way, impetuous and naïve and young.

Sam had helped Reagan pack away Em's belongings into plastic tubs that were taken to the basement. When Cory comes home someday, he can go through them and decide with Kelly what they want to do with them. Simon had told her that Cory kept his sister's gold bracelet, the one that all of the women in the family wear care of Reagan's pilfering of a jewelry store. He'd sent her body home with Simon without it on her small wrist. Sam knows that he has that item tucked away somewhere on his person, wherever he is.

A rapping on the stall door alerts her.

"Hey, Sam," Simon speaks softly.

"Hey, watcha' up to?" Sam asks. He's been very distant and even quieter than usual lately. They all have been. Nobody is dealing well with her loss; everyone is down. The mood of the family is even graver and more morose than when they'd lost Grams. She hadn't been murdered and taken from them abruptly, though. Grams had passed away from cancer. She'd fought it valiantly, and they'd all had a chance to say their goodbyes. Em has been ripped from them.

"Working with Reagan," he answers solemnly. "She didn't feel too well, so she's going in for a break."

"That's weird. She's never sick," Sam says with a frown. "Hope she didn't catch anything working at the clinic."

"Yeah, me, too," he agrees and steps inside the stall with her.

Simon doesn't say anything more but strokes the horse's neck and velvety soft muzzle. It rubs more firmly against his hand hoping for a treat.

"We had a few patients last week that had some kind of flu bug," he reports. "Haven't seen anything like that in a while."

"Great," Sam laments with sarcasm. "What did Grandpa say about it? Does he think it could be another bad sickness like that pneumonic plague?"

"No, he said he thinks it's just a bug, something seasonal. It's just unusual to hit so late in the season," he returns.

"If anybody would know it's definitely Grandpa or Reagan," she says and raises her eyebrows. He's not really her grandfather at all. But when she'd come to live on the farm, she hadn't really known what to call him or Mrs. McClane. She'd started with "Dr. McClane" but that had felt weird after a while. Then she shortened it to "Doc" like most of the adults called him, but that had seemed sort of disrespectful to pretend that she was on the same level as an adult. So he'd just suggested one day that if she felt comfortable enough that she could call him "Grandpa" and his wife "Grams" like their own granddaughters and great-grandchildren call them. As soon as she'd tried it on, it had fit like a comfortable glove. And she's called him that ever since. After all, he's the only grandparent or parent she's ever going to have again.

"Right," Simon agrees. "We treated them with elderberry tea and raw honey and gave them a few Tylenol for reducing the fevers. It's about all we can do for people now."

"Yeah, but you guys are so great with compounding the herbs and making natural remedies for people."

"Reagan gets frustrated because she wishes that we still had an endless supply of pharmaceuticals. We are still saving back some of the important drugs for emergencies," he comments. "But that certainly doesn't mean she's a big lover of herbal remedies, either."

If there's one thing Simon likes to talk about, it's medicine. He would've made a great doctor someday, although he said he wanted to be a scientist. It's the study and research that he gets a kick out of. He'll disappear for hours on end looking for herbs in the forest that he and Grandpa will turn into medicines and herbal teas. During the winter season, she'll usually go to the clinic with Grandpa and Simon if Reagan doesn't go. Sometimes Reagan is called to other tasks such as house calls, taking care of a sick animal on their or their neighbors' farms or working at the farm on research. Sam goes to the clinic so that she can offer assistance to Simon and Grandpa, but she's certainly no doctor. She hadn't enjoyed the massive amount of studying and reading that Simon had taken on in order to become a doctor someday. There is usually a long line of people from around their area waiting outside the clinic for whatever assistance they can get for their ailments, sicknesses, broken bones, pregnancies and just about anything else one could expect.

"I know," Sam agrees. "Reagan says you and Grandpa are turning into a couple of hippy-dippies."

"I've heard that phrase quite a lot during the last year or so as we've run out of synthetic pharmaceuticals. I'm used to it," he says lightly.

"I'm sure you have," Sam adds to lift his mood. "Wanna' go for a walk?"

"Sure," he says on a nod.

Sam pats Blaze on the neck and tugs his halter to return him to his friends in the pasture. She and Simon walk side by side, and he opens the gate for her before they release the gelding. The snow has let up and now they have a light dusting covering the ground. As much as she enjoys riding through a snowy forest when the branches and tops of the tall pines are coated in white, Sam is also anxious for spring.

She is wearing leather riding boots which should keep out the moisture, but Simon's just wearing a pair of New Balance running shoes with mesh inserts. Her down-filled jacket helps to keep out the bitter wind that occasionally whips up.

They walk in companionable silence toward the woods, avoiding deep mud puddles and slushy ground when they can. The trees lost their leaves last fall, making them appear skeletal and angry in shape and form. Sometimes she'll sit in the hay loft of the horse barn where she can view the forest from the wide, open hay door and sketch the farm and surrounding property. Soon the spring season will bring growth and with it the rebirth of greenery and grass and leaves and flowers, which are all preferable to a wet season of snow and rain that breeds on any farm, dark and heavy mud and dampness that clings to boots and clothing and makes all work more difficult and miserable. Grandpa is eager for an early spring so that they can get a good planting season in. And they are all hoping that the snowstorms like the one that hit last week, dumping six inches on the ground are gone for good.

"Do you think Cory's ok?" she asks as they move farther into the forest. Sometimes they'll ride this patrol route together, she, Cory and Simon. Sometimes Reagan and John still do, but usually it's Simon and Cory who handle the patrols by themselves. They even ride along the road that encapsulates their farm, the Reynolds and the Johnson place, too.

Inquiring after Cory is painful. It's like they've all lost him, too. He's gone, and nobody knows for sure whether he'll ever come home or not. Just saying his name brings anguish. He's like her big brother. He reminds her a lot of her real big brother; an unarmed teen boy shot and executed in their horse barn.

"I'm sure he's fine, Sam," he says gently. "He just needs some time to deal with it. Don't worry."

"Yeah, right," she scolds. "How the heck am I supposed to do that? He's our friend, Simon."

She glances up in time to see Simon wince, which makes her feel terrible. If she and Cory are close, Simon and he are a thousand times more so.

"Sorry," she quickly apologizes.

"It's ok," he returns with a lopsided frown. "I'm worried, too. I wish he would've come home with me."

"Yeah," she agrees. "Me, too. I don't like him out there somewhere alone. It's not safe."

"I'm sure he's safe. This *is* Cory we're talking about, remember?" he adds with sad humor.

Sam smiles up at him. This is probably the first time she's smiled at all in weeks.

"True," she concurs. "It would've been more accurate if I'd have said I'm more worried about the people he runs into."

Simon nods on a frown and looks away, looks into the far off distance at nothing. He'd not cried at the burial ceremony of Em. If he has lost his composure over Em's death, then he's done so in private.

John had removed her body from the packhorse, according to Reagan, and had placed her in the bed of the truck. He'd chosen to ride the extra horse beside Simon back to the farm instead of in the truck with Reagan and Grandpa. Reagan had told her that he didn't want Simon to ride all the way home alone. It had taken them hours riding through the dark to make it back to the farm, and they hadn't arrived until nearly dawn.

"Do you want to talk about it?" she asks as she takes a seat on a fallen tree stretching far into the forest and also half across their path. The trunk of it is still elevated a good three feet off the ground which makes her almost eye level with Simon. The soggy bark will probably make her jeans damp, but she wants Simon to take some time and talk with her. He shakes his head and sighs on an unsteady breath. Sam reaches out to him, but he won't take her hand. "It'll help, Simon."

"Doc says that he wants me to draw out the schematics of the solar panels so that we can distribute them to our patients who come to the clinic," he throws out, effectively changing the topic.

Sam lets her gloved hand drop back down to her thigh. Seeing Simon like this is hard on her. He means so much to her. He means so much to the whole family, especially Doc, who often praises what a great deal of help Simon is at the clinic.

"Oh, that's a good idea," she puts in, trying to be less morose. She knows better than to pursue that other line of conversation. He'll just shut down further. "People still need to get their power up and running if they haven't figured it out yet."

"Yeah, that's what we were thinking," he says and swallows hard.

When his eyes meet hers, there is so much pain and grief there that she frowns hard and feels like she might start crying again. It seems like it's all she does nowadays. Simon looks quickly away. He does this so often lately that she wishes she could understand him better. They've always been close, but Simon has become very guarded around her for quite some time now. She's not sure what this is about. They've been through so much together, so much that most people could never understand. He'd fought so hard so many times to keep her safe. He'd not been successful most of the time. But it hadn't stopped him from taking another beating from Bobby or Frank or some of the other creeps with whom they'd been forced to travel, the group the McClane family had called the visitors. He has a fierce sense of right and wrong, and he'd known what was going on within that group and that the way they were treating her and some of the other women and children was so far beyond wrong it could only be described as pure evil. He'd also fought for the twin brothers, Huntley and Garrett, even though Garrett had succumbed to illness and passed away. Thinking of that sweet boy just makes her feel even more depressed. Other than Em, Simon is her best friend on this lonely, scarred and desolate earth. And she's desperate to have her best friend back.

"Simon, why…" she starts.

"Let's head back, ok?" he interjects suddenly.

"Um, sure, Simon," she agrees and allows him to help her down.

He doesn't bring up anything of importance on their walk back to the farm. He is behaving even more distant now.

"I'm going out to the shed to work," he says as they come to the house.

Sam just nods reluctantly and goes inside where she finds Hannah and Sue hard at work in the kitchen.

"Hey, kid," Sue greets. "What's up?"

"Nothing much. Went for a walk with Simon," she replies.

"What's wrong?" Sue asks.

"Nothing really," Sam says but gets a look from Sue that clearly states that she understands that it is not 'nothing.' "I just feel like Simon is being very distant lately."

"Honey, everyone's been through a lot. That's probably all it is. You and Simon are very close. I'm sure it's nothing," Sue tries at pacifying her.

"No, you don't understand. He has been like this for a while now. This isn't just because of Em, although I'm quite sure that isn't helping. He has withdrawn even more since then. He's just been strange. I don't know how to explain it."

Hannah finally says, "It'll all work out, honey. He obviously just has some things he needs to work through. We all do."

Sue places a comforting arm around Hannah's slim shoulders and gives them a gentle squeeze. Hannah tips her head toward Sue's and rests there a moment before returning to her task of chopping potatoes. Her deep sigh does not convince Sam that she even believes her own statement.

"Everything will be ok someday, Sam," Sue assures her. "Here, have a pinwheel. A little sweet never hurts. Since we don't have chocolate anymore, I guess you can have something else that's sweet."

"Thanks," Sam says and accepts the treat. Whenever they have leftover scraps of dough, they roll them in a mixture of honey, cinnamon and butter, and bake them in the shape of little pinwheels. They are crispy yet tender on the inside and oh so heavenly.

"In about an hour or so, Sam, why don't you start herding the kids in for dinner," Hannah requests. "I'm not sure where they all went to. I think some are playing downstairs."

"I saw Huntley and Justin out by the equipment shed shooting bb guns," Sam tells them, earning a chuckle from both.

"Boys," Sue says with a soft smile.

"I'll round them all up in a while, though," Sam agrees and leaves the kitchen.

She goes to her room at the far end of the long second-floor hallway. There she takes up position on a maple chair that she usually uses at her drawing desk. Retrieving her violin from under her bed, Sam opens the black case and draws out the bow, running her fingers along the fine hairs. Then she picks up the instrument and proceeds to play one of her favorite Chopin pieces. It was one of her mother's favorites, as well, one she often requested. The tone is in minor key, a serious piece, not one of light notes used for a waltz. It is a particularly melancholy tune, but somehow seems to fit her mood.

She plays for a long time, losing track of everything but the music and the notes and the timbre of the piece. When she's finished, Sam glances up to find Reagan at her door.

"Careful, Sam," she warns. "Don't go down that road again, kiddo."

Sam knows that Reagan means well. Reagan looks out for her like Sam's her kid sister. She is also one of the few people on the farm who understands what she's been through. Reagan also knows that sometimes she slips into severe depression from time to time. In those periods, she tends to play dark music and sketch rather moody pictures.

Sam gives her a simple nod and says, "I know."

Reagan retreats again without another word, but Sam knows she's right. Even as she recognizes this, it doesn't stop her from moving on to a Handel piece of the same dark undertones. It matches her mood and that of her family and her best friend, Simon.

Chapter Five
Paige

They slept on the floor of a six-story office building last night, and every tendon, ligament and bone in Paige's body is feeling the effects of doing so. They'd tucked Maddie in on a sofa they'd dragged in from the receptionist's lounge, but the three adults had slept on the floor.

She'd startled awake, immediately confused and disoriented. The small, portable heater had shut off sometime in the middle of the night like it normally does when it runs out of juice. Maddie continues to snore softly. Gavin and Talia are out like logs. It's nearly dawn; the light coming through the blinds gray and bleak. Then a noise, a few floors down if she was to guess, alerts her. That is what had awakened her. It wasn't the heater or Maddie's snoring. No wonder she'd startled.

Paige listens intently without moving. Talia stirs beside her, recognizing that Paige is awake and alert.

"What is it?" her friend whispers groggily and sits up.

"Think we have company," Paige relays as another noise sounds below but closer this time. "Let's move!"

She whispers her order frantically, waking Gavin in the process. Talia is already packing their gear as Paige snatches Maddie from the sofa. The four-year-old already knows this routine. They've done this a million times. She knows to be quiet and move fast. Paige has her coat and tiny shoes on in a mere seconds. Gavin is tugging on his boots and simultaneously rolling their sleeping bags. This is a lot more hectic than their departure from the beautiful mansion a few weeks ago. Unfortunately, they had to move on from there. They'll never make forward progress if they stay in one place for long.

Voices filter up from one floor below, spurring them into a frantic exit. Paige listens at the closed and locked door. She can hear numerous voices.

"Go, go, go!" she whispers as they take another door to leave the office.

They run as furtively as they can manage down the hall toward a back exit of the building. She'd checked this hall with Gavin last night before they'd bedded down. They'd tried to plan their exit strategy. Gavin carefully opens the door, pressing the steel bar and pushing inward. He waits until they are all through before closing it softly behind them.

"Go!" he says urgently as he flicks on his flashlight.

They jog down the stairs, careful not to slip and fall or tumble with Maddie, who Gavin carries. The poor ruffian's hair still stands on end, her darling face puffy from sleep. They make it down two entire flights when the distinctive sound of someone opening the door overhead echoes through the stairwell. Gavin immediately cuts the light. She and her friends press against the wall as hard as they can, trying not to be seen in the stairwell. Nobody moves. She's sure nobody else even breathes because she sure as hell doesn't. They only have three bullets. Depending on how many people were coming up those stairs on the other side of the building, they could be in deep trouble. It wouldn't be the first time.

"Thought I heard something," a man says, his voice carrying.

His voice is deep and gravelly. Paige doesn't move an inch as he swings a flashlight around spying for something…or them.

"You ain't heard nothing, ya' dumb prick," someone else says.

This man sounds younger, his Southern accent as thick as Talia's.

"I swear I did, so you shut your mouth, boy," the first one says angrily.

"You just hearin' things, old man," the other one replies.

"Could be the ones we were lookin' for," gravel voice says.

Another man shouts from further away from the two in the doorway, and the door closes again with a much louder clang. They wait a moment and then start descending again in an awkward lope since they carry so much of their supplies that didn't get stowed away properly. They break onto the first floor, going through a door that takes them through the back of the six-story building to the parking deck. This escape route was planned last night just in case. More times than she cares to recall, their 'just in case' plans became set into motion because of danger. She's learned to sleep with one eye open over the years.

Paige leads the way, climbs over the cement wall in the parking deck and takes Maddie from Gavin so he can climb. They run to the next building and rest a moment.

"Do you think they know we were up there?" Talia asks quietly.

Paige shakes her head, "I don't know. Maybe. If they find our camp-out room, they'll know because it was still warm."

It snowed again, not a lot luckily, but enough to be annoying. She squats and zips Maddie's coat, pulls her hat and mittens from her backpack and tugs those onto her, too. She says nothing but stares up at Paige with her pale, greenish-blue eyes filled with an expectant fear and an absolute trust that they will keep her safe. Paige kisses her forehead and tells her that everything will be fine.

"I have to pee-pee, Mommy," Maddie says.

"Ok, Maddie," Paige tells her. She gets a nod from Talia and Gavin, so she goes over to the other corner of the building where she assists Maddie and then uses a small scrap of torn material like they all carry in bunches in their bags to help her wipe. Paige stows it in a plastic bag to be washed later. "Better?"

"I'm hungry. Where's the sun?" she asks.

"Not up yet, honey," Paige answers. "We'll eat soon. We need to get out to our traps."

They join up with the other two and leave the area. Nobody pursues them, thank God. She and Gavin jog through the woods after leaving Talia and Maddie in a safe place.

"Gav, do you think those men were looking for us?"

He shrugs, and Paige can tell that he doesn't want to admit it.

"Probably. I guess it's likely, Paige," he says. "They could've been looking for anyone really."

"Yeah, I guess they could've," she agrees. She's not entirely convinced, either. She also trusts no one.

When they find the traps that they'd set last night less than a quarter mile outside the city limits in the forest, they are empty. Not only are they empty but simply gone. The traps had contained dead rabbits or squirrels or something else because there is blood on the ground. There are also the innards and guts laying near each trap, the blood splattered against the white snow. There are human footprints in the snow.

"Someone took our kills," Paige says angrily.

Gavin nods and points to a place where one trap had connected to a tree. The remnants of four inches of string are still there. Wild animals would've eaten the smaller animals completely and not left a pile of innards. Only a human would've done this. They've been robbed.

"Damn!" Paige hisses through her teeth. They have to feed Maddie. They hadn't had much for a dinner last night, either. She needs food. All four of them need sustenance.

"We have a can of chicken broth," Gavin adds, trying to be optimistic.

She regards him with speculation. This is why she's come to love him so much. He's like this tiny little light of hope in the midst of chaos. Paige reaches over and touches his forearm gently.

"We need more than chicken broth, my friend," she says softly.

They walk back and reunite with Talia and Maddie behind the cover of a short hill. Paige shakes her head which lets her friend know what has happened without alerting Maddie to the direness of their situation.

"I bet it was the guys in the building this morning," Talia observes after a moment of contemplation.

"Why?" Gavin asks. "It could've been anyone."

"I think Talia's right," Paige concurs. "I wonder if they found our traps and came looking for us next, thinking we'd have more or have supplies or…"

Gavin's eyes darken, and he gives a quick, jerky nod of understanding.

"I want to go spy on them, see if they have our stuff," Paige says.

"I don't think that's a good idea," Talia hastily interjects.

"It won't take me long," she argues. "I can probably be back really fast."

"Let me go instead," Gavin suggests.

Paige shakes her head before saying, "No, Gav. Stay here with them. They could need you, and you know that I'm faster than you. Plus, you have the gun, and you know I suck with those."

"Alright," Gavin concedes. "But let's move and find a new place to hole up where you can meet us."

They decide on an abandoned video store which had evidently been looted early on, strangely enough. Many of the racks and shelves are empty, DVD's and discs scattered about on the floor or missing from their cases. Interesting. People with no electricity were worried about stealing movies to watch? In the rear storage room, they do find a few cartons of boxed candy which they stash into their packs. Gavin even finds a box containing twelve unopened packages of microwavable popcorn. This is a rare find. Most places are completely wiped out, every last morsel of food looted by people like them who don't have much of a choice in the matter.

Paige remembers the sketchy television broadcasts when the first tsunami struck in America. For some odd reason, perhaps with forethought or no thought at all, people in large cities had jumped at the opportunity to loot. Mostly what they were stealing were liquor and cigarettes, but it had happened within hours of the first disaster. She would've never dreamed people would do something so lascivious in a bad situation. Of course, neither had she thought anything so horrible could ever happen in her own country. When the second one hit, all hell broke loose. The news feed wasn't good at that point, mostly static. But what she did see, she wished that she could unsee. It went far beyond nationwide looting of liquor stores. She never dreamed people were capable of such atrocities. She'd learned a year later firsthand how intensely cruel they could really be.

"Stay here," she tells them, although she doesn't need to.

"Take this," Gavin says, extending the small gun toward her.

Paige frowns, "You know I don't do well with these things. I can't shoot for shit, Gav. Besides, I've got my knife, and you guys might need this more than me. Just keep it."

"Ok, but don't get too close to them. Come back when you find out something. We'll stay here and see if there's anything else we can find," Gavin says.

"Got it," she says and gives him a quick hug. Then Paige hugs Talia and Maddie.

She takes most of her heavy things out of her backpack, leaving space in it for anything useful she might come across. Paige heads out, pulling her stocking cap low, jogging through the desolate city where a pin could be heard dropping. She and Gavin take turns doing runs like this. It's easier than all of them going, and Talia was sick last fall and hasn't had the lung strength she used to. Paige believes that her damage is permanent, but she'd never tell her friend this. She lets her hope. It doesn't make a big difference in the matter of someone going on runs. One of them would still need to stay with Maddie no matter what, and Talia is simply better at keeping her quiet than Paige.

She takes off at a slow pace, winding back around to the office building where they'd set up camp last night. An older woman, bundled in many layers of mismatched clothing, pushes a metal shopping cart down a side street. Paige shakes her head and keeps going.

Her feet are starting to get wet, soaking through the distressed leather of her ankle boots as she carefully trudges through three inches of melting snow. That's the least of her concerns. It would be nice to find a new pair of shoes for each of them somewhere in this city. Items like that are even rarer than microwave popcorn. She hadn't expected this town to be as big as it is, or was. She tugs her stocking cap down lower, her collar up higher and ventures forth.

Climbing back over the cement wall to the parking garage's first floor where important executives would've parked, Paige sprints to the entrance door. After a hasty search of the first floor and back up to where they'd slept, she realizes that the pre-dawn intruders are gone. Out the front door and down the street, staying close to the building fronts, she jogs and hears men's voices and an engine in the distance, perhaps three blocks away.

She keeps to the buildings but has to cross the street in a rather large intersection. Paige runs low to the ground and takes cover behind a car that has been tipped onto its side. Not seeing anyone yet, she runs to another building where she climbs through the broken window. It's a medical clinic, an urgent care perhaps. Looking around briefly, she realizes that there won't be any medical supplies left. No point in doing a search of the place. The back part of the building where supplies like that would've been kept is burned out which exposes the brick wall of the building behind it. She ducks behind the front window and pulls out her binoculars. They aren't that great, but they are better than nothing.

She spots them near a warehouse, a dilapidated two-story with many broken windows. It's less than a mile from where Paige and her friends had chosen to camp out last night. They were so close, and none of her group even knew those men were out there.

They have a dark blue sedan running, waiting out front for them. Two of them seem to be arguing. One man shoves another, and the fight is broken up by two more who join the scene. Paige is too far away to hear what they are saying. Their group is probably close to a hundred or more yards from her. So far, she's counted four men but no others. There could be more inside of the former manufacturing facility. She decides to creep closer. To avoid being seen, she runs behind the buildings and comes in to the rear of theirs.

The outside fire escape provides the perfect place to view the area down below inside the plant. She climbs the rusty metal stairs and peers inside a window. Only one man remains. The other three have taken off in the vehicle together. They have a ragtag camp of their own, but to Paige, it seems permanent.

She climbs through a broken window on the second story and tiptoes closer, careful not to bump into anything that would alert him to her presence. There are huge machines below her, though she has no idea what they would be used for. This place seems as if it had closed down long before the apocalypse happened. Everything has the patina of rust, old grease, or just plain cobwebs and dust. She waits patiently, takes out her binoculars again and spies silently.

She sees two rabbits on the cement floor near their campfire which is burning at a fairly steady capacity. These men are obviously not afraid of being seen, which means they are always on the offensive and armed. No other men come out of the shadows. It's just her and the man below her in the center of the warehouse floor.

She turns and walks quietly to the end of the raised walkway, trying not to make noise on the grated steel floor beneath her feet. Paige sneaks down the open stairway and hides a moment behind a large machine with greenish-colored paint that has faded and chipped with the passage of time. It looks like a pizza oven like she's seen at pizza shops, but she knows it isn't. She is about to pull her knife but spots a three feet long piece of pipe with a threaded end. Perhaps this is what they used to manufacture here. She doesn't know, but she does pick it up, feeling the weightiness of it in her hand. The pipe is heavy duty steel.

Using the machines that are mostly taller than her, she secrets down an aisle and comes in behind the man, who has now resorted to bending over tending his fire. He turns toward her and Paige ducks behind the big rusted piece of equipment beside her. She counts to five, peeks and finds him with his back to her again. There is a shotgun, or at least that's what she thinks it is, leaning against a cot that resembles the ones she'd slept on in many FEMA camps in the beginning. There are four of them placed in a circle around the fire. Apparently there are only four men as she'd suspected. And three of them are gone, which is fortuitous.

It's now or never, and this man has her rabbits which she needs to feed to Maddie. She takes a deep breath and sprints toward him almost soundlessly. The clubbing she gives him over the back of his skull isn't soundless. It's almost deafening, the thud in the empty building sickening to her ears. He falls forward almost landing in the fire. She doesn't pause to help him. She grabs her rabbits, stuffs them into her bag. She turns to go but sees other items they could use. Paige takes a small sack of rice, half empty. Then she grabs two cans of corn and the shotgun. She doesn't take their other food items, which she's sure are in the boxes and crates scattered about the room. It's not because she doesn't want to. It's because she hears the squealing of tires as the unconscious man's friends have returned.

She sprints toward the back of the machine shop again as voices rain down over her, heightening her fear. She doesn't stick around long enough to hear what they are saying. She doesn't think they spotted her, but she's not waiting around to see. Unfortunately, when she gets to the back door, it's locked. It takes her a few seconds to work the lock since it is mostly dark in this area. The unfortunate part is that the ancient rusted door is stuck. She shoves a good four times before it lets out a loud squeal in protest of its rusty hinges being abused. It finally opens about twelve inches, enough for her to squeeze through. It doesn't matter if they've heard her. She's home free now. This is where she excels.

She knows for certain they are after her now. That door gave her away. Men's voices are behind her. She hears their footsteps slapping at the pavement and slush. Hers barely make a sound. She dashes to an apartment building and blasts through the front door. The shotgun is too cumbersome for her to continue carrying, so she stashes it in a room on the first floor. At least she knows that they can't use it on her since she stole it from them. Running straight, she comes to an exit and uses the door there. Then she's gone again. She can hear the men still pursuing her, but Paige is positive that she can outrun them. This is her specialty, and she needs to lose them before going back to the video rental store to retrieve her friends. There would be no sense in leading them there to continue this foot chase with Maddie and Talia. They'd never make it. Those men likely have other guns that they are carrying and could use against them.

A quick glance over her shoulder proves her right. Only two of them are still chasing her.

"We'll get you, bitch!" one of them yells.

Right before he trips over debris on the road and comes to a skidding crash in the snow where he lands against the side of a parked car. Paige has to suppress a smile and keep going. She darts down an alley and straight into a building there. Jumping over a metal box, she makes her way to the front, road-facing entrance. The door isn't even there anymore. She's running back toward the way they'd come, whether her pursuer realizes it or not. She'll double back again to lead him away from her group waiting for her. A few more stealthy sneaks into buildings where she finally loses him in another big warehouse, and Paige is on her way to collect her friends. The whole chase has taken less than a half an hour. She's barely even winded. Those men should learn the importance of conditioning, or not to steal from people who do, people who are even hungrier than them.

She collects her friends and out the back door they go. They hike through the woods, careful not to be followed again. They were done in the city anyway. They need to keep going since they have around twenty miles still to hike. They make it probably close to five miles before they need to stop for a break and to feed a bit of food to Maddie, even though they've all been snacking on the video store candy of chocolate covered raisins, Sweet Tarts and gummy worms. They take turns carrying Maddie most of the time since she can only walk about a mile or less before her tiny legs give out. It doesn't take long before they come to a small farm which is rather obviously abandoned. A sizable, fenced-in pasture holds a small pony. Strange that it hadn't died in the past years, but it must've had enough to eat to keep it alive. The pasture looks like a good ten acres, enclosed by high-tensile wire fencing. Grass has grown up through the cracks on the front porch of the white house. A black shudder hangs crookedly from a second-floor window and from a wide picture window on the first floor. They let themselves in through the unlocked front door and perform a fast search of the home for inhabitants while Talia stays outside with Maddie.

Gavin finds some sticks and firewood in a shed while Paige roots out some old newspaper. She and Talia locate a hand crank water pump near one of the outbuildings. When they pump it about ten times, water comes trickling out. They find three empty buckets in the barn and fill them. It doesn't matter if the water is stale or contaminated. It's likely that the pony has been surviving on the same water that's in the round, stone basin. It streams out at a steady, continuous pace from the spigot feeding into the trough that overflows onto the saturated, muddy ground around it. The pony laps it up as if to prove a point. They'll still boil the water for a long time just to be safe.

Once they have a low burning fire going in the fireplace, the flue open- which they've learned the hard way over the years to check- and food cooking, Paige tells them of her chase. Neither of her friends is too happy about the perilous danger of which she'd subjected herself to. They are, however, all just happy to be eating food, have a roof over their heads and heat for the night. It is so much more preferable than going to sleep with cold, damp feet and a growling stomach, which they've done so many times.

The four of them will sleep on the first floor near the fireplace to stay warm and close together in case of danger. They spread out the meager few blankets they found upstairs in the attic along with their newly acquired sleeping bags. The blankets are musty but dry. At least the flooring is carpeted which adds some padding. The doors and windows have been secured and locked. Chair backs were placed under the two main entrance doors at opposite ends of the first floor. Noise makers in the form of strung together empty cans were hung on each first-floor window handle or on their ledges to alert her group to intruders. This is just another trick they've picked up over the years trying to stay alive.

Their clothing and shoes are set close to the fireplace to dry out and warm up for another long day of walking. Maddie has an actual pillow under her head for the first time in many nights instead of a rolled up article of clothing. She and Talia found another pillow that they are willing to cohabitate. Gavin removed a cushion from a chair and is going to use it for a pillow.

Tonight their meal was the rice she'd stolen, pan-fried rabbit and canned corn. It had all tasted as good as any five-star restaurant because they were absolutely famished. They'd found a jar of pickled beets and another three of something called potted beef according to the small white label on the front. On another shelf in the basement, Talia had found two bags of dried apricots. Paige is not sure if any of it is still good, but they'll find out tomorrow.

In the amber light of the fire, as they lay cozy and warm and snuggled together, Paige yawns widely.

"Hey, guys," Gavin says, "maybe we could catch that pony tomorrow. We could put Maddie on it. Maybe even put some of our bags on it to carry."

"It might be wild, Gav," Paige says with a chuckle.

"Yeah, bro," Talia agrees. "It's not like we know the front end of a horse from the back."

They all share a soft laugh that isn't loud enough to awaken Maddie. It's good for her to get sleep. She's just a toddler practically. She needs rest. She needs more food most days, too, but they do the best they can with her.

"I know a little," he says.

"Ok, farm boy," Talia mocks.

She and Paige enjoy another laugh at his expense. He's more of a beach boy than a farmer, having grown up in the Carolinas in a posh beach community.

"It's worth a try," Paige admits. "It would be a hell of a lot faster to travel if we didn't have to carry her. Maybe we'd even get there the day after tomorrow or so."

"Sounds good to me," Talia agrees.

They talk a short while longer in the dark, the sounds of the fire cracking and popping and providing more warmth than they've had in a while. A wind gust causes the old house to groan and creak. The windows even rattle slightly. The sky had looked angry enough to dump more snow onto the earth tonight. Paige has a hard time falling asleep and lies awake long after her companions. She feels a certain amount of apprehension at what awaits her at the end of this long journey. It could end joyously or on a tragedy, one of so many that they've shared.

Chapter Six
Cory

He awakens to the sound of his horse blowing through his nose. Cory knows the sound well. This isn't a happy, greeting type of sound or the sound of joyful whinnying. Jet is blowing through his nose hard. It's a loud warning of something out there. Cory climbs out of his sleeping bag already dressed since he slept in his clothing. He's under the shelf of a large rock formation coming out of a hill which had provided shelter from the snowstorm.

This isn't the first time he's had a problem with someone being in his camp. Just yesterday the same thing had happened. Only yesterday it had happened during the day while he'd been gone on a mission in the city. He has no idea what time it is, but it's nowhere near dawn yet. Below him about eight feet, his horse is tied securely to a tree. He's dancing in place. Cory can hear him doing it. This is also a sign of agitation in the stallion. Someone or something's out there.

He stays low, squats near the opening of his homemade cave with the coated canvas tarp acting as a door. Resting his back against the stone behind him, Cory scans the area with his rifle which is equipped with a night scope. Yesterday someone took a keen interest in his camp and had trashed it. He'd come back to find his things ransacked. The only item missing was the remains of a carcass too charred from earlier in the day to be eaten by him. He's not the best campfire cook.

A soft yet menacing growl comes from the forest to his east. Footsteps that are heavy enough to break twigs reverberate through the hills. Owls stop their nighttime communications. The forest falls silent. The hair on the back of his neck stands up. He rubs the gold bracelet, which he'd woven around the black leather cord around his neck, between his thumb and forefinger. He's not afraid. He's just anxious. His camp guest is back. Cory had ensured whatever it was would come back by leaving a trail of cut up innards, raccoon innards to be exact, from about twenty yards out all the way to the campfire below him.

He opted to not have his tiny campfire in his cave tonight but to light one instead below him near the horse. He wants the area well-lit. The fire down below is still burning but at a much less generous strength than he would like. Too late now. He doesn't have the time to go down and throw on more logs. It'll just have to do. The trap is set. Now he just needs to be patient and wait.

This could be a coyote or a wolf, but those sometimes tend to run in packs. They've had numerous run-ins at the farm with both. The wildlife in America has gone into super breeding mode for the last unadulterated three and a half years. There was no such thing anymore as a hunting season or limited seasons to hunt anything. Sometimes it seems more like hunt or be hunted. So much of the human population, the densely populated east coast is gone, just dead in that first wave of tsunamis. He's seen herds of deer in different cities right downtown, like in Nashville one time when he'd gone with John. Another time in Louisville when he was with Kelly, they'd seen their first pack of wolves. That time he was actually scared. It was a few years ago, and he and Kelly weren't too sure they were going to be able to make it back out of the city. They'd taken the Hummer that time or else they may not have made it home. Those wolves had stalked them relentlessly. John actually shot an elk that had wandered too close to the farm about a year ago. There are no boundaries and fences or occupied cities anymore that keep the wildlife at bay. The animals go where they want and hunt what or whom they desire. Most of them have no fear of people left.

Another growl draws his attention away from memories, for which he is thankful. He doesn't like thinking of the family or memories of him and the men hunting together. He buries them and concentrates instead on the sounds of movement and branches being broken.

After a few more minutes, the animal still does not appear. Maybe it wasn't an animal that had ransacked his camp. He is second guessing himself. There were no signs of human tracks. There were, however, signs of animal tracks, multiple sets of animal tracks. The new snow on the ground had made it somewhat difficult to tell what all had been there earlier. But he was able to discern raccoon, possible coyote and something much larger. Perhaps it was a human who'd been good at covering their tracks. Why wouldn't they have taken some of his gear, though? He'd left his sleeping bag and some of his other, heavier items behind at the camp. When he's hunting, he likes to travel light.

Jet stomps irritably and tosses his head against the tether that holds him to the tree branch. Cory knows he'd like to sprint.

"Shh," he whispers which seems to help his stallion calm just slightly.

Nothing. No movement or noise now. It's frustrating to sit in suspended silence like this. He's learned a lot about patience from watching his brother and John during a mission with them. John can be kind of a loose cannon sometimes and tends to go all helter skelter and just kill people. He is much more patient when hunting animals, though. He doesn't, however, have a whole lot of tolerance for people's bullshit. His brother is very different. Kelly is patient and cool. His tactics and maneuvers are calm and collected, well thought out. He's been with Kelly when his brother has let people go that he knows for sure that John would've just killed. Cory knows the time to sit calmly is upon him, even though he'd like nothing better than to go on the offensive and chase down whatever is lurking out there.

Suddenly there is a tremendous amount of noise as dead underbrush is crushed, twigs and branches broken and the sound of receding footsteps echo through the valley where he's camped. It actually causes him to physically jump, nearly out of his skin. They'd gone from complete and utter silence to the crashing of something very large moving through the forest. It doesn't break into his line of sight. It has disappeared into the night like some ghostly apparition.

    He waits a short while longer, but nothing happens. Not even the nocturnal sounds of animals gossiping in the forest start back up. Owls don't hoot. Foxes don't chirp to one another. Nothing moves except his stallion. Jet is still rattled. He continues to toss his head and stamp his front feet in aggravation. Cory decides to wait longer to see if his new friend makes another appearance. Seconds and then minutes tick by, but nothing happens.

    Cory starts to rise from his squatted position when a branch breaks above him, above the ledge of rock and hill where he is hidden. Then another twig cracks in two, followed by the huff of an animal's heavy breath. Something is coming down the hill to his right. It has attempted to flank him. Clever beast.

    The snout appears first followed by its two thick front legs. Cory doesn't think the bear sees him. He swings his rifle slowly right, brings it to his shoulder tightly and takes aim. He's never shot a bear before, but he knows where he needs to hit it for a clean kill shot. It's definitely not a wise move to take a head-shot on a bear's thick skull. He waits another second until it has come down a few more feet. It hasn't spotted him, probably smells him, though. He squeezes the trigger, and the crack of the muffled shot is deafening in the still of the night.

    The black bear falls, tumbles down the hill and comes to a stop near Jet, who freaks out and nearly breaks free of his lead rope. The bear attempts to get up. He hasn't killed it. Cory rushes down the bank and lands on his feet after jumping the last few yards to the ground. He stands over the massive beast and fires a clean kill shot this time, putting the animal out of its misery.

    It is snowing again. The white powder is sticking to the animal's black hide. He is thankful for this bounty, for the meat and for the pelt that will provide warmth. He's going to need a hell of a lot more lighting to gut and skin this animal. Cory piles most of the wood from his stack onto the fire-pit he'd built. Next, he unsheathes his knife and pulls the small sharpening stone from his bag.

Four hours later as the sun is rising, Cory has the bear strung up in a tree, the innards and gut sack removed. The fire is still going at a steady click which is helpful as it enables him to see his work better. He doesn't want to draw any more predators to his camp. It takes him a good while to get the unusable parts hauled away with Jet's help. He ties a length of rope to the saddle horn and attaches it to a plastic tarp where the inedible parts lay and has the stallion pull it behind them.

He has more meat than he could ever possibly need. Some of it, he'll cure with salt. Most of it, he'll leave to the wildlife in the surrounding forest. Now he just has to head into town to find salt or alum somewhere if either are available. He isn't sure of its weight, but if he was to guess, Cory would put it at around six hundred pounds give or take, a very large male. If black bear hibernate, then he must've come out early. And he'd come out hungry, sizing up either Cory or his horse for an early meal.

He hoists the carcass much higher into the tree so that he can travel to town and search for supplies. Ground carnivores won't be able to get to the bear at eight to nine feet in the air. Plus he dumped a large amount of meat and innards about a hundred yards away which should keep thieves busy for a while.

Mounting up, Cory guides his horse through the forest, heading into Louisville, Kentucky, his latest city of choice for raiding. He's been rather busy in this big city. There were more people still occupying it than were staying in Clarksville or Nashville combined. It was surprising when he'd first come into town last week. He camps a few miles outside of the city limits, far enough away from the city and homes where smoke from his fire can't be seen above the tree line.

He stops at a wide, deep stream to wash the blood from his hands, cringing at the freezing water. It's a fast wash. He's been to this particular spot many times collecting water for himself and his horse. After letting Jet drink, he's up again and riding toward town. The snow is deep, close to a foot in depth in drifted areas. It doesn't usually snow this much in Tennessee. Apparently Kentucky gets worse weather than Tennessee. The undisturbed ground around him shimmers when the scant bits of light hit it. He's not sure it was a great time to strike out on his own away from the farm, but there was no way he could go back there, either. He is on a mission, and the mission so far has been successful.

Five days ago before the bear had decided to change up his plans, Cory had sniped a man who'd been in the process of abducting a woman from her children. Cory had left the man's knife and gun with the widowed mother. She was on her own and trying to make it to her family in Chicago. He suggested to her that she stay in Louisville but join up with others that could help her. She didn't adhere to his advice. Cory had then found her an abandoned car and managed to get it started. He siphoned gas from a city maintenance truck and she was on her way, three kids in tow to the windy city. He wished her good luck. She tried to hug him in return to show her gratitude and invited him to go with them. He politely declined both.

Three days ago he'd gone back into the city at night and had taken out a small group of four men who were the kind of people who'd murdered his little sister. He hadn't lost any sleep over it. As a matter of fact, he'd slept better than he had in days because the first dickhead Cory had caught in the act of raping a woman in a dirty alley. The man's friends he'd found later that night robbing an old man.

He guides his stallion into the city and ties him securely where he won't be seen by prying eyes. He'll move on foot the rest of the trip until it's time to go back to their camp. On the back deck of an abandoned home, Cory snags the small, steel grate of a gas grill. He'll need this to cure strips of meat. He raids the home and finds a three-quarter full container of Morton salt. That's hardly going to get it. He hits a half dozen more homes, then two townhouses and finds another seven containers of salt of various measure. He jogs through the snow, no longer being plowed and salted and scraped by city and state snow plow trucks, back to his horse where he stashes his loot in a canvas rucksack.

Cory pats his mount's neck and takes off again. The sun has risen somewhere in the world but not here in the outskirts of Louisville because it hides behind ugly gray cloud cover. The dull, hazy light filters down through the atmosphere which lends a depressing gloom to the city, offering an even more downtrodden appearance than just a post-apocalyptic world.

The next place he loots is a hardware store, which is mostly picked clean. He doesn't find what he's looking for but does hear an engine trolling slowly down the street outside of the building. He ducks behind a check-out counter, the cash register long gone. Some people proved their demonstrable idiocy at the beginning of the end. They would've been better off stealing spools of rope or lighter fluid than a cash register full of worthless money.

The vehicle pulls in close to the curb. A man leans out the passenger window, observing Cory's footprints in the deep snow. He can see at least one other man in the car. They cut the engine and get out. Cory slinks to the back of the store and awaits whatever they might be bringing to him. It could be a fight. It could be harmless. He's not sure, but he's not about to run. He flicks off the safety on his sidearm and slings his rifle over his right shoulder.

A sharp intake of breath off to his left catches his ear, causing him to swing on the person with his pistol up. A young woman and a small girl are standing in the dark shadows of the corner.

"Please, don't shoot us, sir," the woman says.

Her voice is young as if she may still be a teenager. The young girl with her can't be more than five years old. Cory holds his gloved-finger to his lips. The girl-woman nods. The tiny girl buries her face in her companion's stomach. They both resemble homeless orphans. They look like the kind of "street kids" that were used in promo ads for charitable causes that supposedly benefited kids who were homeless before the apocalypse hit.

"Do you think she went in here?" one of the men asks to the other or others.

There is no answer, so Cory has no idea how many men are with him. He backs up to the wall and scoots an aisle closer where he has a better-concealed view of the man. He's lean, lanky and has a shaved head not covered with a winter hat. Another man comes into Cory's line of sight. He's shorter, probably around five-five, stout and has bleached blonde hair that hangs below his stocking cap. Reagan would call him a hippy.

"Little bitch," the first one says.

"We'll find her, man," stout guy says. "C'mon. Let's get outta' here. I'm freezin' my ass off."

He tugs at his friend's jacket only to be shirked away.

"Fuck that!" the lean one exclaims angrily. "Bitch stole from us. I'm gonna fuck her up."

"Hey, man," stouty says. "They were just kids, ya' know? Let's just get going. We got to get back to our house 'fore someone else finds our stash."

Lean Guy comes within one aisle from Cory before deciding to give up the search and leave with his friend. He'll live another day although he never knew it. Cory waits another moment before letting out his held breath. They've driven away without another glance back. Cory clicks the safety back on and stashes his .45 in his holster again.

He asks, "They lookin' for you?"

She nods her head shakily.

"Where you from? Around here?" Cory asks the woman who still cowers in the dark corner.

"Yes, sort of," she answers.

Cory nods and continues searching for things he needs while talking to her. "Yeah?"

"Yes, my daughter and I..."

Cory stops her, "Daughter? She's yours?" She seems too young to have a kid who is likely five or six years old.

"Yes, sir," the woman says. "I got pregnant in high school, seventeen, and my parents threw me out. I was taken in by a foster family in Cincinnati. That's where we're from."

Cory walks away to the tools department, searching for one, in particular. The woman just keeps chattering on.

"Before all this I lived there. My foster dad taught at Cincinnati Bible Seminary. He even got me into taking some classes there. That is until this all happened. My girlfriend and I were supposed to move to Louisville into our own apartment, but that didn't happen."

Cory just gives her a nod. He wishes she'd go away and quit talking to him. He has no desire to make human connections anymore. She talks as much as the women at the farm. Damn, do they talk a lot!

"My foster mom was killed the first week. Me and my foster dad stayed alive with Celeste, that's this one here, for the last three years living in Cincinnati, in the suburbs of it. Then he got sick, like really sick. There wasn't anything I could do for him. It's not like I'm a doctor or anything."

Cory gives her a scowl hoping she'll take her daughter and leave.

"I'm Helen," she says, extending her dirty, gloveless hand.

"How come you're in Louisville then if you're from Cincinnati?" Cory asks before begrudgingly shaking her hand.

"We moved out here to a small farm that my foster dad owned. It was his parents' place. He inherited it a long time ago and told me that if anything happened to him that Celeste and I should go there. Told me to get out of the city. Told me we'd be safer there. So far, we have been. Well, 'cept for those jerks. We've been here almost a year now."

"Did you talk this much back then, too?" Cory chides.

She shrugs impishly and replies, "Yeah, I guess. It's just that you're the first person my age that I've talked to for months. I mean other than those guys. Think they were older than us, though. Right? I mean you are my age, right?"

Cory just gives her another scowl.

"Well, anyways, we packed up what we could into my foster dad's car and came here. It's a good thing we made it 'cuz that car was on fumes by the time I found the farm. So, I'm here. It's safer. It's pretty hidden away. But sometimes I need stuff from town. I came here to find some medicine. She's sick. Has had a fever for a few days now."

Cory grabs the tools he needs, surprised that he can find anything at all that he can use. Most people must not be looking for the tools that he requires for processing bear meat.

"How come you were with those guys?" he asks.

"We weren't," Helen tells him. "We ran into them last night in a drugstore. I couldn't find any medicine for her, and they said they had some chicken broth. I was stupid to trust them, I guess. But we followed them a couple blocks to a house where they were camped out. They did have chicken broth in cans. But when I went outside to use the restroom, I overheard them in the kitchen."

She grows quiet. Cory looks over his shoulder at her. He knows what the conversation was between the men when he sees the look on her face. He nods gravely. Damn. Opportunity missed. He should've shot them, after all.

"The one guy was kind of nice, but the other one..."

"Yeah, you'll find that a lot. You shouldn't trust anyone," he warns.

"I was desperate. She's still sick," Helen says. "So I snuck back inside and grabbed Celeste."

"What'd you steal from them?"

"Nothing! I swear," she says with sincerity. "I was too scared of what the one guy was saying he was gonna do to me that I just grabbed my daughter and took off. We hid in a building and then came here this morning when I spotted their car again."

Cory grunts. "They probably stole from each other. Looked like the types that would."

"I guess so."

"I have some medicine back at my camp," he tells her as he grabs a plastic bucket that looks to have once held nails or screws. "You're welcome to follow me back and I'll give it to you for her. How far's your house from here?"

She seems hesitant to tell him.

"I'm not interested," he confirms for her. "If I was, I wouldn't be volunteering to help you."

"Sorry," Helen apologizes. "We're about two miles from here give or take."

"Which direction?"

"I think east. I don't know for sure. I'm not good with directions. I take this road right out here until it turns left, and then I keep going until I get to our turnoff."

"That's southeast. You probably aren't too far from my camp," he says. "I'm to the south. You want my help?"

Helen nods and says, "Yes, please. I'm desperate."

"Come on. I'm done here. Let's get moving," he orders firmly.

Celeste coughs. Cory doesn't even pause. He flings his rifle over his shoulder and picks up the small girl. She doesn't smile at him or cringe. She just rests her hot little head against the base of his neck. When he gets to his horse, he mounts the stallion with the small girl in front of him. Then he extends his hand down to Helen.

"Oh, no. It's ok. I'll walk. I don't want to burden your horse, sir," Helen says.

Cory chuffs and replies, "He's fine. He can carry the three of us just fine. It's not far that we have to go."

She takes his hand nervously, and Cory yanks her up behind him.

"Just wrap your arms around me and hold on."

He has enough salt and tools for the time being, but he'll have to come back to raid for more later tonight. Right now, the most important thing is to get this kid healthy again.

They arrive at his camp where the fire has died down to just gray embers in the pit. The bear carcass still hangs in the tree. He feels Helen stiffen up behind him at the ghastly sight.

"You guys eat bear steaks?" he asks as he helps her down.

"Can't say that I've ever had it," she admits and continues to stare at the dead animal hanging high in the tree undisturbed.

Cory ignores her and carries the girl up the short incline to his cave. He sets her gently to her feet. She immediately sits on his sleeping bag. Rummaging around in his sack, he quickly locates the bottle of mixed pills. He pulls out the fever reducer. He has no idea how many pills to give her. He almost wishes that Reagan or Simon was here, but they are so far away.

"Get her to take this. It's just Tylenol, but it should help," he tells her mother. "Here."

Cory hands her his canteen full of purified water. He leaves them to collect more of the firewood from his pile. Within a few minutes, he has a small fire inside his rock formation cave of sorts burning again. Helen sits beside her daughter in the dirt and leaves instead of on his sleeping bag. She cradles her child and looks like she's going to be sick herself from distress. Her concern for her daughter is apparent on her face, which is younger looking than he'd thought.

"It's ok, baby girl," she coos softly.

"My ear hurts again, Mama," Celeste whispers raggedly.

Helen looks up at Cory helplessly and shrugs.

"I don't know what to do for her."

"How long has she had the earache?" he asks. Man, where's Simon when he needs him?

"About four days or so," she answers and rocks Celeste gently.

"I don't know much about this stuff, but I have a packet of three-day antibiotics we could give her," he offers. He knows that Reagan used to give kids at the farm medicine like that when they got really sick. He doesn't, however, know if this is the right call for this situation. This kid looks very ill.

"I can't take that from you," she says sadly.

Her sense of honor is stronger than both of the men who'd been searching for her.

"And I can't allow you to *not* take it for her," he says lightly.

She smiles at him. There is so much sadness behind her smile that Cory has to look away and dig out the packet of pills. He reads the instructions, not that it's probably going to help. Hell, these could even be expired for all he knows. They probably aren't even an appropriate dose for a kid.

Helen breaks the large pill in half and lets her daughter take it in two doses to get it down. Cory forgets things like that, like trying to get young kids to take pills that are large. Everything is a struggle for them.

"I have work to do," he tells her. "Why don't you guys just stay in here while I work and then I'll cook us some food."

"Let me help," Helen offers and moves to dislodge herself from her daughter.

Cory holds out his hand. "No, just stay with her. Call me if she gets worse. Rest."

Helen agrees to it, but he can tell that she'd like to repay him for the pills. He pulls the flap of his tarp back down over the opening of the shelter, leaving a gap to free the smoke from the fire. He gets straight to work on the bear carcass, trimming fat, cutting away chunks of meat, strips of meat, sharpening his blade and the new tools on his stone and cutting more. Time speeds by as he continues to work. Some of the thinner strips he sets on the fire where he's added more wood, stoked it and placed the stolen grill grate. The work is laborious. He removes his coat very quickly into it since he's working up a sweat. Mixing about three of the containers of salt into the bucket, he collects water from the nearby stream and mixes and dissolves the salt. Then he places thin strips of the bear meat into it. Checking the meat on the campfire, which is more smoking than cooking it, he places a jar of beans on the grate and lowers it. He would not normally cook so much food, but he has two extra mouths to feed tonight.

He cuts as much of the meat away that he can, only what he'll be able to consume within a few weeks. Then with his horse's help again, he hauls the carcass far away into the woods to attract carnivores away from his camp. When he returns, Helen is waiting for him near the fire. She's removed her small backpack from her shoulders and is squatted on her haunches.

"I said you don't need to help," he says.

"You've been out here for hours. She's out. I think I even dozed off for a minute," she confesses guiltily.

Cory is surprised. He hadn't realized he'd been working so long. Time flies when hard work is the order of the day. This is the kind of day he prefers. It keeps his mind off of memories on which he does not wish to dwell.

"That's no problem. You were probably worn out from hiding from those assholes all night. Didn't sleep much last night?" he asks.

"Not a wink," she admits.

Cory frowns and nods. He can't imagine the pressure she must feel trying to keep her daughter alive.

"Thought I'd contribute," she says.

As he draws closer, Cory notices that she has placed a small loaf of bread on the campfire and has a small pile of eggs near her foot.

"We have some chickens," she explains. "I found them at a neighboring farm. Then my only neighbor who actually still lives in his house gave me a rooster last month, so I guess I can have chicks in the spring. He had to teach me all about them. He's a really nice man, a widow, probably in his sixties. Gus is his name."

Cory just nods.

"What's your name? You never did tell me," Helen asks.

He really doesn't want to tell her. He really doesn't want her and her kid at his camp, either, but he couldn't have left them behind. Tomorrow he'll take them back to their farm. It's too late now to do so.

"Cory," he returns simply, hoping she'll stop with all the personal questions.

"Do you have family, Cory? Around here maybe?" she asks.

He just shakes his head and adds more meat to the bucket of brine water. "You'll need to stay here tonight. I'll take you guys home tomorrow, and then I need to get moving."

"Ok, thanks," she says politely.

"Where do those guys from town live? You said you went to their house," Cory inquires.

She gives him a relatively clear idea of where their home is located and how far it was from the hardware store. He knows he can find it. She gives him an uncertain look, but Cory turns away.

He starts on the bearskin next. He hangs it from a branch so that he can scrape the fat and sinew from the fur. He's going to make a blanket of this. He may need it if this shitty winter never ends. Using a scraping tool he'd taken from the hardware, he gets to work. This is going to take hours. Helen comes over, picks up a tool and starts mimicking his motions.

"You don't need…"

"I know," she says, interrupting him with a grin. "I want to."

Later in the evening when the work is done, they've all eaten a meal that filled their bellies with nourishing foods and Celeste and Helen have fallen asleep in his sleeping bag, Cory lies awake listening to the wolves and coyotes and other predators making meals of the carcass and guts of the bear.

That bear had probably been the biggest predator in these parts. He could've become its prey. Cory is fairly certain that had been its plan, especially when it had flanked him. Reaching over, he feels the child's head and breathes a sigh of relief when she doesn't scorch his hand. He doesn't know much about how to help sick people or how to keep a kid alive. His skills are slightly narrower in scope. If these two need defended in a battle, he's more adept for that. Sick kids and talkative mothers aren't his specialty.

Not able to sleep, he rises, leaves his shotgun on the ground next to Helen in his den, mounts his horse bareback and heads back to town to find the men who had lured this young mother and her ill daughter to their own den under the false promise of helping them. The night's still young, the moon full and the fresh snow will make tracking them easy. The most lethal predator in these parts is on the hunt.

Chapter Seven
Sam

They gallop across the pasture, she and Simon, racing for the barn at a speed not safe with so much snow on the ground. Her pant legs will be covered with slush and mud. It doesn't matter. When they arrive, Simon jumps down first before she even has one foot on the ground. They both secure their mounts to the hitching post at the horse barn. The day is overcast and gray, miserable and cold.

They sprint to the big house as quickly as they can. She slips once and almost goes down. Simon grabs her arm to steady her. They don't take off their dirty, wet and muddy boots but blast through the back door right into the kitchen, startling Sue.

"Good heavens!" she exclaims. "What's going on?"

Sam looks at the counter, taking in the cutting boards and Hannah's handiwork. It looks like they are making beef stew for dinner. Lots of work, stick-to-the-ribs kind of comfort food.

"We need Doc and Reagan!" Simon blurts. "Something got to one of the pregnant mares. She's all torn up."

Sam jumps in to clarify as John strolls into the kitchen, "John! Where are Grandpa and Reagan?"

"They went over to the Reynolds. They're looking at two of their cows that are ready to calve any day. Wayne wanted them to check them out. They've had problems with sickness getting their cows lately," he answers. He's holding papers in his hand. The men have been working on plans for cabin additions and also some improvements on the clinic in town.

"No!" Sam cries. "Sierra is hurt, John. She looks like she was attacked by something, and she must've run and she ran into the wire fencing and she's really hurt and stuck in the fence and freaking out!" Sam says on one breath.

"Let me get my coat," John replies calmly. "Hey, Kelly, we've got a mission, bro!"

He calls this to the other room where Kelly must be watching Mary and some of the other children. Sam can hear them giggling. He's probably tossing them into the air or playing on his hands and knees giving them "pony rides" or playing hide and seek. He's always playing with the kids. And the kids are nuts about him, especially his precocious two-year-old. He comes into the room carrying his daughter on his massive shoulders. Mary holds on by using Kelly's thick hair as handlebars.

Simon adds, "We found her all tangled up in the fence when we were riding patrol. She's way out there, too, near the perimeter."

"Let's roll," Kelly says, places Mary on her bottom on the island and grabs his winter coat.

"Simon, Sam, go grab us some horses, ok?" John says. "We're gonna need fence tools. Meet you at the barn."

"Grab my bag for me, please, John," Simon asks.

He means his medical bag, Sam knows. Grandpa gave it to him two years ago for his birthday.

She and Simon jog to the barn and split up. Within a few minutes, they've caught two horses. These are the ones that John and Kelly usually ride, a tall bay gelding for Kelly and a chestnut mare for John. Sam works on their tack while Simon grabs veterinary supplies out of the cabinets. He joins her a few minutes later, and they finish prepping the horses, as John and Kelly come into the barn.

The four of them ride out at a fast pace to find the mare. She's still where Sam and Simon had left her, tangled, panting, near death with fear.

"Aw, shit," Kelly says as they dismount and approach.

John says, "This one's pregnant, too."

The horse has stopped her screaming and has resorted to soft nickers and whimpers. Sam kneels in the snow near her head. She'll try to keep her calm while the men work to free her. She tunes out the guys as they go about their task and instead tries to focus on the frightened mare. She strokes her head soothingly, concentrating on her forehead. Her large, round eyes stare up at Sam trustingly and with absolute fear for her life.

"Shh, Sierra," Sam croons. "It'll be ok now. We're going to help you, girl."

Her answer is another soft nicker. This is one of Sam's favorite mares. She hasn't ridden her for some time since she's near the end of her pregnancy. She hopes the baby doesn't die because of the trauma to its mother, or the mare who is gentle and sweet.

"Sam, give me a hand," Simon requests near the mare's neck. "Put some pressure against this rag. She's got a very deep laceration there. Let's see if we can't get it to slow down before moving her."

Sam crawls through the snow to where Simon indicates and pushes down on the rag. She doesn't want to apply too much pressure. The pain must be nearly unbearable. Sierra's going to need stitches here. She's going to need stitches just about everywhere. Her stomach is bleeding heavily on the underside which is exposed to them as she lies on her right side.

Kelly and John nearly have her cut free. Sam feels so sorry for her. She's going to have to walk back to the barn. There's no way for any of them to transport her any other way.

Simon is wiping away blood, applying bandages and cleaning her wounds as quickly as he can possibly manage. His hands are covered in blood, but he doesn't seem to notice or care. He's even removed his coat, which is now laying in the snow near him. His pants are soaking through like hers from the snow. John cuts the last strand of gnarled and twisted barbed wire.

"She's free," he declares. "Whether she can get up or not is another thing altogether."

"We'll have to help her. She's too weak from exertion," Simon tells them.

"Let's get her on her feet and back to the barn if we can," Kelly says.

They all line up on the other side of the mare, on the other side of what's left of the mangled section of fence. On the count of Kelly's three, they all shove and rock her. It doesn't do much. She's heavier than normal with carrying the baby. On the second try, the mare realizes that they are trying to help her and is able to help them in return. She gets to her feet, stumbles once but stays up. Her long legs are shaking from the trauma.

"This fence needs repaired," John observes. "We'll stay out here and you guys get her back. I'll run up to the Reynolds and get Doc and Reagan."

"John, look," Kelly says, pointing to tracks in the snow.

They all look more closely.

John says, "Coyote? Looks too big to be coyote. Looks like more than one. Wolves?"

"Not sure," Kelly says, clearly puzzled. "We'll get Doc out here later to have a gander."

Simon explains, "The way she has claw marks and the gut injuries, I'd almost say something like a cat. Mountain lion?"

"I don't know," John admits. "Don't think mountain lions are native to Tennessee, but heck, maybe they are now."

"We've got a perimeter check to do later," Kelly says with steely resolve.

"Good job, guys," John says, praising them. "You did great. I don't think she would've made it much longer."

She and Simon nod and turn with their horses' reins in their hands. Simon clips a lead rope onto the injured mare's halter and tugs gently. She limps terribly from the pain of her injuries. Sam winces with her every falter.

They make it to the barn with some sort of blessed luck and get her safely tucked into a clean stall.

"I'll take care of the tack, Simon," Sam offers. "Just look after her."

"Thanks," he agrees and turns toward her stall.

Sam gets both of their trail mounts untacked and brushed down. She turns them out to pasture. By this time, some of the other horses have gathered near the barn. They sense one of their own is in pain and is down.

"Can you fetch me some hot water from the house or cow barn, Sam?" Simon asks.

"On it," Sam says, jogging away with two empty pails.

She rushes to the house, back into the kitchen where Sue and Hannah fill the buckets with hot water from the tap. They stuff more strips of rags into her coat pockets before she heads out again. When she gets to the mare's stall, Simon is standing outside of it holding his shoulder.

"What happened?" she says on a gasp.

"She kicked me," he explains.

"Oh, Simon!" Sam exclaims with concern. "Are you all right?"

"Yeah, it's cool," he says. "I'm fine. She's just in pain. It's not her fault."

She reaches for him, but he shrinks back, still holding his shoulder. His eyes tell her of his pain, which in turn causes her to feel pain in the pit of her stomach out of concern for her friend.

"I said I'm fine," he says testily and pushes away from the wall.

Sam is hurt by his rejection but nods. They both enter the mare's stall. This time Sam holds the horse's halter, keeping her head pointing toward Simon, who is working on patching together her wounds on her stomach. A horse has a tendency to kick in the opposite direction of where it is looking. This way if she kicks again, she'll kick with her back right leg and hit the stall wall instead of him.

Simon injects a few of the wound sites with a numbing solution he must've loaded into the huge animal syringe. The mare jumps every time he plunges the needle into her flesh. Sam doesn't blame her. If someone tried poking her with that thing, she'd probably kick or pass out or cry. He has three of the gashes sewn up, the wounds cleaned with the rags soaked in the hot water and covered with medicinal salve by the time Reagan and Grandpa appear at the stall door.

Grandpa walks directly over to stand next to Simon. He doesn't try to take over but calmly pushes his glasses a little further up onto the bridge of his nose. He's inspecting Simon's work.

"Good job, son," Grandpa says to him and lays a hand on Simon's shoulder.

It's the same shoulder he'd been holding a short while ago from the mare's kick. Simon winces, although Grandpa doesn't notice.

"She'll need antibiotics, wouldn't you say?" he asks of Simon.

Grandpa strokes the mare's neck to soothe her as Simon works. Reagan, on the other hand, jumps right in to help. The mare has gash marks and an enormous chunk of flesh hanging from her right flank and another smaller wound on her chest.

Simon answers, "Yes, sir. I think so, too. Will it hurt the foal she carries?"

"I don't think so. It's better to err on the side of caution with this. She's due to deliver any day. She's going to need her strength to nurse a baby."

"Right," Simon agrees and just keeps working.

He's rolled up his sleeves to his elbows, mindless of the cold air that feels downright arctic blowing through the barn aisle.

"You've done a good job, too, young lady," Grandpa says.

This causes Sam to smile broadly. "Thanks, Grandpa. I went to the house to get hot water, though, and Simon got kicked in the shoulder by her."

"You ok?" Reagan asks distractedly from the rear of the horse.

"Yes, I'm fine. Sam's just a worrywart."

Grandpa defends her, "No such thing. Not anymore. We all look out for each other. It's all right if Samantha wants to worry about you. Better than not having anyone worrying about you. Don't forget that. Right, Samantha?"

"Yep!" she answers with good cheer. She loves Herb McClane so much that her heart swells with pride and joy and optimism whenever she's around him. He smiles and squeezes her forearm before releasing it.

She thinks Simon might scoff quietly, but she's not sure. That wouldn't be like him to be cocky and sarcastic. He's not like that at all. He's always so cerebral and even-keeled. It causes her to frown. He glances up and gives her a mean glare for tattling on him.

Grandpa moves around the horse, checking her, making comments about different injuries that he finds. Then he kicks into full-blown doctor mode and helps them sew her up, patch her up and get her put back together again. Then he announces that he thinks she'll give birth in the next twenty-four hours. She's dilated, probably from the duress she's been under, he says.

"I'll stay out here with her tonight, sir," Simon volunteers.

"Me, too," Sam adds, getting another half groan and sneer from her best friend. She furrows her brow at him in confusion and tips her head to the side.

"Sounds good," Reagan says. "I'm not too thrilled about pulling a midnight shift in the barn. Been there, done that, got the t-shirt… or the horse placenta."

"Eww, that's nasty, Reagan," Sam says on a laugh. Her "big sister" is lewd sometimes. She is funny, though. Crude but funny.

Simon even grins and shakes his head. Grandpa just chuckles.

"Such a delicate little flower," Grandpa comments. "Hand me another bandage. This one here just needs covered to protect it from dirt. Good. There. We're done. Let's all go inside and wash up."

"Simon, come up to the house immediately," Kelly's voice comes over Reagan's radio in a serious tone.

Reagan pulls it from her belt clip and hands it to Simon.

"Yes, sir. On our way," Simon relays.

"Wonder what's going on?" Sam asks rhetorically. Simon shakes his head in answer as they carefully, so as not to slip in slush, but expediently traverse the trail up to the farmhouse with Grandpa and Reagan.

Sam steals a glance up at Simon, noticing how his dark auburn hair sticks out below his navy blue stocking cap. His mouth is set in a hard line, not the demeanor he would usually radiate. There is no sign of the two deep dimples on his cheeks that are always ever present. Now he sports a glower of despair. She'd tried to get him to talk about Em again this morning on their ride. Perhaps that was what had set him off. Or perhaps it is the injured mare.

Some of the family members are waiting for them when they arrive, and some must be off doing chores, working in the house or hanging out at Sue's cabin in the woods. Molly comes over and begs a petting from her by licking her gloved hand. Sam smiles down at the mutt and gives her furry head and ear a quick rub.

"What's going on?" Simon immediately asks of Kelly, who stands on the back porch with John.

"Got a radio message from the Johnson family," Kelly explains. "They want us to come over. They asked specifically for you."

"Is someone ill?" Simon asks.

John shakes his head and answers this time, "I don't think so, bro. They said there's someone over there who knows you."

"That's weird," Sam remarks.

"Someone from the clinic?" Simon inquires.

"I don't think so," John interjects. "They said we'd better get over there quick. Sounds urgent."

"Let's take the Suburban and go on the main road. John already disabled the driveway," Kelly says as he turns to go.

The four of them go inside and do a fast scrubbing of their dirty and bloody hands and arms. Then they each re-bundle in their winter outerwear and head out to the waiting vehicle.

Disabling the drive means that they've unattached the wiring to the driveway explosives alarms. She remembers distinctly those loud tremors that shook the ground when she'd first come down this same driveway in a stolen RV with her band of criminal captors.

Reagan is also present and apparently ready to go, but some of the family aren't. All of the younger children are either in the music room or playing in one of the basement rooms like they do most days when it's too cold to play outdoors.

"Who's staying to keep guard?" Simon asks.

"Derek will stay here to watch the place while we're gone," Grandpa offers. "He's upstairs in John and Reagan's room so he can see everything better."

"Sue's in the house with Hannie," Reagan offers.

"Can I go, John?" Sam asks of Reagan's husband. He's such a sweet man, but Reagan told her once that he also has another side to him that he doesn't like to show anyone. It's a violent side, and luckily he only displays it when the family or his wife is in danger. Most of the time, he's a lot of fun to be around.

"Sure, kid," he returns easily and ruffles the top of her head, sending her stocking cap askew.

Sam grins at him, and they pile into the SUV. It only takes a few minutes to get to the main road, which is actually just a gravel road surrounded on all sides by forestry. Some of the vines and underbrush has crept onto the road and has clogged the drainage ditch on either side. Without road crews maintaining any streets, roads or alleyways anymore, most roads in America look like this now. The men on these three farms try to keep their road cleared away. The highways and main roads, however, are starting to resemble an unkempt front yard of a repossessed home. They pass the Reynolds farm and come to the Johnson's. Something big must be going down. Even Wayne Reynolds has come over on his ATV to the Johnson's farm. They must've radioed him, as well.

The Johnson family had left this valley when the apocalypse first hit to go and live at their son's farm up north. However, they'd found him murdered and his family barely surviving. They'd come back through Illinois and picked up their other son and his family and returned home to their farm here. They probably figured it was safer in this valley than out there in the rest of the country. Sam can certainly attest to that. And now their family is flourishing, and there are young kids, a new baby, two teenagers and two, single adult Johnson daughters, as well. One of them lost her husband to a sickness a year after the fall, and the other is in her mid-thirties and never married. Em used to go over and hang out with one of the teen girls, Christal, who was the same age as her. The Johnsons work with the Reynolds family and a few of the families from the condo community, which John and Kelly had established, to keep their farm going. It takes all of them pulling together to keep these farms thriving which enables their survival.

Kelly turns down their short drive and pulls slowly to a stop. There is a crowd of Johnson and Reynolds family members hovering around. Getting out of the vehicle, Sam's group makes their way closer.

"Ryan," Grandpa extends his hand cordially and shakes the hand of the Johnson family patriarch.

"Herb," Mr. Johnson returns.

"What's going on, Ryan?" he asks.

"Simon," Mr. Johnson says and turns toward him. "It seems like these young people might know you, son."

Mr. Johnson signals to his son, Zach, who disappears into the crowd to likely retrieve whomever it is his father is referring. He's a kind man like his father and the only living son of Mr. Johnson. He's in his late forties and has two of the teenagers, one of the younger children and a wife.

"Said they've been walking for months to get here. Got lost a few times. Had to ask around in town how to find us out here," Mr. Johnson explains as he smokes a cigar.

"Simon?" a woman's voice says from the crowd as she breaks through, dropping her heavy sack on the ground. "Simon?"

She is emaciated thin, her long, stringy red hair hanging below the wool cap covering her head. Her drab brown coat is in tatters. Her jeans match. She wears short leather boots, but they have seen some mileage and are no match against so much snow and mud.

Sam looks up at Simon, who is standing directly beside her. There are unshed tears in his eyes as he steps forward.

"Paige?" he asks weakly.

The red-haired woman nods and runs for Simon. He lifts her clean off the ground, but as he sets her back to her feet she collapses. Her legs give out as she sobs and smiles and laughs and cries over their reunion. She is nearly hysterical. Simon tries his best to support her. Sam has to look away for fear that she'll start crying, as well. This woman is Simon's dead sister. Except that she isn't dead at all. She has clearly survived the apocalypse and somehow, against all possible odds, has found him again. He's hugging her so tightly, pausing only to kiss her forehead, remove her cap, and run his hands and fingers all over her pretty yet gaunt face. He just keeps repeating her name as if he can't believe he's actually seeing her. They'd all falsely assumed she was dead. They were all so wrong.

Chapter Eight
Simon

Their group has returned to the farm, after introductions were made with the other two families, and now Simon is awaiting his sister and her friends while they get their first hot shower in what Paige said was nearly two years. They had a small Shetland pony with them that they had been using to transport the little girl. Sam volunteered to take it out to the horse barn. Forty minutes later, Paige comes upstairs to the kitchen carrying the small girl on her hip.

She hugs Simon again and shakes her head. There are tears in her light blue eyes again, but she manages to hold them back.

"I thought you were dead," Simon says as he indicates that they should go into the music room where he offers her a seat. Most of the family is there waiting for them. There is much to go over, and everyone is curious.

"Thanks," she says as she takes a seat. "I didn't know if you were dead, either."

"I thought I'd never see you again," he states the obvious but can't help it.

"Ditto," she replies softly.

Simon stares at her in disbelief as if he is seeing a ghost. Many times over these last years, he would've been happy even just to see her ghost.

Paige readjusts the child in her lap. The tiny girl's short curls are springing back to life, and she wears recycled clothing from Sue's daughter, Ari. Nothing is ever thrown away or donated to a thrift shop anymore. Everything is saved, repurposed, reused, patched up and put back to use.

"Where have you been?" he asks as Paige's female friend also joins them in the music room.

His sister gives a sigh and shakes her head. "Where haven't we been would be a better question? Everywhere, I guess."

"Please, sit," Sue offers the woman named Talia Jones.

"Thank you, ma'am," she returns as she takes a seat near the piano, her pale, greenish-blue eyes looking nervously around at the strangers.

Simon is still staring with wonder at his sister. It had taken him a moment to recognize her over at the Johnson's. She's so thin. Her long red hair is drying, but still manages to saturate her clean sweater loaned by Sam. She's also wearing borrowed pants and probably borrowed everything else. Even though she's wearing clothing from women who are also lean, these clothes hang on her as if they are three sizes too big. She takes his hand in hers and holds on tight. Simon can feel every bone in her slim fingers.

"Mama, can I play with those toys?" Maddie asks.

Her face is half buried in Paige's neck, but Simon still manages to hear her request.

"Sure, little one," Simon answers instead. "Play with whatever you want."

She doesn't get down from Paige but does peek at him from beneath her thick, dark lashes. Her light mocha skin is so crystal clear and smooth that it resembles soft velvet. Her frizzy curls are endearing. Hearing the other child interested in playing with toys, Ari gets down from her father's lap across the room while also giving Derek one of her sly looks. Her dad just grins at her like he always does. He's a big softy for his kids. Sue is the disciplinarian, not that she very often needs to be. Ari crosses the room to stand in front of Paige.

"Do you like Barbies?" she asks the new girl, Maddie, with her munchkin voice.

This gets a shrug of indecision from Maddie.

"They're dolls, Maddie," Paige explains. "Go play with her. Make friends. You're safe here, honey-bear. Momma will be right here."

The girl looks once at Paige, then at Simon and then finally at Ari, who she seems more willing to trust than him. She hops down lithely and soon they are engaged in animated play in the corner of the room on the window seat and then half under the huge piano.

"Your daughter is adorable, Paige," Sue comments.

Paige shakes her head and answers quietly. "She's not really mine. I mean not technically. She calls Talia and I both by momma, but the truth is that she's not related to either of us. Her mother was our friend at a FEMA camp in Georgia. Maddie was only about a year old when her mother got sick and died. She doesn't understand. She was too young to. So when we took her in with us, she eventually started calling us both momma when she started talking. We never had the heart to tell her."

Talia adds with a playful grin, "She doesn't call Gavin her daddy, though. We're not sure why. She just calls him Gavin. I think he's too much like a kid himself for her to take him too seriously as a father figure."

She and Paige chuckle, but the family does not because none of them really understand anything about the dynamic of Paige's group. They are all eager to learn more, however.

"Speak of the devil," Talia notes as Gavin enters the room.

"Hi, everyone," he says sheepishly and offers a wave.

"Join us and have a seat, son," Doc says.

Gavin does so, sitting next to Talia on the other sofa. His new borrowed clothing also fit him loosely.

Reagan and John stand near the doorway, and their son Jacob has joined the girls in their game of whatever they are playing under the piano. He's about the same age as Maddie, so hopefully they'll get along. Justin, Sue and Derek's eleven-year-old son, also joins the group after he noisily bounds into the room, earning a warning glare from his mother for the interruption. Sam is sitting on the stone slab of the fireplace hearth beside Huntley. He hangs out a lot with Samantha because he'd also been traveling with the visitors and is an orphan. Her bright blue eyes are expectant and hopeful for Simon. He can see how happy she is for him, for this reunion. He has to look away from her.

"So you were in a FEMA camp?" Simon asks, wanting to know more about his sister's whereabouts for the past three and a half years.

"Yes, for a short while," she answers. "That didn't last too long. I think about a month the first time."

"Yeah, that place went downhill fast. Crime, sickness. It was all spreading like a wildfire through there," Talia says.

"Then we went on to find Gav's parents and family and then Talia's," Paige explains patiently.

Simon notices the flicker of bad memories come across her features, so he doesn't press for more information. He doesn't want her to do a full confessional in front of a room full of strangers.

"Ok," he says complacently and squeezes her hand. The look in her eyes tells him that she's thankful for the reprieve in that line of questioning.

"And then we made our way here," she says with a grim smile. "Took us a while."

"Doesn't matter," he says firmly, shakes his head, and puts an arm around her shoulders, pulling her to his side. "You made it. That's all that matters."

"Where is Aunt Amber?" she asks when she draws back slightly. "You said when we last communicated that you were going with her group to come to Tennessee, to Pleasant View to the McClane farm. I wrote it all down so I wouldn't forget."

"Tell ya' later, ok?" he implores and gets a nod of understanding. There will be much that they will discuss in private.

"This place is amazing, Dr. McClane," Gavin praises.

"We do all right, Gavin," Doc returns with a nod.

"Better than all right," Gavin counters. "I haven't been somewhere this safe and remote and well... anything that resembles civilization for a few years now."

"It takes a lot of work, but we're making it," Derek says.

"There are a few towns here and there and some small neighborhoods that are making it like this, but they aren't too welcoming of strangers," Talia puts in.

"Where have you all been staying?" Derek asks.

Talia takes the lead on this one, "Abandoned homes, apartment buildings, tents when we were out in the woods. Caves a few times. That was scary. I was scared to death we'd find a bear or bats or something. City slicker here! Never been out in the boonies like we've had to be since this all happened."

"Sometimes, back when it first hit, we'd find a FEMA center or an Army base where the National Guard was keeping things under control," Paige provides. "Other times we'd sleep in abandoned cars or sleep in whatever car we were driving. We had a lot of them stolen for their gas, though. Seems like we were always trying to find a running car with gas in it."

"What did you do for heat?" Kelly asks from a nearby chair where Hannah sits, and he stands behind her.

"We had a small kerosene heater," Gavin explains. "Someone stole it a few years ago, but I managed to find another."

"When we camped out in our tents, we'd just start a fire," Paige says. "We got pretty good at starting fires."

"And water?" Reagan asks.

"Creeks, streams, lake water. Bottled water at the beginning, but those ran out. We learned real quick to boil the water after all of us got sick on creek water once," Paige offers.

Simon frowns at this. Some of the sicknesses from tainted water such as adenovirus or leptospirosis can make a person very ill and even kill them. Sometimes other sicknesses can stay in the gut for years and come back in a flare up. He's so thankful that his sister is still alive and, other than being gaunt, appears to be healthy.

"That could've been bad," Reagan mirrors his thoughts.

"It was bad enough," Talia says with a weak laugh.

"No kidding," Gavin agrees.

"And food?" John asks. "What have you guys been doing for food? I mean, I'm no doc like these two, but you don't look like you've been eating much."

"That was somewhat tougher," Paige says. "We looted stores and homes where nobody lived anymore. The disaster centers had food, but when they got too dangerous to live in, we had to leave. The military camps were a lot better, a lot safer. For a while. But then they turned dangerous, too. We found a book in a library about how to set snares and traps and how to clean a wild animal for... well, you know what I mean."

"What did you do with a baby? How'd you feed her?" Hannah asks.

"She was taking formula in bottles, and we did manage to find some cans of formula for a few months," Paige answers again and shakes her head. "Then once we figured out that she could eat soft food, it got a lot easier. We even found jars of baby food and then got her on powdered rice and instant potatoes. Stuff like that."

"You guys are some hardcore survivors," John says with an appraising smile.

"Ha!" Gavin exclaims with a laugh. "I don't know about that. Most of the time, we're barely making it. There have been a lot of days when we didn't eat at all so that Maddie could have a little food. I know she has to be undersized for her age. We've just been doing the best we can."

"Yeah, it's not like any of us three had kids or knew what to do with her," Talia remarks.

"How old are you?" Doc asks, fiddling with his unlit pipe.

"I'm twenty-six," Talia answers.

"I'm twenty-eight," Gavin replies.

Paige speaks next, "And I'm twenty-two."

"Oh? Cory just turned twenty-two, as well," Hannah says with good cheer.

She hasn't had much lately to be cheerful about and rarely acts like herself. It's disheartening for Simon to see this in Hannah.

"Is that your brother or..." Paige asks Hannah with confusion.

"No, and he's not here right now," Kelly quickly jumps in. "He's *my* little brother."

"Oh," Paige says confusedly but doesn't push for further information.

"Dinner should be ready soon," Sue remarks.

Simon knows that she's trying hard not to discuss Cory or let the conversation become depressing.

"Something smells great," Gavin says and then blushes.

He has sandy blonde hair and is somewhat short in stature. The pants he has borrowed drag a few inches below his feet. Simon's fairly sure that he won't complain, though. His brown eyes are warm and full of kindness and humor, which is a stark contrast with Simon's best friend, Cory's.

"Well, if there's one thing you'll learn about our farm it's that nobody goes hungry," Reagan informs them.

"Right!" Sue agrees.

"Really?" Paige asks with a furrow of her pale brows.

"Yep, we'll get you guys fattened up in no time and then we'll see where you all might be helpful," Reagan adds.

"What do you mean?" Talia asks.

"Everyone has responsibilities on the farm," Kelly answers. "Some of us do farm work, some do planting, others work on medical things at our clinic. Some of us work on construction projects. Those who are trained to do it, go on runs for supplies when we need them. There's always something that needs done."

"And when we all work together, we get it done, and that's what enables our survival," John explains.

"Sounds like a coordinated effort," Gavin says.

"We'll figure out whatever it is that each of you is good at, and then we'll get you on some daily chores with the rest of us," John suggests and they nod.

"I don't know anything about farming, but we studied some books from the library about what grasses and plants that you can eat. That was a life saver, let me tell ya,'" Talia says.

"That's great," Simon remarks.

"Yeah, it came in handy when we couldn't find anything else," Paige says.

"You won't have to worry about that anymore. There's always something here to eat," Hannah adds in with a warm smile.

"As a matter of fact," Sue says. "Why don't we head into the dining room and start setting up for dinner while Hannah and Reagan pull it all together."

"Sure," Talia offers cordially. "Let us help."

Gavin nods and everyone slowly disperses from the room, even the children. Simon is left alone with his sister and is content just to hold her hand for a few moments of silent reflection.

"Is it gonna be ok, I mean us staying here, Simon?" she asks and turns to face him. "Do you think this McClane family will want us to leave?"

"I don't think so, but we'll probably have a meeting to discuss it after dinner," he tells her. "It's what we usually do when a tough decision has to be made. We make it together."

"You say 'we' like you're a part of their family," she says on a frown.

"That's because I am," he informs her. "These people have been my family and Sam and Huntley's family for the past... almost four years."

"Really?"

"Yeah, sure. Samantha and Huntley are orphans like me, too. The McClane family is really cool, sis."

"It's just so weird," she remarks.

"Why is that?"

"Because it's just a lot different out there than it is here," she admits. "People are mostly afraid of each other and weren't exactly helpful. We had a lot of problems with bad people."

"We've had our own problems with them, too," he says.

"Yeah?"

Simon nods solemnly and just gives her hand a gentle squeeze.

"Some of the people we had problems with were Aunt Amber and her friends," Simon laments.

"Seriously?" she asks. "Didn't she bring you here?"

"Yeah, she brought me here. Thank God," Simon tells her. "But those men and the other women who were with us were…"

He shudders and can't stop the bad memories of that band of wretched people from entering his thoughts.

"What happened?" she presses.

Simon first looks to make sure they are still alone before continuing, "They were bad, Paige. I mean really bad. They abused women, abused the little kids with us, killed innocent people to steal from them."

"Oh my God, Simon," his sister says and lays a hand on his shoulder.

"Amber was a part of it, too," he says and has a hard time meeting her eyes. "They had a plan to come here and take over this farm. Doc McClane's wife, Grams to everyone here on this farm, her brother was a part of it. They were going to kill all the men and take over the farm. I think that's what they planned. I never heard it discussed, but the McClane family let them stay here. Then that group eventually staged a coup and tried to kill them. It all worked out for the best, though. Nobody was killed. I mean, nobody in the McClane family was killed. They asked us to stay here no questions, no strings attached. They wanted to help us."

"That's horrible," she says.

"Yeah, no kidding. Grams's brother, Peter, was how we found this place. He was as evil as them. That's how that girl with the dark hair, Samantha, came here, too. She was with our group, sort of. As I said, they were really horrible, disgusting people."

"What happened?" she inquires hesitantly.

"The Rangers- that's John and Kelly and Derek- they killed them all. Well, they let three of the harmless ones go. Cory killed Aunt Amber. You know, Kelly's brother that isn't here?"

She nods with understanding and squeezes his hand.

"He's my best friend," he explains and has to hold it together over the absence of his friend.

"Amber was going to stab Kelly, so Cory shot her," he says. "He's like that, sis. He's so protective of everyone on the farm. You'd like him."

"Where is he?" she asks.

Simon can't answer, so he shakes his head instead. Paige just nods again.

"And our cousin, Bobby, was killed, too," Simon says and her head snaps up.

"That's actually not surprising," she says and raises her fair eyebrows in jest. "He was always one step away from prison or being killed by someone. One of my friends at my high school graduation party told me that he tried to sell her cocaine. He was always a loser. Ran in the family. That's why Dad never wanted us around them."

"Yeah, not surprising at all I guess," Simon agrees. He doesn't get further into explaining Bobby and what role he had in destroying Sam's life or his own pathetic inability to stop it.

"Everything's so different now," Paige despairs.

"I know," he says and pulls her close by her thin shoulders and holds tight. "We can talk later tonight when everyone goes to bed."

"Is there an extra room for the four of us? We can just share one room. It's what we're used to."

Simon chuckles. "Not only is there an extra room, there are quite a few. Some of them have bunk beds, too. But I sleep out in a cabin. It's where Cory and I stay. Kelly and Hannah and their little girl sleep here in the big house, down the hallway off of the kitchen. That's what we call it, the big house. Doc sleeps here, of course. Reagan and her husband John also live here up on the third floor of the attic. They have a little boy, an orphan. His name's Jacob. He's a lot like Maddie. He doesn't even know they aren't his real parents. Heck, I guess there are a lot of people here that you'll have to get to know. Sue and Derek and their three kids live in the other cabin out in the woods that we all built. There's plenty of room here for you guys."

"Can I stay with you and this Cory kid? Is there room?" she asks politely.

"Of course, but you might want to stay in the main house for a while. It's a lot nicer than the cabin," Simon says and tries not to flinch at the mention of his best friend's name. "Cory's not here anyways. I'll tell you later about that, too. Stay in the big house for a few days. I might be out in the barn for the next twenty-four hours because we have a mare getting ready to give birth. Plus I don't have a shower out at the cabin."

Her brother chuckles. Paige nods.

"You're gonna help a horse have a baby?" she asks with raised eyebrows.

"There's a lot we need to talk about," Simon adds.

Dinner is called and they all manage to crowd into the dining room but have opted for the children to eat at the island in the kitchen and on the furniture in the music room. Doc leads off with a prayer, and Simon notices that Paige's group grasps hands and bow their heads. He suspects they are even more thankful on this evening than any other in a long time.

"This is amazing," Gavin comments as he helps himself to beef stew.

"No kidding," Talia remarks as she takes a biscuit.

Everyone serves themselves as conversations ebb and flow around them. Talk turns like it normally does to what needs done on the farm.

"There's a tree on the patrol path," Sam mentions.

"On it," John says determinedly.

His wife smiles at him. He leans over and kisses her forehead and sweeps a loose tendril of curls behind her ear.

"I can help," Reagan says.

This gets a chuckle from her husband. "You can watch, half pint. But I'll get it."

Reagan gives him an impudent frown, but it's really more of a grin.

"I'll help," Simon offers.

"Nah, hang out with your sister, Simon," John counters. "You two have a lot of catching up to do."

"I'll help you, sir," Gavin chirps up.

This is a good thing to hear. He's offering to help with something already, and he's only been on the farm a few hours. The visitors' group with whom Simon had been traveling when he'd first arrived on the McClane farm had never offered to help with anything. As a matter of fact, they'd insisted that he and Sam and the ten-year-old twins do all of the work. Simon notices that Kelly and John nod to one another in accord.

"Great," John says. "We'll do it after dinner."

"Good. Thank you for the assistance, Gavin. That is much appreciated," Doc says cordially as he passes the soup tureen to Sam.

She always sits right beside Simon and does tonight. She's still wearing her slim, khaki-colored riding pants and a bulky green sweater. Her long black hair is pulled back in a ponytail. Tonight his sister sits on his other side since Cory's gone.

"We'll get the chores done tonight after dinner since we're eating earlier than normal," Kelly says as he hands the basket of biscuits to Hannah, placing it gently into her hands.

"Momma," little Maddie says from her position on Talia's lap as she tugs at Paige's sweater.

"Yes, honey-bear?" Paige asks the tiny girl next to her.

"What's this?" she questions with avid curiosity and holds up a biscuit.

"It's… it's a biscuit, honey-bear," Paige answers brokenly and inhales sharply. "You've just never had one before. Eat it. It's… good."

Simon catches the look on his sister's face before she hangs her head. Her expression is one of quiet dignity and gratitude on a level that most people could never understand. Her shoulders shake, and she covers her face with her hands as she weeps softly. Simon immediately turns her where Paige sags weakly against him and buries her face in his chest.

"It's ok, sis," he comforts her. "You don't ever have to be alone again. I'm here and I'm not going anywhere and you're safe. You'll never be hungry again, not while I'm still around."

The rest of the family is silent. A pin could be heard dropping. He glances around, while still comforting his sister, and sees that Sue and Hannah have both teared up, as well. Reagan hasn't, but John has put his arm around her for support. They give him space to help his sister. Her friends have also stopped eating. Gavin is comforting Talia in a similar manner. They have been through so much to get here. A plain biscuit has shed light on the depth of their struggle. Her reaction to this simple food item has allowed the McClane family to be privy to their arduous journey.

"Simon's right, Paige," Sam finally says with her usual kindness. "We all take care of each other. You'll be safe here."

Simon knows that she is likely remembering her own violent past and cruelty at the hands of the motley crew who'd kidnapped her. The same crew with whom Simon had hitched a ride.

Paige straightens again and nods.

"Sorry," she says on a sniffle.

Simon hands her a handkerchief which she gladly takes.

"Nothing to be sorry about, young lady," Doc says soothingly. "You've been through an ordeal like none of us has experienced. But Simon and Samantha are correct. You'll be safe here. You don't need to worry anymore."

They resume their meal without bringing up her breakdown. Simon's grateful and he's sure that his sister is, as well. He notices that she doesn't eat much, but it's probably not a bad idea regardless. Her stomach is unused to such heavy, hearty foods. Gavin, however, doesn't need much encouragement to help himself to seconds of the beef stew. The meal wraps up and Talia volunteers to help with the dishes and clean-up while Simon takes Paige on a tour of the farm.

The women have loaned Paige and Talia clothing and hats and coats while their old articles are being laundered, if they are even salvageable. She pulls on a dark navy blue wool jacket and a scarf and gloves. Gavin and John are pulling on their outdoor clothing and shoes to go out and cut up that tree.

"We can do this tomorrow if you're tired and just want to rest," Simon proposes as they walk across the back lawn.

"No, I'm fine. It's good to get out. That house was kind of hot. I'm not used to that much heat," she tells him.

"Oh yeah. I guess that would feel hot. Last week the gas gelled up, so we're using firewood. The gas isn't always too reliable anymore, so we're always chopping firewood. And yeah, it gets pretty warm in there. My cabin's toasty warm, too. Cory and I have a small wood-burning stove out there," he adds.

"Not like Arizona. I miss the warm weather," she recalls sadly.

"Yeah, this was hard to get used to at first. Doc wonders if the warm weather out west and down south is still as warm as it used to be or if it changed," he says.

"I can tell you that the weather in Georgia and the Carolinas is still the same," she informs him.

"That's good," he says. "That means that the nukes haven't disturbed our atmosphere here in the states."

"How do you guys have electricity? I haven't seen that in a while. A few homes here and there have it, but if you try to approach them…. well, you just don't try to approach them if you know what I mean," she says.

"Solar power, so we always have to be really careful when there's not much sun for days on end in the winter," he tells her. "What about the disaster centers and the military bases? Didn't they have it?"

"For a while. Once the generators gave out, that was it. And that was when it got bad, too," she says with a shaky sigh.

"Let's feed the horses, all right? That'll help with the evening chores," he explains to guide her off subject and receives a grateful nod.

They spend the next half hour tossing flakes of hay to the horses outdoors and pouring grain and dumping hay to the two pregnant mares in stalls in the barn. Simon carries buckets of water and pours them into the small holding containers inside each mare's stall.

"Do the ones outside need water?" his sister asks.

"Nope. They have a spring that feeds into a big cement trough up on the back hill. The cows have two in their pastures. That's how the cabins have water, too. It's fed in from a spring."

"Oh. That's good. This place is efficient. I gotta say that much," Paige says on a grin.

"Yeah, well we have to be. If it wasn't set up like this, we'd be in trouble," he tells her. "It's a lotta' work. But it's worth it in the end because the animals provide us with transportation, food and when the tractors don't work we can use the horses to pull plows. Luckily we've only had to do that a few times. It's kind of hard on them. They aren't exactly draft horses. But they're pretty cool. I like riding. I can teach you, too."

"Hm, I don't know," she says and wrinkles her nose. "Seems kinda' scary. I prefer to keep my feet on the ground."

Simon laughs. He actually laughs aloud for the first time in a long time. "Scary? After everything you've been through? You're a nut."

Paige shrugs and grins.

"Wanna see my cabin? It's kind of a hike out there, but we could check it out if you want to," he suggests.

"Heck yeah!" she says. "I want to know where you've been hiding out the last three years."

"Zip up your jacket, sis," he orders and gets a peculiar look from his sister in return. "Think it's gonna storm later. Don't want you gettin' sick when I just got you back."

"Oh, so now you're gonna be my protector?"

"I sure am," he returns with a nod and a smile.

"Great," she adds sarcastically but smiles, too.

He chuckles as they leave the barn. He can't stop looking at her. He still can't believe she's here and alive and safe. He's going to do everything in his power to ensure she stays that way.

Chapter Nine
Cory

The next morning Cory loads Helen and Celeste onto his horse with all of his gear and packed meat. He will see them safely home and settled in before moving on. He is leading them on his horse while trekking through the snow on foot.

"Won't you stay on a few days with us, Cory?" Helen asks. "It's the least we can do for helping Celeste."

Her daughter is already feeling considerably better with the one dose of antibiotics in her system. Her color has come back to her small pink cheeks. It's an encouraging sign that she'll not get worse. Unfortunately, she still seemed too weak and fatigued for them to walk home on their own, so that's how he ended up on this route. And even more unfortunate is the fact that her mother literally woke up this morning in full chatter mode. And she's still doing it.

"No thanks. Gotta keep moving," he declines for the tenth time.

"We're almost there," Helen says, ignoring his refusal. "See that place?" she asks, pointing to a small, shake shingle cottage tucked away behind brambles and ivy. "That's my neighbor Gus's place. He's a sweet, old man."

Cory grimaces as she recounts more stories of her neighbor who looks after her and Celeste. They come through a small meadow dotted with oaks and maples and apple trees. The tree groupings becomes denser, forest overgrowth takes hold, but he finds her narrow, snow-covered path that she tells him leads to her own place. Her small white house, shed and chicken coop come into view. It's a picturesque setting surrounded by tall oaks and overgrown, unmanicured bushes. The door to the one car, attached garage is pushed up and has been left open.

He is just about to clear the forestry around them when Jet startles, planting all four feet wide so that he can take flight if need be. Cory reins him in and backs the stallion up. It snorts angrily. They circle back while Cory keeps a keen eye on the house and their surroundings.

"What is it? What was that all about?" Helen asks, not aware of the horse's warning of danger. "Did I kick him by accident?"

"Something's not right," Cory tells her. "Get down."

He reaches up for Celeste, places her behind a wide elm tree and then collects Helen from the horse's back. He makes her stand next to her daughter.

"You live here alone?"

"Yes, yes, of course. I would've told you if someone else lived here with us. I swear. I didn't lie to you, Cory," Helen says, pushing a strand of brown hair back under her pink stocking cap that is embroidered with white flowers.

He is quite sure she would've told him in great, blathering detail of her housemates had she any.

"There was a truck in the drive, and the garage door was open. Is that truck yours?" he asks.

"What?" she asks hysterically. "No! We don't have a car at all. Remember? I told you that it died right before we made it to the house. Ran out of gas. I left it up on the road about a mile from here."

"Stay here," he orders. "Hold the horse. Know how to shoot?"

"Um, a little. My foster dad taught me after things got bad."

He hands her the easiest gun to manipulate, the shotgun, and tries not to roll his eyes with impatience. Jet is prancing with agitation. Cory jams one into the chamber for her and tells her to just pull the trigger if she needs to. Something is wrong, or his horse

100

wouldn't behave this way. If it's just a squirrel, he may have to shoot Jet for being such a contrived imbecile.

"Don't try to follow me," he warns. "If you hear shooting, just stay here. I don't need help. Keep her hidden. Keep the horse hidden. If I don't make it back, then leave with her and my horse. Go to your neighbor and get out of the area with him."

Helen's eyes are wide with fear, the brown color darkening slightly as her pupils enlarge.

"Do you understand?" he asks for confirmation and gets an erratic nodding in answer.

Cory turns and jogs to the edge of the woods again, pulls out his binoculars and squats down behind a holly bush. He waits at least two full minutes before he spots a shadow through a small window moving around in the house. Then he watches a second shadow take the same path. A moment later, a man comes out the back door, letting it slam on its squeaky hinges. Cory flanks him as the man heads to the chicken coop. He remains hidden for the time being just quietly observing. The man has a .38 pistol shoved down in the back of his pants. He doesn't wear a coat, even though it's freezing cold and the snow is deep. His hair is wet. His long-sleeved shirt is damp in the back as if he's just come from the shower.

"Gimme' those fuckin' eggs, you dumbass chickens," he shouts.

One of Helen's brown chickens goes flying out the door as if he kicked her. The hen had some air time that chickens just don't get on their own. Cory screws the silencer onto the end of his pistol and slings his M16 behind him. He stalks up behind the coop and rests his back against the outer wall, staying concealed.

The man, in his early thirties or so, emerges from the coop and jogs back to the house. Cory follows silently and stays outdoors. He needs to do recon on them and see if they are a threat or if they are just squatting on her property out of desperation. He peeks into a nearby window and spots them. Two of them including chicken-man are in her kitchen raiding for food. There is a fire going in the fireplace in the next room which appears to be a living room. A man lounges or is asleep on the sofa. Cory slinks around to the other side of the house where he spies through the windows there but doesn't find anyone else.

He steps onto the porch railing, pulls himself up and climbs onto the lower roof line of the front porch, careful not to slip on the snow. He eases up an unlocked bedroom window. Nobody notices his entry. And after a quick perusal of the entire top floor, which is just two bedrooms and a narrow bathroom, he finds it empty. He can hear the men talking downstairs from his position on the landing of the second floor.

"Don't burn my eggs, you two bitches!" the man, presumably from the sofa, calls to the others.

"Fuck you, asshole!" one of the men in the kitchen yells back. "I ain't the cook around here."

Quieter conversation comes from the kitchen as the other two converse without their alpha male leader. Cory inches closer so that he can hear them.

"Hope that woman comes back," one says.

"If there was a woman here," the other comments. "He could be full of shit, man. There might not be no woman livin' here."

"Sure there is, man," the first one contradicts. "Her shit's still upstairs. Undies, bras, soap, all that women type of shit."

"Can't wait to see what goes in those panties and bras, if you catch my drift," the sous chef says.

"No shit. I get first dibs, though. Hey, maybe she's got an ugly sister for you."

"Who says you get first dibs?" the second one whines.

"You know how it'll go, man. I don't even know why we're arguing. He's gonna claim first dibs. You know how he is," the first one says more quietly than before.

"The only reason he gets first dibs is 'cuz he's got more bullets left than us since we only got one each," one of them says.

Their conversation becomes more muffled as Cory's ire becomes more intense. They mean Helen harm. Hell, they may mean her small, sick daughter harm, as well. This isn't the way he and the other men at the farm talk about women. This is aggressive talk reeking of implied rape.

    He backs away, purposely knocks over a small stack of books resting on the ancient, scarred hardwood floor on his way to the bedroom farthest from the stairs. Putting his back to the wall on the other side of the open door, he waits. It only takes a few seconds. They've heard him, which was the plan. One set of footsteps clambers up the creaky stairs. Then one of the men is in the first bedroom and then in the hall, the bathroom and Cory's room will be last. The man appears, the one from the sofa. A shotgun is the first thing Cory sees coming through the door. Then the man's body is next. Cory shoots him point blank to the back of his skull. He falls with a hard, loud thud. Cory wastes no time and exits through the window again and down to the ground, the snow muffling his drop.

    He jogs around back where he climbs the four porch stairs and tries to open the screen door with the noisy hinges as quietly as he can. He knows for sure that at least one of the other men would've pursued the noises of a gunshot and a clatter on the top floor since his friend wouldn't be answering his calls by now.

    The head chef, he catches in the kitchen. The man manages to get a round off before Cory hits him with a round of his own point blank to his narrow chest. By now the chicken-man has figured it out and found the upstairs vacant, probably discovered the open window. He comes sprinting into the kitchen where Cory gives him the same treatment as he offered his friends. They weren't exactly difficult to take down and obviously had no tactical military training on clearing a room. Helen's kitchen cabinet took the cook's bullet instead of Cory's body for which he is thankful.

    He feels no remorse over the killings. These men were going to use Helen and probably kill her eventually. They've trashed her tiny house, her sanctuary for herself and her young daughter. And Celeste they probably would've abandoned or killed, as well. These are just like other groups he's run into and taken care of. They don't care about stealing from people. They don't lose sleep if they take food from women and children and old people. These are the new cockroaches of society. And Cory has appointed himself as their personal exterminator.

Taking a minute to make sure there aren't any other men on the first floor or lurking in the basement, he then jogs outside and does a quick perimeter check, as well. He tells Helen to stay put a few extra minutes. He needs to carry the cockroaches out of her house and dispose of their corpses. The first two men are easy to carry to the bed of their truck. The third is a little heavier, but he manages. They conveniently even left the keys to the truck in the ignition, which makes his disposal job easier. He doesn't know the area but drives out to the main road where he makes a left turn. A few miles away Cory dumps their bodies in a small ravine and returns to Helen's house. Then he retrieves her and her daughter. He even helps her get the splatters and puddles of coagulating blood cleaned up with old rags she finds in the basement while Celeste is put down for a nap in the guest room on the second floor.

"Thank you, Cory. Again," she says over and over as they dip rags into buckets and scrub the hardwood floor.

"No problem. Stop thanking me," he utters. "Why don't you fix us something to eat while I finish?"

He's mostly sending her to another room because she's driving him nuts. At first she'd wept uncontrollably that men had broken into her home. Then she'd cried because they'd wrecked it looking for anything of interest. Her dining room chairs were knocked over, the drawers of all dressers and desks opened or dumped onto the floor, and her pantry raided. Cory understood her frustration. He also wouldn't like it if people had ransacked the farm. That would've got them a short rope at the end of a sturdy branch.

When he finishes in the bedroom a short while later and rings out the bloody rags, he goes back downstairs where he finds a strange man in the kitchen. His hand automatically jumps to his pistol.

"Hey, wait!" Helen says and dashes between him and the other man. "This is our neighbor, Gus. Remember? I told you about him?"

"I'm not a threat, young man," the old codger says. "You could just about do me in with a good pistol whipping. No need to waste a bullet."

He chuckles which puts Cory a bit more at ease. Cory removes his hand from his holster. He looks down and realizes that his hands are covered in blood, the men's blood that he'd mopped up. Gus extends his hand to shake Cory's, but Cory doesn't mirror his movement. He holds up his hand to show him what he'd be shaking. Gus grimaces, gives a nod of understanding and takes a seat. Celeste bounds into the room in good spirits and rested from her short-lived nap.

Gus is a slim older man, his hair totally silver, what's left of it, and he smells of stale cigarette smoke. He has an awkward gate as if he has a bad back. Celeste obviously trusts Gus because she sits on his lap at the small dinette set in the kitchen. She's resting her cherubic face against his chest. He has his arm wrapped around her and is gently bouncing his bony leg soothingly to comfort her. He is obviously not worried about catching her illness.

"Guess I owe you a big thank you," he says. "I had no idea there was anyone over here. By the looks of the place, I think they were here for a couple days. Maybe they got here right after she left. I told her to leave Celeste with me, but she couldn't bring herself to do it. Nobody leaves their family, I suppose. Not even for a few days."

Cory tries not to cringe at the comment that he knows wasn't meant for him.

"You have about ten acres between your house and hers," Cory notes. "That's too far apart to keep an eye out for each other. You should really think about condensing to one house for safety. If those men came here, others will, too."

"I've lived in my house for over fifty years. It would be kind of hard to leave it," he says.

"It might be a good idea, Gus," Helen says from the stove.

Cory notices that she has started a new meal for them, having disposed of whatever concoction those fuck-heads were preparing. He's glad she did, too. No telling what diseases those creeps were carrying. Her tiny kitchen is immaculately clean. The whole house is actually, minus the disaster that those men caused. He understands why she was so upset at them causing the mess they had. This orderly, neat house is the only thing she probably feels like she can control. The rest of the world has fallen into chaos, but this young woman, who is his age, has managed to create a tiny haven of security and safety and cleanliness tucked away from the dirty, vile world out there. They are still discussing a move-in together situation when she snaps him out of his psych evaluation of her.

"I left some water in the bathroom sink, through there, for you to wash up, Cory," she says, indicating with her spatula through to the other room.

He nods and thanks her then heads into the dining-living area and into the small half bath. Leaning his hands against the sink a moment, Cory gazes into the mirror at the feral man staring back at him. His reflection is frightening. No wonder he scared Gus. There are speckles of blood on his forehead. His hair is long and wild. His brown eyes are dark and haunted. Circles that look like an NFL player's black, under-eye cheek paint blend almost seamlessly into his untrimmed beard.

He'd only slept about an hour this morning before dawn because he'd spent the night tracking and then killing the two men who were after Helen and her daughter for supposedly stealing from them. Then he had stolen from them. If they were going to accuse someone of doing it, he figured he'd at least make the accusation legitimate. He'd stuffed everything they owned of value, including their food and guns into his pack. When he'd left, he'd given them a proverbial Viking burial at sea and torched the disgusting, rundown house where they'd been squatting with rats and mice and whatever else that wanted to come in through the broken windows. It wasn't necessary, but it had given him a clean, uninterrupted exit from the city since people would be distracted by the tall, violent flames licking at the night sky.

Cory plunges his bloody hands into the sink, turning the water into malevolent pink and ruby swirls. She's left soap on the ledge of the pedestal sink for him. He scrubs, repeats the process twice before getting it all removed. Then he drains the water and uses a small towel to dry his hands. The white porcelain of the sink is stained and smeared as if someone has poured a glass of red wine down it. He uses the towel to wipe it clean. He doesn't want Celeste to see blood stains in the sink. She's just a kid. They need preservation from such darknesses.

He joins the others in the dining room where Celeste has brought bowls of food. They say grace. Cory refrains. He and God are not in good standing of late. He has no wish to have Helen's nice dining table burnt to a crisp from a lightning strike.

"How do you have power?" Cory asks when Gus passes a bowl of scrambled eggs his way. The lights of the chandelier, circa 1960 something, flicker but don't go out. The ones in the bathroom had, as well.

"Wind turbine on top of the house," she answers and hands him a platter of bear meat. "It's pretty good. Sometimes it doesn't draw enough power for the stove, so then I just cook over the fireplace. But most of the time it's reliable as long as we use it sparingly."

"Helen told me how much you've helped her, Cory," Gus says, observing him quietly.

He just frowns and gives a brief nod. "What do you do for electric?"

Gus shrugs and says, "Haven't had electric for years. Never wanted to let those electric company people on my property. Don't get mail, neither. Don't trust the government. Never have."

Cory considers him a moment. This guy is kind of strange. Was he some kind of off-grid survivalists or something even before the fall? He sure as hell doesn't look like it now. He looks like a crooked, bent, skinny old man.

"Retired with disability from the railroad. Got hurt on the job back in '12. Some young punk hit me in the back with a coupler, not paying attention to what he shoulda' been doing. Half o' me is metal and pins and screws, and the other half is piss and vinegar."

Cory has no idea what he's talking about with the coupler thing but also doesn't ask. He's not enjoying their conversation. He wishes that he would've left already. This is beginning to feel comfortable, domestic. He fidgets in his chair, itching to flee.

"You two young pups should think 'bout gettin' hitched!"

That startles Cory out of his daze about splitting the scene. He nearly chokes on his tough bear meat.

"Gus!" Helen exclaims. "Goodness me. That's not very subtle."

"She's a good girl, Cory. You could do a whole lot worse. Seems like you could take care of them," Gus replies, looking directly at Cory.

"I'm not stickin' around. I'll be leaving later today. I have places I need to go," he says.

"You shouldn't take off. Stay till spring. It's not safe out there," Helen says.

"Yeah, you and your horse would do well to winter here. I have hay out in the barn for that big stallion. Brought it over here for Helen to bed down her chickens. But I could bring more. I keep a few beef cattle. Always have. Got a couple goats at my place, too. Good for the milk. Goat meat ain't bad, neither. Not as good as this bear steak. Haven't had bear since I was a young pup like you, Cory. Used to hunt up in Alaska every year with my pop."

Cory refuses to make eye contact with her or Gus. He wishes they'd stop talking to him like they are all some big happy family. He keeps his head down, shovels his food and then leaves the table in the middle of the conversation to go outside. There he removes Jet's saddle and tack and places him in the small barn, which isn't much more than a shed. He even finds the hay there which doesn't seem moldy. The stall he places his horse in is small and rickety. Jet could easily get out, but Cory doesn't think he will, not with three flakes of hay to fill his fat gut.

He leaves some of his items, including the bear skin on the dirt floor of the barn. He'll work on the bearskin some more tomorrow once he's gone from here and set up somewhere on his own. There is still a good amount of fat clinging to the skin that will need to be removed before he cures it with salt water.

When he's done, he checks the area again. He takes his rucksack to the house where Helen is finishing with cleaning the kitchen. The home is warm and cozy. No, he definitely isn't going to hang around here.

Gus and Helen join him at the dinette again where he unloads a pile of items from his pack. He retrieves the weapons from the other room which he'd confiscated from the men earlier.

"Where'd you get those other guns?" Helen asks.

He gives her a look that clearly lets her know that she really doesn't want the answer. Her dark eyebrows rise as she nods with understanding.

"Look, I'm gonna leave you with most of these. I don't need them, and they're just taking up room in my bag."

"I've got a shotgun at my house," Gus offers. "We been talkin' and I think I am gonna move in over here, especially if you're not staying…"

"I'm not," Cory reiterates firmly.

"Well, then I guess I better move over here. Seems like we should keep a better eye on each other," Gus tells him. "House is plenty big enough for the *four* of us, though."

Cory shoots him a glare for the added hint. "I take it you know how to shoot?"

"Was in the Army for four years straight outta' high school, young pup. I can shoot just fine. And Helen, here, does fine, too."

"Good. I'm leaving you with another shotgun, two .38's, a .45 and three 9 mills. There's enough ammo in this other bag," Cory says and digs out a smaller canvas bag and also places it on the table, "to get the job done. Whatever job that needs done, I suppose."

He also removes the stolen food items, mostly just canned goods and some dehydrated fruit pieces mixed with nuts.

"Cory, why don't you just get a hot bath, ok?" Helen suggests. "We can go over all of this later. Stay the night at least. You're exhausted. Your horse seems tired, too. Just take a day and clean up and rest. There's clothing in the spare bedroom. Men's clothing. I have no idea who they belonged to, probably my foster dad or his relatives. But you're welcome to them."

"I need to get going," Cory argues, even though his legs feel about ready to buckle.

"Please, don't," Helen pleads. "Just one night. Look, I'm not trying to pressure you. I would just like to pay it forward for everything you've done for us. The hot water tank is small, but it works most of the time. Might not be the hottest water usually, but it works. I don't have a shower, just a tub, but at least you can clean up and rest up before you leave. I'm gonna put a big pot of stew on the fireplace for later. I'll make some bread, too."

The idea of spending a night clean, indoors and with a full belly draws him in like a sweet, mind-altering drug.

He nods and says, "Ok, one night. Then I'm gone."

"Deal. And I won't try to stop you again, either. I promise," Helen says.

Upstairs he runs a shallow bath full of moderately hot water, conserving for the rest of them to do the same. Cory makes a quick scrubbing job of it, using Helen's soap. When he's done, he uses it to scrub his face and beard and hair. The water has turned murkier than he would've thought. He lets out the water and wraps a towel around his waist, leaving the bathroom to the next person.

"Oh, hey!" Helen says.

She's standing in the open door of the guest room where he is rummaging through the drawers. Cory notices that she takes a second to look him up and down, pausing extra long at his stomach.

"I… I was just going to lay out some clean clothing for you. They might be too big, the pants I mean," she stammers.

"Got it. Thanks," he says and stands aside to let her dig out clothing. She probably has a better idea of where the different items might be.

"I can wash your dirty stuff for ya' if you want me to," she offers kindly. "I was going to wash some of our things, so it's not a problem. I do it by hand in the tub and then hang them by the fireplace."

"I can do it myself," he declines the offer. This is all way too comfortable. "I'm going to Gus's house to help him get whatever he wants to bring over here. I don't want you two to have to do all that work when I leave. Is he still here?"

"No, he left to go home and start packing," she answers.

"I'll head over there with that truck. It'll go faster," he says as he surveys the plethora of clothing she has placed on the double bed. The room is sparsely decorated with a bed, covered in a hand-sewn quilt in navy blues and reds, a bedside table and lamp, and two antique-looking dressers. There is a Bible on the nightstand.

"You should just take all this when you leave, Cory," she says. "It's not like I'd ever be able to wear any of it."

"No, but you can cut some of it down, re-sew them and repurpose them. It's not like you can go to the mall anymore," he reflects.

"I wasn't much of a mall-goer before," she explains and then lays her hand on his forearm.

Her thumb rubs a few times against his skin. Cory looks down at her small, pale hand against his darkly-tanned flesh. He pulls away, and Helen takes cue and leaves him to his privacy. A few minutes later, he packs up for Gus's house and drives the chicken kicker's truck over there. His house is slightly bigger than Helen's but not as neat. As a matter of fact, his home is kind of cluttered and messy and even disgusting. Tall stacks of newspapers, yellowed with age create narrow paths from one room to the next. It's a fire hazard. The curtains and walls are coated with a brownish glaze in places from nicotine staining. The acrid smell of tobacco smoke hangs in the air. Cory is surprised that Gus wasn't more excited to get the hell out of his home and into Helen's.

He helps Gus get his four goats loaded into the bed of the pick-up truck along with his small flock of chickens. Then they load his food items, which are mostly crates and boxes full of canned vegetables and a box full of apples from his special tree- as he'd called it- in the grove. The four cows, they will leave in the small enclosed pasture until Gus and Helen can move them in the spring.

The work takes a few hours and four trips, but he and Gus get his belongings, the ones he cares to take, moved into Helen's home. Cory checks on his horse again, helps milk the two nanny goats, gets them settled in and feeds the chickens. The sun set hours ago, and his body is feeling the effects of no sleep for the last few nights.

He joins the group at the dining table again, this time noticing that Celeste sits next to him. Her color has completely returned, and before dinner he saw her sitting on a braided rug of muted red tones on the living room floor playing with her dolls. She smiles up at him through her long brown eyelashes, exposing baby teeth and dimples. She's looking at him with some kind of parental hero worship. Definitely time to move on.

They share in a meal of bear stew based in a thick broth of stewed tomatoes, braised carrots and potatoes. Apparently Helen knows how to keep a garden and how to can the harvest. If not, she would've been dead three years ago like so many others who hadn't known how to take care of themselves and had died from starvation.

He offers to help with the dishes when the meal is over but is rejected and ejected out of Helen's kitchen. Gus is sitting in the living room in a recliner snoozing, snoring softly. Celeste is sent upstairs to start her bath water, and Cory makes a mad dash to his own room.

Helen comes into his room an hour and a half later as Cory is reviewing his map.

"What are you working on?" she asks.

Cory glances up as she sits next to him on his bed which is still made. She's wearing a simple, pink cotton nightgown that comes down to mid-calf. Her hair is still damp from bathing.

Instead of answering her or acknowledging why she sits so close, her knee touching his thigh, he asks, "So what's Cincinnati like again? Dangerous? Safe? Still people living there?"

Her face falls slightly, but she answers, "There are a lot of people there, but it's not safe at all. That's why I came here."

"Not safe like how?"

"Like the men that were after me and Celeste yesterday morning, like the ones in my house earlier. Dangerous, bad people that will kill each other and anyone they have to just to survive. Some of the men are…" she shudders her answers.

That's all he needs to know. Her confession's good enough for him. Now he has a new course to plot.

She touches his leg and says, "I know you aren't like them, Cory. You're a good man. I want you to stay. Can I convince you?"

Her hand gives the meaty part of his thigh muscle a squeeze. Then it travels higher before he clasps his own over top. He shakes his head and tries to temper his rising lust.

"It's nothing against you. Trust me," he says but watches the rejection settle in on her features. "I can't stay. It's not that you aren't appealing. You are. This whole… everything," he tells her, gesturing with his hand around the room, "is great. But I can't stay. I have things I need to take care of and someday… someday I have to go home to my own family."

A new understanding etches creases into the corners of her brown eyes. She nods once, leans forward and kisses his mouth softly. She's not looking for more, Cory knows. It's more of a thank-you than another sexual invitation.

"I hope you find what you're looking for out there, Cory," she says and rises from his bed. At the door, she turns back and says, "You're still a good man. Remember that, ok?"

He nods again, and she leaves. Cory listens and waits until her bedroom door closes with a soft click. He commences with a few hundred push-ups to alleviate his sexual frustration. Then he gets back to work. He also oils down his rifle and cleans his pistol before going to bed and turning off the low-wattage lamp.

Before dawn, he rolls out, dresses, packs and pulls on his boots. He slings his backpack over his shoulder, grabs his rifle and heads out to the rickety barn. Most of the bear meat he leaves for Helen and her little family of three. Cory keeps one small bag of dried bear jerky for himself. He's not worried about food. He can always hunt a deer, squirrel or a rabbit in a few days. He cracks three raw eggs from Helen's coop straight into his mouth. The protein will keep him warm and metabolizing for a few hours until he can hunt.

He doesn't want any more sad goodbyes. If Celeste were to ask him to stay, he might. She's a damn cute kid. He's glad that he could be of service to the single mom, her kid and the old man, but staying here would prevent him from accomplishing his goal of ridding the world of as many scumbags as he can. He can't stay. Although her offer had been enticing. He has a new destination calling his name.

As he's riding away, he glances over his shoulder one more time at the tiny cottage tucked away in the apple grove. They'll make it, he tells himself. He's left them enough firepower for a few years. He turns back around and steers his horse toward the east. There are people out there upon whom he will exact his vengeance and the vengeance of his dead sister. Next stop on the train of death: Cincinnati.

Chapter Ten
Paige

She's been living on the McClane farm for a full week and still doesn't really feel as if she belongs. The family has been more than welcoming, but she just doesn't feel connected to them. They have a very specific way of doing things and have strict schedules and seemingly important family time. Mostly she stands off to the side and observes like a useless tool. She works with Simon on whatever he needs help with, and every day she tries to aid with food preparation. Hannah is by far the easiest person on the farm to get along with, even if she does seem sad and depressed most of the time. When they work together in the kitchen, however, she tries hard to put on a happy face for Paige.

She is standing in the massive kitchen, hanging back somewhat in a corner as the other women work. Sue breezes around her sister Hannah at the island. Paige has no idea what they are working on preparing, but the whole house smells good. The smell of food cooking had actually awakened her.

Sue says, "Paige, turn the sausage over on the stove."

Paige hops to attention, "Oh, yeah sure."

She quickly crosses the room, picks up tongs and turns the long, fat links of some sort of sausage onto its other side to brown. It smells divine.

"Excuse me," Hannah says as she pours a container of something into a pot of boiling water.

"Oh, sorry," Paige blurts and backs up.

Hannah grabs her arm without hesitation and says, "No, you're fine. Stay here. Stay right where you are. I'll work around you."

"Oh, sure," Paige says. This kitchen is hopping at six a.m. The children aren't awake yet and running through the rooms of the grand, old house. The noise and being around so many people has been a bit difficult to adjust to. It's sometimes hectic for her.

"What was that you just poured in there?" she asks Hannah, who has gone back to the island where she is rolling some sort of dough into a roll.

"Grits," Hannah answers.

"Just give them a few stirs now and then, would ya,' Paige?" Sue requests kindly as she crosses to the fridge.

"Oh…oh… ok," Paige answers. What the hell are grits? She bites her lower lip and uses the wooden spatula that Sue jabs at her to stir the grits. It looks like medieval porridge. She stirs it anyway.

She was awake downstairs for a while and was going to head up earlier, but everyone keeps telling her to take it easy and rest. It is difficult to sleep for more than a few hours at a time, which will be a hard habit to break.

"What are you doing there, Mrs. Alexander?" she asks.

Paige doesn't get an answer. She thinks perhaps she's gotten Hannah's last name wrong.

Sue laughs, "Hannie, she means you, silly!"

Hannah laughs once and says, "Oh yes, I guess that is me. Nobody uses my married last name. Just call me Hannah. Making? I'm making glazed cinnamon rolls for Reagan, well, for everyone. But these are her favorite."

Sue chuckles and says, "She's a sugar addict, so we've had to learn how to be creative since we don't actually have sugar anymore."

Paige nods and replies, "Those smell better than the ones my local bakery near my college used to make. They would smell up the whole block with the scents of sugary baked goods."

Sue bumps her hip against Paige's, "Scooch. We gotta share the stove. I need to get these eggs on. The guys will be in soon from chores, and the then monsters will be up. I say that with the utmost affection, Paige."

Paige smiles unsurely. Sue is a very warm and open woman and the oldest of the three McClane sisters. She has a charming way about her, motherly and tender. Maddie had even allowed Sue to tuck her into bed last night.

Reagan comes blasting into the kitchen from the mudroom with frosted red cheeks and a matching nose. She coughs once and blows her nose on a handkerchief. Her hair is damp with snowflakes. She has some seriously untamable curly hair. Paige used to whine about her light red color, but it's not as bad as Reagan's frizzy, wild curls. At least her red hair usually lays in soft waves. Paige had asked her brother about the faded white scar that runs the length of Reagan's cheek, but he hadn't known how she got it and told her that she's had it since he'd come to the farm.

"What up, chicas?" she asks in a joking tone.

"Breakfast, cooking, cleaning, trying to survive, you know, just another day in the apocalypse," Sue teases with her.

Paige smirks and shakes her head disbelievingly. The two women laugh, but Paige notes that Hannah does not.

"Brats up yet?" Reagan inquires presumably after their children.

"No, thank God," Sue jokes again. "Do you notice that it's peaceful in here? The guys still working?"

"Yeah, they'll be along in a minute. Then the really annoying noise will start," Reagan teases.

"The chest beating will commence," Sue says waving her spatula like a sword before going back to scrambling the pan full of eggs next to Paige.

Hannah chuffs this time and says, "I thought you liked the chest beating."

"Only in private," Reagan jokes bawdily.

Paige furrows her brow. These three women are kind of rotten and ornery. It is homey and comfortable hanging out with them, but she still feels mostly like a stranger.

They get everyone fed, the kids on dishes and clean-up duties with a lot of groans, and the men back out the door to work on whatever the hell those crazy dudes are working on. Paige is highly intimidated by the three men on the farm. They are like military badass barbarians. She chooses to tag along with her brother.

Today Paige is working in the woods collecting herbs with Simon, Talia and the neighbor Chet Reynolds. He seems like an honorable man. His sense of loyalty to his family is strong, and Talia seems to get along well with him. He comes over to the farm rather frequently to help out with projects and for the company of the McClane men. His brother Wayne and his wife and daughter visited a few days ago to discuss some sickness that has been affecting their dairy cows. Paige had been confused about two minutes into that conversation. She knows nothing about livestock but is starting to appreciate the cows, in particular. She hasn't had milk in almost four years, so it is welcomed commodity.

Another snow storm blew through the valley the other day, leaving them with a thick blanketing of fresh white powder. The temperature is miserably cold, probably only hovering around twenty-five degrees, but the sun is shining brightly through the trees in the forest and reflecting brilliantly off of the snow. She has her hair pulled back in a braid and covered with a black stocking cap. She borrowed a coat from Sue's stash of clothing that says "Carhartt" on the front, but Paige has no idea what that means. It's warm enough, however. Simon and John had gone to some nearby neighborhood and raided for a few small boxes of clothing for her and her friends. Most of the clothing is baggy and loose, but she's appreciative anyway. All of the pants are too short for her since she's on the tall side. She just tries to wear longer socks to fill in the gap and not have cold skin on her bare legs.

"Look here, Paige," Simon calls over to her.

She joins him near a tree as he picks off the bark with his knife.

"What are you doing?"

"See, sis, this is wild cherry bark," he tells her and turns the piece of bark over in his palm

"So what do you do with it?" Paige asks of her brother who wears a long navy blue wool dress coat and a ball cap that advertises the Tennessee Titans football team. He was never a football fan, so it's obviously just something he's picked up. He's always worn baseball caps since she could remember. They were usually emblazoned with some comic book title, video game, or science equation. Simon has always been more self-conscious of his red hair than her, and their mother used to get mad that he kept it covered. The long wool coat is out of place, but he'd explained that his short winter coat is being repaired by Sue, patched in many places. His worn and threadbare jeans have patches sewn on them at the knees and on the back of one thigh. His short black rubber boots are practical but don't go with the rest of his unusual get-up. His preppy gray sweater is just one more mixed up part of his ensemble. Of course, nobody really thinks much about what they wear anymore.

"It's good for medicinal uses," he tells her. "We'll also try to find a verbena tree- really more of an indigenous shrub actually. You can boil them together and make a tea. Doesn't taste too great. But we can also mix a little cinnamon with them. Helps the taste just a tad. And cinnamon is great for lots of things. Keeps blood sugar low, good for metabolism."

He's in full-blown nerd mode. He was always like this. Even when they were kids, he'd be studying something and almost unaware of other people and what they thought. He'd had a few friends in school, but not many. Paige often wondered if that was the reason her parents sent them to a small private school.

"What kinds of medicinal uses?" Paige asks him, genuinely wanting to know. All of the information her brother has in his head about medicinal cures would've helped her small group greatly over the years. She feels like it's very necessary to learn this. Anything could happen. She and Simon may need to leave this farm someday. He could become ill. She may be his only source of help.

"It's good for respiratory illnesses, colds, sore muscles. Most of the herbs we grind will be made into teas. It just makes it easier for our patients because that way they don't overdose," he explains patiently.

"Overdose? Seriously?"

"Oh, yes!" he says with enthusiasm. "There are a lot of herbs that can kill people if they consume them too heavily or too frequently."

"Like what?"

He smiles patiently and stops searching for a moment before answering, "Well, for instance, licorice root can be dangerous in large quantities. It can cause an irregular heartbeat or cause it to stop altogether. Foxglove is another plant that's highly poisonous. Pharmaceutical companies used to make Digoxin with it. That's a heart medicine, but it can stop your heart, too if taken in the wrong dose. Hemlock, of course, is deadly. Wolfsbane is highly poisonous, as well. As a matter of fact, the Chinese used to tip their arrows with it to ensure their enemy died in case the wound hadn't been fatal. In old folklore, they used to believe that you could kill a werewolf with it."

Her brother chuckles.

"Right, werewolves. I wish that's all we were up against today. Did you learn all of this from Dr. McClane?"

"Some," he says with a shrug. "I went on raids with the guys and would hit the local libraries to bring books about herbs back home. I guess I just like studying it."

Paige regards her big-little brother with awe. He's so different than when they were young. He's so mature and responsible now. His physique is also much different. His body is bulky and thick with muscle and a new height he didn't have when he was fourteen, which was the last time she saw him before leaving for college.

"That's good," she offers forth. What he hands her looks like something that would taste like the tree from which it came. Her brother is excited about the find, though, and stuffs the brown bark down into his distressed leather messenger bag he carries with him everywhere. "It seems like you're always reading a lot of Dr. McClane's medical books."

"I still have a lot to learn," Simon says with a shrug.

"Reagan said you've been reading and studying twelve hours a day for the past four years," she says on a chuckle but gets no reply from him.

"Cory reads a lot, too, but it's all military stuff."

"Sorry about your friend. I can tell you miss him," Paige offers and gets a nod and grimace from her brother. "I never would've thought you'd be a medical doctor someday."

"I'm not. That's why I study hard. We need more doctors. The population is going to continue to die off from diseases that we conquered a hundred years ago if we don't push hard to fight back."

Paige nods solemnly and stares with wonder at this strange man in front of her. His sense of responsibility is unprecedented.

"Sometimes I find wild thyme out here," he tells her as he climbs over a boulder sticking out of the hill.

"And what would you do with that?" she inquires.

"It's helpful with the flu and cold symptoms," he supplies. "And there's ginseng out here, too. It grows in the ground like a root. Doc says there used to be a big issue with people growing it and fighting over it and stealing each other's harvests. Not around here, but elsewhere. You can find it at the base of elm and oak trees. It's good for digestion, your immune system and overall health."

He's like a walking herbal encyclopedia. Something occurs to Paige, though.

"Hey, where are your glasses?" she asks. He used to wear black-framed eyeglasses.

"Oh, I don't wear them all the time," he says distractedly as he bends to pick at more weeds, carefully scraping away the snow with his bare hand.

"How do you see?"

"I can see just fine," he tells her. "My eyes have strengthened without wearing them constantly. I still have them. Sometimes I wear them at night when my eyes get tired and I'm trying to study. Sometimes I wear them at work. But I'm also kind of worried that if I wear them too much and they get broken, then I'll be out for good. The optometrist office in town is destroyed. It was burned down really soon after, I guess, and the doctor fled town to… I don't know, somewhere."

"That's interesting," Paige says as she watches him cut a limb from a bush with his knife. By "work" she knows he means the clinic. She's heard a lot of talk about this clinic of theirs.

"Well, that and Bobby would hit me and then I'd lose them or they'd get broken and I'd constantly have to keep fixing them. So I just learned to live without them," he adds quietly.

"I can't believe you got stuck with them," Paige recalls sadly and places her hand on his forearm. "I'm really sorry about that, Simon. I wish I had been there for you."

Simon shakes his head and frowns. "It's not your fault. Heck, I sure am glad you weren't with me, sis. Aunt Amber was a horrible human being."

"From what you told me about the men she was with, they sound pretty horrible, too."

"Oh yeah, they were sickening freaks. Drug addicts, thieves, murderers, rapists. The worst kind of people imaginable. She probably would've let them…"

"I can imagine. We ran into a lot of those types," Paige recalls.

"I'm glad you finally made it here safely. There were a lot of times I thought about taking off to find you, but I didn't know where to even start. I don't care what you had to do to survive. I'm just thankful that you are alive."

"Me, too," she concurs. "I still can't believe Amber was that bad of a person. I mean I know that Mom and Dad didn't like her, but I had no idea she was that evil."

Simon nods sadly and looks away for a moment before glancing off into the distance, into the serene and peaceful forestry around them.

"I just wish…" he starts.

His blues eyes dart to where Talia and Chet are strolling. It doesn't seem as if they are looking for the things that Simon told them to look for. They are mostly engaged in talking, although Paige cannot tell what about because they are too far away.

"What is it, Simon?" Paige prompts. She searches his face for some hint of what is troubling him.

Unfortunately, he just shakes his head and looks away from her. Whatever it is that haunts her brother, Paige fears that she may never know. A muscle in his long, strong jawline flexes.

She stays on topic and says, "All of us have regrets and things that we wish had gone differently, things that we could go back and change."

"You just have to move forward, Paigie," he says.

He's changing the tenor of their conversation by using the nickname he used to call her, which causes her to smile and nod. He walks forward again, forcing Paige to follow or be left by the tree. He's clearly not going to tell her what had caused him to look so forlorn. She wants to help him if she can. He's the only family she has left.

They pick herbs and bark for a while longer until they come to a stream where Simon picks a few more weeds, or what looks like weeds to Paige. Then they turn back for the farm and run into Samantha on the way. She's carrying a sketch pad, something she seems to have at all times. She sports a bright smile and flashes it at Simon who looks away with a crease between his dark brows.

"What have you been drawing, kiddo?" Chet asks her.

This man is very comfortable with the McClane family, and he looks very protectively at Samantha. He regards her as if she's his kid sister. There is a smile in his eyes and a grin on his face. She's hardly a child. Simon had told her that Sam is almost nineteen. Paige can understand why the men look at her like a child, though. The bone structure of her face is delicate and child-like, her big blue eyes set against porcelain. Chet even ruffles the hat on her head.

"The horses," Sam replies shyly.

She and Simon seem to be very tight. The girl hangs on his every word like he's her big brother. According to Simon, Sam had been with him and the group of people with Aunt Amber. He did not expound on it further, and Paige hadn't pushed him. She knows exactly how he feels. Some things are just too hard to remember, the memories too painful to dredge up. She can't help but wonder what happened to them both while in the custody of Aunt Amber.

Sam tips her sketch pad toward them, earning praise. But when Chet tries to flip a page further, she quickly shuts it.

She even attempts to lie badly to cover up for it with, "Sorry, that one's not done yet."

Simon frowns hard at her which causes Sam to shrug for some reason. These two have an unspoken body language that transcends words sometimes.

Reagan is just returning a horse to the barn when they arrive there, and Simon holds open the stall door for her.

"He's got a limp, Simon," the short, pretty doctor explains.

"Yes, I thought he was favoring his back leg yesterday," her brother agrees with a frown.

"Are you ok, Reagan?" Sam asks.

Upon further scrutiny of the other woman, Paige can see that Reagan's forehead is broken out with beads of sweat, her face seems pale and the skin around her eyes is pink and puffy. She even sniffs and then coughs twice, hard. Her cough sounds wet and full of phlegm.

"I'm the picture of health," she states on another cough.

"Has Doc looked at you?" Simon asks.

Her brother has a lot of faith and respect for Dr. Herb McClane. He talks almost non-stop about the older man. Herb is clearly the patriarch of every person on this farm, even the ones who aren't related to him by blood. Her brother also told her that the people in the community revere and trust his opinion on most issues involving their small town. To Paige, however, just being a part of a community feels too surreal.

Reagan shakes her head and answers, "No, I'm fine. Really, Simon, it's probably just a seasonal cold or something like that. I never get sick."

She uses a handkerchief from her pocket and blots her forehead and then her nose. Even though Paige is freezing her butt off, Reagan is wearing only a t-shirt and flannel shirt over top and seems to be sweating profusely.

"You look like you're burning up, Reagan," Simon argues further and reaches out to feel her forehead.

"Stop!" she hisses with impatience. "Just help me get his leg wrapped. I don't need your help, but this gelding sure as shit does. He has to have stepped in a hole or got kicked by a mare. Look, it's swelled up near the hoof. That's not good."

Simon nods, but Paige notices that it is with great reluctance. The neighbor Chet also seems concerned. Everyone in this small group cares greatly about each other. It makes them all seem like a family instead of distant relatives, married into the family relatives or just neighbors.

The other night, her brother had come to retrieve her before dawn to witness her first horse birth. That had been about as disgusting a thing as she's ever watched. He'd been fascinated and had even assisted Dr. McClane with the birth. The mare was a mess, all cut up and sewn back together, also her brother's handiwork she'd found out. The mother and new colt are in one of the stalls in the horse barn still, being kept away from the others for the time being. The baby horse is cute. Getting it into this world hadn't been.

"Let's just take care of him now while we're out here because Grandpa said that first heifer should be calving soon," Reagan points out.

Paige has certainly never watched or wanted to watch animals birth their babies, but if she and her brother stay on this farm it seems as if she'll need to get used to it. Maybe she can phone in sick for the cow birth. Gross. There was a goat that gave birth the second night she'd been on the farm, but thankfully Simon had taken her out in the morning to look at the baby. She missed all of the excitement, thankfully. She's only been here a week, but all they talk about is animal care, barn maintenance, medicine, chores and community. The life here is simple, but it sure as hell is tiring. When she turns in at night, she sleeps like a dead person for the few hours that she can. Of course, that could be because she actually feels safe for the first time in a long time and is catching up on three and a half years' worth of it. The McClane family has been more than generous and has offered many times for her to not help out with chores and projects until she's stronger, but then she'd just feel like an even bigger freeloader. They worry that she's "too thin" or that she's "just getting stronger." But their concerns aren't necessary. The hard work that doesn't involve running for her life, hiding, trying desperately to keep a small child quiet and alive, scavenging for food and constantly looking over her shoulder is a welcome relief. She doesn't feel for even a second like she fits in with this family of tough farmers and badass soldiers, but at least she has her brother.

The three of them work with the gelding while Paige, Talia and Sam take a rest on the hay that blocks the huge back doors.

"You're a really good rider, Sam," Talia praises.

Neither Talia nor Paige have enjoyed the riding of the horses. At all. Talia explained that she grew up a city slicker, but Paige just genuinely fears them. The horses are muscular and strong and seem kind of stupid most of the time. Her brother put her on one the other day, and it had just stood there. She couldn't get it to move. When it finally did, the dumb animal had trotted back into the barn as if the ride was over. For her, it was. She got off.

"Oh, thanks," Sam says graciously. "You guys will get the hang of it, too!"

She's a sweet girl, innocent and kind. The younger kids cling to her as if she is the center of their worlds.

Talia laughs at her comment and adds, "Nah, no thanks for me. I don't think I'm ever gonna be too popular with the horses around here."

"Right. Me, either," Paige says. And then she asks, "Did you ride before this," she gestures around her, "happened, or did you just learn it when you came here?"

"Um, no, I knew how to ride before," she mumbles evasively and begins hastily packing her art supplies into her backpack.

"Where are you from, Sam? I mean if you don't mind me asking," Talia says.

"Yeah, because we're from all over!" Paige jokes to lighten the mood. "New Orleans, the Carolinas, Arizona and Maddie's real mother was from Florida."

Maddie is in the big house with Gavin playing in the music room with the children. It had taken her less than a full day to adopt every member of the McClane family, especially their children. She's also enjoying all of the new food selections that she's experiencing for the first time. Paige's stomach hasn't adjusted yet to the rich, hearty home-cooked meals that the McClanes serve. Not that they aren't great. They certainly are, but her body isn't used to the heavy cuisine just yet. She hasn't even had beef for over three years. Vegetables, canned vegetables, the occasional fruit like apples, and wild game were the staples they've grown accustomed to. The women in the McClane family serve fresh breads, oatmeal, tons of eggs and meats, potatoes, root vegetables from their cellar and canned vegetables and fruits and jams. It's all too much for her. However, it's all rather delicious, too. Talia has complained about it bothering her stomach, as well, but Gavin had needed about ten minutes to grow used to the substantial portions and rich quality of the food.

"I'm just from right here," Sam evades again and points with her short index finger to her bale of hay.

Paige knows that she is not a McClane, nor is she from this farm. Simon had told her as much, without telling much about Sam at all. But her last name is not McClane; it's Patterson. Talia looks at Paige, and they both realize that they need to drop the subject. Not a problem. Everyone has a past, a dark story they don't wish to share with anyone. She and Talia have their own long list of things they'd like to forget. These are the stories that keep her up some nights and encompass past occurrences that she'd like never to remember again.

"That's cool," Paige offers almost reflexively. "Simon says how great you are at the clinic in town."

She figures the girl would appreciate a reprieve from the torrent of unwelcome questions being fired at her. She gets a sheepish smile from Sam in return.

"I don't know how he gets that I'm 'great' out of what I do at the clinic," Samantha air quotes while grinning. "I just try to be helpful to him and Grandpa, and Reagan when she goes."

"I still can't get over the fact that any of you travel to this Pleasant View town. That's nuts!" Talia remarks with honesty.

"Oh, no," Sam says with a frown. "It's very safe. And it's not far from here, so that's good. We always have guards at the clinic. It's important to work there and offer our services, too. It's sometimes the only medical care people have had in years. They need our help."

Paige scoffs quietly. "He also said you were like this."

"What do you mean?" Sam asks, her black eyebrows raising.

"Generous, overly so sometimes is what he says," Paige says with a sly grin. She watches the small waif's bright blue eyes narrow suspiciously, but with good humor toward Simon. Her black hair hangs down below her wool winter hat, which is also black and blends seamlessly into her hair. The dark pink puffer coat she wears just makes the flush of her cheeks and the blue of her eyes stand out even more. She's a strikingly lovely young woman.

"He's so silly," Sam answers with a soft sigh and a gentle smile that reveals her straight white teeth.

Talia and Paige regard each other again. Sam's response is strange and not what they would've expected. She behaves as if she has a funny little secret that she's keeping all to herself. She's still distracted with tucking her art supplies away into her pack. There are articles littered everywhere on the bales of hay, where she has apparently been sitting and sketching for some time in the cold barn.

"We're ready to go in!" Chet calls from the other end of the barn.

"Well, looks like we'd better get going," Sam remarks.

The young woman slings her yellow floral sack behind her back. Her backpack is mostly brown and grungy, giving it the appearance of being carried by a homeless person for about ten years. Most everything that people own now looks this way. Tattered, holey, patched many times over. This is the appearance of most people's clothing, bedding, bags, or anything made of cloth that Paige has come across. The McClane family seems to have a plethora of extra clothing and bedding items, but they are very conservative with the usage of them.

When they get to the other three, Sam asks first, "How is he doing?"

"Reagan says he'll be just fine," Simon answers her. "Don't worry, Sam."

Her brother's concern for Samantha is endearing. He doesn't even want her to worry about a stupid horse. Of course, they all actually seem to enjoy the horses, unlike Paige.

"Good," Sam says and then coos as if she's talking to a baby. "He's a good boy, aren't you? Yes, you are!"

She rubs the huge horse's muzzle through the open stall door into which she's moved. It makes a funny nickering through its nose against her hand and pushes at the front of the small woman's jacket, leaving a dirt mark. Sam just giggles quietly. Simon, however, gives a short, pained grin and turns away.

"Let's head inside, everyone," Reagan says. "Wanna' stay for dinner, Chet?"

"Hm, yeah, sure," he says. "If you're gonna twist my arm and all."

Paige catches the slide of his eyes toward Talia. Interesting. Her friend smiles openly back at the handsome neighbor with the permanently reddened, leathery skin of a farmer.

"Let me shut the door," Reagan says.

She coughs again as she slides the heavy stall door closed. Then she turns around, sways hard and then passes out altogether. Chet catches her halfway down.

"Oh my goodness!" Sam shrieks.

"Holy shit!" Paige nearly yells. "Is she ok?"

"Get her to the house!" Simon orders loudly. "Never get sick my ass," her brother swears prolifically through his gritted teeth.

They all move quickly through the snow toward the back of the house where Reagan's husband John is unloading firewood. He's laughing loudly at something Kelly is saying to him. Those two always seem to have something to laugh about. She's overheard them reminiscing funny stories from their military pasts. The older brother, Derek, is more serious than John, who seems to find humor in everything. When he turns around to find them coming toward him, the color drains from his face instantly. The humor is gone immediately from his handsome, bearded face. He literally drops his firewood, runs at them, grabs his tiny wife from Simon and races into the house yelling at the top of his lungs. Paige hangs back on the porch with Talia. They've seen this type of situation before. Many times. It never ends well.

Chapter Eleven
Cory

The chipped white lettering on the faded green sign in the shape of the state of Ohio reads *Welcome To Cincinnati* and hangs askew on its post. He stands beside his horse, overlooking the city through binoculars from the crest of a hill. Cory pulls the thick bearskin up over his shoulders to guard against the arctic winds whipping through the valley.

They are leaving Kentucky and moving at a steady pace northward. Cory mounts his horse again, leading him down the incline. The terrain is treacherous and slick, but they manage to get to the bottom where the pavement starts without falling end over end. Jet's hooves clip-clop on the blacktop beneath them and echo noisily throughout the desolate area. Cory pulls the hood of his coat down over his face tighter to keep out the chill of the bitter wind. The softened bearskin is tied around his throat to aid as a subzero wind barrier. It hangs down over Jet's rump, which Cory is sure he appreciates, as well. The road is empty, deserted as usual, but he's not taking any chances. He unbuttons the catch on his rifle scabbard just in case.

They travel further north on route 71 until he comes to a massive suspension bridge with steel girders overhead. There are two tall sandstone towers with strong, steel cables connected to them. It's an amazing structure to behold on foot. He's never been to this area of the country before. His family hadn't traveled much before the apocalypse, not like Kelly, who'd been around the world many times over with the Army. His own plans of joining were thwarted by the shit hitting the fan in a worldwide sweep. He'd been angry at first.

Then he'd reconciled himself to what his life would be. Until Em, he'd been fine with the choices that fate had decided to deal him for a future life. Now he's back to being angry but for different reasons this time. Now he's looking for a reckoning, not a career.

The bridge seems like it could be a potential danger, but there's no way he's crossing the flooded Ohio River down below them on horseback. Many of the neighborhoods are flooded from the Ohio, the banks having long since swelled over from the wide river not being controlled anymore. The bridge has to be close to a hundred feet high, the water below it rushing and roaring along unhindered by man-made locks in the North. Abandoned cars, taxi cabs, buses, motor-homes and semi-trucks are littered about on the long structure. Beneath him, Jet snorts and prances in place. He does this when he's nervous, but Cory urges him forward onto the bridge.

"Don't be a pussy," he scolds. The horse tosses his head angrily as if he understood the insult.

They move slowly, weaving around the vehicles, but staying far away from the edge so that the horse doesn't further spook. He has no wish to chase down his mount if he gets unseated. It doesn't happen often, but when it does it pisses him off.

Cory glances right and sees another bridge, older and one that looks to have been built for trains. This one, unfortunately, has collapsed and now lays partially in the city and partway in the Ohio River. The steel support beams of the old train bridge have apparently buckled and weakened with time and without regular maintenance. This isn't the first time he's seen such huge, seemingly unbreakable infrastructure in ruin on the ground, but it never fails to shock him. This is not even the first destroyed bridge he's seen. He just hopes that the one he's on doesn't decide to do the same thing- at least not until he and his horse are off of it.

There is a long barge which has been left unattended and has crashed into the side of the collapsed bridge, just floating and bobbing there. The freight is still perched rather precariously on the flat surface of the heavy boat.

As they pass the open door of an older model motor-home, a cat scurries out of it, startling his stallion. Cory laughs at him, even though the horse damn near dumped him when it lurched forward.

"Chicken-shit," he reprimands and gets an indignant snort in answer.

At least the vehicles are empty. Sometimes when he's with the Rangers, they find dead people in them. A wild animal calls out to another, drawing his attention to the source. He whips around in the saddle to look over his shoulder. There is a massive buck standing on the other side of the freeway divider about sixty feet behind him. His rack is wide and majestic. His chest is nearly all white. Cory could use those antlers to make knives, but he'll let this one pass. He's too noble to take down, and Cory doesn't need the meat. Besides, the big stud has some balls on him to walk onto the same bridge as Cory and his horse without fear.

They make it to the other end of the bridge where they pause behind a school bus to spy with binoculars toward the downtown district of Cincinnati. There is a professional football stadium and a major league baseball stadium nestled within the city center, both of which had once stood so proudly to draw in excited spectators. Tall office buildings surround the perimeter which will put him on edge if he heads that way. He doesn't like feeling closed in by buildings, narrow streets or… people. The windows of these structures are covered in dirt and filth. Ivy grows wildly up the sides of nearly every building, marring their sophisticated status. This area of the city is very tight and crowded. Cory makes a note to stay close to the buildings for protection and to prevent himself from standing out as a target if he goes in there.

Gunfire in the not too far off distance startles his stallion and alerts Cory at the same moment to potential dangers. He pulls his mount to a swift halt.

"Easy," Cory says softly. "Settle down, knucklehead. Easy."

It is essential that his horse not give them away, bolt and leave him in the dust, or whinny loudly. That gunfire hadn't sounded more than a few hundred yards away. Time to go and investigate.

He weaves around vehicles, a city bus, a semi on its side, which looks to have contained liquid oxygen, and crosses many lanes of the congested freeway as quickly as possible to get to an exit ramp since his horse isn't winged and they are still at a relatively elevated position. Cory takes the first exit he comes to so that he can make progress through the city. He starts heading northeast, crossing streets that contain more vehicles with their gas caps open, letting him know that the city has been well-pillaged. A man sits behind the wheel of one such vehicle, a skeletal corpse really. A spray of dried, brown blood smears the inside of the driver's window. There is a shotgun wedged between him and the steering wheel, and his skull is mostly missing. Apparently nobody wanted a shotgun used in a suicide, and neither does Cory.

He glances right and notices that a section of the freeway he's just come from is destroyed about a quarter mile further east. He would've needed to get off of it regardless. He can't tell how big and broad of a section is ruined, but what he can see is laying in a pile of cement rubble on the city road he's on. It looks to have taken on full mortar fire or a missile or about a ton of dynamite. The cracks all around on the pavement below him, some of which are sizable tell him that it was possibly an earthquake ranking about a solid twenty on the Richter scale. He'll be glad to get out of the city later and back into the forest where he feels safer. First he has work to do, probably a lot of work.

He circles in between buildings covered in moss and black dirt and mold and vines. Many abandoned vehicles line the streets, and one that he passes even has another decomposing dead man in the back seat. His stage of decomposition indicates that he isn't a victim from four years ago, but perhaps four days ago. Likely this one froze to death, thinking he'd survive the cold Ohio winter in a car.

Cory rides down a short alley which has more grass growing from the cracks than some of the lawns he's seen. The gunshots could be a harbinger for help, or it could just be bad people doing bad things to others who are unarmed and incapable of defending themselves.

As he comes closer to the source of the continued commotion of gunfire, he rides his stallion directly through and into an empty building's man door. Jet is used to being pushed forward into buildings and shelters. He's never known the difference between where man should be and where he should go. He's trustworthy, even for a stallion. The building looks to have once been some sort of manufacturing plant. He dismounts, ties Jet to a piece of steel poking out of the wall and rests his hand a moment against the horse's muzzle.

"Easy, boy," he says quietly. "I'll be back. Think about hot chics and getting laid." The stallion snorts at him impatiently and paws at the cement floor.

Cory removes three extra magazines of ammo for his rifle from the saddle bag and heads back out into danger. A woman's cry of terror comes from his west. This is the direction he jogs, using the buildings and vehicles as cover and to prevent himself from being shot. It doesn't take long to find them. They are less than a hundred yards from him. A dead body is on the sidewalk already. There are four men with guns who appear to be terrorizing a small group of people outside of a Gothic style stone church. There are women and children crying and huddling close together. Another woman and an older man are leaned over the dead body of a man and sobbing. He needs a good fighting position.

Cory spots the perfect place, an apartment building with many windows facing the area he needs to view. He sprints low to the six-story building, moves quickly inside and scans the area. The building seems empty. Nobody is squatting on the main level that he swiftly previews. No lighting source comes from anywhere that he can see. The long hallway leading to the first-floor apartments is eerily dark, but no movement alerts him. The smell of mold is overwhelming. Fungus grows up the walls and doors like black stains expressing the torment of the once-inhabited structure. This building has apparently flooded, likely the first winter after the apocalypse. There are two suitcases sitting unattended near the elevator. He's guessing that special vacation to the Bahamas or some other exotic destination was never taken.

He runs up two flights, taking the stairs two and three at a time. Not a soul is in sight. He jogs left down a hall toward the west-facing façade of the building. He cautiously opens an apartment door and scans the rooms within. Nobody resides here anymore and likely have not for some time. Fortunately, the dead smell isn't residing here, either. He hates that nasty smell. He goes back to the entrance and locks the door so that nobody can come up behind him. As he assumed, there are no people still living in apartment 2C. He crosses the main living room still dotted with furniture and belongings covered in a thick blanketing of gray dust, slides up a narrow window and cuts a hole in the screen with his pocket knife.

The hoodlums are still yelling and frightening the group of people below him across the street. One of the men has a woman held to his front against her will. He's holding a gun to her head, has an arm around her waist and is threatening the others. Another man has a woman on her hands and knees and is simulating what he'll do to her later. The other three are laughing and egging him on. She's crying and trying to crawl away. The man just yanks her back by her blonde hair. Her clothing is wet from the snow, her palms an angry red from being cold.

Cory calmly screws his silencer onto the end of his rifle. He doesn't feel rushed, but he wastes no time in taking action. These assholes are enjoying their monologue showmanship and fear-mongering. A short creep screams in a rage at one of the people and then shoots the man point blank to the chest. Apparently their negotiations aren't going well.

Cory takes a few breaths to slow and steady his heart rate even further. Kelly gave him books on snipers like Carlos Hathcock and Chris Kyle so that he could further educate himself even beyond what the men had taught him. Simon is a natural sniper, though. He is probably by far the best long distance shot on the farm. Cory's specialty is hand-to-hand combat and stalking. All three of the Rangers at the farm believe in self-improvement through education and have encouraged him and Simon to work on their skills.

He flicks off the safety, hooks his index finger into the trigger slot and takes aim through his Zeiss scope. A firm squeeze and pop, one target down. The woman he'd been holding lets out a bone-chilling scream as blood and brain matter splatter against the side of her face. Cory aims again, this time on the asshole who'd just murdered an unarmed old man. Another pop and target two is down. The other two realize they are being sniped and turn to flee. Cory shoots and kills the first with two quick-succession shots to the man's back. He knows they are both kill shots. He watches the man's blood and tissue spray against the wall of the building he'd been running toward. The fourth is out of range as he avoids the building his friend was running toward. He changes direction and runs northbound for his life. Time to stalk on foot.

Cory sprints down the stairs of the apartment building, this time using the back exit. It brings him around slightly to the south of the terrified people who had still not spotted him. Cory jogs at a steady pace down an alley, turns left and keeps going. His heavy duty boots give him good traction in the snow, and he's not too worried about being tracked, not when he's the worst sort of death stalker this city's ever seen. He's never been in better shape in his life. For almost four years, he's been in constant training mode on the farm. He's gone up two sizes in clothing, now wearing an XL. His shoulders are wide and strong and match the muscles in his back from chopping and hand splitting firewood, handling livestock and loading and unloading thousands of bales of hay. The men took him and Simon on every mission immediately following their basic training. He knows how to kill a man with a gun, a knife, an improvised weapon like a piece of metal or glass, or hell, just his bare hands. He can build and set human traps, animal traps and snares. Weapons training was not the only drills that he'd been put through. He also knows how to build explosive devices and small bombs and how to detonate them. Knowing when to do E & E is also important. Escape and evade isn't one of his favorite activities, but he understands the importance of knowing when he's outgunned and outmatched. It doesn't happen often. Cory feels no fear. His heartbeat is even. His composure is not ruffled in the least. This will be an easy hunt. Unless Cory's opponent has a time travel escape pod, he's fucked.

 He must find the runner. The man could be joining back up with others. He may report back to a larger group to tell them that someone has killed the other three men. He could possibly bring others back to attack the people in front of the church. There can be no quarter offered to this man. He pauses and listens at the corner of two streets, waiting for his perp to give himself away. It doesn't take long.

 Cory hears the faint rattling of metal or steel being shaken or tested and turns in that direction. It only takes him a second to find the other man who is disappearing into a short, square building's front door as Cory rounds the corner. He will try to enter through the rear. He runs to the back of the small, cement block building and finds the door already pried open. Easy enough. He steps gingerly around debris, careful not to kick anything and alert his prey. He's in some kind of a restaurant. Cory leads with his rifle and moves into the dining area, finding the man peering frightfully out the front display window.

 "Hey," he calls softly, startling the other man.

The perp swings his shotgun toward him, and Cory drills him in the right shoulder, causing the man to drop his weapon. Then he shoots him once more in the left thigh, disabling the man which makes him cry out in anguish. Sliding down the wall and window and leaving a trail of blood from his shoulder wound, his prey drops to the dirty linoleum floor.

"Please, man!" he screams and begs. "Please, don't kill me."

Cory steps around an overturned table and walks closer to the bleeding man. He kicks his shotgun away and checks him for a pistol. He finds none. Bummer. He could always use another handgun or really just ammo for his.

He asks the man who is bleeding out, "What were you doing with those people?"

"We was just lookin' for some help," he lies.

"Help? You mean by raping their women?"

"What?"

"I saw you," Cory admits. "You were the one with the woman on the ground. You like raping women, fucker?"

"Who cares? What are you some kind of saint? Like you ain't never taken a woman. My woman was killed a year ago. We just wanted food, and then we saw their women. Ain't no big deal. They was just with an old man and some young punk."

"Not now, dumb-ass. You killed their men," Cory states with irritation.

"Hey, hey, we can go back there. You know, me and you. Yeah, man. Help me and we'll go back there together," he suggests.

Bad move on his part. Cory nudges him in the arm with his rifle tip. The man yells loudly from the pain. He grits his teeth and tries to scoot away. Cory doesn't want to kill him, though. He needs more information.

"How many others are with your group?"

"Please, don't shoot me again. I'm not a bad person," the guy says while trying to stem the blood pumping out of his leg.

The leg wound, left unattended, will be fatal. Blood squirts between the man's thin fingers and splatters the black and white checkerboard pattern on the floor.

"Answer me and I won't shoot you again," Cory warns. His eyes dart above the man, watching the street cautiously so as not to be come upon. "You don't answer and you get shot in the other arm.

You don't answer again and I'll shoot you in one foot and then the other. Got it? Give me their position. Where are you camped? How many are with your group?"

"Aww, man, fuck! I'm bleeding to death!" the man whines loudly as tears stream down his face. "Help me, man! Help me tie this off or something!"

Cory kicks the jerk's foot and lifts his chin in a gesture that the man should start speaking and quickly.

"Ok, ok, just don't shoot me again!" he bleats hysterically. "They're up in a neighborhood. We've got a house up there. 'Bout a mile from here or so. We was just out… looking for supplies and shit."

"How many others are there?" Cory inquires. He has no doubt that this man and the other three were looking for women, not supplies. He's seen this more times than he'd like. They take women and use them until they die. They give them just enough to keep them alive while they repeatedly rape and abuse them.

"Five guys," the other man answers.

His eyes are a dark brown, almost black and remind Cory of that little fucker Bobby, Simon's cousin, who John had killed in the forest. This man's eyes, however, are filled with fear. They should be.

"Give me directions," Cory demands and the other man starts rapid fire spilling forth details about their compound. He gives him the directions to the house, where it's positioned in the neighborhood and everything Cory demands. When he stops answering questions, Cory steps on his leg, the wounded one.

"Aigh! Stop! Ok, ok," he whimpers in defeat.

Cory asks, "Any women or kids with your group?"

He only gets a shake of the head in answer. So they were looking for replacement women.

"Don't kill me, man," he pleads again. "Please, man. Who are you? What the fuck? You just go around shooting people? Shit! *What are you, the new police force around here?*"

Cory smiles ruefully and states, "To scumbag sons a' bitches like you? I'm the Angel of Death."

And with that, he head-shots the creep and takes his weapon.

Chapter Twelve
Reagan

Her eyes peep open and then close again as if heavy weights are attached to her eyelashes. When she opens them next, she is greeted by Hannie's gentle face, covered with a surgical style cotton mask. A hand squeezes her own. Reagan clears her voice, which comes out more like a weak croak.

"She's waking up," Hannah calls over her shoulder.

Reagan tries to speak, but her voice cracks and her mouth feels dry. Her body aches but not as badly as it had the last time she'd awakened. She coughs weakly. Her sister's different colored eyes are filled with unshed tears and raw emotion. Hannah blows out a long sigh and then shakes her head as if relieved.

Someone on her other side holds a cup to her mouth so that she can take a sip. It's Grandpa.

"Now you just hold still, honey, and let me take your vitals again," he says gently.

His voice sounds strange, full of worry and concern.

"Again?" she croaks out. "When did you take them before?"

His eyes refuse to meet hers. He's also wearing the protective mask over his mouth and nose, but his eyes are giving away his distress. The corners pinch, the lines between his gray brows deepen.

"Just lie still and rest, Reagan," he tells her.

"How long was I asleep?"

"Just take it easy, sweetie," Grandpa says patiently.

"What…" Reagan begins to say but succumbs to a fit of coughing. Her chest hurts, and her body feels cool, cold almost.

"It's ok, Reagan," Hannie says on her other side.

Grandpa listens through his stethoscope to her chest, takes her pulse and checks her for fever with a thermometer.

"I'll be back," he says before leaving.

"What's going on, Hannie?" she asks her sister.

"You've been very sick, sis," she answers patiently.

Hannah rubs her thumb over Reagan's hand through a rubber glove. As she wakes and becomes more alert, she realizes that Hannah is also wearing a protective gown.

"I don't remember," Reagan says weakly and tries to sit up.

"No, no," Hannah says. "Don't get up."

Her sister presses her shoulder more firmly down again. Reagan frowns and sniffs hard. Her sinuses are burning and feel stuffy.

"What's wrong with me? What do I have? How the hell long was I out?" The questions just start pouring out of her mouth. "Where is everyone? Where am I?"

"It's ok. Calm down," Hannah says gently. "You're in the shed. See?"

Her sister indicates with a wave of her graceful, gloved-hand around the room. Reagan frowns.

"You've been out for a while," Hannah provides.

"What's 'a while'?" she asks with trepidation.

"Four days. Well, four and a half days since today is almost over," Hannah explains.

"Holy shit," Reagan murmurs and gets a scowl from her delicate sister. She rolls slightly to her side and realizes from the pinch in her arm that an IV drip is hooked up to her. "What the hell? An IV, too?"

"It was necessary," Hannah says. "You were dehydrating."

Reagan sighs and swallows hard around her sore throat.

"Do you remember what happened?" Hannie asks.

She thinks for a moment, trying to recall anything about four days ago. "I was in the barn. And… Simon and I were taping a gelding's leg. Is he ok?"

"Simon?"

"No, the horse," Reagan clarifies.

"Oh," Hannah says with a smile behind her mask. "Yes, silly, he's fine. He's back out in the pasture. But that was the least of our problems, Reagan Harrison! You passed out! John about lost his mind."

Reagan winces. She doesn't like to think of John being distressed. She looks around again.

"Passed out? I don't remember that part. Where is John?"

"Oh, he's inside with Jacob," Hannah says.

Reagan nods. It's difficult to focus. Her mind feels fuzzy.

"Grandpa sent him in about an hour ago when I came out," her sister explains.

"How is he?" Reagan asks of her husband, worried about his state of mind.

"Not great. He's been sleeping for the past four days in this very chair," Hannah says honestly. "None of us have been doing too hot, Reagan. You were… you were really bad."

"What did Grandpa say it is?"

"That first night when you had fevers over one-o-four, he went to town with Kelly. He said there were some patients that you both took care of at the clinic who had the same symptoms," she says.

"And?"

Grandpa's voice interrupts them as he comes into the shed, "I wanted to know how they were doing, if they were better. Two of them died, honey. They had influenza. You have it, too. That's why I had to quarantine you. This isn't just a seasonal thing. This is full-blown flu A, but not like I've seen, not in my lifetime."

"Shit," Reagan whispers. She sure as hell doesn't want to get anyone in her family sick. Her little boy has never been exposed to anything this bad. It could kill him.

"Your fevers were spiking so high that I couldn't get them down," Grandpa says as he pulls down his mask. "As you well know, there are no anti-viral drugs to give anymore. This is more like the Spanish flu or H1N1 or H2N3."

He looks weary and ragged. His face is unshaven, and a growth of four days' worth of gray whiskers is present on his cheeks. His eyes are hooded and tired behind his glasses.

"How did you treat it?" Reagan asks.

Grandpa smiles and presses his hand to her cheek and then her forehead.

"Doctors always make the worst patients, Miss Hannah," he says with a smirk, glancing at Hannah.

"In her defense, Grandpa, she was mostly out," Hannah jokes lightly. "She missed all the exciting stuff."

Her sister air quotes to which Reagan scowls.

"Take a few sips, Reagan," Grandpa orders.

He presses a mug filled with warm liquid to her mouth. Reagan takes a small drink and grimaces. Grandpa just smiles at her.

"Great, now I'm going to be treated with yours and Simon's hippy-dippy teas and shit?" she asks with sarcasm and then coughs. Her congestions does sound pretty damn bad. "What's next? Gonna do a dance around the fire-pit and go streaking?"

Grandpa chuckles and pushes the hair back from her forehead. It feels damp and matted there. That probably looks attractive.

"You're cool. Finally," he says. "Temperature is back down to ninety-nine."

"I feel cold actually. Yeah, I think I remember having a fever. I kind of remember waking up a couple times. I thought I was just having some kind of trippy, hallucinogenic dream. Thought I must've drunk some of your hippy tea," she teases again. Her grandfather grins.

"We'll get you a warm blanket in a moment. I told John that you're finally awake," he says as he pauses to take her pulse, "when I went to get your tea- that you *will* drink, young lady. He'll be out shortly. Jacob's giving him some trouble going to bed. Your son's been worried about you. I think we had a harder time keeping him out of here than your husband. We gave up on John. He wouldn't leave at all."

"Yeah, I miss my guys," Reagan says. She'd like to get up, go into the house and shower away her germs and the general grimy feeling she has from sweating through fevers. Her body doesn't seem to want to respond to that idea, though. She just feels weak, like she's been run over by a stampeding herd of cattle and boat anchors have been attached to her limbs.

"I'm hooking up another bag," Grandpa says.

She knows he means a saline drip as she watches quietly while he works. How the hell had she become sick? She never gets sick.

"Is anyone else presenting symptoms?" she asks the inevitable.

"No, no, sweetie. Just you," he says with a wink. "You're the lucky one."

"We were so worried," Hannah says on a soft cry.

Grandpa swiftly rounds the bed and puts an arm around her sister. Reagan squeezes Hannah's hand reassuringly.

"She's fine now, Hannah dear," Grandpa says.

Hannah nods and wipes at her eyes with a handkerchief. It already looks very used.

"Wait a minute," Reagan halts them. "How the hell sick was I?"

Grandpa's eyes meet hers. He shakes his head slowly. Well shit. She hadn't known she was even sick. She'd written it off as a cold.

"Sorry, Grandpa," she explains. "I thought it was just seasonal or a cold or something. I had no idea that I was getting that sick."

"You may have just had something mild, but when you were exposed to the flu it took hold hard on you since your immune system was already compromised."

Reagan nods and feels depressed.

"This is quickly becoming pandemic," he explains further.

She furrows her brow, and he continues.

"We went into town again yesterday, Kelly and Derek and I. There are over thirty families down with this. Even Zach Johnson's daughter has it. Three others have died, as well as the two we treated at the clinic."

"Shit," Reagan swears as her eyelids begin to droop again. "Hey, don't put any sedatives in my IV. I don't want to get too tired to stay awake again."

Grandpa just chuffs softly through his nose.

"Told you doctors make the worst patients," he says to Hannah, which makes her smile.

"We need to go and re-sanitize the clinic and our..." she starts but is cut off.

Grandpa states, "We already did, Reagan. We also sanitized the house, the laundry, the bedding and the vehicles. We've got it under control, Dr. McClane. The only problem I could foresee is the family who had contact with you, physical contact with you, within a few days to a week before you started fevering."

Reagan frowns hard. "Yeah, that's not good. What about Jacob? I mean, I hold him and kiss him. And John! Shit, they could both get it."

Grandpa's eyes tighten, and he says, "I know. But we're taking preventative measures. They are both drinking my teas."

Reagan laughs, actually laughs out loud and rolls her eyes at him. Grandpa chuckles. It makes them both feel a little better, but she knows that they also both understand the danger her family could be in. A moment later, Kelly pokes his head into the building.

"Hey, baby," he says softly to Hannah. "Brought another load of firewood, Doc."

"Thank you, Kelly," Grandpa says as he rises to greet her brother-in-law.

"Baby, I told you that you could come out for a few minutes," Kelly cautiously says to Hannah. "It's been almost an hour."

"Kelly Alexander!" Hannah scolds harshly.

Wow, Hannah never talks so meanly to anyone, especially not to her husband. Reagan watches the interaction with curiosity.

"She's my sister," Hannah states emphatically. "I'll leave when I'm good and ready!"

Kelly sets the armload of firewood next to the small, compact wood-burning stove and backs away toward the door. He places his hands on his hips through his thick parka.

"Five more minutes, woman, and I'm coming out here to carry you back to the house if I have to," he threatens and then quickly retreats.

Reagan chuckles. She wasn't sure how much of Hannah's sass Kelly was going to tolerate. Apparently not too much. Grandpa chuckles once, too, as he finishes adjusting her IV drip. She still wants to know exactly what he's been pumping through it.

"I'll leave you girls for a minute," he states. "Going to get John for you and some more of my hippy-dippy herbs."

He smiles, winks at her and leaves.

"This sucks," Reagan complains. Her voice sounds scratchy, even more so than normal. Hannah just squeezes her hand.

"Grandpa says we'll need to watch for a relapse," her sister says.

"Hm, I'm sure I'll be fine," Reagan says, trying to reassure her lovely sister.

"You were so very ill, Reagan," Hannah says again and then lays her head against Reagan's hand on the bed. "I can't lose you. We've already lost Em and Grams. I can't lose you, too."

Reagan places her hand on Hannah's head and strokes her soft hair. "You won't, Hannie. I'm tough. Hell, look at me. I'm in peak form."

Hannah raises her head and chuffs softly.

"I wouldn't be bragging too loudly right now if I were you," Hannah chides gently.

"I'm not going anywhere," she emphasizes again. "I'm here to stay. You're stuck with me."

A short time later, her husband bursts through the door. Reagan can immediately tell that he hasn't slept much during the week that she's been sick. His hair stands up on end, and his eyes are hooded and exhausted. He rushes toward her bed and, without thinking, gathers her into his arms. He plies her face with kisses and leaves a final one on her forehead. The rough beard he's grown this winter rubs against her cheek.

"John!" Hannah exclaims. "You could get sick. Don't do that."

Before John can rebut her sister, Kelly reappears at the door and escorts Hannah away. Reagan can hear her arguing with him all the way to the house. John grasps her chin and turns her toward him. He has taken up residence in Hannah's chair.

"Don't you ever do that to me again, Reagan McClane Harrison," he threatens.

His blue eyes are bloodshot. His brow is so tightly knitted together that she fears it'll stay that way.

"I'm fine," she says weakly. Maybe not fine but doing slightly better in her opinion. She's getting a blinding headache, one of the many symptoms of the flu.

"We weren't so sure yesterday morning," he tells her and kisses her hand. "You were at your worst yesterday. All day your fevers were so high. Doc said one time that you were up to one-o-six. That's dangerous high, he said."

Reagan nods. "I know. That's pretty bad. I remember feeling like I was on fire," she acknowledges.

"He said there could be complications, a relapse, infertility issues, pneumonia still," John frets with full-blown anxiety.

"I'm feeling much better, babe," Reagan says. "You know I can't get pregnant, so that doesn't even matter. Is Jacob ok? Are you? Have you felt any of the symptoms…"

"Reagan, we're all fine. You're the one that's sick, honey," he says with a soft smile. "Don't worry about the rest of us. Just get better."

"Shower when you go inside, John," she orders softly.

She blinks heavily and then the next thing she knows she's snapping back awake. Grandpa has returned, but John still sits beside her. Reagan has no idea how long she was out. A warm blanket is covering her. It feels delightfully cozy. Having John beside her and Grandpa taking care of her makes her feel safe.

"There's our girl again," Grandpa remarks with wit.

"You two don't have to stay out here," Reagan says weakly. "You can go back in. It's not like I'm going to be doing anything other than lying here, maybe dying a little bit."

"That's… not funny," John scolds as usual. "I'm not leaving," he states simply and squeezes her hand.

"I need to use the restroom," she tells them.

"Just a moment, honey," Grandpa says. "Let me get your stats again and then you can go."

The men added on a small, rustic bathroom to the med shed a few years ago so that the house bathroom would not have to be used by sick people or the medical staff taking care of them.

"How long was I out?" she asks.

"A few hours," John tells her.

Reagan frowns lightly. Damn, she thought she'd only been out for a few minutes not hours. Her throat feels like she's swallowing razorblades.

"Can I get a drink?"

"Sure, babe," John agrees.

He holds a glass of cool water to her mouth, but Reagan takes it from him. She even pushes to a slightly elevated seated position.

"Take it easy, Reagan," John complains with worry.

Reagan shakes her head. "I actually feel a little better..."

"It's my tea working!" Grandpa states with zeal.

She rolls her eyes at him, earning a chuckle from John.

"Anyone else sick?" she nervously inquires after her family.

"Sue is feeling a little down, but she's not running fevers," Grandpa tells her.

"Oh no," Reagan says on a sigh. "She's not getting this, is she?"

Grandpa places his hand reassuringly on her shoulder and smiles gently.

"I don't think so," he says. "But if she is, we'll treat it the same way."

Reagan feels sick with guilt now instead of fevers and body aches. What if she's infected her whole family? What if one of them dies?

"My granddaughters are tough cookies, little missy. Everyone will be just fine. You don't need to worry about any of that. Just get well," Grandpa tells her.

"Right," John agrees with her grandfather. "Don't worry about everyone else. Just concentrate on getting better."

Reagan nods but can't help the frown she knows is on her face. If Hannah contracted this, then she might not be able to have any more children. Sue already can't conceive more. After her mid-term miscarriage that had gone so badly almost four years ago, Grandpa and Reagan had come to the conclusion that she would likely never conceive again. She'd been so devastated, but at least she and Derek have their three healthy munchkins. Reagan's still not convinced that people should just continue procreating as if nothing has changed in the world. Grams had not agreed one iota with that philosophy and had told her so many times. It's not like it would've mattered, though because she can't have kids. It doesn't bother her because she has Jacob, and he's all she needs.

"You should go in and sleep in the house tonight, John," she tells her husband after he's helped her to the bathroom and back to her bed again. Her legs had felt like rubber and had given out on her when she'd stood. Her husband, her husband with the huge arm muscles and strong back, had insisted on carrying her. Just being in his arms again for a few brief moments had made her feel like everything would be ok. He always makes her feel this way.

"Not a chance, boss," he says with a handsome grin.

She just gives him a jeering look. "If I'm not fevering tomorrow, do you think I can go back to the big house, Grandpa?"

"We'll see, honey," he says as he writes something on her chart.

Reagan almost laughs. He's so thorough, even if he's just taking care of his own family. Some doctorly habits must be hard for him to break. She would also like to get her hands on those notes.

"Let's not push this, ok?" he says and touches her shoulder again.

Reagan nods and feels that familiar tug of fatigue enveloping her in a warm embrace of restful promise. She slips away again to that place where she doesn't have to think about the world as it is now. Where she can believe that everything's still unicorns, rainbows and teddy bears and not death, deconstruction and devastating diseases.

Chapter Thirteen
Cory

A late winter snowstorm explodes with a vicious fury as Cory battens down and takes refuge from the torrent of snow and icy sleet that started over three hours ago. His shelter of choice is a beauty salon and spa in Cincinnati. It's unlikely that anyone would suspect a man to take shelter there. He has no particular destination in mind other than to stay as far away from people as possible. He has tied his stallion right outside the front door under the overhang of the roof line.

A few days ago when he'd first arrived in this city, he'd found two, fifty pound sacks of grain in a tractor and farm implement supply store. He also salvaged a ten pound bag of chicken feed in the warehouse section of a huge pet supply company. His stallion doesn't need to lay an egg, but Cory knows that it's not much different than the mix they use at the farm for all of the livestock as long as it hasn't molded. It's just compounded differently and packed together into pellets instead of loose corn and crimped oats. The other bags he'd found had mold spots in them from where the roof had leaked and ruined an entire pallet. When he'd decided to head out on his own, he only had a few coffee cans full of feed and one bale of hay. It hadn't lasted long, and he'd had to stop for hours on end for the horse to forage on wild grasses. Then he'd come through a few small towns and had stopped in northern Tennessee where he finally found suitable, dry hay in an abandoned barn. It was a few years old, but not ruined. He'd found more in a cow barn in a small town in Kentucky. Luckily for him, there had been many other abandoned barns there since it used to be such a big horse breeding state.

He'd found three more scumbag creeps that he'd killed yesterday morning in this big city. They'd been messing with an old lady, robbing her of her tiny supply of food she had stashed where she was apparently living in a small, two-room former furniture and appliances rental store. She'd unnecessarily told Cory her whole life story including the fact that she'd been forced to leave her first-floor apartment a few years before because it had flooded. She'd confirmed his hypothesis about the earthquake. He'd dragged the dead bodies away and stashed them in a parking lot where she wouldn't have to look at them. She didn't have much food, so Cory had snared a rabbit for her later and took it back to her. She'd been so appreciative that she'd cried.

He'd also finished the job on the group of thugs who'd been terrorizing the people in front of the church when he'd first arrived in the city. The one in the restaurant had confessed about their whereabouts, confessed because Cory had shot him in the leg. They'd been hiding in an abandoned home just like their friend told him. He'd taken care of them at night. It had been easy. Then he'd redistributed their weapons and ammo to the family near the church who had been attacked. He had carried away their former pastor, removed his dead body from the sidewalk.

He'd gone back to the restaurant where he'd killed the sidewalk rape simulator turned snitch and found two cans of something called *Skyline Chili* on the floor near the deep fryer. The name on the blue-labeled can had matched the sign missing two neon letters on top of the restaurant that looked more like *yline Chili*. Later that day he'd eaten the one can of unusually flavored chili, heated over a low fire in an abandoned warehouse after he'd scrubbed his hands clean with cold snow. The other can he'd taken back and given to the small group at the church. He'd also given them a squirrel carcass he'd killed earlier that morning and the last of his bear meat.

There were three little kids playing in a pew. He couldn't exactly justify eating food when kids were hungry.

Yesterday he'd stayed at the Red's stadium and had allowed his stallion to free-range graze on the field around the baseball diamond. It was very overgrown, gone to seed numerous times in the last years and not maintained by anyone. Jet had made quite the feast of it, too, pawing through the snow to graze. He'd galloped and bucked and ran around like a maniac for the first few minutes of his uninterrupted freedom. Then Cory had found bats and a bucketful of baseballs down in the dugout. He'd taken some time to crack a few around the field. It wasn't like he was worried about someone attacking him. He used to play baseball in school but had given it up for the full contact sport of football instead.

Cory had slept down in that dugout and had allowed Jet to roam around the field throughout the night. He'd had shelter, and the horse had his freedom for about twelve blissful hours. When he'd left there this morning, he'd taken two of the bats and a few of the signed balls. The bats can be used as a weapon if need be. But if he doesn't use them, he can always take them home someday to the farm for the kids. If he ever goes back there.

The sun has almost set outside of the beauty salon, so he moves fast at securing the back door to prevent anyone from sneaking up on him in the middle of the night. Then he works to get a fire lit. He rushes to one of the ceramic bowls meant for washing and rinsing a woman's hair in and kicks once, twice, and three times to free it from the plumbing works jutting out of the wall. There's no danger of flooding the place. The water in this city probably stopped working within the first few weeks after the apocalypse when the electricity failed. Most people trying to live here at that time had probably used up most or all of the water they had, thinking it would simply keep pumping out of their faucets forever. Those who hadn't drained their pipes or who hadn't been home had paid the price of frozen and broken pipes and a flooded home the first winter.

He plugs the bottom of the bowl with a few small rocks from outside and then proceeds to build a base for kindling, a handful of dried hay and twigs. Then he lights the tiny structure with a match taken from the inside pocket of his coat. Once it sufficiently catches, Cory adds more sticks and then three small logs. It's good enough for tonight. He just needs to warm up and dry out his gear and hopefully his clothing. He places the saddle, pad, and blanket on the back of a salon chair that once used to swivel to enable the big reveal. The front door of the salon, he leaves about half open to ensure proper ventilation and to not kill himself from fumes in the middle of the night. He sets a trip wire across the entrance to add to his security. He'll not add any more logs to this fire tonight. Once it has burned down, he'll zip up his cold weather sleeping bag and be done with it.

He rummages through the break-room, finding two old cans of soda, which he's fairly sure have no expiration date and takes them. He also finds a snack size bag of pretzels and then a pack of four-year expired, strawberry yogurts in the fridge. Everything in the refrigerator is spoiled and stinks like a dead person. He does spy three bottles of water, so he snags those, too. He quickly shuts the door and exits that room, which he's already ascertained has no windows.

Cory strips out of his soaking, drenched through clothing and hangs them around the room on furniture and lighting fixtures. He's stripped to his thermal underwear. Pulling dry socks out of his pack, he puts them on quickly and sets his boots closer to the fire. The first thing he needs to do is get food into his empty stomach. He removes the squirrel carcass from his sack. He uses one of the counter-tops, which he first wipes clean with a towel that he finds in a cupboard, to cut thin strips of the meat from the body. He cuts as much of the meat from the bones as he can and places them in a small cast-iron skillet that he and the other men from the farm always carry on a mission run.

He makes a fast meal out of squirrel meat cooked on the fire and canned green beans from the farm. His food supplies from the farm will be gone soon. He has a jar of dried oatmeal, some applesauce, three granola bars, a bag of beef jerky, two jars of creamed corn and three apples from Helen and Gus's house. Cory eats his meal of squirrel and green beans and finishes it with a granola

153

bar as it is more perishable than the canned goods. He uses another towel, meant for drying a freshly shampooed client, to wipe out his skillet, clean his fork and put it all back into his bag. It's best to hide all evidence of cooked food and the aroma of it. They've had quite a few problems back at the farm and out on supply runs with wild dog packs, coyotes and even a few stray bear. Wild dogs had even killed one of the dogs on their farm. Reagan and John had found its remains in the forest behind the farm. They'd chosen to tell the children that it had run away. After that, the security at the farm had been amped up against wild animals. They'd had to set snare traps, leg traps and other devices to dissuade the wildlife from encroaching.

He slips his boots back on and slings his rifle behind his back. Once outside, he checks on his horse in the dark. Cory removes the feedbag from his halter. The horse nickers appreciatively to him as he sets a flake of hay on the ground in front of Jet and then re-checks the lead line holding him secured to a pole.

Once he has the area secure, the horse fed and he double checks the back door again, Cory sets about wiping down his rifle and pistol with an oiled rag since they'd also been soaked in the icy rain. A rusted or dirty weapon can cause it to malfunction, something he can't afford. This machine will keep him alive and allow him to do his work.

When he's finished with the guns, he raids the upscale salon using his small penlight. He's able to take two pairs of scissors, a bottle of shampoo that will also double for him as soap when next he finds a stream in which to bathe. He also takes a small round mirror, not for gazing at himself all day but for use as a diversionary device as a reflector. Next, he throws the six remaining, white towels into his pack. They're small but handy. He finds a straight edge razor and folds it closed, places it in his cargo pocket. Two boxes of rubber bands are next. He knows from learning from John that he can mix these with gasoline in a metal can and create a small incendiary device that will burn hot like napalm. He locates cotton balls, a bottle of peroxide and a brush and stashes those, as well. He hasn't used a brush in a while as he's not too concerned with his appearance at the moment, but the rest could prove useful.

He removes three cotton cushions from a nearby sofa and places them on the tile floor below the front windows of the store. He'll sleep right there for the night to ensure the security of his horse since the stallion was too big to fit through the narrow door. Cory lays out his sleeping bag on the cushions, then pulls on dry clothing and his boots before he slides down inside the awaiting comfort. He knows to be ready at a moment's notice. Kelly had taught him and Simon this. They always sleep fully dressed and with their shoes on when they are on the road.

His rifle he places beside him and his pistol right under his makeshift pillow which is just a balled up shirt. He zips the sleeping bag up to his chin, pulls the bearskin up, as well, and hunkers down. The low burning fire will help to ward off the chill, but by morning, he'll be freezing his ass off. As soon as the sun rises, he'll be moving on from this spot.

This is the worst part of the day for him. It's quiet, nothing is going on but the silent, still of the night. It's when his mind races with memories, good and bad. He remembers all the hours upon hours of training that Kelly, Derek and John had put him and Simon through. He can field strip a rifle, shotgun, or pistol of any make or caliber. He knows how to track and hunt animals... and people if need be. He knows how to set up a secure perimeter no matter where he is at the time. He's proficient with just about any weapon including a shotgun, hunting rifles, handguns, grenades- which they'd found a small box of one time in the dirt basement of someone's bug-out shelter. First they'd found the owner's dead body in the woods and had traced him back to his shelter. The man had a damn arsenal which included older rifles which he'd converted to fully automatic. There was even a SAW, which Kelly used to frequently shoot in the Army. They'd loaded it all onto their horses and the two extra pack horses and had taken the bounty back to the farm. He and Simon also know how to reload their own rounds for each of the weapons at the farm. Simon doesn't really have the stomach for killing people, although he's done it a few times. Hell, he'd even stabbed his own dirtbag cousin who'd attacked Reagan. But he's softer than Cory, which is fine. Cory never judges his best friend. John had explained it to Cory that some men just have the ability to lock that shit down. Simon doesn't. He's more adept at healing people and studying herbs somewhere out in the forest than killing people. He's a peaceful kind of person and soft spoken unless they are in danger, or the family is in harm's way. He's the complete opposite of Cory.

He remembers the last years of his life with acute detail. Kelly became a father for the first time and nearly lost his mind over it as a consequence. He'd helicoptered around Hannah twenty-four seven until he'd driven her nuts. And on the day that Mary was born, he was a complete mess. Cory thought Reagan was going to kill his big brother. Kelly vowed never to get Hannah pregnant again. But once Mary was born, he'd miraculously forgotten all about his vehement protestation of Hannah's pregnancy and any future pregnancies. And no wonder. Mary is probably about the most precious little girl ever born on the face of the earth. Being her uncle, Cory's opinion is just slightly biased, but she's still damn cute. Her black hair mimics her dad, but she gets her light eye color from Hannah. And she has everyone at the farm, himself included, wrapped around her teeny tiny, two-year-old pinkie finger.

Sometimes he thinks about Sam, but he tries not to. She's like a kid sister to him and reminds him so much of Em. The girls had been very close, which makes his guilt tear away at his heavily-weighted conscience. She's already been through so much bad shit that he hates thinking about how this new loss could be making her feel. He's not sure what all happened to her when she was held captive by those bastards that had squatted on the farm. Simon never talks about it, and neither does she. Either she's sworn Simon to secrecy or perhaps he also doesn't wish to speak of it. Sam hangs out a lot with Reagan, too. He's not sure why, though. He's always been a little scared of Reagan. She's not quite right, but she's come a long way since Cory first came to the farm with his brother, Em, and John. Sometimes she's even nice, which must be the side that Sam sees in her. They go to the clinic in town often together where Sam acts as the clinic nurse.

Em had been a girly-girl, though. She'd preferred hanging out with Sue and Hannah in the kitchen or hiding from the younger kids up in one of the hay lofts. She'd never taken to medical work or gardening, but she did help out a lot with cooking with Hannah. Sam and Em shared a bedroom on the second floor of the house, his old room. He wonders tonight if Sam is lying awake unable to sleep because she, too, is missing his sister.

A wind gust blows a fine mist of snow into the salon through the partially open door. Sleep is alluding him, as it does most nights. The last few weeks have been nothing but hunting and stalking and then usually killing. He's killed another seven men. Men who were murderous, thieving low-lives. Two of those men in Kentucky even had a woman chained to the wall of their shelter, which happened to be a former lawyer's office. He'd freed her, gave her some food, and let her go. The men he had not let go, nor did he offer them any sort of compassion. He'd shown them the same mercy they'd shown that poor woman. The other five had been in a group of sorts in another town in Tennessee. He'd watched them from afar for a few hours one night through his night scope. They were raiding house to house in a small neighborhood where it seemed a few families were trying to survive. After the first few rounds from one of their guns had pierced the silent night air, Cory had jumped into action. He'd taken out the first two, who were supposed to be keeping watch at the end of the street, with his rifle. The attached silencer had afforded him the opportunity to do so without drawing unnecessary attention to himself or the muzzle flash. The others he took out one by one, catching them unaware, and finishing the deed by killing the last man with his knife. Some of the people living in that small neighborhood had come out to thank him. Cory had given one of the men the dead raiders' guns. He'd made a quick exit, grabbed his stallion and took off. He didn't want or need their gratitude.

A mewling near the door alerts him, and Cory springs to his feet with his pistol aimed. It's just the damn dog again.

"I said get outta here, ya' damn dog," he hisses through clenched teeth.

The German shepherd just stands there.

"Go on! Get!" he shouts this time.

It whines which further irritates Cory, so he throws an empty shampoo bottle from the floor at it. This method of getting rid of her is effective because she scoots around the corner and leaves. No sooner does he get back to his sofa cushion bed, does she poke her head inside the salon again. She's whimpering softly and crawling on her belly trying to cross the threshold.

This is not their first run-in. She's been shadowing him for a week, even though he's chased her off a dozen times. She's also underweight and skinny. She'd followed him the other night in freezing rain and sat patiently under a tree while he slept in a cave. The stallion doesn't seem to mind her, but Cory doesn't need another mouth to feed. Plus, she could give him away when he's trying to stalk creeps.

"Damn dog," he gripes.

She belly crawls closer until she's right at his knee where she licks his hand.

"Damn it. Fine! One night, ya' damn dog," he complains, and she whines louder.

Knowing he's never going to get any sleep unless he does something, Cory retrieves the squirrel carcass and tosses it over to her. She wags her tail vigorously and goes to work on the remains.

Cory returns to his sleeping bag and within a short time, finds restful peace from his memories. He rubs with his thumb and forefinger at the gold bracelet on the leather cord. He notices that the damn dog has curled up and is sleeping on his feet. He doesn't kick her off, though. The extra warmth isn't such a bad thing tonight.

Chapter Fourteen
Sam

It's been almost a full month since Paige and Simon were reunited. For the first full week, they'd been stuck together like two peas in a pod. Wherever Simon had gone, Paige had trailed after him. He has become frighteningly protective of her. He'd taken her with him and Sam to check on a sick cow at the Reynolds farm. That was almost two weeks ago. One of the local, single dads who had stopped by to visit Wayne Reynolds had made a pass at Paige. Simon had nearly come across the cattle gate and had the guy by the scruff of his shirt. His soft voice and refined behavior had instantly disappeared. Sam's eyes had grown wide and then she'd just smirked and shook her head. He has such an old soul. He's always been protective of everyone on the farm, but it's never been anything like what he displays for his sister. It's almost comically endearing. The single dad had originally come in to the clinic the month before with a third-degree burn on his arm. They'd treated him as best as they could. That day when he'd hit on Paige, Simon had simply handed him more bandaging and cream out of his satchel and sent him on his way, even though he certainly had no right to do so since they were at the Reynolds' farm. Wayne had just chuckled at his distress.

It wasn't as if the man had meant any harm. His wife had been killed the first day of the tsunamis. She'd been in Los Angeles for a modeling gig. The tsunami that had blasted California had set off the San Andreas Fault again, causing it to split open and once again shift. What wasn't engulfed by the tsunami was soon destroyed by aftershocks and fires that reached inland hundreds of miles. She distinctly remembers listening to the radio and sketchy television reports with her mother and father and feeling sick to her stomach at the images. Sam can understand the widower's heartbreak and loss. He's probably just feeling desperately lonely. He'll just have to find someone in the surrounding communities, though. These are the neighborhoods that the men on the McClane farm have worked so hard for the last few years on getting re-established. There are over six hundred people now thriving in Pleasant View. The community has rebuilt, and the people pull together to help one another, most of the time. Everyone has turned their manicured lawns once full of neatly trimmed hedges and shrubberies and decorative flower beds into thriving vegetable gardens during the summer months. Many of these families have resources like electricity from solar power, running water and heat, care of chopping firewood from whatever source they can find. It's nothing like it was before, but Sam knows that it may never be again, at least not in her lifetime.

Today they are riding together through the forest as the early morning sun glares blindingly bright as it shoots shafts of light onto them. It's finally a more temperate day than it's been in the last few months. Sam tilts her head back, letting the warm rays touch her skin. Her denim jacket almost feels too warm for the weather over her blue hoodie.

"Are those tracks?" Gavin asks as he points to his left.

Paige's friend has also tagged along and is fitting in just fine with the rest of the family. The men have said he's rather thoughtful when it comes time for chores, even though he hasn't caught on to most of the work yet. His heart's in the right place, and Sam's sure that he'll eventually get it all figured out. It's not exactly an easy transition to go from city slicker to apocalypse survivor to farmer.

"Those are just from deer," Simon explains patiently. "See how they kind of slide in the mud? These are from a cloven-hoofed animal. Not a threat."

They still haven't found whatever animal attacked the pregnant mare, which is why she has been forbidden to ride alone for the time being.

Paige rides behind her brother. She's not at all a lover of the horses. Simon literally has to coerce her to ride with him. She's only done it twice, including today.

"Oh, sorry," Gavin remarks with embarrassment.

He's catching on to the riding and seems to enjoy it. They've also given him an older gelding, who is slightly sway-backed and very mellow. Sam's mount is spirited and fun to ride. Her chestnut coat is a lovely tan color that contrasts with her lighter mane.

"No problem," Simon returns with a friendly grin. "Took me a while to learn this stuff, too. Hey, you'll get it. No big deal."

"Yeah, we've all learned some pretty strange things on this farm," Sam agrees.

"Oh yeah?" Paige asks from behind her brother's back where she holds around his waist with a death grip. "Like what else?"

"How to make butter and bread and soap," Sam says with a chuckle and disbelieving shake of her head. "I never knew how to sew before and now I do. Even know how to sew stitches on someone if I have to."

Simon breaks in, "How to birth a calf if the cow can't do it on her own."

"Ew, gross. Man, I don't know about that one," Gavin says.

They all laugh. It's good. It's a good thing. Laughter has been gone from the farm for so long and had come so few and far between since the death of Grams and then Em. Neither of them would want the family to be so sad and mournful all of the time.

"Simon's great with the animals!" Sam praises with a smile.

When she looks over at him, he turns in another direction and coaxes his horse farther away from hers.

"I'm getting the picture on that one," Paige says.

Sam knows she is thinking of the other day when her brother had taken her to the neighbor's farm again to deal with a sickness that seems to be plaguing the cows at the Johnson's. There is a vet in town again, but his services are already spread so thin that many of the bigger farms are trying to keep their livestock healthy without his aid. He is also a heavy drinker of homemade alcohol of some kind and not reliable. He'd lost his wife and son when the world fell apart and has not been the same since. Sometimes he also disappears for days and even a week or so at a time. Nobody knows where he goes, but they also don't question him. Grandpa explained that not everyone deals with grief in the same manner and to give him time. Sam remembers him distinctly, though, being a different man before the apocalypse happened because he took care of her show horses. He'd always been professional, mild-mannered and courteous. On the rare occasion that she has encountered him since, he is unshaven, scruffy even, and ill-tempered.

Most of the townspeople and the small neighborhoods have chickens, and some of them are keeping pigs or a few cows fenced in on the surrounding properties. Any and all animal antibiotics that were found on raids by the Rangers are being stored on the McClane farm, though. They are perfectly fine, according to Grandpa, to use on humans in different dosages. The people who'd needed them hadn't seemed to mind that their sick child would get well again versus not being able to use the antibiotic on an ill hog.

Gavin doesn't notice the aloof and detached interaction between her and Simon and chuckles again.

"No kidding. You're like a doctor and a vet and a botanist all in one," he says.

"Nah, I'm not that skilled. Not like Reagan or Doc," Simon returns with a shrug.

He is being very modest, and Sam would like to point that out but knows Simon will only argue. Grandpa says that Simon is quite accomplished and a very fast learner. She, on the other hand, needs to be shown many times how to do a particular procedure. Sewing sutures had taken a ton of practice. Her hands always shake, too. She doesn't particularly like getting in the trenches. She'd much prefer to stand by and offer assistance than be in charge. She's just not that kind of person. She'd actually much prefer to be at the farm riding or sketching to working in the clinic at all but understands the importance of what they are doing there for their small community.

They ride a short while longer talking about the farm and how different it is than being out where Paige and Gavin have been.

"We were offered shelter here and there. Usually it was from nice people like the McClanes," Paige explains.

"But most people didn't want three more people and a little girl to feed," Gavin says.

"We don't let people stay here, either," Simon says with a solid shake of his head.

"I can't blame the family," Paige says. "The McClane family has a good thing here. It's safe, safer than anywhere I've been that wasn't guarded with a couple hundred Marines. But that was a long time ago that I've felt that safe. Those camps didn't last long. People aren't looking to take in a bunch of orphans right now. Mostly they are just trying to keep themselves alive."

Gavin says, "Right. This place is like a utopia compared to what's out there. The best place we ever stayed was that old farm up in Pennsylvania. We were the only ones there, but at least nobody found us and tried to rob us or kills us or..." he stammers and stops.

Sam wonders at what Gavin isn't saying, which sometimes tells a person more than what someone does say. He looks troubled by his thoughts. Paige looks away, too. She fiddles with the thin strips of leather she has tied around her wrist. She seems to wear these constantly like a piece of jewelry, and Sam has wanted to ask her about them but hasn't had the chance yet.

He continues on, "I never used to be like that, ya' know? I used to want to be around people all the time. I'd go to my dad's job sites and interact with the guys and work alongside them and shoot the crap and go out for a beer after. It was a social life. It's not like that anymore. Being secluded and away from people is the way to go now. It's just so weird."

"And I hung out with my friends in college and was social. You guys probably had friends and social lives before, too," Paige admits.

Sam smiles sadly, remembering her old life which is sometimes too painful to do.

"Science Club, Chess Club, those were fun," Simon acknowledges and gets a few chuckles, although he frowns unknowingly.

"We try to help where and when we can, though," Sam says brightly. "We take as much food that we won't need at the end of the harvest to the local food bank. It's just the library actually. But people know to go there at the end of summer if they need supplies to make it through the winter. Everyone does. Some of the older people in town can't take care of themselves, so we all try to help and look after them. The men, you know the Rangers and Simon and Cory, see to the distribution on those days. That way it all gets passed out evenly and nobody fights over it. Right, Simon?"

"Uh... yeah, right," he agrees.

He looks away again. Why is he so distant and strange? It doesn't have anything to do with his sister's return. He was acting this way before she came to the farm.

"That's really great, Simon," his sister praises.

He chirps up when Paige talks to him.

"Yeah, it's the right thing to do. We have so much land here, and all of us guys can put in the extra vegetables. As long as we keep the beef in production, it's good to share that, too."

Sam smiles at him with a nod. He just gives her the slightest of grins before turning the other way again. She's going to have to get him alone and discuss this. He's her best friend. She can't stand his aloof behavior.

"Our herd size has increased significantly, and the guys have closed off a big section of the forest with fencing so that the cows can graze there, too," Sam tells them. Gavin nods and comments. Paige adds a comment. Simon doesn't say anything.

The small talk goes on a while longer until they reach the paddock, where they pull the horses to a halt. Simon allows his sister to swing off first. It's comical because Paige squats and grimaces.

"Whoa, owies," she jokes. "I need to ride a narrower horse."

"You'll get used to it," Simon says with a laugh and ruffles her light red hair.

Sam pats her chestnut's furry winter coat. She'll start shedding this soon if the weather continues to improve. She hasn't worked up a white, foamy lather from the ride, which is good. It'll make brushing her down and getting her turned out a faster job. They have only been gone about an hour, but this day is long from over.

They laugh at Paige's drama while Gavin gets off of his mare more easily. He's not a particularly tall person, but he has a sturdy build. He's even put on some weight, which is a sign of forward-moving progress and that life goes on, at least on their farm. All four of Paige's group have gained some weight, but Paige is tall for a woman, so she definitely still looks really skinny.

Gavin comes over to Sam and reaches up for her. She frowns but takes the offered help. She's not sure why he's trying to help her. She could out ride him any day of the week and twice on Sunday, but apparently he doesn't know this. She reaches down anyway.

"Thanks, Gavin. I could've…" she mumbles as she steps away from him. She turns quickly back, still in the middle of speaking, as Simon grabs Gavin's shoulder rather roughly.

"Hey!" he barks in an irate voice. "She doesn't need your help."

"Oh, sorry," Gavin apologizes and backs away.

He holds up his left hand in a posture of surrender. There is a sudden fear in Gavin's brown eyes. Sue had cut his dishwater blonde hair when he'd first arrived. She'd basically buzz cut it as was his preference. Paige had explained that they all four had lice once that they'd contracted while staying at a temporary FEMA camp. It had taken them weeks to get rid of the pesky bugs. Sam remembers shuddering at the thought. Gross. She'd cut her own hair once with a semi-dull knife. She'd cut it for an entirely different reason than invading bugs, but she doesn't like remembering that part of her life.

"Simon!" Paige reprimands and pulls her brother back.

"Samantha doesn't need his help," Simon explains through gritted teeth.

His blue eyes are alight with a fierce and sudden anger. He never acts like this. The look in his eyes is maybe even worse than the sneer he'd given the single dad over Paige, and Sam can't imagine what has set him off like this. Gavin is a harmless, kind man.

"He doesn't know that, Simon," Paige rails on. "He was only trying to be nice. Calm down."

Simon's eyes narrow on his sister. They are almost eye to eye. Paige must be at least five nine or five ten. Her long red hair is pulled back today in a single braid.

Simon finally nods and says, "Sorry, Gavin."

"No problem, Simon. Look, I didn't mean anything by it. I just thought she seemed kinda' small to get down by herself," he explains.

Sam frowns at him. "Hey! I'm plenty big enough, thank you very much. And I've been riding since I was two."

"Oh, sorry," he says again.

"It's fine. No harm, no foul," she returns and tugs her gelding toward the barn. When she glances over her shoulder, Simon is still looking at her. "We'd better get moving! Going to the clinic today, remember?"

Simon nods but still seems sulky about the harmless incident with Gavin. Sam's not. Gavin's a nice guy. He's been generous and considerate since he arrived that first day and every day since. Before everything fell apart, he'd worked for his dad's construction business and was in Georgia on a big commercial build. Repair work seems to be the one thing where he is actually helpful on the farm, according to the men. Gavin also gets along with and is very kind and affectionate toward the children on the farm which is a good quality in Sam's opinion. Even though Paige trusts him, she knows that the men were wary of Gavin at first. He seems to be a man of strong moral character and is a big cut-up, which certainly doesn't hurt anything. He and Talia are always joking and having fun. Even though he is not a particularly good singer, he joined in the other night when Hannah had played the piano and John his guitar. He'd even danced around with the kids.

Paige tugs at her brother's sleeve and Simon nods and follows her into the barn, as well. It doesn't take long before they have the three horses turned out, the tack put away and are heading in to pack for the clinic. They make the trek twice a month to the clinic in town. It's the only available medical care for miles. There are usually people waiting outside for them when they get there.

Sam takes Paige to the shed with her to pack what they can while Simon convenes with the men for a security meeting. They have a security meeting before every clinic day. They have a security meeting once a week to discuss the farm. They have security meetings to go over the surrounding neighborhoods they've established into sections. They basically have security meetings on a near constant basis. The ex-military men in the family take security very seriously.

"Here, Paige," Sam instructs. This is Paige's first trip to the clinic with them. "Take a crate. We need certain supplies for the clinic. We don't keep anything at the clinic because it could be stolen or looted when we're not there. So every time we go to town, we take the supplies with us."

"Ok, sure," Paige says and takes the wooden crate. "What do we need?"

"We'll fill my crate and then yours. We try to keep the supplies separated by their uses so that when we get to town it's a lot easier than having to sort it all out. We usually take bandaging, which we're getting low on," Sam remarks as she checks the third shelving unit. They've added five metal shelving displays in the med shed for storing hospital supplies looted from surrounding, deserted medical facilities. "This shelf is all for wound care, so there're syringes, rubber tourniquets for blood draws, needles and thread for stitching, bacterial swipes and bandaging. Oh, and we need antibacterial cream."

Sam starts adding items to her own crate as Paige stands by watching. She's unsure of herself, but she won't be for long. Sam hands her items to stow in her crate.

"This unit," she indicates the next set of five shelves, "has the most surgical types of supplies. This shelf has forceps, scalpels, canisters of oxygen, surgical staples and, well, just about anything else we might need."

"Do you usually use all this? I mean does it get that bad?" Paige asks.

"Oh yeah," Sam says on a sarcastic chuckle. "But then sometimes it's not too bad. We've delivered fourteen babies there!"

"Really?" Paige asks with cynicism. "That's kind of ignorant. I can't believe people are even still getting pregnant."

"Grandpa says that life has to go on, so we should encourage it," Sam says.

"I noticed that you call him that," Paige comments after she shrugs.

"Yeah, I know. He's not really my Grandpa, but he's kind of everybody's grandfather if you ask me."

"Yes, he's quite the patriarch of this place," Paige admits.

Sam notices for the first time how pretty Paige's eyes are. The color isn't exactly blue like hers, but more of a pale bluish gray. Sam has officially found her new muse. She'll sketch Paige with pastels instead of charcoal so that she can capture the interesting light to dark red shades of her hair, the tiny brown freckles on her cheeks and nose, her excessively high eyebrows and her deep-set pale eyes.

"Grams was great, too. It's just too bad that you didn't get to meet her. She had a soft spot for Simon. She was so sweet and wonderful," Sam explains. She frowns and shakes her head, trying to get rid of those thoughts. Remembering Grams is difficult. "This shelf is full of Simon and Grandpa's medicinal concoctions."

She points to the display of herbs and pastes, balms and talcs all stored in baby food jars or pint sized canning jars. This unit looks like an eighteenth-century apothecary's shop. Everything is labeled with small pieces of paper or stickers that are beginning to yellow with the passage of time. This shelf holds special meaning for her. It represents all of the time that she's spent hunting herbs and berries and plants with Simon. Those cherished, safe moments with him are suspended in her memories forever.

"Simon or Grandpa usually come out and pick what they want to take to town from this shelf," she tells his sister. "Then we have this last unit and a half, give or take, of bottled medicines from before the apocalypse hit."

"Wow, you guys have a ton of shit out here," Paige exclaims as she rounds the final corner.

Sam chuckles, "You better not swear in front of Hannah. Since Grams passed, she's the cursing police around here. Oh, except for Reagan. Nobody's ever been able to clean up her language, not even her husband. Not for lack of trying, however."

"Good to know," Paige returns and raises her eyebrows.

"...I said I'm going," Reagan's voice spills into the shed.

"Babe, you're still very weak. You're just getting better. Why don't you just stay home this time, sit this one out?" John retorts.

They both come into the shed; Reagan flailing her arms while speaking and John scowling.

"I'm fine!" she argues. "I've had a little more energy the last few days."

Her recovery from that intense flu has been very slow, indeed. She'd been down for almost two full weeks. Everyone was surprised at how ill she'd become. John and their son Jacob and then Sue had also come down with it, but they'd each kicked it within forty-eight hours. Reagan still carries with her a slight cough and seemingly chronic fatigue.

John tugs her arm, effectively halting his wife and swinging her around to face him. Then he plants a big kiss on her mouth. He's not exactly shy about showing his affection for her. Reagan wraps her arms around his neck and kisses him back.

"I'm going!" she says when she jerks back.

"All right, you hard-head," he says before kissing her cheek. "I'm going too, then."

"That'll work. Tell Kelly, though, because I heard him say that he was going with us."

"Right," he says and takes off at a jog.

Normally Kelly, Derek, John and Cory take turns going in teams of two to the clinic with the medical crew. However, with Cory being gone, they can't afford to have both Kelly and John go. Grandpa, John, Reagan and Simon will have guns to defend the practice should a problem arise. But Kelly will need to stay on the farm to keep it protected with Derek. They also offered to work with Gavin on firearms training since they found out that he's not very experienced with them. He mostly hunts with a bow.

"Got everything packed up, Sam?" Reagan asks.

Sam notices that she doesn't offer to help but instead sits on a nearby folding chair.

"Yeah, I think so. You aren't feeling ill? Are you sure you want to go? If you're tired, then we…" she asks of her friend and adopted older sister. They have become very close over the last few years.

"Nah, it's cool. That bug's just taking its time exiting my worthless body. Nothing to worry about," she admits.

"We treated those people, the ones from section four, when you were still down," Sam says. They've named the different areas of the town by numbered sections. Small towns within the town almost. There are five of these separate areas.

"Yeah, I know. I wish I could've helped. Grandpa said a few more of them died. It seemed like bronchitis, and a few had strep when it all started. I didn't have what some of them had," Reagan answers. "I think it altered itself, became a nasty flu bug."

"Right, but you've seemed kind of tired the last few days, too. It's hard telling what we're running into out there when we work at the clinic. Perhaps you *should* stay here. We don't want you to come into contact with another stupid sickness, Reagan."

Reagan waves her hand, dismissing that idea.

"You are a hard-head, you know," Sam teases and lays her hand gently on the top of Reagan's head, which is a messy braid of frizzy curls. She gets a pat-pat to her hand in return.

Before she'd gotten to know Reagan so well, she'd have never felt comfortable joking around like that with her. She used to be a lot fiercer, frightening actually. Sam also wouldn't have attempted touching her, either. Reagan has come a long way in the last few years. Grams used to say how time heals all wounds, but sometimes Sam has a difficult time understanding that theory.

"Yeah, so I've been told," she jokes right back. "I'll be ok, though. Don't worry. We need to get these sicknesses under control. We don't want a full-blown pandemic on our hands."

Sam nods and adds, "No kidding."

Paige interjects, "When we went to one of the FEMA camps about three years ago or so, there was an outbreak of measles."

"Measles? Really?" Reagan inquires.

Her nerd brain isn't going to let this one pass her by. Sam grins and returns to the shelf where she collects more supplies.

Paige nods and continues, "Simon and I were vaccinated for it when we were kids, but Maddie never was, of course. So they recommended that anyone who never got the vaccine should vacate the camp. It seemed really bad. We got out of there, but not before I saw behind the camp that they had put a lot of dead bodies in a pit there."

Paige takes a deep inhale and stares at her worn black boots for a moment. Sam can just imagine what that pit had looked like.

"I thought measles wasn't something that could kill you," Sam contemplates with worry. If measles hit a camp a few years ago, it could spread again.

"Normally, it isn't," Reagan says. "But that's back when we had plenty of antibiotics and vaccines to go around. Those kinds of medical supplies at a big disaster center wouldn't have lasted long."

"Exactly. They didn't go far at all," Paige agrees and changes direction in the conversation. "We stayed one time in another camp in South Carolina and some kind of weird virus went around. Maddie got it. We were scared shitless. I wasn't sure if she was gonna make it. She got so sick. They gave her stuff for the fevers, but there wasn't anything to give her for the flu, which is what they thought it was. I wasn't so sure. It didn't seem like a flu to me."

The sadness in her light eyes is deeply ingrained there. Sam doesn't think that time has healed any of Paige's wounds yet.

"Not to sound like a smartass, but how come you didn't head this way sooner? How the hell did you end up going to New Jersey first?" Reagan asks with her usual flair for tact.

Paige just laughs once. "We didn't. We went to South Carolina first. But that's a long story."

"We've got a few minutes," Sam coaxes. They've all been curious about why her group hadn't come to the farm sooner. She's quite sure that Paige has discussed it with Simon privately, but nobody has felt comfortable enough around her to just butt into her business.

"Well, I didn't exactly start out with Gavin and Talia and a baby," she says and then blows out a deep sigh. "I was a student at Georgia Tech. I'm not sure if you knew that," she says and pauses as Reagan nods. "I had a boyfriend in college. I lived off campus with him and my two friends and one of their boyfriends. We all shared a three-bedroom loft in the city. When we heard about the first tsunami hitting the east coast, we didn't know what to do. The radio stations were repeating the same emergency broadcast over and over on a repetitive loop."

"We heard that, too," Sam tells her.

"They just kept saying things like stay inside, stock up on water, don't travel, don't be out after dark. We knew about the nukes overseas, of course, but never thought it would get bad here in the states. My mom was pissed that I wouldn't come home. Hell, by then it was too late anyway. I wouldn't have made it to the state border."

Sam frowns as she realizes that Paige's tale will be full of hardship and despair.

"We saw from our apartment on the eighth floor what was going on. There were fires, people were shooting, cars kept crashing, stores were being looted. That was all the first month. It wasn't like we could hop a flight out. Remember? Flights were grounded after the nukes. The two guys with us would take turns going out and trying to steal food and supplies for us. Then we ran out of food and water. That was it. We were done. It's not like we had weapons to go out and defend ourselves. Our friends took baseball bats with them to hunt for food. But there was nowhere left to go, and the violence was beyond what two college boys could handle with a baseball bat. We heard from a neighbor about a National Guard outpost that you could go to for help. The last email communication I had with my brother told me that our mother was dead and that he was coming with Aunt Amber to your town. I told him I'd meet him, but he told me when I first got here that he never got a return email from me."

"Yeah, communications went down pretty fast," Reagan says.

Paige frowns and says, "I thought: simple, right? I'd just head here no problem and probably beat him here since I was closer. Like I'd just roll in here in a few days. What a dumbass," she almost whispers and takes the package of bandaging Sam holds out to her.

"Yeah, we heard about those camps. The guys- our Rangers- were working in some of those out West somewhere before they came here. They worked security there when they weren't sent out on missions to control the populous," Reagan says.

"We didn't exactly make it to the outpost," Paige says, shakes her head and looks away.

Sam can read the fear in her eyes as Paige recalls the events of that day. She has a feeling that Paige has never told anyone most of this.

"It was only about twenty miles from where we were. It wasn't like we had a long way to travel to the outpost. We were carjacked, and my boyfriend who was driving was shot and killed. My two girlfriends were literally pulled out of the car windows and taken. The only thing that saved me is that I got out the other door in the back seat and ran. My girlfriend's boyfriend wasn't killed, either. We both escaped. Within a few seconds, a herd of people were fighting over our car. It was just he and I left, left with no car and none of our stuff, no food, no water, and no friends. I literally only had the clothes on my back."

"Oh, Paige," Sam says and touches her arm. "I'm so sorry."

When Sam looks at Reagan, her eyes seem guarded and darker suddenly.

"It gets worse," Paige returns and frowns. "Gary was his name, my friend's boyfriend. We ran and ran forever, weaving through the city streets. It turned dark. We managed to find another route that was safer. We found a car, too. We were able to get to a grocery store because we were hungry and tired. There weren't any police around. We saw a few cop cars with their lights on, but when we got to them, they were empty. Maybe the police were chasing people down. Maybe they were dead somewhere. I don't know. We didn't have any luck at the grocery store, either. There were people in there looting. Three men came at us with guns, so I dropped the things I had, which wasn't much, a few cans of soup and a candy bar. The men were yelling at us from the other end of the grocery store aisle. Then other people started shooting at the guys coming at us. It was chaos. I ran out the back door. Gary took off the other way and ditched me. He took off in the car, too before I could catch up to him."

"Holy shit," Reagan exclaims. "What a dick."

Sam can't imagine being left to her own defenses and abandoned. When her family was murdered, at least she found comfort from Simon.

Paige scoffs. "No kidding, right? I never really liked him all that much, but my girlfriend was head over heels for him. I always thought he treated her badly."

"How did you get away from those men?" Reagan asks and coughs a few times.

"I ran track in high school. When I went to college, I used their track to stay in shape. It wasn't hard to outrun them, but I was afraid they were going to shoot me in the back."

"You were lucky, I guess," Sam comments. "Either that or your guardian angel was watching over you."

Paige nods and gives a grim smile before continuing, "Anyway it was dark, so I just hid out until it got really late. I figured a lot of the people roaming around would head back to their homes or cars or wherever. Then I tried to sneak around the city looking for a car. I didn't find one. I didn't find any help, either. I went to a police station, but there was nobody there. I mean nobody and the doors were all locked. So I just kept walking all night until the sun came up. An Army truck spotted me on the road and picked me up. I don't know what would've happened to me if they hadn't. I didn't have a gun or even a knife. Who knows? I could've been killed or taken like my friends."

"You *were* lucky," Reagan states with a scowl.

Paige sighs heavily and says, "I know I've been lucky many times. They took me to the disaster center that my friends and I were trying to get to. Gary wasn't there. I don't know whatever became of him. I never saw him again. But it's there that I met Talia and Gavin. And then we got custody of baby Maddie. We've been together ever since."

"But why didn't you come straight here?" Sam asks.

"We literally had no way of getting here… or anywhere really. Finding a vehicle that still had gas had become nearly impossible. Plus we were kind of hoping things would improve. After a few months of floating around to different FEMA camps, we kind of figured that it wasn't going to get any better. They kept pumping us full of false promises and even falser hope. But there was no denying what was happening. When each camp became too dangerous, we'd leave. Then it just didn't feel safe at all to go to them. So we found an older minivan in a neighborhood and headed for Gavin's family's home. It was the closest to go to first. We had to learn how to siphon gas from the empty cars on the freeway. We never even found his parents. They could be dead, but we'll probably never know. His town was pretty much under water. They lived right on the coast, on the beach actually. We found two kayaks, and Gav and I rowed as far as we could toward his family's home. That was the most horrific thing I've ever done or seen. There were dead bodies floating in the water here and there. Some of the homes were leveled like toothpicks. Again nobody was around. No one. Not even emergency management organizations. All you could see of some of the homes that were still standing were the top floor windows, barely. His home was gone, ruined, hardly anything left. We never found their bodies."

"Poor Gavin," Sam sympathizes. She'd never seen her family's bodies, either. The McClane family had buried them for her.

"He took it really hard. I guess he was really close with his dad. He was depressed for weeks. Talia and I had to do the foraging. I even shot a deer, and the two of us girls skinned and gutted it. We found canned food in some of the flooded homes, too. And then from there, we heard about a group that was headed to the Northeast. So we figured it was probably a good idea to join up with a group. They had three buses, and two Army trucks that were leading the way. At that point, I think the military fell apart, and the men left their posts."

"That's probably about right; summertime is when the men showed up here," Reagan says.

Paige tries to offer a smile, but it comes off as morose.

"The men leading us were Marines. They said they didn't have family. They just wanted to help people. There were four of them, very kind men. They were trying to reunite people with their families up north. None of us three felt it was a good idea to set out on our own, and since that group was going, and the opportunity was there, we took it. Our caravan was attacked in northern Virginia, though. We spread out, and everyone got separated. It was a mess. The military men went into an all-out battle with these really violent people. They were organized, not just a few looters. We didn't stick around. We learned to keep moving. We hit the ground running. Literally. We walked for a few days until we found an abandoned car. Talia's family's home was inland in Jersey, so we felt like maybe we'd have better luck finding hers. We made it to her sister's house, but she was gone. Nobody was there. She didn't leave any information on where she went with her son. Talia's brother-in-law was in Thailand when it all hit, so we know he never made it home. But her sister was just gone. We talked to a neighbor, and they told us they saw her pack everything into her SUV and leave. Maybe she was coming south to find Talia, but we'll never know. Her mother was in a nursing home, so we went there next. She was only in her early fifties, but she'd had a stroke the year before. I guess it was really bad, and she was put into a care facility. Her parents were divorced, and her dad was in England when it all happened. She never made contact with him, either. We had Talia wait outside the nursing home for us. Gavin and I went in. Everyone was dead. The staff was long gone. Most of the patients looked like they starved to death or died from not having whatever medicines they needed. The staff must've left the nursing home months before we got there. We found her, but she was long gone. She must've died right after it all started."

Paige's eyes take on a haunted appearance as she remembers whatever that nursing home had looked like. Sam regards Reagan, who frowns with understanding. Sam can't even imagine the horrors that Paige has seen in the last three years. Paige shivers and rubs her arms.

"Where'd you go from there? I mean that was a long time ago," Reagan asks.

"By then it was almost winter, so we knew we couldn't keep traveling with Maddie in the winter. She was still just a baby then remember," Paige says.

"What did you do?" Sam asks. Simon's sister has a lifetime of stories to tell from her cross-country venture.

"We ended up in an abandoned farmhouse that year. We only made it to the border of Pennsylvania and West Virginia. We didn't know it was going to be such a rough winter. There was firewood in the barn and even some canned goods like you guys have in your cellar. Well, not quite *that* much," she says with a grin.

"Really? What the hell happened to the people who lived there?" Reagan asks bluntly.

"Um, I'm not really sure," Paige answers honestly. "There were dead animals in their barns; chickens were still running around the barnyard. That was actually good because we were able to have eggs. Never collected eggs from a chicken coop before. That was interesting. When we first got there, there were eggs all over that place; in the barn, in the hay mound in the top of the barn, even in the stalls. We ate them, but we didn't even know if they were still good. We were that hungry. We also never built fires in a fireplace for heat, either. We all three learned a lot that year. Gavin and I went looting for us, too. We both got very good at being quiet and sneaky. We'd bring back bags of food, canned goods mostly. There weren't any more rescue camps or centers to go to at that point, so we were on our own."

"Yeah, I was a city slicker for all intents and purposes before the apocalypse, too, Paige," Sam says. "I have learned a lot of new skills since then."

"Yes, I suppose we all have," she agrees. "The owners of the farm maybe went out for supplies and were killed. I don't know."

"Or maybe they left looking for their family somewhere else in the country," Reagan says. "Our neighbors, the Johnsons, did that. But then they came back."

Paige shrugs and says, "Perhaps. Who knows really? But most times I'd go with Gavin and let Talia stay with Maddie. We found enough food and supplies to make it through that first winter by raiding homes in the area that were deserted. One night some men came there. Luckily our fire had burned out. We could tell immediately that they were up to no good. They came in the first floor of the house, kicked in the door. We were upstairs sleeping, but we heard their loud truck pull down the long drive. Saw the three of them get out of the cab. They knew we were there. There were signs of life on the first floor like empty jars, baby bottles in the sink, a smoking freaking fireplace. We yelled down the stairs at them to leave. They kept trying to talk to us like they weren't a threat, like we could just all live there together. It got heated very quickly. Then one of them got mad and shot his pistol up the stairwell at us. Little did they know, though, that we'd found two old guns in a gun cabinet in the master bedroom. It looked like there were a lot of other guns there at one time. About a month before those men showed up, we'd figured out how to load them. Gavin and I took some time to familiarize ourselves with them. Even shot a few rounds each to practice out behind the barn. The worst part about that night was dragging their dead bodies back out of the house. They were big men, heavy."

Sam's eyes widen at the realization of what she is hearing. She can just imagine the fear they must've felt, the fear and desperation they lived day in and day out. She doesn't comment, but naturally Reagan does.

"So you guys killed three men? Have you killed any other people?"

"A few," Paige answer honestly. She shakes her head with forlorn memories. "We stayed there the rest of that first winter until we felt like we could get moving again. Then we walked until we could find a vehicle to use. Gas was harder to find than a car. We crossed farther into Pennsylvania and finally ran into a caravan of people. It was safer to be with them. They were good people. Travel was really slow. You gotta understand. Sometimes we were lucky to make it twenty miles a day. We were always stopping for a lot of different reasons; gas scavenging, cars or vans breaking down, food and supplies runs."

"I can't imagine," Reagan says, furrowing her brow.

Paige sighs heavily. "We stopped at a big camp in Ohio. And then we hit sickness. I don't know what the hell it was. People were puking, fevering, had horrible rashes. The group's plan was to continue all the way through and go to Colorado. We were going to head south and leave them because we knew we needed to get here. They'd heard there was power out West. None of us made it further than the border of Ohio and Pennsylvania. It was bad. There was a small hospital there that was trying to run an emergency medical facility to help people. I think most of the people there weren't even doctors or nurses. They were just people from that small city who were trying to help each other. We shouldn't have stopped. But some of the people in our group were tired of being on the move and wanted to rest and hole up for a few weeks to gather supplies. Some of them felt like we should try to help the sick ones there. Well, that didn't work out so well. There were twenty-seven of us when we got there. I convinced Talia and Gavin to leave within the first week. We lost seven people in our group. Whatever the sickness was, it was killing people that fast. They were having seizures and…"

Her voice drifts off, and she doesn't restart her tale of horror. Her story reminds Sam of the sickness that had struck down her traveling companion-captors. She still can't reconcile in her mind that the wretched people she hated within that group hadn't contracted the illness, but that Huntley's young twin brother had and had also succumbed to it.

"We saw the pneumonic plague hit here," Reagan recounts. "But that doesn't sound like what you saw up north. That sounds like some sort of fast moving virus. Sometimes prolonged high fevers can cause seizures. Something pretty damn deadly to kill people so quickly, too."

"No kidding," Sam agrees.

"There was a veterinarian working there that said he thought it could be typhoid fever, whatever that is. I mean I've heard of it, but I don't really know what it is."

"Hm, maybe," Reagan says thoughtfully. "It's usually spread through contaminated food or water. It will spread through third world villages quickly because they are all drinking and eating from the same source of contamination. It's not all that deadly, unless, of course, you don't have the right antibiotics to treat it."

"Yeah, they didn't have anything to treat it. They were just trying to keep the sick people hydrated…"

"Well, there you go," Reagan states. "If they continued to drink the contaminated water, then of course they weren't going to get any better."

"We left in the middle of the night. Gavin went into the hospital and stole some medical supplies for us, especially for Maddie in case she got sick. It wasn't much. A few aspirin tablets and a tiny bottle of little kid Tylenol. We stopped down below Columbus, Ohio next."

"That's where I went to college," Reagan offers and then furrows her brow.

"Yeah, Simon told me that you did. Sorry, but there's not much left of that town. We stopped at another settlement below Columbus and stayed there for a few weeks. At that point, it was getting harder to find food and clean water. This settlement was homes, tents and campers all in a small town. They were nice people. They welcomed us in. Most other established communities did not."

"That's terrible," Sam says.

Paige vehemently shakes her head. "No, it's understandable. It was so dangerous. I don't blame any of them at all."

"Where did you go after that?" Sam asks.

Paige toys with the leather strings on her wrist before answering, "We tagged along with another caravan going down route 77 south. We ended up staying with them for the winter in Kentucky, which was a hell of a lot easier than the winter up farther north."

"No shit," Reagan swears, getting a smile of all white, straight teeth from Paige. "I hated those freagin' Ohio winters. They were a whole shitload harder than here."

Sam recalls how she used to ride during the winter with her best friend and teammate from her riding academy. She never minded the weather back then. Snow and cold weather were the least of her worries in her former life. She never worried about much of anything other than winning at a riding event. Her life had been sheltered and protected from the harshness outside of it. She was always just happy to be out riding or spending time with her family.

"There wasn't a lot for food at that point. It took everyone working together in that whole group to scavenge and produce food. Gavin and I decided we needed to leave. Talia wanted to stay. She liked the security, but we took a vote and left. Gavin's great with his bow, too. We found a lot of books at a bookstore about what plants you can eat in the wild. We would've starved after that without those books."

"That's actually good knowledge to have," Sam speculates as she places the last few items in her box. "We should probably all learn that from you."

"Trust me, it's mostly what grasses in a yard or field that you can eat. And berries, wild mushrooms, that kind of thing. But we'd have starved for sure."

"Where'd you go from Kentucky?" Reagan asks.

"We left our group and made our way here. It was rough and mostly on foot with a toddler, but we finally made it. Even though I don't like horses, one of those would've come in pretty damn handy back then. Tennessee isn't very on-foot friendly terrain."

"No shit!" Reagan agrees. "That would've been a bitch for sure."

"What's a bitch?" Kelly asks from the door, startling them.

"Hey!" Reagan yells. "We're having a private moment here, Hulk! Do you mind?"

Kelly just laughs at her. Sam smiles. Reagan and Kelly have become like brother and sister over the years. He watches over Reagan protectively when John's not around or on a run or at the clinic when she's not.

"You girls finish your moment and then you're haulin' ass. John's ready and so is Doc," he informs them.

"Beat it, or I'll tell Hannie you were swearing," Reagan teases.

"Yeah, yeah. Takes a cusser to know one, half pint," he razzes her. Reagan good-naturedly punches his big shoulder. He just smirks before leaving. Sam believes that Kelly may have been just as worried about Reagan during her bout with the flu as John.

"We're glad you made it here, Paige," Sam says, trying to make her feel welcome. She's been rather standoffish since her and her friends arrived. This is by far the longest conversation they've had with her.

"Thanks," she returns. "There were a lot of other bad things that happened and things we had to do to stay alive, but I don't really want to talk about any of that."

"I don't blame you," Reagan says. "And we've all had to do bad shit, Paige. That's why we're still alive, too."

Paige nods and there is a sadness in her gray-blue eyes. Sam understands it well.

"We should get going," Reagan tells them. "There are bound to be people waiting for us. Besides, we don't want our men to get their panties in a wad."

Paige laughs heartily, but Sam refrains. She certainly doesn't want to be overheard laughing at Simon or Kelly. She wouldn't want to hurt their feelings.

"Right," Sam mumbles. "Ready, Paige?"

She gets a nod in return from Simon's sister. They leave the shed, find the men waiting for them near Grandpa's SUV, pack in the crates and all pile into it. John drives while Grandpa sits shotgun. Reagan and Paige share the middle seat. Gavin has stayed behind with Kelly and Derek, and Talia is also remaining at the farm to watch Maddie, who is fitting in just great with the other McClane kids. The milder weather has driven the children out of doors, which is a benefit to everyone's ears. The backseat is reserved for Sam and Simon. As usual, contingency plans are being covered.

John starts it off with, "If there would be any people that come to the clinic with weapons, I'll disarm them before they get in."

"Roger that," Simon agrees.

"We've never had a problem yet, John," Reagan says. "We'll be fine. Everyone's thankful that we're doing this."

"Doesn't matter, honey," Grandpa argues. "John's right. We could have other people from farther away who will hear of the clinic and want help but don't know our rules."

John adds, "So we all know the procedures, right? If anything goes down, Doc will secure the back entrance and.... well, it will be me and Simon who will hold down the front. I'm going to stop by the Reynolds and pick up Chet. We could use an extra set of eyes at the clinic today."

Chet and John have become friends, despite their rocky start. Sometimes he'll come over to the farm and hang out with the men in the evening. He also helps out with road security and like today since Cory isn't around, he'll come to the clinic with them.

John goes on and on about security as they drive down the rutted oil well road between the two farms. When they hit a particularly deep hole, Sam is jostled against Simon. He looks down at her and scoots farther away. The narrow double seats in the rear of the SUV are less roomy. Unless he climbs over the seat and into the trunk, there's nowhere else to go.

"Sorry," he mumbles and resumes reading his medical book.

The conversation in the car is loud as Reagan explains more about the clinic to Paige; and Grandpa and John converse about security and procedure. Sam figures it's a good time to try to talk with Simon.

"Is everything ok, Simon?"

"Yeah, sure," he says without turning toward her.

"Did I do something wrong?" she asks as she twirls a loose thread from the hem of her sweater.

"No, everything's fine, Sam," he responds and finally turns toward her.

He offers a grin that reveals it was born of a pained effort. Sam is disheartened by this. He's normally so full of good spirits and is easy to be around. He's quiet-spoken, but always tries to find the bright side of most situations. He's night and day different from their beloved Cory. Sam believes that's why they get along so well. Cory has always been cynical and just... darker. Despite everything that he's been through, Simon tries to see light and goodness in the world.

"Wanna' go for a hike and look for some herbs later when we get back?" she suggests with a hopeful tinge in her voice.

He quickly points out the window without answering her, "There's the Reynolds farm."

They pull in and park, taking a moment to track down and pick up Chet.

"Have you met the Reynolds yet, Paige?" Grandpa asks.

"Yeah, I met the brothers and Bertie and their little girl the other day," Paige offers.

"They're good people," Grandpa adds.

"Yes, they seem very nice," Paige agrees.

Reagan scoots to the middle as John comes out of the barn with Chet. He gets back in the driver's seat as they all wait for Chet to come out of his house with his shotgun. He also has a pistol strapped to his hip when he emerges. He jumps in the SUV beside Reagan and jovially blurts a greeting to everyone which is returned.

He shoots a smile over his shoulder at her which Sam returns with one of her own accompanied by a wave. He's like another adopted big brother, one of so many that she has now.

The conversation of security picks back up as she and Simon still brood silently in the back seat. His mulish behavior and withdrawn attitude doesn't sit well with her. She tries to clear her mind of the issues between her and Simon, and there are definitely issues, of that she is certain. She just needs to concentrate on the clinic and doing her job as a nurse for Grandpa and Reagan.

Simon almost always takes care of the children with Grandpa, and Reagan tends to the adults. Her job is usually more gruesome and involves a lot of suturing and broken bone settings. Many of the men in their community will injure themselves but put off seeking medical attention at the clinic or calling on the radio for help. It makes Reagan's job of fixing their injuries even gorier and difficult. So many people rely on their little clinic, and Sam is always happy to be going there to help them. Helping others is all that matters right now. Helping those less fortunate. Helping those who can't help themselves. Helping the good, kind people of their tiny, deconstructed and broken community.

Chapter Fifteen
Paige

It takes slightly more than twenty minutes to make it to the small town of Pleasant View where the family used to interact, shop, go to church, attend high school and have a medical practice that served their small community. It's quaint and has a real hometown cozy and comfortable feel about it. Or at least it probably used to look that way. Now it looks more like a deserted ghost town with some of the streets barricaded off to keep outsiders from getting in. They pass three of those areas. And as John drives slowly through the small burg, Paige spies through the cracks and crevices of those barricades and sees children playing here and there, people milling about and walking around and some others doing outdoor chores. Some of the barricades have graffiti spray painted on the sheet metal and wood that in no friendly terms lets trespassers know that the area is secured by heavy firepower. She doesn't blame them.

"Here we are, everyone," John announces.

He pulls the vehicle around to the back of the clinic. Paige takes note of the thirty or so people waiting for treatment at the front door of the building that was explained to her as being Herb's old practice. It's his practice again. The services just come a bit cheaper.

"All ashore who's going ashore," Dr. McClane adds in a light tone as he alights the big SUV.

Sam chuckles behind her. Dr. McClane is always making jokes and being funny. Sam told her the other day that she loves him as much as she'd loved her real parents. She feels the same about the rest of the family. Paige thinks that the McClanes are very generous people, but she doesn't feel any certain connection to them yet other than being eternally grateful to them for taking care of Simon and now for opening their home to her and her friends.

Paige tips her seat forward so that Simon and Sam can exit the SUV. He holds out his hand to help the other girl down. She jumps to her feet and her long black ponytail swings side to side like one of those huge horses' tails back at the farm. Her bright blue eyes regard Simon with hopeful expectation. He just turns away from her and guides Paige through the back door. Paige finds his behavior odd. He's told her quite a few times how close he is with Sam. She glances back in time to witness Samantha's face fall with disappointment

He's also close with the absent kid, Cory. He also explained why that guy is gone. That story had been about as depressing as one could get. Paige had even wept for her brother's pain at losing this young girl named Em, although he did not. There was a cool hardness in his deep blue eyes that had left Paige feeling as if she was looking at a stranger instead of her younger brother.

"Hey, when we get back to the farm, could I move into the cabin with you?" Paige asks. She's been meaning to ask this of him. She doesn't like being in the big house while he's out, what seems like, so far away from her. She'd lost him once. She doesn't wish to do it again. Paige knows that he's never going to be her kid brother again, but she still wants to keep him close.

"Oh, um sure, sis," he answers as he holds the door for her and Sam.

They are lugging the full crates into the back room of the building. Reagan rushes around opening the blinds and setting up the rooms. Sam follows after her with supplies and things they'll need to treat patients. This is weird as shit. Such a short time ago, she'd been worried about where they'd get enough food for Maddie for the day. For the day! And here she is volunteering at a clinic in some small, re-established community.

Simon had been right about the food at the farm. They certainly have enough to go around. She'd cried like some sort of lunatic when he'd taken her down to the basement in the big house and had shown her where the food pantry was located and the root cellar that holds packing crates full of vegetables and apples. He'd just comforted her again. As usual.

"Don't like it in the big house? Is there anything wrong there? Here, ditch your jacket in this closet," her brother says as he swipes a clump of hair from his forehead.

His red hair has darkened so much in the last four years since she's seen him. He used to have a lighter red like her. She used to like to get blonde highlights painted into her own. That seems like a hundred years ago. After a week of hot showers at the farm, she'd broken down when she'd picked up the bar of homemade soap and the small bottle of shampoo. She'd cried over that, too. Luckily, Simon wasn't there for that one. She'd been standing under a warm stream of water in the shower and had been naked, of course.

"No, no," she's quick to explain. "It's not anything like that. I just thought since maybe that kid Cory isn't out there with you that I could just stay there. I mean if he comes back, I'll move back out. I know it's your place... and his. I don't mean to barge in. It's just that I missed you."

"When," he mutters to himself mostly and sets a crate on an exam table. "*When* he comes back."

"Oh, right!" she corrects. "Sure, when he comes back. I could..."

"Yeah, sure," he offers. "I'd be glad for the company out there, but it's not as comfortable as the house. We don't have a full bathroom with a shower or a tub or anything. It's rustic. You've seen it. Just a toilet and a sink."

"I'm cool with that. Simon, I've had to go to the bathroom in the great outdoors for much of the last four years. Your cabin is awesome as far as I'm concerned."

Simon gives her a grin that reveals his adorable dimples.

"All right," he says with a nod. "It's up to you. If you end up not liking it, then you could go back to the big house. I won't be offended."

When Paige meets his gaze, she is dumbfounded by how adult he is now. There is no trace whatsoever of the young teenager she'd left four and a half years ago to start college in Georgia. There is even dark reddish stubble on his cheeks, which had surprised her the first time she noticed it a few weeks back. His square jawline is hard and strong, a dent prominent in the center of his chin. There is still just the slightest hint of boyish charm about his face, but he is mostly serious and diligent. He'd been so naïve and carefree back then. He'd hung out with his very small circle of friends and went to comic book conventions and studied science with a passion. He was always close with their mother. To say that he was a momma's boy would've been an understatement. Paige can't even comprehend what Simon had been through when he'd lost her. They haven't broached that subject yet. Paige isn't sure she's ready. She's not sure if she'll ever be ready. She doesn't think he is, either.

"Thanks, bro," she teases about getting her way and nudges her shoulder playfully against his. He doesn't return it but grins down at her as if he is being tolerant. Her smile slides away as he shows her where to take the items and what needs to be distributed to which room.

"I'll be right back," Simon tells her. "Gotta get the wood-burner fired up 'cuz the practice is too cold."

"There's a wood-burning stove here like the one in your cabin?" Paige asks and stands out of his way.

"Yes, John and I installed it since there isn't any other way to heat the practice in the winter," he tells her.

Paige is dumbfounded by her young brother's newfound skills. She offers to help carry firewood from under the back overhang, but he declines it. Once again, she just stands in a corner and watches the McClane family march about in military fashion readying their clinic for the day's work. She fidgets with the leather ties on her right wrist.

A short time later, John exits through the front door and calls out the instructions to the awaiting patients. Mostly he's telling them to mind their manners and not try to skip line or they won't receive care. Simon goes through the crowd and hands out numbers on slips of papers so that order can be maintained. Chet stands guard on the front, overgrown and dead lawn, and John takes up post on the corner of the porch. He'll allow people to come in one at a time until three exam rooms are full. Once patients are filed back out, he'll allow more in. It's a system that seems to work for the family, and more importantly, helps to prevent chaos. She feels bad for them, though because the temperature has to be hovering at less than forty degrees.

Paige shadows Simon for a few hours as they take care of people who are ill with everything from fevers, sore throats, children's earaches and tummy troubles to rashes. He explains that they are hoping for a reprieve soon from the seasonal illnesses since the weather is starting to improve.

Later she moves over to Reagan's exam room and offers help. They examine pregnant women. Reagan stitches up three different men who've cut themselves and did piss poor patch jobs on themselves. That had been completely unpleasant. Two of the men had infected wounds. Paige had averted her eyes. They don't have the capabilities to do an x-ray, although they do have dim lighting from the solar panels that the men installed a few years ago on the roof. The x-ray machines pull too much on the power source and do not get used. Reagan explains that every once in a while either she or her grandfather will use an ultrasound machine for a pregnancy that they suspect could be a problem.

"Mrs. Wagner, you're doing just fine," Reagan tells her patient and notates on a chart.

The charts are just pieces of paper that will go in a file folder when they are done in the exam room.

"Your baby's heartbeat is strong and steady," she says as she presses her stethoscope against the woman's distended abdomen. "Keep up with the vitamins. I know you were sharing with your sister, but she's not pregnant. You are. So quit sharing. You need the extra nutrients right now. She'll be fine without them."

"My sinuses are so stuffy and miserable. Can I get some of that tea that Dr. Simon makes?" the woman with the dark blonde hair says.

She's thin but still seems healthy. She looks a hell of a lot better than some of the pregnant women that Paige had run into on the road. Hell, she looks better than Reagan now, who is still slowly recovering from her illness. Although she doesn't know Reagan that well, Paige has taken to her. There is something about her, something about the sadness that Paige can see in Reagan's eyes that make her seem like something of a kindred spirit. Sam is the same way, but she knows how to hide it better.

The pregnant patient can't be more than thirty. Her husband, Roy, is hovering just outside the exam room door. He's a big burly dude, not one to mess with in Paige's opinion.

"No!" Reagan retorts. "Don't drink any of that crap till you pop out this kid! It has licorice root in it. If you'd drink too much and overdose yourself, it could stop your heart... or the baby's."

Her bedside manner could use some softening, but Reagan seems like a good doctor. She also seems really young to even be one. Simon told her that Reagan's some kind of mega genius or something. He'd worried and worked around the clock with Herb to heal her from the flu. His feelings for Reagan are apparent. Sam had told her that Simon had saved Reagan's life from their awful, psychotic cousin Bobby. When she'd pressed Sam for more information, the girl had just smiled and turned away.

"Oh!" the woman exclaims with fear. "Oh, ok, Dr. Reagan. I won't drink any of that until after the baby comes."

"No!" Reagan snipes again. "Not then, either. You'll be breastfeeding. Once you're done, then you can go back to drinking it. Your stuffy sinuses are just from the pregnancy. A lot of women complain of it. Just flush them with some warm water. You can also place a warm washcloth on your face, too, or humidify your house by placing a bucket of water near your heat source with a wet towel hanging out of it. It will draw the humidity into the air. That should give you some relief, but no weird teas or herbs!"

A few minutes later, Reagan helps her patient carefully down from the exam table. She's nearly eight months pregnant and a bit awkward. Paige notices a bead of sweat on Reagan's forehead. She wonders if this long day is too much for her new friend.

"Now, I'll see you again in…."

"Everybody get down!" a shout interrupts Reagan. It sounds like her husband, John. Paige feels a pang of fear deep in her gut.

A moment later, gunfire comes from outside of the building followed by more than one woman screaming and then return fire. Reagan rips off her face mask, something they all wear. She also pulls her gown away and tosses it to the floor. Paige pulls her own mask down away from her mouth but lets it rest against her neck. Reagan eases toward the door in a hunched over position. She pulls it open so that the doting husband can enter to protect his pregnant wife. It sounds like a war zone out there. Shouting and gunfire continue to pop off, some rapidly and some in single shots. Some of it sounds like it is smacking into the side of the practice. The sound of shattering glass exploding into millions of shards comes next. Paige is fairly certain that some or all of the windows of the building are being shot out. Her heart is pounding so hard she can hear it in her ears. The acidic bile that comes with uncertainty and fear rises in her throat. This is the time that she'd normally start running. Only a few seconds have passed, but it feels like a lifetime. Her flight instincts are kicking into high gear.

Simon comes racing toward their room. He has Sam by the hand. Her pretty blue eyes are wide with fear. The pistol from her hip is in her hand.

"Sam, stay here with Reagan and Paige," he orders and pushes the girl into the room with them.

Paige wants to shout at him to come back. She wants to grab her brother and run, get the hell out of this war zone.

Behind him, Dr. McClane holds a shotgun. He's still wearing a white lab coat. The irony of his appearance is not lost on Paige. They both leave them before anyone can even retort an argument to the contrary. Paige wants to run out of this building with her brother, convince him to escape with her through the back door. Apparently running isn't in the McClane family vocabulary, or her brother's.

Sam huddles with her against the inside wall of the office while Reagan stays near the half open door. Sam still holds a pistol, but Paige notices that her small hands shake.

The husband says, "Stay down! Stay low in case a bullet comes through the wall."

They obey and squat lower as more shouting and shooting ensues. Car tires squeal. An engine coughs and sputters and then dies.

"Fuckers!" Reagan hisses as she peers around the corner, holding her own handgun.

The young doctor is about to breach the doorway when Sam calls out to her.

"Reagan, no!" she shouts. "Stay here. Please don't go out there."

The doctor with the vibrant green eyes glances worriedly at her and Sam and then at the door before deciding not to go through it. She and Sam are the only protection that any of them have should those people in moving war machines, formally known as automobiles, get into the building. Paige's palms sweat. Perspiration runs down her forehead and also trickles down her back. She wants out of here. This feels like a trap being in this building.

Gunfire follows again before the sounds of more than one vehicle speeding away reaches them.

"What's going on, Dr. Reagan?" the husband of the pregnant woman asks.

"Not sure, Roy," Reagan answers him.

Paige notices that he's drawn his knife. It's a serrated style with a long blade. He looks like he could be quite crafty with it. She's had to use a similar weapon before, as well, but Paige certainly has no wish to do so again.

A second later, John blasts into the building and appears at their doorway. His wife throws herself around his waist, hugging him close. He doesn't return her embrace, but nor does he push her away.

He's too busy digging something out of his pocket. His eyes are troubled.

"Charlie Tango to Alpha Company," he shouts into the radio. "Charlie Tango to Alpha Company."

His tone is impatient and loud, not something Paige has ever heard from him before.

"Alpha Company, go ahead," Derek's voice comes over loud and clear.

"Charlie Tango under attack, three wounded, one casualty," John shouts.

"Sit rep on Charlie Tango party," Derek returns with more calm than Paige feels.

"Charlie Tango clear. I repeat, Charlie Tango party all clear. Civilians wounded, some casualties. Send the Hulk to JF1. Rendezvous and reinforcements ASAP in case of repeat assault," he says more calmly this time.

"Roger that, Charlie. Right away. Over and out," Derek says and ends the transmission.

Reagan has stepped away, and Sam and Paige have risen from their low squatting positions. They all go into the main waiting room of the practice where panic and chaos has ensued and twenty or so people have taken safe refuge. Women are crying. Children are screaming and crying and clinging to their mothers. Simon runs through the front door and heads straight for them. He's scanning his surroundings as if looking for someone. Her brother seems unusually subdued for what just went down. His eyes connect with hers, and he nods curtly. He's carrying some sort of military rifle in front of him pointed toward the floor. He touches her shoulder briefly but squeezes past her in the crowd, scanning.

"Sam!" he calls out.

"I'm here, Simon," Sam returns and rushes forward from behind other people.

Her brother hugs the younger woman fiercely to him. This strikes Paige as unusual. He'd told her how close they are and how they'd been through so much together. He hadn't expanded on anything beyond that, however. Paige can only speculate on what they've been through to make him so desperately protective of Samantha. Of course, Sam is small and delicate in nature. She hardly seems capable of taking care of herself. Paige joins them near the wall where her brother regards her over Sam's head which is still stuck to his chest like it's been glued there.

"That's never happened before," he tells her.

"Who were they?" Paige asks.

Other members of the McClane family join them. Reagan and Doc are flying into motion trying to treat the innocent victims who'd only come today for medical care, not to be shot at.

"We're not sure yet," Simon answers.

"Kelly's on his way with back-up from the Johnson farm," Sam says when she pulls away.

Paige notices that she doesn't relinquish Simon's shirt tail.

"We gotta help these people," Simon tells them. "Paige, take my rifle. The safety's on. Keep it with you for now so I can help John carry people inside."

He shoves the heavy rifle into her hands whether she wanted it or not. Guns have always scared her, but she has been glad that she had one a time or two… or three or four during the last few years. One time her group hadn't been lucky enough to have one. That had by far been their worst experience together.

"Um, yeah, ok," Paige answers and slings the rifle behind her shoulder like she's seen him do at the farm. She hopes she doesn't accidentally shoot herself with it.

Chet Reynolds rushes into the room carrying a child. She can't be more than ten years old. Her long, single blonde braid is dampened with blood.

"Reagan!" Chet yells. "She's been hit. Right shoulder."

"Come with me," Reagan says in a rush. "Sam!"

Samantha races after Reagan and Chet as they disappear to the back of the clinic. Her brother has already gone back out the front door and is carrying a woman who has also evidently been shot. It's so surreal seeing him like this. Her once youthful, silly kid brother is carrying a woman in his strong, capable arms.

"Paige," he calls over to her. "Come with me."

Paige follows him on legs that quake from the waiting room where they end up in Exam Room 2.

"Protective gear," he orders her firmly. "Set the rifle in the corner."

He quickly dons a surgical style gown, rubber gloves, and a face mask. He pulls a hair cover out of a drawer and puts the funny looking cap on.

"Mimic everything I'm doing, sis," he states. "We don't want to risk our own infection or our patient's."

Paige would like to explain to him that she's not a nurse, that she has absolutely no experience with this sort of crap, that she feels like she's going to puke her breakfast all over the nice clean floor at the sight of this woman's blood. She doesn't. She simply follows his dictate and tries her best to be helpful while their patient gasps and cries from pain. The McClanes, of whom she now fully realizes that her brother is a part of, do not seem to allow for weakness, hesitation or indecision.

Her brother takes a hypodermic from the drawer, removes the plastic cap, squirts a tiny amount of liquid into the air and plunges the needle into the fatty tissue of the woman's lower calf area where she's been shot. She looks to be in her late fifties and is moaning loudly.

"Morphine, pain blocker," he explains patiently. "It will help to relax her and also block pain to the whole area."

How the hell is he so cool and collected? Their practice was just attacked, he ran outside to return fire, perhaps killed some men, and here he is so steady and sure.

"Now, Paige, I'm going to need you to hold her still and mop up the area for me as I go. The bullet's lodged in there. It needs to come out. Then we'll get her stitched up. All right?"

Paige nods shakily but would like to tell him "hell no!"

She uses the gauze blotting pads and clean linens to keep the area as dry as she can while her brother digs through flesh and muscle and tendons or ligaments or whatever the hell she's trying so hard not to look at until he finally finds the small lead bullet. He places it in the porcelain sink behind them. Paige pats gently at the woman's wound while swallowing hard. The poor lady is weeping softly. Paige would like to run from the damn room. Maybe run all the way back to the farm.

"Got it. It was only a .22 round, so that's good. No hollow-point. Not a high caliber large cartridge," he notes.

The patient moans loudly from the pain. And no wonder. Her wound seems deep and painful. Paige assumes he's learned so much about guns and bullet sizes from the Rangers on the farm. They certainly didn't grow up shooting guns and hunting in Arizona.

"Load that syringe," her brother says.

It takes a moment to realize he's talking to her. "What? I don't know how to do that!" she whispers hysterically.

Simon smiles gently behind his mask. "Ok, sis," he says.

Then he proceeds to calmly show her how to load a shot vial. This time it's called lidocaine something or other. She barely has time to read part of the label.

"Now, Mrs. Parker, I'm going to administer some stitches, ok? We'll wait just a minute to give the shot a chance to kick in. If you start feeling this, let me know, and I'll hit the wound again with another shot of lidocaine."

The woman mumbles something incoherently, leading Paige to believe that she is nearly out. Apparently that shot of numbing solution had been powerful. Either that or she is in shock. There are cries of pain and agony and likely grief coming from different areas of the clinic through the walls of the small building.

Simon says to her, "Make sure she doesn't roll off the table, Paige."

He turns his back to them, threads a needle, returns to the table and begins carefully yet swiftly sewing this woman's small wound together. Paige watches in amazement as her once bookish brother sews an open, gory wound so neatly and precisely until he has the hole closed.

"See that bottle over there?" he asks her.

"Um, yes. Got it," Paige says as she brings the bottle of disinfecting solution to him. He also treats a few abrasions on his patient's knee and left arm where she'd taken a hard fall on the concrete from the shooting.

"Take a few cotton balls and moisten them so I can clean the area and get this covered," he orders softly, his voice muffled through his cotton face mask.

They work side by side until the woman's wound is covered with fresh white bandaging. Then Simon helps her down from the table to escort her out of the room. A nervous young man is waiting on the other side of the door, obviously a relative or friend of the patient.

"If there's blood on the table, try to get it cleaned before I come back with another patient," he tells her.

She can hear her brother giving the woman instructions on her wound care as he helps her down the hall. After he departs with the limping woman, Paige assesses the room. What the shit? There's freagin' blood everywhere. She quickly grabs a stack of rags from a box and starts mopping it up. She's about halfway through it, when a wave of nausea hits her so hard that she has to run to the rear exit where she expels her stomach contents on the gravel behind the building. When she's done, she hunches there in the same bent over position taking deep breaths. A hand on her back startles her, but it's only Sam.

Her kind blue eyes smile into hers. "You all right?"

Paige nods, "Yes, thanks. I'll be right back in to help. I'm just not used to seeing that much blood."

"Oh, it's fine," Sam conciliates. "It takes a while to get used to working here. We've never had anything like this happen, but we've seen a lot of bad things over the years. A lot of shooting victims, too. That seems to be one thing people haven't run out of."

"Bullets?"

"Ways to hurt each other," Sam elucidates with sadness.

"Right. I'll come back inside in just a moment," Paige says. Sam just rubs her back another second.

"Take your time. We're safe now. Kelly's here with three of the Johnson clan. He brought your friend Talia, too," Sam says kindly. "Oh and Paige? Don't come back in and work with Reagan. She's a bit abrasive sometimes. She'll not tolerate you puking. She'd just say something crude like 'nut up or shut up.' She can be harsh, but we still love her. Trust me, work with Grandpa or Simon," Sam says with a smile and turns to leave.

When she feels calm enough, Paige pushes her braid over her shoulder, goes back inside on shaking legs, and helps her brother with a little girl who has minor abrasions and scrapes from the broken glass. Talia is working with Doc. And they've allowed Sam to continue to work with Reagan.

The anxiety everyone feels is just slightly subdued by the time they are done with the girl. Reagan is called to work with Doc, and Talia is sent outside. Moments later Simon sends Paige to join the others in the main lounge. She tries to be helpful where she can, offering assistance, a blanket to an elderly woman who is mostly in shock, a lollipop to a small, frightened child from the stash that Sam gave her to hand out to the children, and cleaning up glass debris from the windows.

Reagan emerges from the room where she has been working with Simon and Doc. She and John are conferring. Kelly stands at the entrance to the clinic, effectively blocking the wide doorway. Paige joins Reagan and her husband.

"He didn't make it," Reagan relays.

"Yeah, I wasn't sure about that one. His wound was pretty bad. That makes the death toll three, counting the woman who was killed out front," John says. "Kelly and I will go get him out of Doc's exam room before he tries to do it by himself."

Her husband sprints away with Kelly.

"What happened?" Sam whispers as she joins them.

Reagan explains it quietly, "One of the shooting victims died. He bled out before we could get the artery sewn."

"Where's Simon?" Paige asks next.

"He's still with another patient," Sam explains.

"It's gonna be a long day," Reagan says and swipes a hand through her ponytail. "We still need to treat the people who came here for help. Cleaning up is going to take hours today. You two, make sure you take precautions. We don't want any germs or blood borne pathogens coming back to the farm."

"Right," Sam agrees.

"What was that all about?" Paige inquires. "I mean the shooting? Does anyone know anything yet?"

"John said that there were three vehicles. Two trucks and a car. Maybe ten or twelve men total. He and Chet took out four or five of them I think. Simon got two. John said he thinks they were here to raid for drugs. Or hell, who knows what they came here for...." Reagan states with a frown.

"Oh my," Sam says on an inhale of surprise. "I didn't know it was that many people."

"Where'd they even get gas for their vehicles?" Paige asks, still reeling from the comment about her brother shooting two men.

"Probably the same damn place they were gonna get their drugs or whatever the hell they came here to raid for," Reagan answers with her usual fondness for swearing.

"Reagan," Chet comes over and is followed by Talia.

Paige smiles at her friend, who also looks very put out by this whole situation. Hanging around for gun fights and sewing people back together isn't exactly their thing. If it had been the three of them with Maddie, they would've run for a nearby house and hid out. Then they would've got the hell out of this town. It isn't that they don't feel charitable or obligated to help their fellow man, but they have learned to flee when danger strikes. They are simple survivors with little to no skill other than staying alive another day.

"There's a sick kid out there. He doesn't look so hot. I mean he's not shot. He's just really sick," Chet Reynolds tells her.

"Thanks, Chet," Reagan replies. "You better get back out of here, though. You don't even have a face mask on. You, too, Talia."

They both nod and go out the front door again. Paige notices the shotgun that Talia carries. Other men loiter around outside with guns and bravery. She recognizes one of them as the son of the

Johnson family, Zach. The other two must be with them, as well, but she doesn't remember meeting them. She notices that Talia stays close to Chet.

A tapping on her shoulder causes her to swing around. Simon, still in head to toe protective gear, gestures.

"You ready to come back and help again?" he asks.

Paige nods. Yeah, it's going to be a long day.

Chapter Sixteen
Reagan

"There's a guy hog-tied out back, babe," John tells her as their day is coming to a close.

"What?" she asks with a bit of hysteria. They've been working all day at the clinic, and the sun is nearly set. They don't typically linger this many hours in town, but with so many extra patients needing attention, they had no choice. "What the hell do you mean that someone's tied up out back?"

"One of the men that I shot," her husband says. "Kelly and I took him next door to the feed mill so we can interrogate him."

"What the fuck?" she asks as she removes her protective gown. "When were you planning on telling me this?"

"Now," he says with a silly grin.

Reagan rolls her eyes at him. Then she can't help the smile that creeps onto her mouth. It quickly gets replaced with a frown. She's still a doctor, after all. "He's shot?"

"Yeah, not fatally. Well, it could be if he didn't treat it," he says with a shrug.

"Do you want me to treat him or bandage it or…?" Reagan asks and gets a raised eyebrow in return. She nods. Although she doesn't like this side of her husband, she knows that it's what keeps them all alive. "I'll come with you."

John's hand shoots up to her arm with lightning speed. She'd like just to collapse into his strong arms from fatigue. When she'd planned on coming to the clinic today, she had thought they'd only be working a few hours, not all day.

"Look, boss, I don't think that's too good of an idea. You don't need to see this," he says, the corners of his blue eyes crease with worry.

"I'll be fine," Reagan argues and shakes her head.

John sighs loudly and with great over-animation. "Why do I even bother?"

"I don't know," Reagan replies. "You'd think that you'd have learned by now."

John pulls her in for a quick kiss and adds, "Oh, I know, woman. I know."

Twenty minutes later while the rest of the family cleans, sanitizes and locks up the medical clinic, and others repair the broken windows with pieces of salvaged plywood, Reagan walks to the feed mill with John to observe and possibly help with the interrogation of the prisoner. She's exhausted. She's sweating profusely from the exertion, although she has no intention of telling her husband. Kelly is already waiting at the mill. The hostage is tied to a chair, his arms and legs bound. There is a wound in his side which continues to drip blood onto the old hardwood floor of the grain store.

"Hey, little Doc," Kelly greets her.

"Who's this?" Reagan asks.

"This is our new friend," Kelly says with a false cordiality. "He was just about to tell me where his other friends are camped."

"Fuck you!" the man shouts.

Kelly punches him to the side of his face, sending a spray of blood onto the wall near them. The Hulk has on short, black leather gloves for the job, and he's hung his winter coat on a hook. His shirt sleeves are pushed up to his elbows. Reagan doesn't envy this dirtbag. Kelly's fists are huge. That had to hurt. He's lucky Kelly's punch didn't break his jaw or knock out a few teeth.

"You'll talk, dude," John clarifies with confidence and bends over to speak directly into the man's now bloody face. "This ain't our first interrogation. No, way. Not us. We've had some experience with interrogations. Right, bro?"

"Yep," Kelly agrees and moves to stand behind the man.

John continues, "Sure did. We used to do this with terrorists that didn't want to tell us information."

"I ain't tellin' you shit," the dirtbag answers and spits blood on the floor in front of John.

The man is maybe in his forties, dark-haired and tall and skinny. He's no match physically for the Rangers, but he may be mentally. They need him to speak. They need to know where his group is from and if they would come back. Reagan would also like to know why they attacked them in the first place.

"You'll talk," John argues softly.

Her husband nods to Kelly, who returns it. Then he places a threadbare dusty canvas grain sack over Dirtbag's head. Kelly tips him back by tugging easily on the spindles of his wooden chair.

"Hey!" Dirtbag states with surprise. "What the...?"

Her husband, her loving, wonderful husband who'd healed her wounded spirit, proceeds to perform a modified water-boarding on Dirtbag. The man coughs and sputters and gags as John slowly trickles water over his face and into his mouth and nose through the bag. He's literally using a bucket to do the job. Reagan notices that there are six buckets of dirty creek water lined up against the wall.

Right when the man seems as if he's going to drown to death, Kelly tips him upright again. He coughs and spurts water inside of the cloth. Kelly removes the bag from his head. The man's face is red from the strain; the veins in his forehead and neck stand out angrily.

"Where are your friends camped out?" John asks calmly.

Reagan is still surprised at the tenacity of her husband. He'd certainly pursued her with this same unbridled relentlessness.

Dirtbag coughs two more times and then expels another expletive at the men. John nods to his best friend again, and the process starts all over. This time Reagan has to look away. She hadn't thought it would be this hard to watch. It also goes on longer this time. John questions him again and gets nothing. He gives the signal to Kelly once more. When they sit him upright again, his shoulders slump in defeat.

"Now, we can do this all day, or we can show you mercy, my friend," John says quietly.

Her husband squats in front of the chair and speaks slowly and with clear enunciation. She notices that Kelly doesn't speak to the man. She highly doubts that this is by accident. Everything these two soldiers have ever done is calculated and planned out.

"Where are your friends?"

"Can I get a shot or somethin' for the pain? Damn, I'm shot, you know! I'm bleeding to death!"

"That's not gonna kill you," John explains. "You're fine. It was barely a graze. Now tell me where they are."

That's a total lie, Reagan knows. But she also knows that her husband has a low tolerance for sissies. The man's wound is bleeding at a fairly steady rate, however. This will undoubtedly kill him.

"They'll kill me," Dirtbag whimpers. "They'll kill me if I tell you."

"No, they won't. You're here with us," John says. "Where are they?"

"A…about ten miles from here," Dirtbag says.

"Where?" John asks.

"Over in Coopertown. We've got a Target store over there all to ourselves," he relays.

"How many?" John asks next.

Dirtbag seems reticent to answer, so John kicks his shoe.

"There's twenty-two with me. Well, 'cept you killed five of our people today," he says and hangs his head.

"How many are armed?" John interrogates further.

Reagan recognizes the intensity in his blue eyes. This frightens her. Does he mean to go after them? She sure as hell hopes not.

"Armed? Not everyone. Well, everyone's armed but not with guns. Some have clubs, bows, knives," Dirtbag explains.

Snot drips from his nose and hits his thigh, blending into the blood already staining there.

"Why'd you come here?" John asks next.

"What?" Dirtbag returns with a question.

He's not functioning well. Reagan wonders if it is from blood loss or the trauma of the water-boardings.

"Why did your group come here today? Did you come here for us? For the clinic? Or were you here for something else?"

"We heard 'bout this place," the man admits and then shakes his head with regret. "We didn't know you fuckers were armed."

"And?"

"Thought you might have drugs," he says. "We ain't had nothing for almost a month. Found a stash in a house over in the big city."

"Why else did you come here?" John asks.

"We needed medical help. Yeah, someone in our group was sick," the man lies.

John nods to Kelly and they proceed to nearly drown the man again. This time Reagan is sure he is dead until he finally coughs.

"Don't lie to us," John says with grit.

"Sorry, sorry, man," Dirtbag cries. "Please don't do that again. Please."

"I asked you why you came here. You aren't being truthful," John says decidedly.

"Ok, nobody was sick. We just came here for the drugs," the man says. "We heard from some people that there was doctors here. Doctors and medicine and drugs and shit."

"And?" John asks with impatience as if he's after something different.

"And we heard there was women here, too," he says.

Dirtbag's eyes dart to Reagan's, and she looks away.

"I wasn't in on that, man!" he says nervously.

John regards her with a smirk. He clearly doesn't believe this man. Neither does she. This isn't the first time they've had trouble with bastard men who wish to rape women.

"Hey, you gotta believe me," he pleads.

"Who told you about the practice?" John asks patiently.

"A guy from this town told his cousin who lives over there with us," he says, his eyes jumping around between Reagan and John.

"What is this cousin's name?" John asks.

"Huh? His name? Um, Lowry, Lavery, somethin' like that. I don't remember, man," Dirtbag explains.

"Does he have a family here or is he alone?" John asks.

"No, man. I think he lives out in the boonies somewheres," the man says. "He don't live in town. He's out in the woods in his shack or some shit."

John looks at her and Reagan nods with understanding. She knows exactly who this man is talking about. Her grandfather also knows this cousin of Dirtbag's friend. He's a junky loser who they treated about a week ago. He'd asked a lot of questions about them, about the practice, about medications although his small wound hadn't required any. Tim Lafferty is the cousin. He's just signed his own death warrant. Reagan hopes for his sake that he cleared out within the last few days because he's got a bounty from two Rangers on his head now.

"What else do you want us to know about your friends?" John inquires.

"Nothing, man. I'm not like them, ok? Just let me go," he says. "I'll never come back here. I swear!"

His eyes are full of dread. His facial tension and feral behavior remind Reagan of a wild animal that's been caged.

"Are there any women or children over there? Old people?" John asks.

"Nah, no old people or kids. A... few women," he admits.

"Are they with your group because they want to be?" John asks through clenched teeth.

"Um…"

"Don't lie again," John warns.

Kelly tips his chair just slightly.

"Ok, ok! No! They aren't there 'cuz they wanna be! They're with some of the others. That's their women. But we protect them! We don't let nothin' happen to 'em."

"Uh huh," John says with understanding.

Reagan sees his fist clench.

"Six of your group died today," her husband clarifies.

"What?" the turd asks. "What do you mean? There was only five that got killed."

John says nothing. He stares at the man for a moment until it sinks in. Then the begging and pleading starts as John leads her away.

"You like raping women, motherfucker?"

These are the last words that she hears from Kelly as John helps her down from the loading dock behind the feed mill. Then she hears the distinctive sound of a single .223 round being stifled with a silencer.

They load into the SUV and Grandpa's pick-up truck, all of them packed in cozy and tight. She's sitting next to John in the front, while Grandpa shares the middle seat with Sam and Simon, who are still holding hands. Reagan doubts that he's let go of her hand since the attack. He's taken it upon himself over the last few years to be her guardian. Sam, although she's now an adult, still resembles a little China doll. No wonder Simon feels protective of her.

Paige rides in the rear with her friend Talia. Her friend had been quite helpful at the clinic, but from what Reagan overheard, Paige wasn't too keen on it. In her defense, it's not usually a damn war zone at their peaceful clinic. They usually treat minor illnesses or self-inflicted accident wounds, not gunshot victims.

When they get to the farm, everyone takes armloads of crates and materials back to the shed. Then they convene in the dining room, allowing Chet and his brother Wayne, who has also come over on his four-wheeler, to join them.

Kelly leads off, "We need a plan, guys."

"Agreed," John says.

Grandpa rubs his hand over his forehead wearily. Reagan can tell that he isn't going to be thrilled with any plans that involve family members being put in danger.

"What are you talking about, John? What kind of plan?" her grandfather asks.

"We gotta go over there," her husband clarifies. "We can't allow people like that to live so close to us. That town's less than ten miles from your town. Too close."

"Right," Kelly agrees. "They gotta go. If they're hurting women and robbing people, they can't…. live."

He almost whispers the last word. He doesn't like to upset Hannah, although most days her sister walks around the big house like a zombie going through the motions.

"Right," John agrees. "We need to formulate a strike."

Her lovely sister, Sue's face, turns down into a deep grimace. She clenches at Derek's sinewy forearm. Her brother-in-law places his hand on top of Sue's and nods.

"You're right," Derek agrees with the other two Rangers. "It's been a while since we've had to do this, but we're ready."

"Wait, why can't we just let them be?" Hannah asks quickly.

There are dark circles under her different-colored eyes. She hasn't slept well lately, not since the death of Em. Kelly wraps his arm around her shoulders and comforts her. Many times when Reagan can't sleep she's found Hannah sitting in the music room in the middle of the night.

"No, baby," he says gently and tucks an errant strand of pale hair behind her ear. "They could come here. They could attack the clinic again. More innocent people could be killed. Or your grandpa or Reagan could be taken for their medical knowledge. Or the women could be taken, not just our women, but women who come to our clinic could be taken."

"Right, Hannie," Reagan says to quiet her sister's worries. "They're real shitbags. I was there when John and Kelly….questioned one of them. These are dangerous men. They have women captive over there. We have to do something."

Hannah nods but is clinging on to her husband as if she's afraid to let him go. Even though her sister is blind, Reagan can still read the fear in her eyes. She's already lost Em and Grams. If she lost Kelly, too, Reagan's not sure she'd recover. Nevertheless, there's no way in hell that he's not joining this fight. He'd never let John go into something like this without him.

Reagan's eyes dart to Sam's. She feels terrible for having said the bit about captive women. She knows what Sam has been through. She sure as hell doesn't mean to dredge up nightmarish memories for her. If there's one thing Reagan understands, it's bad memories. The girl doesn't acknowledge the comment, but Simon squeezes Sam's hand on the table reassuringly. His eyes pinch at the corners as if he, too, is remembering something horrific. They are still holding hands. She's not sure if Sam will let him have his hand back. His sister sits on the other side of him. She's quiet, pensive. She's usually pretty quiet, though, and Reagan is sure that Paige is just trying to figure out the family and whether or not she'll fit in with them, how they operate and get things done. It must be difficult for her to acclimate into a new group of strangers.

"What's our plan?" Simon asks.

Now his sister is looking at him like he's insane. She even mouths the word "what" to him, but he ignores her. Simon shakes his head at her to subdue her questions. Her pale blue eyes are troubled, and she bites her lower lip with nerves. Paige is likely questioning everyone's sanity because they mean to go on the offensive. Reagan gets the impression from what she's learned about Paige and her group that they weren't the confrontational types.

He and Cory go on every mission and have for the last three years. They'd been put through every kind of military training the men could put them through other than jumping out of planes. They are both crack shots, too. Simon isn't the kind of person who enjoys killing for any reason, but Cory is a natural born killer according to John. He's done so many times. He never comes back from a mission looking forlorn, not like Simon. Reagan can tell how heavily his decision to take a life weighs on his mind, but he never backs down. He takes his responsibility of the family's safety just as seriously as the other men. And the fierce look of determination in his bright blue eyes tonight tells her that he's ready again.

"We'll go in tomorrow night," John says. "What do you think, Derek?"

"Yeah, let's not go blasting over there tonight," his brother concurs. "They'll be expecting us. Let's all get a good night's sleep. We'll work on a plan tomorrow and get it all laid out."

"You can count on us to help, too," Wayne says and gets a nod of ascent from his brother Chet.

"I know, Wayne," Derek says. "Why don't you all come over tomorrow evening for dinner, and we'll go over the plans. That'll give us guys a chance to work on it. Bring Bertie and Sarah, too. We don't want you to leave them at home if you're both coming with us."

Sarah is Wayne and Bertie's two-year-old daughter. Bertie had miscarried while John and Reagan were in the city together, but she had conceived again about six months later and gave birth at home to a lovely baby girl. Reagan had assisted Grandpa, just as she had with the birth of her sisters' babies. Now Sarah is close to Reagan's son Jacob's age, and they love playing together when the adults gather for meetings and planning. Even though Jacob is almost five, he still plays with Sarah. And so does Sue's three-year-old son, Isaac. Reagan smiles as she thinks of those two toddlers and their silly, make believe games and their tiny voices when they talk to each other. But her husband's deep voice interrupts her thoughts.

"Bring a rifle and a pistol each. Make sure you have full mags. Also bring your night vision gear," he says to the Reynolds brothers. "This is going to be a night raid. It's the safest way for us. Gives us the advantage."

"Sounds good, John," Chet replies.

There is the added element of surprise and the advantage of seeing the enemy without them seeing the Rangers when they go out at night. John and Derek have seen to the extensive training of some of their closest friends and allies. The Reynolds, the Johnson family, some of the men in town, as well as, some of the people at the condo community have been trained.

Chet's sitting next to Talia, who chirps up. "I'd like to go, as well. I can contribute to this. I know how to shoot all right."

"No, we don't take any of the women on raids," Kelly corrects her.

"Um, ok... what is this, the 1800's? I can shoot. I won't be in your way if that's what you're thinking. I want to be able to help," Paige's friend responds as she pushes back a frizzy black curl from her forehead.

"This really isn't a democracy, ma'am," Derek explains. "No offense, but I'm in charge of security around here. We don't take women. It's just one of our rules. It's not a sexist thing. If we can avoid putting you women in harm's way, then we do. If every one of us men is killed, then the enemy could take you. We've seen it before with other creeps. It doesn't happen on our watch. I'm not saying that you aren't competent, but if you don't have the proper military training you'll be a distraction and could cause us to make an uncalculated mistake."

John offers more politely, "If you want to go on supply runs, you'll need to start with basic training, tactical maneuvers and everything else that Simon's been through. We have a very specific way that we move, a way that we operate as a team. If you don't know it, then you'll just be in the way."

"Besides," Reagan adds, "if everyone leaves the farm, then nobody would be here to protect it in case something happens."

Reagan knows they won't ever take Talia out on a gunfight, maybe on local runs for supplies but not into an all-out battle. Supply runs are dangerous enough. Hell, she doesn't even want her husband to go tomorrow. But she knows that he'll never abide by people like the man they'd water-boarded a few hours ago living so close to them, especially if they are criminally-minded bastards who attack innocent people waiting for medical care. Talia nods but still seems disappointed. Reagan notices that their friend Gavin doesn't volunteer to go. Perhaps he doesn't feel as if he's adequately trained for a mission. That's good. The men don't need him getting in their way, either.

When the meeting wraps and everyone goes their own way, the Rangers and Simon reconvene in Grandpa's office. Reagan also sits in on it.

John immediately starts off the conversation with, "Tim Lafferty. Do you guys know this man and where he lives exactly?"

Reagan feels a sense of dread.

"Sure I do. Tim Lafferty," Grandpa acknowledges as he puffs on his pipe. "Why do you want to know about him?"

"He's the one who told that group about the clinic, about our women, about the center having drugs," John clarifies.

"Great," Derek says with sarcasm. "Sounds like a real dickhead."

Kelly sighs loudly and then says, "You guys figure this out. I'll get our gear."

And with that, Kelly leaves the room, which leaves Reagan feeling profoundly unsettled. Her heart starts racing. The idea of them going tonight to deal with Lafferty because he squealed to scumbags about their helpful medical clinic makes her queasy. She feels overly hot in Grandpa's office, and a coughing fit takes her. John rubs her back soothingly, and she shoots him a smile.

Grandpa proceeds to draw out directions to Tim Lafferty's cabin on the other side of town. There isn't much out his way, just other hunting cabins, rural farms and a few homes peppered here and there. It's mostly forest.

"Wait a minute," Reagan interjects. "What if he's not alone? What if he's holed up with a bunch of people like the ones who shot up the clinic today?"

Her body is starting to give in to the extreme fatigue she's been fighting all day.

"Then we'll assess the situation when we get there and do some recon, babe," John says and rubs her shoulder gently. "Don't worry. We've got this."

Less than an hour later, she watches with nerves in her stomach as John and Kelly leave with Simon in the pick-up truck on the oil well road. Derek stays behind, as does Gavin and Grandpa. A short while later she overhears Gavin talking quietly with Derek about the possibility of him going tomorrow with the men on the raid.

She paces for an hour. Then she falls asleep in a chair near the fireplace, which Derek had lit before the cold evening air permeated the walls of the old house. When she awakens, she tries to busy herself with getting Jacob ready for bed in his shared room in the basement with Ari, Justin, Huntley and the new tyke, Maddie. The bunk beds will be full for the next few nights since Sue and the kids will be staying in the big house instead of out in the woods in their cabin while the men are gone. It's just safer that way. She and their three children sleep in the house sometimes when the Rangers go on a night run.

Talia offers to go to bed in her room next to the children's in case one of them needs her. Everyone else ends up in the music room together either pacing or trying to make small talk to distract themselves. Samantha and Paige pair off together in the corner to chat. Simon's sister is clearly worried about him, and no wonder. She just found him again. Reagan's positive that Sam is reassuring Paige that he'll be fine. He's damn near a Ranger himself now. Grandpa tries his best to engage Reagan with a discussion about a different animal virus they've been seeing more frequently at some of the local dairy farms, which are still miraculously in production. And Hannah sits in a rocker with her daughter, who is asleep in her arms.

"It'll be ok, sis," Sue says a while later as she comes to stand next to Reagan at the window.

"I know," Reagan says, although she doesn't really feel it.

"You ok? Derek said you weren't feeling well again," Sue asks.

"I'm fine. Just sort of feeling run down still, not used to working all day yet," Reagan answers distractedly. "Don't worry about me."

Sue rubs her back soothingly, so Reagan wraps her arm around her sister's back and lays her head against her arm.

"Sleep in tomorrow, sis," Sue practically orders. "I'll take care of Jacob."

Paige walks to the next window over from them, biting her thumbnail and staring out into the darkness with worried eyes.

"He'll be fine, Paige," Reagan offers.

The other woman with the wavy red hair doesn't nod or agree. She looks pissed and confused and scared.

Headlights on the horizon startle them out of their trance of staring out the window incessantly, and they alert the rest of the family. Reagan scans the vehicle before they all even exit. Then she exhales through her mouth. Everyone does. They are all back and safe. Derek is outside at the truck in a flash. The men talk a moment before coming inside.

"They found him," Derek says as they gather in the kitchen.

Reagan knows what the outcome of that would've been. She doesn't need to ask what the men did to the snitch.

"He had two other men with him," John says.

"And a woman," Simon says with downcast blue eyes.

"She didn't exactly wanna' be there," John explains. "They had her out in a shed."

Her husband's voice lowers in register. She can tell that he doesn't even like telling this part of their eventful evening.

Grandpa immediately asks, "Where is she?"

"We dropped her over at the Reynolds with Wayne and Chet," Derek says. "I figured they could take her in. Right now, I don't think we should add any more people to our group. No offense."

"None taken," Gavin agrees with embarrassment.

"She's not very old, maybe twenty. Besides, they were happy to take her in," John says to alleviate Gavin's awkward and sudden discomfort.

"Good, that's good," Grandpa says. "Simon, you should come with us, too, son. Reagan and I should shoot over there and give her a thorough examination."

"Agreed," Kelly says. "I'll take you. She's in pretty bad shape, docs. There wasn't a heater in that shed, either."

"Let us get our bags," Grandpa says. "Reagan, you should pack some extra supplies. We don't know what all she'll need."

"Yes, sir," Reagan says to her grandfather.

"Why don't you stay here, babe?" John suggests. "You're exhausted."

The fact that her husband is contradicting her grandfather is a rare thing, indeed. He is genuinely worried about her health.

Grandpa immediately jumps in to say, "John's right, honey. Let me just take Simon. You wait here. In fact, go to bed, young lady. This will be good for Simon."

She's certainly not going to argue tonight. She's beat, dead on her feet.

"Ok, I'll stay. Let me go and get the supplies for you guys, though."

"Wait a sec," Derek says.

Her beloved brother-in-law looks to her husband, his brother. Sometimes Reagan thinks they can read each other's minds they are so close. And the same goes for Kelly.

"Our friend from earlier today was apparently lying, after all," John says with a downturned set of his mouth.

"What do you mean?" Sue asks nervously.

"There aren't a few dozen men over there holed up in the Target," Kelly says and looks at John.

"There's more like fifty," her husband says.

John regards her with uncertainty in his eyes. He's never had this look in his blue eyes before, and it scares the hell out of her.

Chapter Seventeen
Simon

The planning starts at dawn. John, Kelly and Derek are in the armory room of the med shed taking stock and loading magazines. This will likely be the most dangerous mission they've ever been on. They've never taken on a group of this size. Some of them could be killed and may never return to the farm again. His sister has been pleading with him all morning already which mimics the begging that went on until after one a.m. last night. She doesn't want him to go with the team.

He'd helped her move last night into the cabin that he normally shares with Cory. It hadn't taken long. She hardly owns anything; one backpack and a small duffle bag full of her precious articles. She sleeps in Cory's bedroom, which isn't really a room. They share a one room cabin. There are drapes that they draw which serve the purpose of being wall-like room dividers. It hadn't ever mattered before. It was just him and Cory. The only room is the bathroom, which is just big enough for the commode and sink. There is a wood-burning stove with a flat cooktop where they sometimes heat up food that was usually prepared in the big house first. Other times they'll cook wild game on it that they've caught. But most of the meals are communal and shared in Doc's house with the rest of the family.

"I'm going," Simon tells his sister as they walk together to the house. Chores are finished, of which she'd helped, and it's time to sit in on a meeting after breakfast.

"I don't want you to," she complains again.

She's wearing a blue bandanna around her head, holding her hair back from her face with it. Her baggy jeans are being secured with a belt as usual. She's still too skinny. Her sweatshirt is borrowed from him and hangs like a burlap sack on her. It is dark navy blue and stitched on the front with bright yellow lettering that reads *Nashville*. He's never visited there as a tourist, however. He and Cory did a run last year for supplies and had hit a huge, trucker's rest stop and gas station off of the freeway where such shirts, mugs, bumper stickers and hoodies were once sold to promote tourism. The entire family has plenty of clothing to loan Paige and her friends. Unfortunately, most of it doesn't fit her too well. The pants are always too short, the shirts too big. She never once complains, though. As a matter of fact, she always says how great everything is and how they smell clean. On runs that he and the others have done over the years, there has always been plenty of clothing still left in stores, malls and second-hand shops. He'd like to make a run and find her a few pairs of jeans that might actually fit. Simon can't imagine that his sister is very comfortable wearing clothing that doesn't at all fit her.

She's still in full-blown nag mode, "We could just leave, Simon. Me and my friends and you. We don't have to stay here…"

"What?" Simon asks angrily. He'd like to shake his sister until her teeth rattle but refrains from doing so. She's so skinny she might just rattle all the way apart. "Don't even suggest anything like that. These people are my family. Just like you're my family, Paige. You know they took me and Sam and Huntley in. Why would you even suggest anything so ridiculous?"

She nods and bites her lower lip just like she used to when they were younger and she was worried about something.

"I know," she admits. "I just don't want anything to happen to you. I just got you back, Simon."

"It's ok," Simon tells her and pulls her in for a hug. When he draws back, there are tears in his sister's eyes. "Hey, don't do that. I'll be fine. This isn't my first raid, Paige."

She squints her eyes as if she doubts him.

"Trust me, I'm not the Simon you used to know. I have acquired a few new valuable skill sets thanks to the guys," he says trying to quell her fears. He also runs his hand tenderly over her cheek and kisses her forehead.

"I've noticed," she admits and frowns at him.

"Come on," he says and tugs her hand to get her to walk with him once more. "You can sit in on the strategic planning meeting. You'll feel better if you hear the way we plan things out."

Paige nods but goes back to the lip biting. He bumps her shoulder playfully.

"You know you kind of sounded like Mom back there with all the nagging," he chides. He receives a light punch to the shoulder. He just laughs at her distress.

"Shut up," she orders softly but has finally smiled.

As they enter the kitchen, the usual chaos is occurring. The younger kids are already eating at the island, Sue is holding Hannah's daughter while her sister finishes something at the stove, and Reagan is carrying trays of breakfast food into the dining room. She also seems stressed out.

"Here, Hannah," Paige says. "I can do that if you need to do something else."

"Thanks, Paige. That's very helpful," Hannah returns so gently and touches his sister's arm.

Simon is glad to see his sister jump in to help. He remembers that she used to like to cook with their mother sometimes.

"Simon, darling, do you know where the men went off to?" Hannah asks. "This should be ready soon."

"They said they'd be right in," he tells her. He doesn't elaborate on the fact that they are preparing weapons for tonight. There's no sense in frightening Hannah even more than she clearly already is.

He would normally hang out with Cory during this transition to breakfast, but his friend is long gone. He scrubs up in the mudroom and decides to rest for a moment of quiet solitude in the music room until breakfast is called. It doesn't last but a scant few seconds before Sue rushes in. She's carrying Isaac, who is covered in food mess as if he's been at the pigs' slop heap instead of at the island in the kitchen.

"Hey, have you seen Sam?" she blurts without preamble.

"No, I've been out in the barns with Paige," he reports. Sue looks flustered and stressed out, too. All of the women are probably worried about their husbands going into a battle tonight.

"Can you find her, Simon?" she asks as she tries at wiping her son's small face. "I can't seem to find her and we're about ready to sit down to eat."

"Sure, no problem, Sue," he offers.

"Maybe she didn't come down yet," Sue suggests. "That would be unusual for her, but I haven't seen her all morning."

"I'll run up and check on her," Simon decides and takes off at a sprint up the long set of stairs to the second floor.

He traverses down the long, wide hall, passing the set of stairs that goes up another floor to Reagan and John's suite, then passes the bathroom. She's not in there. The door is open, the light off. He comes to her closed bedroom door and knocks softly. After a moment with no answer, he cracks the door open and, unfortunately, catches Sam in the middle of dressing.

"Oh crap!" Simon screeches and slams the door shut. "Sorry," he calls through the closed door.

Oh God, how embarrassing. Now he feels terrible. He hadn't thought he'd find her up here at all. His next move was to head out to the horse barn to look for her which is where she usually hangs out. Instead, he'd caught a glimpse of her bare stomach as she pulled a shirt down over her head. He'd also seen a glimpse of more than he wants to admit.

A moment later the door opens and Sam stands there, this time fully dressed. Although she is buttoning her jeans.

"Hi, Simon," she says brightly. "What do you…"

"Sorry about that," he interrupts with a quick apology. "I didn't think you were in there. I was just coming to get you for breastfast… I…I mean breakfast, breakfast!"

Sam laughs haughtily at his gaffe. "You're such a prude."

He takes offense at her impudence and says, "I am not."

"Yeah, ok," Sam remarks as if she doesn't believe him. "Simon, it's fine. I'm sure you didn't see anything of importance," she says and lays a hand on his forearm.

"I actually figured you were outside already," he says with confusion. He doesn't want to admit what he saw. He doesn't want to tell her that he'd seen part of her black bra and the pale skin of her smooth, flat stomach.

"I want to show you something," she remarks casually.

Sam turns her back to him and simply walks into her room again. Simon trails after her, but only hesitantly so.

Her bedroom is equipped with an art desk that he'd found for her in an architectural firm over in Nashville. He'd insisted on making Cory help him get it into the pick-up truck, even though, his friend had protested that it took up too much room. It was worth it. Currently, it's littered with sheets of paper covered with her incredible artwork. He wanders over to take a closer look. She always shares her art with him, but not always with everyone else. She goes through dark phases sometimes that she doesn't want the family to see. What he views on her desk is not dark at all this time. There are at least a dozen angels drawn in different angles and positions and scenarios. Some of the figures are of women with long wings and ethereal clothing that is nearly transparent. Some are of men with swords and armor and mighty wings.

"I had to finish this," she says as she joins him at her desk.

She is casually running a brush through her long black hair as if it's just a normal thing, him being in her room. They don't hang out like that anymore. Not since she'd become an adult.

"Finish this drawing?" Simon asks her and picks up the one in front of him. It's a charcoal of an angel with dark hair and a gauzy gown of fine, thin filaments. She's holding a spear and is hovering above the ground. She is no peaceful angel. She's a warrior of strength and purpose.

"Yes," Sam confirms beside him.

She places the brush on her nightstand and stands next to him again. Her large azure eyes gaze up at him with nervous agitation, worry and something he can't put his finger on.

"She's for you," Sam tells him. "She'll protect you tonight while you're gone, while you're on this mission."

Simon tries to keep his expression stoic like he does whenever he's looking at Sam. It's not always easy anymore. Her head tips slightly to the side, causing her long hair to fall forward and frame the side of her face. His jaw clenches reflexively.

"You drew me a guardian angel to keep me safe?" he asks and hates the fact that his voice sounds so full of emotion.

She says nothing but moves into him and lays her head against his chest. Her arms wrap around his middle.

"Come home safe, Simon," she demands softly and then sniffs.

"Are you crying?" Simon asks and pulls back, his hands at her slim shoulders. There are tears streaming down her cheeks. "Hey, don't do that. Don't cry, Sam."

"I can't help it," she says on another sniff. Then she throws herself against his chest again. "You're my best friend, Simon. I don't know what I'd do if I lost you. I heard Kelly telling John that this could be bad. He said you guys have never taken on a group this size before."

Simon strokes her head and down her back trying to soothe her. He doesn't pull her closer. She couldn't exactly get any closer if he's being honest. He shushes her, tries to get her to see reason.

"Sam, everything's gonna be fine. You stay here with Paige. I need you to help me with her," he tries another approach. "She's not used to this. She wants us to run. That's what her group's always done. They run. But you know, sweetie, that we can't do that. We have to help people. It's our duty. Those men are way too close to our farm and the clinic. If they found out about this place, they could come here next. They could try to take you. We have to stop them before it ever comes to that. You understand, don't you?"

She raises her head from his tear-soaked t-shirt and regards him pensively. Simon steps back to put room between them. He wipes at her tears with the hem of his shirt.

"I don't like this," she complains.

Good grief. Is every single woman in the house going to do this? He's not sure he'll make it through the whole day if they all start crying. He hates it when they get upset.

"I know, but we'll be ok," he tries to reassure her. "You know we've been trained. We've done this before, right?"

This gets a nod, but her eyes tell him that she's still not sure of this plan to do a full-scale raid on this group of marauders.

"We'll be fine, all right?"

"Take her with you," Sam says.

She turns away from him, picks up her drawing and proceeds to fold it four times until it's a small square.

"Don't do that," Simon scolds. "You're wrinkling your art, Sam."

"She can't keep you safe if she's not with you," Sam tells him.

Then she goes too far and jams it down into the front pocket of his jeans.

"Hey there!" he exclaims. "I can do that myself, young lady."

Sam chuckles at him.

"You're such a prude, Simon," she says with another laugh. "I'm not trying to get in your pants. I'm just trying to put something *into* them!"

"Uh huh, well I don't need your help," he says nervously. "I still wish you hadn't wrinkled it all up. That was a really good one."

"Of course it was!" she says with charm. "I wouldn't draw you something shabby to watch over you, silly."

"It's excellent. One of your best," Simon says to her and watches a shy grin of praise creep onto her small, Cupid's bow mouth. Reagan's always saying how Sam looks like a Japanimation comic book character with her big blue eyes, dark hair and tiny red mouth. This comment usually irritates Simon. She doesn't look like some cartoonish character. She's lovely and delicate and feminine. And she thinks she's his best friend. Simon has to look away for a moment, over her shoulder out the window.

"What is it?" she asks with concern.

"Nothing," is his standard answer for this. She asks him this question or similar ones a lot lately. "We should head down for breakfast."

Sam frowns slightly but nods in agreement. They return to the boisterous first floor where breakfast has commenced in the dining room. It doesn't take long to finish the meal of grits, smoked sausage, eggs and homemade bread and then clear out the children. The men get straight into the planning and coordinating phase.

"I'd like to go, too," Gavin chirps up and says out of the blue.

All eyes fall on him. He's been unusually quiet the last twenty-four hours. His sister's friend is normally quite the talker. He's full of funny stories, and Simon has come to like him.

"I'm not so sure that's a good idea," Kelly says.

"I can shoot my bow really well," he says. "I can hit a squirrel, so I'd say I could hit a person, too. I've had to use it in that capacity before. I just never wanted to again."

"This isn't exactly a bow and arrow kind of fight," John puts in with a frown.

Reagan nods and seems concerned.

"I can shoot a gun, too," Gavin offers. "I'm a good navigator. I'd like to contribute to this. It's important to me. You all have been so good to us. I'd like to be of some help, pay you back. If we're going to stay here, it only seems right."

Kelly and John regard one another. John whispers something to Derek, who nods.

"Actually, Gavin," Derek says. "We need you here. We don't usually all leave the farm at the same time. Understand?"

"Sure, I can do that, Derek. No problem," Gavin states but looks disappointed.

Beside him, Paige fidgets in her seat. She clearly isn't comfortable with her friend wanting to go on this raid any more than she is happy that Simon is going.

For the next few hours the men go over plans while the women take care of the children, the chores, cooking and also come and go in the dining room to pick up on snippets of their ideas. Sue has helped by offering forth information on the exact layout of the Target store, each area of the interior and what they used to contain, the location of departments, and entry and exit points. It could all be completely useless information since the fall of the country and the occupation of the store for who knows how long by a band of fifty or so people, but it may help. Every little bit helps. Simon offers his opinion where he feels that it would make a difference. The men respect his opinion, and he does theirs, as well. They work together until every last detail is hashed out. It's almost noon when they finish, but this day is far from over. They'll need to finish loading weapons and ammo, make sure that the people staying on the farm are also locked and loaded in case something was to happen while they are gone, and go over the plans with the Reynolds when they arrive later for dinner.

It is nearly six p.m. when they all say their final good-byes in the driveway and review once more how to handle any bad situations with the family who will be left behind. His sister clings to him for a long time. Hannah is weeping as she holds her baby girl and Kelly close to her. The Reynolds men are saying good-bye to Bertie and the young, abused woman they'd taken in yesterday. He'd gone over last night with Doc to treat this woman. Her abuse had been severe, but she will survive. Doc gave her a preventative dose of three-day antibiotics in case Tim Lafferty or any of his friends whom she said had also raped her were carrying any diseases. Simon felt sick to his stomach when she'd disclosed her severe abuse at their hands. He could literally feel his blood pressure rising with anger and malice toward those men. He's glad Kelly and John had killed Tim and his two friends. He only wished they'd suffered more. Tonight he'll let his anger fester on the ride over to the Target store where the same types of vile men dwell. And then he will unleash his fury upon them.

Doc is going over plans with Derek while Sue stands patiently beside her husband with their three children. Reagan is arguing with John. That's nothing new. She always gets tense and snippy before he goes out on a run. It's how she deals with it. Anger and stress are her go-to emotions. Whatever works for them, Simon supposes. John allows her to go on another moment before he snatches her into his arms and hugs her tightly.

"Simon," Sam whispers.

She tugs his sleeve, which causes him to pull away from Paige. He kisses his sister's freckled forehead and turns away from her. He tries not to notice that her eyes are bloodshot and puffy. Talia comes over to comfort Paige and to lead her toward the front stairs of the house where Gavin awaits them.

"Yeah?" he asks Sam. Instead of answering, she takes his hand in hers and pulls him to the side of the house where it is more secluded and private. "What is it?"

"Have your angel?" she inquires with huge, hopeful eyes.

He offers a pained grin. There are so many ways he could answer that. But instead, he goes with, "Sure. I've got it."

She blows out a breath she'd obviously been holding. She's wearing a short red jacket to ward off the evening's chill in the air. It creates a stark contrast against her pale skin, dark lips and black hair.

He and the others have changed into black or very dark clothing. He is dressed in black cargo pants, a long-sleeved, dark navy blue thermal henley and black combat boots. His auburn hair is covered with a black stocking cap. None of them wear coats. Adrenaline will keep them warm, and a bulky coat could get in the way. His rifle rests against his back. Two extra mags fill his cargo pockets. A 9 mm Beretta sits comfortably on his hip. Another two magazines full of ammo for it reside in his back pocket. His shotgun is in the bed of the truck. He's ready. He's always ready. He may not like killing people, but over the years he's learned the necessity of the kill or be killed mentality. Normally once he's in the beginning phases of a fight, all he has to do is allow his mind to wander back to the time when he and Sam had been with his aunt's group. It's enough to quiet his nerves, steady his hand and turn him into the cold-blooded killer he needs to be. He only wishes that he'd known what he does now back when he'd first found Sam hiding in her home.

He joined the other men on the farm today for a three-mile run after lunch to prepare for tonight. They always work out. When they aren't laboring on the farm chores, they all work out together. John says it's important to stay in top shape. It's nothing for them to pump out a few hundred push-ups on any given day along with hiking, running and chin-ups in the barn. Simon's glad he's become accustomed to their difficult forms of exercise over the years. The men had even found free weights that are now in the top of the cattle barn for working out. When they'd put him and Cory through their modified version of boot camp, he thought he'd blow a lung. Now he's used to hard work, and his body has toned up, filled out and added bulk muscle which makes him better able to handle most of what comes their way.

Without asking permission, Simon reaches under Sam's short jacket to find the pistol on her hip. He takes it out of its holster, checks to make sure a round awaits her in the chamber, secures the safety again and replaces it back into the holster. He even takes a second to button the snap again. He tries not to notice the gentle curve of her hip through her slim-fitting blue-jeans or the narrowness of her small waist.

"Don't take this off at all, not even for a second," he orders softly, trying not to frown so hard. It's difficult to do so.

"I won't. I promise," she says softly.

When Simon finally meets her eyes, he wishes he hadn't left the crowd of the family making their final goodbyes. He deals with Sam better in crowds. Her long black lashes nearly touch her eyebrows when she looks up at him.

"Don't take yours off, either," she teases half-heartedly.

Her delicate brows knit together with stress.

"Don't worry, Sam," he tells her.

"How can I not worry?" Sam returns his question with one of her own. "You're my best friend, Simon."

She's staring so intently at him that Simon flinches. Her knowing, intelligent eyes regard him as if she can read every thought on his mind, every emotion he tries to hide, every secret he harbors. Simon worries that sometimes the shroud of guilt he wears where Sam is concerned will be visible like a smudge of black paint on a white canvas.

"Come back," she says with a tad more grit.

Then, without preamble or much apparent forethought, Sam leans up on tiptoe and places a soft kiss against his closed mouth. It lasts less than two full seconds, but she closes her eyes- or does a long blink. She immediately rocks back down onto her heels. What the heck? He's too startled to do anything but stand there scowling down at her as if she's gone mad. Then she grabs his hand again and practically drags him along after her until they are rejoined with the family.

They are leaving early so that they can pick up more men from town and from the condo community where Paul and his son reside. They have always helped out when they can and have proven trustworthy and steady in a gunfight.

Everyone loads into the vehicles, but nobody speaks. Everyone is silent and reflecting on the mission. He knows they are thinking about where they will take up position, how they will handle their orders that Derek's laid out, what they'll do if it goes south. It's always like this before they head out on some dangerous raid or another.

Simon's mind is buzzing with questions, however. Why had Sam just done that? Had she just missed his cheek? That was highly unacceptable behavior. He'll have to correct her on it when he gets home tonight. If he gets home tonight.

Chapter Eighteen
Cory

"Son of a bitch!" Cory swears under his breath.

They shot his fucking horse! And now Jet is freaked out beneath him and trying hard to stay upright. Cory vaults from his back, landing on his feet while returning fire and pulling the horse to the safety of the brick building's wall. It's dusk, the sun setting rapidly which he'll use to his advantage.

"Easy, boy," he murmurs. "Easy."

He backs him down the street a few meters and ties him to a water line coming out of the wall where he flashes his penlight into the wound. Looks like a possible .38 shot size. He's bleeding pretty good and blowing through his nose in pain and fear. He's even doing his agitated prancing in place, although Cory can tell it pains him to do so. It infuriates Cory. However, the stallion is still on his feet. He's a warrior through and through. All this horse needs is armor befitting that of a knight's brave steed. He grabs his medical pouch from his saddle bag and rips open a gauze patch, pressing down the sticky edges against the stallion's dark coat. He has one eye on the road and alley behind him so as not to take on more gunfire while checking his horse. None comes, which is fortuitous for whoever was shooting at him.

He'd been riding down the street in a small suburb of Columbus called Powell. It's a fairly crowded metropolis, Columbus. He'd arrived in town yesterday and found the downtown district and the Ohio State University area too crowded for his taste. There were sections that people had reclaimed and were working together to survive. Some places were gated off with fencing, others with vehicles and debris. All of the exclusive areas were advertised as such with plywood signs tacked up that suggested people should "keep out" or "stay out." One such sector even had razor wire at the top of a chain link fence. Cory didn't need to be told twice. If they were keeping to themselves, then so be it. He hadn't run into trouble with anyone. Until now.

He is positioned around the corner of a former mattress retailer. It looks identical to the one in Clarksville that they'd looted a few years ago. Doc had suggested it since so many children are on the farm, and the family seemed to be steadily expanding. They'd also taken a crib mattress for their neighbors.

Cory grabs two extra mags from his saddlebag and slings his rifle behind his shoulder. Next he grabs his nightvision headgear and pulls it on. He clicks off the safety on his sidearm. He pats Jet's neck one last time.

"Stay," he orders Damn Dog. Her response is a soft mewl, but Cory's sure she'll stay put. She seems to listen well and has turned out to be a good travel mate. She lowers onto her stomach next to the gelding. He sprints in the opposite direction of the threat.

The dog had also alerted him the other day when he'd been camped out in the woods below the city. A group of nomads was moving through. Cory hadn't troubled himself with them because it had only been a band of families, harmless enough as far as he was concerned. They were noisy once they got closer to his camp, but he'd hidden himself and the dog and horse by then. They were moving on foot mostly but had four horses and two gray donkeys which carried two small children each. Their belongings were packed and tied onto the horses. He hopes they get to wherever the hell they thought they were going.

For tonight, though, he knows that the shots came from across the four lane road that holds scattered and abandoned and a few torched vehicles and a motorcycle on its side. He'll flank them quickly and assess the situation. He may not have gone after or bothered with these people, whoever it is that had shot at him. That was before they'd shot his horse.

Moving surreptitiously around three different buildings including a taco restaurant, a lighting supply center, and a smoothie bar, which is enshrouded almost completely with an entanglement of dark vines, Cory comes out behind the area where the three shots originated. The green haze of his night vision capabilities makes it easy to spot a scurry of movement inside of a former 24-hour gym. Most of the two story tall glass windows are gone, broken and shattered. A mini-van is permanently attached to the gym, bumper to the cement block façade of the building, having crashed there long ago. One of the men decides to leave the safe cover of the building to pursue Cory. He is of average height and build, which makes him smaller than Cory. The man steps cautiously out the front door, which hangs on its hinges. He fast walks in the direction they'd fired shots and hit Cory's stallion. Not smart.

Cory takes a breath and shoots his rifle. The man goes down on his knees and lets out a piercing scream. Cory hits him again in the back. He's not going to get back up from that one. The silencer on the end of his rifle has subdued the sound slightly. Unfortunately, his muzzle flash has given his position away, so he sprints across the street and ducks behind the service pump of an abandoned gas station. Two bullets ping into the side of the smoothie bar, chipping away at brick and mortar and poison ivy leaves and vines. They obviously hadn't seen him move to his new spot. A flashlight gives away the second perp as he swings it frantically left and right trying to spot him. Also not smart.

Cory takes aim again and… pop. A clean head-shot on number two, and the man slumps back into the dark recesses of the gym below the front knee-high, cut block wall of the building. Panic quickly sets in on the group in the gym. There is shouting, the sounds of scampering feet, things being run into or knocked over. A few men even boldly shout expletives out the front window.

Cory can make out the entire building, front to back exit. There is an alley for deliveries to the strip mall next to the gym. He has the perfect position to take out anyone else who comes out. He waits patiently, but nothing happens. Seeing an opportunity, Cory creeps to the rear of the building and tries the door there. Bingo. Unsecured and unlocked. Also not too smart. These people have the tactical aptitude of a toddler.

Moving stealthily through the back of the gym, passing the doors for the men's and women's locker rooms, Cory peeks around the corner and doesn't see anyone. Suddenly out of nowhere one of the men appears less than a few feet from him to his left. He takes him out quickly enough, but it alerts the rest of them to his presence in their building. He ducks behind a short wall of loose weights and a Nautilus machine for leg exercises, fully expecting a barrage of bullets. It doesn't come. They are panicking and scattering again maybe a hundred feet or so away toward the front of the building. A single shot, which sounds like a .38, hits the wall very far to his left. He believes it to have been fired out of frustration. They are yelling angrily, threatening to take everything he owns and kill him.

"Psst," comes from behind him.

He swings on the man but finds him hiding around the corner where Cory dust departed. He's been flanked, but he's down behind the equipment. He inches to his right, taking further cover from both opponents, the new man, and the creeps in the front.

"We're on the same team, bro," the man whispers to him.

Cory doesn't trust him for a second and doesn't lower his rifle.

"Been tracking these fuckers for a week. Don't shoot, man," he whispers.

"Stay back," Cory warns quietly. "I'll shoot you dead."

"I'm alone, guy," he says nervously.

"Then I'll only have to shoot one of you."

"No, bro, Semper Fi," the other man whispers.

Cory knows the man is trying to ascertain whether or not he was a Marine.

"Not a Marine, dude, so back the fuck off," Cory warns. He really doesn't want to shoot this guy. The other man could've shot him in the back, possibly, and chose not to.

"Think these fuckers took my sister," the Marine says. "She's been gone for almost a week. They took her right out of our car while I was getting water from a creek. Been tracking them. Let me come up beside you, and we'll flank them."

Hearing this man's horror story, Cory changes his mind about the other man. He's not sure if it's the part of his story about his sister or that a woman is in danger. Cory nods in the near dark to the Marine. The single lantern in the front right corner of the building illuminates that area but mostly casts ghostly shadows around the two story building with the low ceiling. Stairs to the front and left of him would indicate another floor above them. He's not sure if anyone is up there. Could be a hot spot.

The Marine joins him near the equipment, and Cory immediately takes in his appearance. There's no doubt in his mind that this guy was a former Marine. He's carrying a carbine, has a 9 mill semi-automatic pistol and night vision gear similar to his. He is of a solid, stocky build like Derek. His hair is still buzz cut like he's awaiting his orders to re-up.

"Think there's eight of 'em," the Marine tells him.

That's a number higher than Cory had anticipated.

"Five now," he shares and gets a surprised nod in return.

"Cool," Marine says.

Up front, the group of five has settled down and are formulating some sort of plan. Cory can hear them whispering conspiratorially. There is a clattering of metal or equipment, causing a ruckus of epic decibels.

"Who else is with them?" Cory asks.

"Hopefully my fucking sister," he swears. "Assholes. I don't know about anyone else."

"I'll cross to my right, come along the wall of mirrors toward them," Cory states. He's not asking this stranger for permission on military tactical moves.

"I'll go left and flush 'em out from there," he offers.

As the Marine has been speaking, Cory removed his penlight from his cargo pocket.

"Hey," Semper Fi says softly. "Don't shoot me, ok?"

"Got it," Cory acknowledges and turns to move out of his hunkered down position.

He low sprints toward the wall of mirrors, placed there for vanity viewing. Squatting behind an incline bicycling machine, which also makes a good gun rest, he gets ready to make his move. Hiding his hand and the penlight from view by using the back of the padded seat will work to conceal it from its origin. He flicks on the tiny flashlight, also hoping at the same time that it still works. He hasn't had any recharging capabilities for some time. A very faint spray of light hits those mirrors thirty feet down the way from him. Instantly a peppering of gunfire blasts into the mirrors shattering them but also giving away his targets by their muzzle flashes. Squeezing once, twice, three times, two targets are taken down. It reminds him of that arcade game at the once popular, annoying pizza chain Chucky Cheese called, "Whack-A-Mole." He's hitting people as they pop up into his line of vision.

Position forsaken, he moves closer to the wall, avoiding incoming fire from a higher caliber round than the other two were using. A single shot from the familiar blast of a carbine, followed by a scream, lets him know that Semper Fi has taken someone down. Hopefully, it's the asshole who'd just shot at Cory and missed.

"Don't shoot! Don't shoot! Please, mister," calls a woman from near the front wall.

A man's voice barks, "Shut up, bitch!"

Another bark of the carbine tells Cory that Semper Fi has disabled another person. Perhaps it was the woman. He jogs quickly, taking up position behind a counter, probably meant for checking in gym goers.

"All clear," the Marine calls out.

He waits another thirty seconds or so before coming out from behind the desk to join the group of three. Apparently Semper hadn't shot the woman. And now there are two women. One of them is hugging onto the Marine tightly. One sister found: check. Assholes who'd shot his horse taken care of: check. The other chic, however, is still standing there with her hands raised to shoulder

232

height in surrender. She's crying. Apparently the Marine has killed three of them unless Cory counted wrong.

Cory dashes upstairs, careful not to take a bullet, and does a speedy and thorough sweep of the second floor. Mostly he finds articles that would imply that the group had stayed here for a short time. Backpacks litter the floor as well as their supplies and boxes of ammo and food. In one particular wooden crate, he finds boxes of ammo that he can use. Stashing two boxes of it into his cargo pockets, he moves to the food supply next. There are three people downstairs, so he only takes a few items, placing those in the interior pocket of his coat.

He jogs back to the group which has moved toward the center of the first floor away from the windows. They've brought the lantern and another over closer and set them on the workout equipment. The Marine is examining his sister thoroughly while the other woman stands close by. She's weeping softly, shaking violently. She probably thinks they will rape or kill her. As long as she's not pointing a gun or knife at them, Cory won't shoot her. And rape? Not a chance. He's not into that kind of thing. Too much crying. That and the fact that he prides himself on killing those kinds of men.

It's been a while since he's had sex with a woman, since a few weeks before he'd deserted the farm. He and the Johnson's widowed daughter, Evie, would sometimes meet out in the woods or in his cabin if he could get rid of Simon for the night. Neither of them expected anything out of the relationship, which was good because he has nothing to offer anyone. She was lonely since her husband had died of sickness at the beginning of the end, and Cory was young and virile. She was older than him by almost seven years, but he hadn't minded. Evie had also taught him more about sex than he'd ever learned from high school girls back in Arkansas. Their relationship was not one of public discussion amongst their families. Her dad was just as religious as Doc, so they'd kept it a secret. They didn't want or need a commitment or the entanglement of the families' opinions interwoven into their affair. She was a kind and good-hearted woman who was simply needing companionship, just like him. Simon knew about them, but he'd never tell a soul. Besides being his lover, she'd become a good friend to him, as well, and he trusted her older, wiser opinion on many issues that had troubled him. Also, she wasn't in the McClane clan, so he felt like he could discuss subjects with her that he couldn't with the family. He'd like to think that their relationship, or whatever it really was, had helped her to heal from the loss of her husband, whom she'd loved deeply. She'd cried many nights in his arms while he held her close and tried his best to comfort her.

"We should get out of here," the Marine's sister says in a panic, peering over her shoulder.

She looks road weary and tired. Her clothing is dirty and unkempt. She's also clearly frightened. Cory tries not to notice the deep bruise on her right cheekbone or the split lower lip.

"Ok, we will, sis," her brother says to her.

He wears the remnants of his old uniform mixed in with civilian clothing. He and Cory have both removed their night vision gear. Cory's hangs from his neck on a cord, but he's not sure where the Marine's has disappeared to. His gear was smaller and more compact, so perhaps he'd folded it away somewhere.

"There's plenty to loot upstairs," Cory explains. "Food, ammo…"

"Cool," he returns, his eyes widening with anticipation.

"We'll divvy it up," Cory states.

"Seems fair to me, dude," the other man says with a nod. "You helped me… hell, you damn near did it for me before I got here. You Special Forces or something?"

"Nope. Just a grunt," Cory says humbly. He's sure as shit not Kelly, nor will he ever be. But he can certainly aspire to be a better soldier every day.

"Well, grunt, you can be my wingman any day," he says with admiration and shakes Cory's hand. "We've been traveling a long while."

"Yeah?" Cory inquires as he jams a few rounds into his magazine to replace the ones he'd used. "Where you been?"

"We came down from upper Michigan. We were gonna head South but heard that ain't any better. Now we're going West."

"What's out West?" Cory asks as he slaps the magazine back into his rifle and slings it behind his back.

"We heard there's power out there," the Marine says. "Going up into Washington State."

"Hm," Cory mumbles. There isn't power in Washington just like there isn't power anywhere else that people aren't manufacturing it with supplemental sources like solar.

"Wanna' stick with us? We could…"

"Nah, no thanks," Cory says. "I'm headed North. I travel alone."

The Marine nods with a frown. "Too bad."

This always happens. They have heard so many this place or that place "has power" or "it's safe in Colorado" or "upstate New York is getting back on its feet" stories over the years that they've become fairy tales. The promise of restoration is no more real to him than Hansel and Gretel and that witch's cottage.

"What are you going to do to me?" the forgotten woman asks, still quivering like a fragile leaf hanging by its gentle petiole.

The Marine looks at Cory, who shrugs.

"What were you doing with these creeps?" Semper Fi asks.

She shakes her head, her short, cropped black hair swishing around.

"I didn't have anybody else," she says. "They picked me up a few months ago in Virginia."

"How the hell'd they travel from Virginia to here in a few months?" Cory asks.

"They just stole cars and gas. Sometimes they stole gas out of people's generators. That made me feel terrible. They didn't care, though," she relates. "I didn't really want to go with them, but they didn't give me much choice."

Her voice is child-like as if she's not much more than a teenager. She looks to be about twenty-five or so, maybe less. It's hard to see her clearly. Her lumpy coat is at least two sizes too big and engulfing her. The apocalypse has aged some people much faster than others. Not everyone has had it as good as Cory has at the farm. Some people have literally been living on the streets and on the move for years, always in search of what could be better. Keep searching, he'd like to tell them. It doesn't get any better. It all looks the same. That elusive promise of hope on the horizon in the form of a restored power grid is a fantasy. The reality is harsh. The reality is death, rape, pillaging, disease and eventually losing the only people you care about.

The sister speaks up, "She's cool, Terry. Let her go with us."

Apparently Semper Fi's real name is Terry. Cory won't commit it to memory, though. He doesn't care to join up with them or anyone else's group. He's alone now, and that works just fine for him. Groups imply bonding which leads to friendship which will inevitably lead to watching one of these three die. He's done with that part of his life.

"You guys go on upstairs and get whatever you can get," he tells them. "I'll be right back."

He turns to go, snags one of the rifles from a fallen man. It's a bolt action 30-06. He loots his pocket for more ammo and keeps going. He'd taken a box of .223 rounds for his M16 and a box of 30-06 cartridges from upstairs. His plan all along was to confiscate that rifle from whoever had it. He'd guessed that someone had a 30-06 in the gym by the loud, distinctive crack. Apparently the man had not been proficient with it, but Cory is. It's a good rifle, good for long range shots. He doesn't wait for an answer but leaves, using the front door.

Cory hopes the Marine and his two female companions don't stay there for the night. It's hard telling how many others could've been with this group and just weren't there for the big game. Semper Fi is probably smart enough to figure that one out. Cory also has no intention of coming back here to ration out the booty.

Jet is waiting for him. His horse needs medical care, and Cory has no wish to make him wait any longer. He was on his way to the Columbus Zoo to take shelter for the night, so he's hoping that he'll find animal medical supplies there. When he'd chosen that destination, he hadn't known he would need it for that reason. He'd simply wanted an obscure place to hole up for the night where he'd be safe and, more importantly, not bothered by anyone.

He unties his stallion and walks beside him, wincing every time the horse missteps or falters. Stopping for just long enough to give him a break, Cory adheres a patch of material on the horse's wound with some tape. They are leaving a trail of blood drips, easily traceable in daylight to their final destination. He pulls down his night vision goggles again. Damn Dog plods along beside him.

They arrive on the northeast side of the zoo as he cautiously makes his way down the hill toward it. The expansive blacktopped parking lot sits empty of vehicles, all except for the two abandoned trams meant for escorting people too lazy to walk to the entrance. The blacktop looks as if someone has seeded it in a half-assed attempt at growing a lush pasture. It is damn near deep enough to mow. Poison oak grows up and around a shelter where people could wait for the tram to pick them up. A sun-faded poster for a polar bear exhibit is hanging crookedly beneath the ivy. The front gates of the zoo stand wide open, but there are no workers present to sell him a ticket for admittance. The once decorative grasses and ornamental landscaping has become disorganized and overgrown. Long tendrils of dead grass poke up through the cracks of the pavement near the entryway. The sign overhead that reads "Columbus Zoo" hangs askew and is missing the last "O." To his left is the elaborate entrance to a water park called Zoombezi Bay. He bypasses the turnstyle entrance like the ones used in subway systems and uses an employee breezeway three stations over to gain his entry. Directly in front of him is a pond in the center of the zoo's massive layout. Cory can hear ducks quacking to one another, likely floating lazily there. One of them could make a good dinner. He's not too fond of fancy things like pate de foie gras, but hell, duck meat's not too bad cooked on an open fire. A screech, likely from an owl or some other exotic bird, pierces through the night sky.

Grabbing a map of the zoo from the plastic display rack, Cory quickly scans it and comes up with squat for a med center. He'll have to find the "zoo personnel only" areas on his own. It's not like they would've let people tour those places unattended. He heads to the right, using a flashlight when he needs to find his way better. He comes to a sign that reads, "African Elephants," but no majestic animals bleat through their trunks to greet him. According to the map, he's in the African animals section of the zoo. If he veers off further to the right and up the hill, he should come to the children's petting zoo and the North American animals. He remembers going to a zoo like this with Em when she was young. There is usually a section in each zoo with domesticated farm animals. She'd marveled at the baby goats, ponies, chickens and horses. Little did either of them know that farm life would become their futures. A gurgle of thunder ripples forebodingly in the distance. That's just what they need. Damn Dog even whines a few times. He needs to find some shelter for the night, in out of the rain or icy rain more likely since the temperature feels like it's hovering near forty degrees, maybe less.

When they reach the crest of the hill, surely enough, a faded red barn awaits them. The petting zoo is unequivocally and permanently closed. He pulls open one of the wide barn doors and flashes his light inside. A small swarm of bats swoop and dive at Cory and his group and, more likely, his flashlight. It's all clear. Apparently nobody has thought to take refuge in the zoo. There is even a horse stall, and luckily no dead carcass awaits them there. However, there are bales of hay stacked at the other end of the barn that he'll make good use of as long as it hasn't molded. This barn is like something out of a catalog for gentlemen farms. There aren't any long, wide cracks between the wall slats that let in a cold draft. No dirty floors with hay, grain and specks of straw scattered around. It's dusty and covered in cobwebs but not anything like the barns at the farm which were built for function and use and not aesthetics and grandeur to impress city slickers. The floor is even cemented. To his left are small animal cages, some of which open to the paddock.

He leads his limping stallion into the stall, not bothering to shut the gate behind them. Cory quickly removes the load of supplies of which is being transported by Jet. Then the tack, saddle and pad are next and get hung over the short oak wall of the roomy stall. The bridle comes next which earns him a grateful nicker. He rummages through his supplies and lights his small lantern. Then he inspects the stack of old hay, smells it for mold, ascertains it's still good and gives two flakes to his horse. He closes and locks the stall door this time upon retreat.

"Let's go," he says firmly to Damn Dog, who jumps to her four feet.

There has to be a medical facility for the animals of a zoo of this size right here on site. He needs a few shots or even a dose of relaxing sedative so he can dig out that small bullet if it's still in there. Then he can stitch up his friend. He extinguishes the lantern and closes and latches the wide barn door. Jet will chomp contentedly on that hay. He could probably care less about his wound now. Doc always gives injured livestock hay to work on. He calls it nervous food. It helps to take their minds off of their pain and eases their discomfort.

He and his dog sprint around the zoo, this time with his night vision gear down so that he doesn't run headlong into the wall of an animal pen. They trot through the North American animals section of the zoo where Cory sees what's left of two polar bears' carcasses, which aren't much more than snippets of hide and bone still in their glass enclosures. When he gets to the grizzly bear display, however, he's surprised to find them gone. As a matter of fact, he runs through section after section finding the same empty cages and gates. The Asia display, Congo, the snake enclosure, which is a long maze of a building with empty glass display cases, and finally the Australia area are all the same, empty. The zoo's employees must've freed the remaining living animals, or at least what they could. Perhaps some of them escaped on their own, realizing that their handlers were no longer going to be sliding open those secretive hinged doors and rewarding them with morsels of raw chicken, hay, grains or whatever other sustenance they'd needed. The idea of running into a grizzly bear or a rhinoceros is slightly humorous, although also a tad creepy.

Arriving at the aquarium, he decides to go inside out of idle curiosity. As soon as the door opens, a smell so foul hits him that he gags and hides his nose and mouth with the flap of his shirt. Damn Dog mewls softly and swings her head back and forth.

"Come on," he badgers her and raises his eyebrows. "You know you want to know."

The taunt must work because she follows him in but stays low to her belly. The massive water tanks are green, blending in with his night vision. Cory removes his goggles and turns on his flashlight instead. Inside of the murky tank that goes on for probably close to a fifty yards are the decayed and decomposed remains of three manatees. Enough seen. He backs right out the door again with Damn Dog on his heels.

"Why'd you want to go in there?" he reprimands his dog with a grin. She just looks at him and whines once before they trot on.

Finally, when he figures he's never going to find the veterinary care building, he does. He lets himself in by ramming the lock on the rear door and busting it with the butt-stock of his rifle. The composite material of it is tough. It can take and give quite the hit. Kelly and John have told him some funny stories over the years regarding that particular piece of the gun and what they'd had to do with theirs. He clicks on the flashlight again and begins a thorough search. It doesn't take long to discover the items that he needs. Apparently most people weren't raiding their big city zoos for medical supplies for themselves and their animals. He actually can't believe his family hadn't thought of this before. They'd sure as hell raided enough other places over the years.

On top of a supply cabinet, Cory finds a discarded canvas bag and fills it with some needles and thread and bandages. Twenty-three small bottles of antibiotics from inside a metal cabinet go in the bag next. Cory knows damn well that animal antibiotics can also be used to treat humans. Next he rams seven large tubes of antibiotic creams, more unopened packages of bandaging, and clear medical tape into the bag, stuffing it full to the gills. Surely that should work for supplies. He's no doctor like Reagan, Doc or even Simon, who is more nutty professor than doctor, but he knows enough to take care of most of the animals on the farm.

A bolt of lightning streaks across the black sky, and within a few minutes he can hear the rain tapping against the metal roof. He doesn't mind the snow, but he sure as hell hates rain. He'll need to come back in daylight for more supplies. He jogs at a steady pace back to the petting zoo barn and wastes no time prepping and also sanitizing and cleaning his dirty hands. It's still relatively early, but he has a long night ahead of him. Damn Dog takes up residence lying near the barn's partially open door and doesn't move. She's got his back while he attends to his ghastly task.

A few hours later when he's lying in the hay with the dog, and Jet is sewn up and resting peacefully, Cory hears the familiar clucks and murmurs of chickens on their perches somewhere in the barn. He hadn't spotted them earlier, so they must've been outside free ranging. They make these little sounds like coos and gentle clucks at night to one another when they are tucked away snug as bugs in their rugs. Chicken breast sure would taste great tomorrow with the can of lima beans he'd taken from the gym pukes. He falls asleep with a grin on his face and a dog on his feet.

Chapter Nineteen
Simon

There are three vehicles full of McClane warriors headed into the city of Coopertown to take on the creeps at the Target store. The men from there had ambushed the McClane medical clinic. They'd come there to kill them. They'd come there to rob them. They'd come there to take their women. And, unfortunately for these rats, every man in the Ranger caravan is willing to lay down his life to ensure that never happens, Simon included.

Three men including Paul from the condo community are in the truck behind them. In the bed of the truck are another four men from the different sectors in town. The Reynolds brothers ride together in their small car with the muffler that is much quieter than their big dually pick-up truck from their farm. Zach Johnson and his friend are with them. They've all been thoroughly trained by the Rangers, each and every one of them. These men have gone at one time or another on missions with them, and the Rangers had deemed them ready and worthy in the field.

Simon is riding in the bed of Doc's pick-up truck with Kelly while Derek and John ride up front in the cab. The night air is frigid, but he barely feels anything. His adrenaline is high, pumping him full of a vibrant metabolic heat. He doesn't think about the family. He doesn't worry about his sister. His mind does not wander to Sam, as it so often does. The only thing he thinks about is the mission. He's reviewing the plans over and over in his mind until they are melted into his brain.

John's voice comes across his ear piece, "Five minutes out."

"Wish the Death Stalker was here," Simon comments about Cory.

Kelly's eyes meet his, and he replies, "I know, brother. He's a good fighter."

Simon nods solemnly and tries to get his head back in the game.

"Sound check," Derek says into his throat mic.

Simon repeats him, as does Kelly and Wayne. Nobody else except Condo Paul has a headset. Everyone has night vision gear, though, or they wouldn't be on this mission. They can't afford to go haphazardly swinging a flashlight around and alerting the enemy to their location. The men from their small town have gear raided from Fort Campbell Army base. He, John and Kelly had gone up there about three years ago, but the place had been deserted. The men had been hoping to connect with others from the Army. Not a soul was in sight. A few of them had left notes explaining why they abandoned their posts. They'd all left for their hometowns or to find their loved ones. Simon could hardly blame them. If it hadn't been for the promise of someday finding Paige, he never would've come this direction so far east of his hometown. Being a sixteen-year-old boy on his own in Arizona hadn't seemed like too brilliant of an idea, either. He'd initially hoped that his father would make it home to Phoenix. That hadn't happened, and instead he'd lost his mother, too. He's quite sure that his father is in the same place as his mother. He'd been in England when the shit hit. It wasn't like he could catch a flight out. Great Britain had been nuked.

They'd found a few provisions at the fort but not much. A couple thousand rounds of .223 ammo, the night vision gear for their comrades in arms, some disgusting MRE's- which they'd promptly stored in a crate in the basement for emergencies only- and a Hummer were the more relevant items they'd found. The Hummer had actually started, and Simon got to drive it back. They don't use it too often, though because it's a bit of a gas hog, not as efficient as the old pick-up truck of Doc's.

John pulls the truck into an alley and puts it in park, cuts the engine as the other two vehicles do the same. They know the layout of this town fairly well. They've been here a few times but not recently. Doc and Sue had filled them in on information about areas of which they weren't yet familiar so they could make an escape plan if it comes to that. Simon jumps over the side of the bed, landing on the balls of his feet. Everyone meets up at the corner of Doc's truck.

"Everyone clear on what to do?" Derek asks.

He gets nods of ascent or verbal replies to the affirmative.

"Tonight we ring the bell of justice on these fuckers," Kelly asserts and gets a lot of "hell yeah's" in return.

"We're about three blocks from there. Let's move out," John states.

"Hooah," Simon, Kelly and Derek call out softly.

Kelly and the four men from Pleasant View are moving in their own group. John and Simon are leading the men from the condo units, minus Paul. The Johnsons and Reynolds will work as a four man team. They do this frequently on their own, so it's not a good idea to split them up. And Condo Paul and Derek are on their own. Their positions will be taken up at higher elevations for sniping at first, and then they'll join the skirmish. For communication purposes, Paul has been given the headset and throat mic that Reagan had worn years ago to help out on the raid of the neighbors when they'd been overrun.

They move out, some in one direction, some in the other. Paul and Derek will be taking up spotting positions for the time being, watching the front and back exits of the building. About a block from the store, Simon's group pauses to scout for a rooftop sniper or movement. None is discovered. Derek and Paul will be watching their sixes now so that they can accomplish phase one of the mission. They slow jog to the back of the Target where John and Simon split away from their group, leaving them to wait behind the cover of a building and two knocked over dumpsters. The four men fan out so as to provide cover fire if needed.

"No security detail on the roof. All clear," Paul says through his throat mic.

244

"Roger that," Kelly returns for the rest of them.

When Simon and John get to the back entrance of the retailer, they ignore the closed garage-style doors. John reaches for the handle of the man door, but there are a chain and lock covering it. Simon quickly whips out a set of bolt cutters from his pack. He crimps down on the lock and snaps through the tough steel. John pulls the chain away and lays it quietly on the cement. Surprisingly the door pops open easily enough with a gentle tug as nothing else on the other side is keeping it from being opened. They creep inside, sweeping left and right and spreading out.

"Clear," John whispers.

Simon muzzle sweeps his own area and repeats, "Clear."

This storage room is much bigger than Simon would've thought. Shelving units are knocked on their sides, some in a domino effect lying against others. There is literally nothing left of the retail giant's overstock. Every available area is cleaned out, which makes it easier to do a quick sweep. Also, no people reside in the rear part of the store, which makes phase one easier. He meets back up with John at the swinging doors that lead to the store floor. Simon places two rubber doorstops under the threshold of each door so that it cannot be opened. They do this so that their enemies will not be able to get away from them after this starts.

A whoosh and a solid thump sound behind them outside of the building.

"Target down, rear entrance still secure," Derek comes across their headsets.

John's brother is set up at an angle near the back entrance with his silencer-equipped rifle, but far enough away that he won't be in danger of being shot. He and Paul will watch both entrances until John has this one secured. Then Derek will move forward toward the front, providing cover fire in the same manner he's just done.

"Roger that," Simon whispers back to Derek through his throat mic.

He and John exit through the man door again where they are met by two of the men from their group. This is a damn near impossible task they are up against. It's not like clearing a single house or a building occupied by one family. This is a full-on military assault on a crowded retail store full of possibly more than fifty men with hostages. This could potentially turn chaotic and hectic very quickly.

"Got it?" John whispers.

"Yep," Roy replies.

He's a good man who has a family and lives within Pleasant View's city limits. He has no military experience but used to hunt, never missing an opportunity. He is broad-shouldered and built like a bull.

The big man hands John a piece of heavy steel pipe that he was left to scout around for in the alley by the dumpster. John slips the thick pipe through the handle, further preventing the rear exit of a hasty, panic-ridden freak. Now the only way out is through the front where Condo Paul should already be in position.

Simon hand signals to the group to move forward. He and John lead the way. Everyone in their group wears body armor, care of the Fort Campbell supplies. It's not full-proof. A few years ago, they'd lost a trusted friend from town, a former sheriff's deputy, who'd been killed on a supply run that he'd taken, a run that John and Derek had warned him not to do. He'd gone anyway and been killed. He'd been wearing similar body armor.

They jog quietly to the front of the building, passing a dead man on the ground. Simon lithely hops over him and continues on. This is probably Condo Paul's handiwork. He's a great shot and a deadly sniper.

Two men come at them from their left, and he and John take aim and quickly disable them. However, one of them has gotten off a round. It wasn't silenced, so it could likely alert the rest of the fifty men inside to their presence. It sounded like a 9 mill, and Simon notices the fallen man's semi-automatic pistol on the ground near him. It was loud enough to awaken people. No time to lose, they pick up the pace. A softer ping tells him that Paul has taken someone else down, followed by two more pings and the dull thuds of bodies slumping to the concrete. He's not one to miss, so Simon's confident that three more men are dead. They reach the front of the store, stay low to the knee wall and climb inside over the broken glass of a huge window. The whole team moves in. Kelly's group mimics them from the other side.

Simon spots two men off to his right near the restroom sign and speedily takes them out, head-shots to both. Inside the building, the sound is louder than he'd care for. It's too late now. The fight is on. There is light, either from a campfire or a torch of some kind coming from the far right corner of his vision. Shadows dart around back there.

One of the men from Kelly's group shoots another freak, hitting him in the shoulder. They spread out, moving in two-man groups. That is everyone but Kelly, who will remain near the entrance for a few extra minutes, giving Derek enough time to come in and take up position. Simon and John move forward, leading their team into the right half of the store. Kelly's team will work to their direct left, and everyone will hopefully meet in the back middle, successful with clearing their sections.

They are immediately met with gunfire, so Kelly gives a little back, laying down about fifty rounds from the S.A.W. The red tracer rounds popping out every fifth round cause the freaks to lose their nerve and start scattering like rats. A woman starts screaming. Another follows her lead. The freaks begin shouting to one another.

He and John and their small group are in the women's clothing department with little to no cover, so they push forward. One of their group takes a bullet, but they don't completely stop. Kelly is still laying down the hate at the front of the store, and apparently he's having some success because at least two men are shouting for help, shouting from pain. John fires to their left, hitting another thug. Simon swings right, covering them as their group helps their wounded comrade behind a display case that used to house jewelry.

"Fuck!" Roy says through gritted teeth. "Winged my leg."

"Tie it off," John orders hastily. "Move it."

They both squat beside Roy while the others cover them with suppressive fire.

Simon whips a strip of material from his cargo pocket and ties it tightly around Roy's calf muscle. It is Simon's job to act as the field medic when they are on a raid.

"I'll cover you guys from here," Roy demands. "Leave me here."

"Move out," John commands to Simon and the others.

Their group half rises and shuffles forward. Simon signals to their left and the men spread out slightly and move as one through women's accessories. The S.A.W. is silent, but Simon can pick up on other guns being fired. Derek's loud 30.06 is barking steadily, as well, without the silencer on anymore. He's in the building with them and should be set up over in the far west front corner near the Starbucks. He's not there for a latte, though. He's picking off perps who are trying to either flank them or sneak out the front doors or through the broken windows also at the front.

Simon switches weapons, setting his rifle sling against his back and pulling forward his sawed-off shotgun. He notices tents and backpacks and boxes set up as if each man has his own small section of this store. Areas have been cleaned out and reorganized to accommodate their "homes" better. One such man crawls out of his tent trying to pull up his pants as he goes. Simon hits him square to the chest with a buckshot round from his shotgun. For up close contact like this he likes his shotgun with the short barrel better than the M16. John and Kelly still use their military rifles for almost everything, but that just didn't feel as comfortable to Simon. He does all of the reloading of everyone's shotgun shells, too. It helps him to relax doing tedious jobs like that. Plus he likes being able to control the grain count.

"Shit," Derek says into the mic. "Group moving your way."

Nobody has time to answer, give away their positions or offer assistance. They all have specific instructions to follow out on this mission. Straying from the plan could jeopardize more lives. They make it almost to the back wall of the store separating it from the warehouse behind it. John holds up a hand to call a halt halfway down the third aisle as they close in on the electronics department. Simon hears them talking frantically, too. Sounds like a group of freaks trying to make their move on them, likely the group Derek warned them about. The freaks are attempting to be quiet, but they fail miserably. Simon signals to the three remaining men in the group and then follows John. They'll flank.

Gunfire continues at a steady pace coming from the other side of the store. Simon hopes that Kelly's group is having the same luck so far that they are. He rounds the corner, and he and John open up on the men they find there. The other three men with Simon and John's group do the same. The perps either go down with a scream of pain or try to scatter to the winds. John takes out the final one with a shot to his center back as the perp tries to run down the wide middle aisle while shooting at them over his shoulder.

Suddenly a woman runs at Simon. She isn't armed, but he doesn't want her coming at him so fast. John has warned him many times not to trust women just because they are women.

"Help me, please," she cries frightfully.

Simon shoves her away, and John pushes her down.

"Stay there," he orders firmly. "Don't come back out till we call out an all-clear. Ya' got me? Stay down."

The skinny woman with the dark, stringy hair nods frantically and ducks lower behind a shelving display of how-to books. Apparently cooking French cuisine or hand-crocheting a winter hat isn't popular reading material in the apocalypse.

Simon circles his right index finger in the air, and they move out again. Derek's rifle rings out loud and clear again. Their group has come to the sporting goods section as he and John cautiously lead down each aisle. Not only do they need to clear every aisle in the store, they also have to watch out for the mini tent cities for movement. A bead of sweat runs down his back. Someone at their rear takes a shot at them as they move back into the main aisle leading out of this department and into the next which used to be grocery items. Another man in their team is hit. He smacks against the floor with a fatalistic crash.

Simon and John jump to their right, but the other two men in their team dive left. John squats low and Simon hunkers over the top of him. His friend and mentor fires on fully automatic at the band coming toward him as Simon fires off two rounds straight into the crowd. The other two men in their group mimic and do the same. The group of thugs dive for cover, but not before four of them end in a heap of entangled arms and legs and dead bodies. These men don't have military experience, Simon's sure, but they have numbers that the McClane group doesn't. Simon reloads at lightning speed, jamming five more rounds into the shotgun's magazine.

John moves forward, and Simon covers him with his rifle this time, providing suppressive fire. David, one of the men in their group, also moves forward and jumps back behind cover after about five feet, mirroring John's smooth tactic. They both provide fire as Simon and the last man move forward, this time jumping an aisle ahead of John and his partner. Simon spots one of the freaks scurrying again and takes a shot but misses. Damn it! He fires again and misses again because the angle is too severe. Another stands up, issuing orders to his group, and Simon takes another shot, hitting this one center mass. An important rule of battle is always to take out their leadership. If this man was a leader, he's not anymore.

Simon jogs to the end of his short aisle and comes up behind John, who'd been expecting him. Together they go back the same way and start moving against the cement block rear wall of the building. They'll flank these punks if they can. Their two remaining team members keep the freaks occupied with distracting cover fire while he and John make their move. They come to the men's clothing department, still stocked with items hanging on hangers, surprisingly enough. John indicates with two fingers that Simon should continue in a wide arc while John goes straight forward. They've done this move many times over the years. It always works. Simon leads with his shotgun again and low shuffles further east, making a circuit of the men's clothing and coming almost to the corner of the building again. He can see them clearly enough. There are around ten or so.

"At your twelve, Doc," Kelly says to John through their headsets, referring to John as Doctor Death.

"Professor's in the east corner moving in," John alerts their friend.

He's letting Kelly know their exact positions so they don't take on friendly cross-fire. For some reason, he's earned the nickname Professor over the years.

"Roger that," Kelly returns. "Lead us off, tiny."

Even during a firefight those two make jokes. Simon just shakes his head and sneaks even closer. John fires first and within a minute or so, they have commenced in taking out the last band of men making their stand in the former ladies' lingerie department.

Together the group finishes the sweep of the area since they'd been interrupted by being shot at from the rear.

"We've got company," Condo Paul comes across their headsets.

This statement is followed by Derek's rifle and likely Paul's silenced rifle, as well. Their group jogs to the front of the store again where they assist with disabling a truck with three men in it that was heading in as back-up, presumably. It ends with the truck on fire and three more dead creeps.

They finally give an all-clear after a thorough search of the area. A small group of women has huddled together near the front entrance with them. One of the younger ones doesn't even have on shoes.

"Roy's down but alive. Dennis isn't," John states to Kelly.

"I'll get him," Kelly offers.

Simon's glad for the offer. Roy's almost as big as Kelly. He isn't exactly going to be easy to move. Kelly takes two of his men with him, and they jog away.

"Pack it up?" Simon inquires.

"Roger that. Do a clean sweep, mop up. Make sure we don't have stragglers," Derek explains. "We need to get back to the farm."

"Wait. Something's not right," John says as he raises his night vision gear to rest on top of his head.

"What is it?" Derek asks.

They are traversing toward the Starbuck's kiosk. Two of the women trail after them as if they are too afraid not to.

"I didn't count fifty men," John says.

"Kelly, what's your k.c.?" Derek calls over his headset to the Hulk for his group's kill count.

"Think it was nine," comes the return.

"Where are the rest of your men?" John barks angrily at one of the women.

"They left!" one of the younger women says quickly.

"When?" Simon demands.

"About an hour ago," another answers.

"Where'd they go?" Simon petitions and can't stop the tension from entering his voice.

Another woman steps forward from the crowd and says, "The man that had me said that they went to get revenge on the people of Pleasant View, the ones from that clinic."

John demands, "Were they going to the clinic?"

She answers quickly with a flash of fear in her dark eyes, "I don't think so. I heard him say that they found out about some farm or something."

It only takes a nanosecond for that to sink in. Kelly, who'd just joined them again with Roy, shouts orders.

"You three stay here and get our dead and injured to a vehicle."

"Let's roll!" John shouts with definite worry in his voice.

Sprinting in the pitch dark, headless of being cautious, they run for their truck. Derek jumps in the driver's door. Kelly hits the passenger side, and he and John literally jump over the bed's sides. Paul and two other men grab the truck from the condo village, and they speed away.

The cool edge of apprehension that Simon had felt earlier about their mission has now given way to an icy cold hand of dread.

Chapter Twenty
Paige

They've been on pins and needles all night waiting for the men to return. They haven't been gone all that long, but it feels like hours. This is way worse than when they'd gone to the creep's cabin in the woods last night. That was one guy they were after, the snitch. This is a small battalion of armed men. Paige paces from room to room restlessly while intermittently biting her nails. Sam and Sue do the same, but Reagan seems calm as she spies through binoculars. Doc is on the back porch doing the same thing. Hannah is in the basement with the children. They'd sent her downstairs to sleep with the children, but Paige highly doubts that she is doing so. She'd been just as worried about the men. Talia is hanging out in the kitchen brewing a pot of tea on the stove for everyone. Paige is a nervous wreck over Simon being gone. Gavin is standing on the front porch with a shotgun. The two women from the neighbor's farm are trying to play a hand of cards to pass the time.

Paige strides down the long hall from the back porch door to the front entrance. Then she takes the same path again. The pistol that she wears on her hip feels awkward and slightly uncomfortable, but they've all been relegated to the task of being the farm's militia while the men are gone. She's not too worried about the McClane compound, but her nerves are fried over Simon's absence.

"Here," Talia says to her. "Have a cup of tea. It might help. Something warm's always good for nerves according to my Nana.

She used to say stuff like that all the time. She was full of old wives' tales and mostly just, well, her own tall tales."

Paige grins and takes the proffered mug of hot tea.

"Thanks, Tal," Paige says. "Did you have any trouble getting Maddie to bed?"

"No way," her friend says. "She sleeps so hard here. Sometimes I get up to check on her in the middle of the night just to make sure she's still breathing."

They both smile.

"I think all four of us sleep like that now. Been a long time since we could," Paige says as she blows on her tea and adds a smidgen of honey. She'd gone last week with Sue to check on the bees. That had been interesting, to say the least. She's never been too fond of bees. She also hasn't had anything sweet for a long time, so the honey is appreciated. Sue was very patient while explaining the bees, even as most of it went in one ear and out the other. Paige has only ever swatted at the nasty buggers, not tried to co-exist with them as if she needed anything from them. The McClane family lives like pioneers. Thank God the bees aren't producing yet and are just in their hives surviving the remainder of the winter until spring when they can fly out and about and collect pollen and produce nectar and breed and work and sting people. This honey collecting thing is one chore she's not looking forward to at all.

"I see them," Doc declares as he bursts through the porch door into the kitchen.

Out of everyone on the farm, Paige likes Herb McClane the most. He's so kind and even-tempered. She sees so much sadness in his blue eyes, sadness that she understands all too well. He's lost the love of his life, and it shows in the crinkles and lines around his eyes, even when he smiles. Paige had certainly not felt anything like that about her boyfriend in college. She'd been sad when he'd been killed, but there really wasn't any time to even process his death. She had been too preoccupied with just staying alive after that. But once her tiny group had settled into the old abandoned farmhouse for the winter, she hadn't mourned him then, either. She had even begun to feel like true love was just a phrase people liked to throw around. Her parents had been more like partners than great lovers. Her dad respected her mother and likewise, but they were very distant and cool with each other. They had also married quite young, and Paige believed them to be more like good friends than crazy-for-each-other lovers. Her faith in love has restored exponentially since arriving on the McClane farm, however. She sees love all around her. The three Rangers and their wives and, unfortunately, Herb have renewed her belief that love is still out there and attainable. She's not, though, sure if she'll ever actually find someone. Having Simon back in her life is plenty good enough for her. And thank the good Lord, he's back.

"Yep, I see 'em…" Reagan agrees but pauses. "Wait, there's an extra vehicle."

"They're moving really slow, too," Doc says on a hard frown as he moves to another window. "Something's…"

Sue and Talia have joined them in the music room. The family dog, Molly, begins barking. The hair on her back stands up like she's been shocked by electricity. Doc shushes her, which gets an immediate response of her crossing the room and sitting at his feet. The other dog is tied at Sue's cabin in the woods. He's a lot more hyper and playful, so he gets secured out at their cabin a lot to keep him from being a pest when the situation on the farm is hectic. He also doesn't listen as good as his mother.

"Wait a minute. Shit!" Reagan yells. "That's more than one extra vehicle! I don't think that's them. There are three or four trucks coming, and nobody radioed in. Those aren't our men!"

"Everyone, get ready," Doc says calmly though his eyes read an underlying fear. "Sue, get downstairs and tell Hannah. Make sure Justin and Huntley have their guns ready and keep the door locked unless we call out for them. Then get back up here and take up position. The rest of you secure the windows with me. Quickly now!"

What the hell? They gave a gun to Justin? And Huntley, too? Those kids are like pre-teens or young teens. And Hannah's blind! How the hell could they possibly defend themselves?

Everyone springs into action. Reagan, Talia, Gavin and she run from room to room on the first floor securing the windows by shoving up and opening the ones that face the oncoming traffic, but closing and locking the steel bars on the inside. Simon had explained the windows to her after she'd freaked out about the black bars that close from the inside in the big house making her feel caged in. He'd said that after the assault by the visitors, which she knows was her Aunt Amber's group, the men had welded and screwed bars on the insides of every window of the house to ensure an impossible entry from anyone on the outside. Bolts have been screwed into the floor right behind every exit door so that they either lie flush or are able to be pulled up and turned to prevent the doors from being opened from the outside, too. Talia makes sure to double check those bolt mechanisms. To say that the McClane men take the security of this farm serious would be a massive understatement. The cabins in the woods don't have similar security systems, but the forest alone conceals them from even being viewed.

When they are done, probably less than a full minute later, and back in the main hall with Sue and Doc, they all nod.

"Go now," Doc says quietly. "Sue, kill that light."

His voice is grave and speaks volumes as to how he feels about this situation. Paige is scared shitless. Why don't they just pile into that big SUV out back and take the hell off? The light he was referring to was a single oil lamp in the music room. They'd wanted to conserve their solar power for this very reason. This family always seems to have some sort of contingency plan or another, but they hadn't really counted on something this bad. How could they?

Gavin goes out the front door where he'll cover the house from there, squatted down behind shrubbery. She and Reagan sprint out the back door. Strategies were reviewed about five times with the men about scenarios like this should it happen that creeps would come to the farm while they are gone. Nobody really thought it would happen. According to Simon, it never has before. This could all be for naught, though. Those could just be people out there looking for help.

They are almost to the cattle barn when Paige suggests, "Why don't we just take that car and go? This is crazy." Her voice shakes with a fear that she can't help. The anxiety she'd felt waiting for the men to come home safe and sound has turned into full-blown fight or flight survival mode.

Reagan stops and painfully yanks Paige's arm, pulling her to a halt.

"We don't run," the shorter woman says vehemently. "We're McClanes. This is the *McClane* farm. We aren't leaving. This is our farm. This is *your* farm now Paige. The only people leaving are them. In body bags."

Paige nods but still feels scared. The vehicles are less than two hundred yards from them. Reagan reaches for Paige's pistol and flicks off the safety.

"When you need this, just aim and pull. It's ready to go," Reagan tells her with one firm nod before returning the handgun to the holster on Paige's hip and turning away.

They continue on through the dark until they reach the barn where they both carefully climb the ladder to the hay loft. Reagan gives the ladder a hard shove, and it tumbles over into a big pile of loose hay below them. A cow moos softly, probably thinking she's getting another meal. The headlights draw closer as she and Reagan take up position at the opening of two different wide slats. Simon explained to her earlier today when he'd brought her up to the loft to discuss her role should this happen that these wide slats were made wider by the men so that they could be used for this exact purpose. She'd barely paid attention because the idea of this happening was unimaginable.

"Remember, three shots each. Quick. Then we move," Reagan reminds her.

"Got it," she affirms. "Reagan, I'm not that good of a shot. I've only ever shot a gun twice in my life."

"You've got that rifle. It's good enough for the both of you. Just aim center mass. Don't try for head-shots. Just aim to their center."

"What if they aren't bad people?"

"They are," Reagan says with decisive irritation. "Take a few deep breaths. Take a breath before squeezing that trigger and let it halfway back out. It'll help to steady your shot. You can do this, Paige."

The other woman pokes her rifle's barrel through the slat and pushes her cheek against the black stock. Paige copies her.

"You *will* do this," Reagan demands without taking her eye away from the big scope. "You're one of us now."

And with this one poignant sentence, Paige realizes that she *is* one of them. She and her brother and friends may never be able to leave this farm. She certainly doesn't think Simon would ever even want to. His heart is embedded into this farm and these people. The security and sense of family and belonging are like nothing she's ever had, not even with her boyfriend from college. This McClane family has opened their home and their arms to her, and she'd held back. Not anymore. Reagan was right. This *is* her family, and she's willing to fight to her dying breath for them.

The four trucks of variable size, yet with similar loud mufflers, pull straight onto the back yard of their farm, leaving their headlights on. A man jumps out of the passenger seat and crawls over the side of the bed to stand in it. He has a megaphone in his hand. This is apparently their leader. This is obviously not a group of people looking for their assistance. Other men also alight their vehicles and the beds of the trucks. They are all armed with guns or baseball bats. There must be close to thirty of them. Paige takes more than one deep breath to steady her nerves and stop the quaking in the pit of her stomach.

"Light 'em up, Grandpa," Reagan says to herself softly.

A moment later, Doc has hit the switch on their breaker that illuminates the whole entire outside property with spotlights and floodlights without giving away any easy viewing of the house or outbuildings. Hopefully, it is blinding them.

"Nice," Reagan whispers. "Hey, assholes."

"Should we shoot?" Paige asks nervously.

"Steady," Reagan returns. "You know the plan. I lead off."

"'Kay," she says, her voice shaking.

"Easy, Paige," her companion whispers. "We've got this. They don't know our farm like we do. Nobody knows this farm like us. We've got the biggest advantage in that. Keep it in mind when you start moving."

Her logic makes sense enough. These men have never been here before tonight. They are at an extreme disadvantage.

The man on the megaphone turns it on and begins monologuing, "Hey, inside the house, we don't come meaning no harm."

Reagan scoffs. Paige even smirks with derision.

"Just come out with your hands up and nobody has to get hurt!" he continues. "We know your men ain't here. Surrender now and…"

"Fuck you, asshole. We don't surrender," Reagan says with fire in her veins and squeezes the trigger.

The speech giver takes a head-shot from Reagan's high caliber rifle. His body falls over the side of the pick-up, landing out of view. Simon told Paige always to take out the leader of any group first. Apparently Reagan also knows this. Paige had really not listened that closely when he'd lectured her on tactical maneuvers. Most of it was going over her head. She'd always figured on running away with him if it came to that.

Instantly there are shots fired from all positions within the McClane home and Paige pulls the trigger of her own rifle. Beside her, Reagan reloads and fires again, hitting another man in the back. Paige's shot isn't as clean, but at least she got one of the men in the shoulder who'd been brandishing a shotgun. He's lying beside the first truck screaming in pain or perhaps shock. It looks like every member of the family has hit their intended first targets as close to a dozen men go down and then another from Reagan's second shot. Unfortunately, the men are returning fire now and ducking and hiding and spreading out, making it more difficult to get them. Shots hit buildings but are completely ineffective since they haven't quite figured out where she and Reagan are hidden. Good.

Paige squeezes the trigger again and wings a guy in his leg who'd thought he was hiding behind the third truck a whole lot better than he actually was. After sighting in, she finds another one near the back porch, takes a breath, and shoots him, too. Reagan takes her final shot, hitting a man in the side of his neck as he runs toward the big house. The farmhouse is taking more gunfire than they are, which scares Paige that a bullet will go through the wall and strike one of the family. The only thing that makes her feel any better about it is the fact that the children are all safe in the basement.

"Let's go," Reagan says in a rush.

They both leave their heavy rifles in the hayloft and grab the short-barreled shotguns that were waiting for them next to the hay pile.

"Remember, these aren't good for long distance," Reagan reiterates as her husband had earlier today. "You use your pistol for that."

As they exit the barn a different way than they came in, Paige hears the continuation of people firing at one another. Sue is on the attack in John and Reagan's room. The neighbor, Bertie Reynolds, is in the other bedroom on the second floor, doing the same. The new woman who'd been chained to a freak's cabin is on the first floor using the windows there with Doc. Talia is in Sam's bedroom on the second floor shooting out of the two opposing windows sporadically to add to the enemy's confusion. And little Samantha is behind the med shed moving furtively around in the dark sniping people. She is to cover all of the buildings near the house, including the house and flanking up around behind it to the equipment shed, as well. Gavin is ensuring that no men come around the front of the house to sneak into it or onto the porch. Paige and Reagan are covering the horse, hog and cattle barns, using them for cover and to add to the overall chaos of the scene. They split up, and Paige goes toward the back of the chicken coop while Reagan runs for the area near the horse barn. Nobody shoots at them, which is nothing short of a giant miracle. They haven't been spotted yet thanks to the spotlights likely blinding the men.

Just as she is rounding the corner, a man comes barreling toward her from around the other end of the coop. Paige barely hesitates before blasting him with the shotgun. She steps back for just a second, hiding around the building again before risking a peek.

The sharp recoil of the shotgun surprised her. She hadn't expected that. Two more men reveal themselves by standing under a spotlight maybe twenty yards from her. She's not sure if that's out of range for the shotgun, but she's about to find out. Her indecision is interrupted by a loud explosion followed by the horrific sound of men shrieking and bawling. Sections of the farm are booby-trapped for fights like this. They've apparently wandered into one and are either on fire or blown to bits.

Both men under the light turn to look, so Paige shoots the one in the back. The range is fine. The other man she grazes to the left rear shoulder. She fires again and misses. Damn. She can't remember how many bullets this shotgun holds. She doesn't want to be wasteful. He goes down bellowing in anger and pain. He is literally cursing her out, although he has no idea where or who she is. Now her directive is to move again per the soldiers' battle instructions. They are only to take a few shots from any one position. She's pretty sure she needs more bullets for the shotgun from her back pocket but doesn't have time.

Paige hears Reagan popping off three more rounds in quick succession. She certainly doesn't know whether or not that is from the shotgun or the pistol she carried. Guns were strategically placed around the farm before the men left. Reagan told her that this is what they do every single time the men leave the farm for any reason. If the house is attacked and overrun, they can get out and hopefully get to one of the guns. She sends up a prayer that her new friend is all right.

Moving quickly, avoiding the lighted areas, Paige sprints behind the detached garage. It's almost pitch dark in this area which creeps her out. She draws her handgun and slings the shotgun over her shoulder. She needs to add more bullet thingys to it. She low shuffles to the edge of the garage and glances around it. Men are scattering everywhere. Paige watches as one climbs the back stairs to the main house but is met with a round from Doc's rifle or shotgun. He immediately re-shuts the kitchen door and probably locks it.

Another man shoots and shatters the glass somewhere near the front of the house. If things get any worse, then everyone outside is to make their way closer to the house to protect the children inside. They have no idea what men like this would do with them or their precious children. They could kill them, abandon the kids, kill Doc or destroy the farm. After killing so many of their men, Paige is quite sure that her fate at the hands of these men will not be kind. Her small group had run into men like these before, but not in such big numbers. It hadn't gone well for her group. It was before she and Talia had learned to defend themselves better, or learned just to run.

Paige chooses a small cluster of men who look like they are thinking about flanking the farmhouse. They sprint around the back of their pick-up truck to apparently regroup. Paige presses her back tightly to the cement block wall and doesn't dare take a breath. A high-power rifle round sings out from the horse barn area, followed by more screaming from a man. Reagan has made her way there to her favorite rifle, as she calls it. From what Paige saw on that furtive glance around the building, there are still close to twenty men in the scattered group.

A trickle of sweat runs down her forehead. She's too scared to move in order to wipe it away. She hears the men drawing closer. She holds her breath, lest the vapor of it hitting the cold night air will give her away. They darn near walk right past her hidden in the concealing shadows of the garage wall. She waits until they pass. She waits another second until they are basked under the illumination of the garage's single flood light spilling into the barnyard. Then she raises the pistol and takes aim. She squeezes off one round and hits a man in the buttocks. Her next shot misses her target. A long range round hits the man from Reagan's rifle. Then all hell breaks loose for Paige. Men she hadn't seen before come running toward her from the last remaining truck and are shooting rapidly at her. She shoots three more quick rounds and dashes. She doesn't even know if she hit any of them, and she's not sticking around to find out. Paige literally dives down into the weeds and crawls on her stomach away from the danger. Another window explodes in the McClane house, followed by a woman's scream this time.

"Don't shoot 'er," a man shouts loudly behind her.

"Fuck that," another yells. "She shot Mac."

Paige knows they are talking about her. They ensue in an all-out argument as Paige finally manages to get to her feet. She stumbles over something, almost falls but keeps her balance long enough to run. Peering over her shoulder, she sees one of them coming at her. She barks off a round from her handgun while trying to continue running forward. That's when she runs into a wall. Although it's not a wall. The wall is a man, a very large man.

"Got 'er," he yells.

Paige tries to swing her pistol up to shoot him, but the man knocks away her hand, causing her gun to fall somewhere. Then he grabs her by the throat.

"How many of our men did you shoot, bitch?"

Paige doesn't answer. She can't. He's nearly crushing her esophagus. Instead of waiting for her reply, he slaps her square on the cheek. Then the man yanks her arm roughly, throws her shotgun to his friend and hauls her along with him to the spotlighted area. She makes a break for it, wriggling free. A second later he has her around the waist as she kicks and fights against him. He's too damn strong. He's holding her like a sack of potatoes as if her wrestling around is just amusing him.

Men in his group are hiding behind the trucks and lighting bottles with rags sticking out the top. He joins up with them. One of them runs forward and tries to throw the flaming bottle onto the front porch. He takes a shot from Sue in the attic and falls dead. Unfortunately, the bottle explodes right at the base of the porch. If it isn't put out, the fire could spread onto the wood porch and into the house. Talia and Maddie are in that house. Her little Maddie is in the basement where she wouldn't be able to get out if the house is engulfed in flames. Paige's heart races harder, and she feels like vomiting as she watches another man run toward the front of the house where Gavin should still be.

"You people come out or I'll kill this bitch right now!" her captor shouts above the melee and comes out from behind the shelter of the trucks.

"Let me go. Don't come out! Stay inside! Don't come out here, Dr. McClane!" she calls to Herb. Paige fights against his hold, causing the big man to club her over the head with the butt of his gun while still keeping her upright.

"You got to the count of twenty to throw down your guns and come out!" he calls out.

His words come out fuzzy. Paige's mind is cloudy, too. She wonders if he hit her with his pistol hard enough to cause permanent damage.

His group starts to merge and gather in a cluster near them as her vision blurs. Some come out of hiding. Paige wants the family to shoot them, even if it means these men kill her in the process. The freaks are feeling more confident since he's holding a gun to her head. They begin jeering the family, her family, as the end of Paige's life moves as if spinning on a slow-motion real in a bad action movie.

Chapter Twenty-one
Sam

The bad men have Paige. Sam can see them from her concealed position at the dark, farthest end of the equipment shed. A big man has Paige, holding her like a rag doll. He's yelling and carrying on, but Sam can't really tell exactly what he is saying because they are too far away. The way he is motioning with grandiose, she believes that he is using Paige as a bargaining chip to get what he wants. She's going to have to do something. They're on their own out here. The men are long gone in another town fighting other bad men who'd attacked their clinic yesterday. It's up to them to save Paige and themselves, as well, from whoever these horrid people might be.

Her hands shake violently, matching the breaths that she expels. She has to do this. She's a better shot than Sue, so she knows that her older adopted sister won't take it. Reagan is an even better shot, but Sam has no idea where she is and why she hasn't done so already. Do one of these men have her somewhere, too? Has she been killed, or does she just not have a good enough angle for a clean shot? And why hasn't Gavin done something? There haven't been any shots fired from his position for a while.

Sam has shot and killed two men already tonight. She knows she killed them and not just injured them because they fell hard and never moved again. What would Grams think of this? Would she be disappointed in her? Would she be worried about Sam's soul? She sure as heck is. Taking a life is a sin. Freely giving your life to another without putting up a fight for it should be a sin, too. She knows what it feels like to be in Paige's position. She also knows what it feels like to lose this fight, and she has no intention of allowing that to happen to her best friend's sister. Simon would never forgive her if she didn't do everything she could to save Paige.

Sam takes a deep breath, rises from her squatted position, intending to slide inside the building and move closer. A hand grabs her from behind, covers her mouth as another large hand slides around her waist, lifting her clean off the ground. She yelps a stifled scream of fright and surprise. Now she'll never be able to save Paige. She's gone and gotten herself captured, as well. She'd been so careful not to get flanked.

"Shh, it's me," a familiar voice whispers into her ear. "Don't move, Sam. It's just me."

Sam nods and Simon releases her. She looks over her shoulder to also discover John a few feet away with his back against the wall of the shed.

"How'd you guys get here?" she whispers unsteadily as her poor heart beats like that of a hummingbird's.

"We found out that they were headed this way and came in off the main road," he says. "Did they use the oil well road?"

"Yes, yes, they did!" she says, not letting her voice get loud. "They drove in from the oil well road that comes in through the back of the Johnson's."

Simon looks over to John and they both nod. "That's what we figured. We're parked up on the road. We ran in. The other men are here, too."

"Thank God, Simon," she frets as two tears escape her eyes. "We're not doing so good."

"Everything's going to be ok now, honey," he says and touches her cheek with the back of his hand.

His hand has gun powder residue on it that matches the black paint mixed in with green covering most of his handsome face.

"They have Paige!" she says in a low voice.

"I know," he grinds out fiercely.

John motions for Simon to move out. The women all know the same military hand signals as the men. Sometimes the women will go on supply runs with the men but never on a mission for blood. These signals are important for them to understand so that nobody makes a mistake or gets hurt during times like this one. Except that they've never been through anything this dangerous together.

Simon tugs her arm, and she goes with them. They sprint as quickly as they can in the dark. They climb up the side of the gravel driveway toward the top grazing pasture. The men both have night vision goggles on, but she's literally in the dark. She stumbles once over a rock or a divot, but Simon grasps her arm before she takes a fall. They climb through the barbed-wire fence near the steep driveway, and Sam's jacket catches on a steel barb. Simon frees her quickly enough. They walk slightly downward until they are at the crest of a small hill. Simon tugs her arm gently until she kneels. They end up on the cold, wet grass on their stomachs. All three of them have a rifle with a scope. Hers is outfitted with one that enables her to see in the dark, but she can't remember what it's called.

"Sam, you see those men by the front porch?" John asks in a rush of breath.

"Yes, sir," she answers in a barely audible whisper. Her heart is racing again from the run up the hill and the high levels of adrenaline pumping through her system... and mind-numbing fear.

"Try to take out one or two, honey," he tells her.

"Yes, sir," she squeaks to John. If there was ever a time that she was going to feel pressure being a part of the McClane family, it's going to be right here, right now. They need her to be fast and accurate. They need her to help kill their enemies. They all need each other if they're going to make it out of this alive. Her mind begins conjuring up the horrible, possible outcome of losing this fight.

Simon butts in to explain, "Derek and Kelly are down behind the cattle barn. Kelly's in position with Reagan. They'll take out the guys over there. He's probably already got a few taken care of."

She can breathe a little easier knowing that those two members of her family are still alive and unharmed. She hadn't heard shooting over there, so she is left to assume that Derek and Kelly have killed them in an alternative way. She doesn't want to dwell on that. Her oldest adopted brothers are too kind and sweet and gentle for her to even ponder them being cold-blooded killers. When the men go on assault missions together, they never discuss what happened out in the field when they get home. *Never.*

John says into his mouthpiece, "In position."

She knows the other men in their family will echo him when they are ready. She knows they are somewhere on this farm, moving around like stealthy thieves of the night. Cory is the most stealthy of them all, thus the nickname Death Stalker. But Simon is the deadliest, most accurate shot, other than John.

"Just breathe, Sam. Steady now," John says to her softly.

"Yes, sir," she answers.

"The Reynolds brothers will get the ones behind the truck," John says as he rises to one knee.

"Where are you going?" she cries out with urgency.

"Got this?" John asks of Simon in a calm voice, ignoring her question.

"Yeah, I've got this. Go on," Simon says firmly.

"Slow breaths, little brother," he says and places a hand on Simon's shoulder. "Slow breath. I've got your back-up. Lead us off, Professor."

And with that, John jogs away, going down the hill toward the back of the house until she cannot see him anymore because the light from the spotlights don't reach there. She worries for him. He's like her big brother. All three of the Rangers are like her protective, older brothers; Cory, too.

Down the hill in the light-flooded side yard, the man still holds Paige's body somewhat upright while yelling and promising false security in exchange for their complete surrender. Sam wonders if Simon's pretty sister has a concussion from the blow from that jerk's gun. She is no longer fighting him. Sam had seen the whole thing go down but hadn't been able to do anything to help her. That's why she'd been coming around the equipment shed. She was planning on sneaking up behind them so that she could at least try to get off a shot. Surrender is not an option for them. They can't risk the children and women being harmed, taken captive, raped or killed for just one person. It was just the cold hard truth of the life in which they all live. The children have to come first. They are the future, the survival of their country and this family. Sam could never sit back and watch what happened to her at the hands of the visitors, happen to one of the McClane children. It would break her heart. She's willing to give her life before watching that happen.

"Ready?" Simon asks calmly.

"Yes, Simon," she responds with full faith in him.

He glances at her in the dark, the tension and strain so readable on his handsome face. His blue eyes resemble icy, glacial shards in the moonlight. The dark black paint under them makes him appear more menacing than she knows he is. Tonight, however, like so many nights, he's become someone he doesn't like having to be. She knows he's killed people tonight. She's seen this intense look in him many times before. It never sits well on his conscious. He's just not like Cory or John. He wrestles with this side of him that he must tap into at times.

"I'm ready. I trust you," she tells him with more steel in her voice than she feels at the moment. Although she does trust him implicitly, it doesn't stop her fear from rising like a dark bile from the pit of her stomach.

"Just relax," he whispers to her as he pulls down his goggles again.

Sam isn't sure if he's actually talking to her or to himself. She has no doubts that he is positioned on this hill to take out the man who has his sister. He wouldn't want it any other way. It's going to be a tough shot. He's more than capable of doing it. She's seen him make tougher ones when they go hunting wild game together. Mostly she goes as his spotter and doesn't actually shoot the animals. It feels too unkind because she'd rather be drawing them than shooting and then gutting them. Tonight they are hunting different animals, but animals nonetheless.

She listens a few seconds as he does his weird breathing. It sounds the same as the breathing method that Reagan does when she's doing her yoga. She knows Simon is slowing his breathing in order to steady his shot.

A moment later he squeezes the trigger and just clips the man in the shoulder who is dragging his sister around. Then shots come from all directions on the farm. Presumably John finishes off Simon's victim by administering an injection of lead to the man's skull who had held Paige and abused her. This second kill shot comes from the area where John had sprinted, and he'd told Simon that he'd back him up. He's always been a man of his word.

Simon's sister slumps to the ground lifelessly and doesn't try to rise and run away from the dangers happening all around her or the man who had her and now lies dead near her. At least she's not in danger of being shot accidentally since she's on the ground.

The bad men return their fire with an angry vengeance because the McClanes have just taken out their number two in charge. They are quickly running out of a chain of command. Nobody else seems excited to take on the newly-vacated position, either. Sam breathes steadily, draws in a deep breath, lets it half out and squeezes the trigger without jerking it. Her intended target goes down, but he's not dead. Simon shoots him again. Movement just to the right of her felled opponent catches her attention. She spies Kelly through her scope. He's killing a man. He's not using a gun. Instead of dwelling on that macabre scene, she moves on. Swinging her rifle in a controlled, short movement to the left, not worrying about her huge, older adopted brother, Sam spies more bad men. She fires at one but misses. Simon covers her miss and shoots the man, finishing the demon off.

Some of the invaders jump into a truck, but the Reynolds brothers close in on them and do what needs to be done. Derek and Reagan have also moved forward. She sees them sprinting toward the med shed. Men must've moved toward it. It is the second most important place to secure on the farm. The family's arsenal is in there along with their medical supplies.

Simon leaps to his feet, drags her along and together they run as carefully as they can manage toward the scene of bedlam below them. Other than sporadic lighting from the moon, it is pitch dark where they are and she slides on the gravel and falls all the way down, down a short incline in the driveway before Simon can catch her. They don't maintain much of the driveway anymore since nobody really uses it other than for moving the cattle and horses from pasture to pasture. The drive is deeply rutted from the winter months of snow, melting snow, and ice running downhill and causing uneven ruts and gullies. The rocks and gravel sting and bite into her palms. Her face skids on the fine, pea gravel mixed in with the bigger base rocks. Simon literally skids to a halt in front of her.

"Sam!" he calls in surprise.

"I'm fine," she tells him as he helps her awkwardly to her feet again. "Just go, Simon! Go!"

He looks hesitant but nods with great reluctance before turning away. He keeps running toward their farm. She watches in awe as he pauses a moment to take aim and shoot out the back window of another truck that is trying to escape. It was quite a long range shot, but he'd made it. Then he takes out their back tire before jogging forward into the fray again. Sam knows he could care less about these men but is only trying to get to his beloved sister. She can't even imagine what he must be thinking right now looking at Paige's prone, unmoving body lying on the grass. Sam prays she is not dead. She asks Grams to watch over Simon's sister.

Sam pushes on, moving at a slower pace down the hill until she comes to the front of the equipment shed where she hides in the darkened shadows. The men in the family are moving at an all-out military assault pace and don't seem to need her help. She knows to stay out of their way in a situation like this. Unfortunately, one truck does manage to get away with the flurry of commotion and confusion. Dust is flying, bullets are flying faster, and the shouting of the evil men to one another is near deafening. She's not sure how many men were able to get into that truck, but she is very sure that the Rangers will not stand for it. If they have to hunt those men to the ends of the earth, their days are still numbered.

She creeps closer and hears Kelly call out for a recon of the area. Some of those jerks could be hiding in their barns and buildings or trying to escape on foot. She waits impatiently behind some bushes.

Hearing John, Derek, and then Kelly calling out "clear" or "all clear" a few minutes later, lets Sam know that she's safe to come out of her secure hiding place. Kelly is dragging a captured man into the light. Chet Reynolds walks over to him and kicks the guy in the stomach as if he has some personal vendetta against him. Grandpa and Derek begin filling buckets of water and using the garden hose near the back of the house to put out the porch fire. Kelly joins them, leaving Chet to watch their hostage. It doesn't take them long to get the fire put out, but it leaves a charred, smoking mess and half of the grand back porch in ruin.

A few of the family from inside the house start emerging to join them. Hannah will stay inside with the children to ascertain their safety and reassure them of their security. Likely the gunfire had awakened those who were still asleep if Hannie hadn't already done so to help them hide. John is embracing Reagan affectionately under one of the lights. Simon is on his knees beside his sister, his rifle discarded haphazardly near him. Sam joins him there, kneeling and supporting Paige's head. She is just coming around. Her light eyes are unfocused.

Grandpa comes over to the cluster of family members. Condo Paul has another man held at gunpoint. He's bleeding from his right shoulder. Nobody offers the man assistance to slow it.

"Everyone ok?" Derek quickly inquires after the family.

"Yes," Sue replies as she hugs her husband around his waist and cries unashamedly.

"We're just fine, Derek," Grandpa declares. "Were these the men from the clinic yesterday?"

Derek leads Sue a few feet away, and Kelly nods to Grandpa to answer his inquiry before jogging away again. He's going back to the porch to ascertain that the fire is completely out.

"Crap," John notes, "the house took a beating."

"It'll be easy to repair," Grandpa says reassuringly.

Sam's not sure if it will be or not, or if Grandpa is just trying to make everyone feel better about their beloved home. It looks scorched and black, charred to a crisp. She's not even sure if it is safe to walk on the porch deck or stairs to get in the back door. John offers a comforting, strong hand to Grandpa's shoulder in return for the motivational words regarding their home.

Reagan joins her on the grass near Paige's head and takes over. Sam stands and backs away, giving the doctors space to work with Simon's sister.

This was not a random attack. These men had outmaneuvered them. They'd allowed the soldiers to leave the farm abandoned and had waited for their opportunity to strike. How had they found them, though? She's not sure where the escapees are going, but she is quite sure that the men in the family will apprehend them soon. Single gunshots ring out periodically for the next few minutes. Sam believes the men are finishing off the wounded. They've left one man alive to be questioned, but the rest are being killed and put out of their misery. It's a brutal act, one that she's not so sure Simon's sister or friends would approve of since they are new to the family. But Sam especially understands the importance of annihilating their enemy absolutely. These men had come here to kill them, rape them, God knows what else. They had formed an army of over fifty people before and built up a stronghold at the Target store. They could do so very easily again if they are allowed to go free. Again she wonders what Grams would think of this? Would she want them to show these injured men mercy or finish them off? She misses her so. She misses the wise counsel she offered the family, the humanity behind her reasoning, and most of all, her warm hugs.

Talia and Bertie have also joined them from the house. Sam hugs them both, each offering the other what small amount comfort they can.

"Where's the other lady?" Sam asks Talia because she can't remember the woman's name who has been staying at the Reynolds' place. She must be even more traumatized than she was last night when the men had rescued her from Tim Lafferty's cabin in the woods. She has been through quite the ordeal.

"Vicky is in the basement with Hannah trying to get the kids to calm down," she explains patiently.

"I'll go in and help," Sue volunteers as she comes over to them. She has settled down considerably under the care of her devoted husband. "Hey, are you ok, Sam? You look pretty banged up, sweetie."

"Oh, yeah, I just slipped and fell down in the driveway," she stammers, not wanting or needing any of the family's worry. There are bound to be more important issues to deal with tonight other than just her own clumsy foolishness.

"Well, all right, honey, but you'd better let Reagan or Simon get you cleaned up later," Sue tells her and pushes a lock of Sam's hair back, tucking it behind her ear affectionately before jogging over to the house.

"Hey, where's Gavin?" Talia asks her.

"Oh, I'm not sure. Let's ask John if he saw him. He went that way after he left me and Simon on the hill," Sam suggests as they walk past Simon and Grandpa, who are both now helping Paige to sit up very slowly. She's awake again, thank goodness. His sister looks very surprised to be on the ground, so Sam believes that she's just had her bell rung, as the men always phrase it.

"John, where's Gavin? Didn't you see him at the front of the house?" Sam asks when they find him in the crowd. Reagan and he have parted, and she is now looking at Chet Reynolds, who has been shot.

"Just grazed your shoulder blade, Chet," Reagan is saying as they pass her. "Hey, Talia! Give me a hand here, would ya'? Let's get him and Paige over to the shed."

"Sure, but where's Gavin?" Talia inquires again.

John averts his eyes and then says, "I'll find him."

"Oh my God!" Talia exclaims. "Where is he? Is he dead? Where is he?"

"Stay here. Let John find him," Reagan orders her.

Grandpa rubs his forehead roughly and asks, "Any others wounded, John?"

"We lost a few, and a few are injured," John recounts with a furrow of his brow. "This place is about to be bombarded with shot up men. They'll probably bring whatever women or kids are left over there to our town until we can get them set up permanently and get it all straightened out."

Grandpa nods with understanding. "Right. Let's get moving, people!"

Chapter Twenty-two
Cory

His injured horse is tucked away safe and secure in a dilapidated, run-down barn just outside of the Columbus city limits. They are within a few miles or so of the city and well within the areas that he will raid. Damn Dog is with him tonight on this run. He's curious to see what this farthest northwest side of the city has to offer.

He and the dog stick to side streets and as close to the walls of buildings as possible to avoid being seen. Last night hadn't gone as well as he'd have liked since assholes had shot his horse, so he's hoping for better luck. Voices in the distance catch his attention, and he and the dog come to an instant halt near a McDonald's restaurant complete with the indoor play place. What he wouldn't give for a box of grease sticks, otherwise known as French fries. Or a milkshake, he reminisces. That would be good about now, too. And just to mock him, his stomach gurgles loudly in protest at missing lunch and dinner. Damn Dog cries softly.

"Shut up," he growls in a subdued tone. "You got your dinner, remember?"

She hangs her head in shame as they continue to move forward. He'd caught a rabbit earlier this afternoon in a snare and had given the whole thing to her. He'd been too busy tending to Jet's gunshot wound to be bothered with the rabbit. They'd made the trek away from the zoo and found a farm where they can rest a day or two. He'd risen before dawn and grabbed the rest of the medical stash in the veterinary clinic. A group of people had shown up at the zoo midmorning, and he highly doubts they were there to tour it and gaze at caged animals. He didn't stick around to find out. They were likely just using it as either a shortcut to get somewhere else or as a temporary shelter like he had. He'd led his limping horse and the dog away as quickly as he could. He hadn't even had enough time to snag a chicken or duck in the process, but he had grabbed a few flakes of hay. Getting the stallion to safety was priority number one, so he had no time to venture around too long before invaders had ascended on his peaceful reprieve.

The sound of voices is getting closer, so Cory opens the door to one of the taller buildings, an office building of some sorts and slinks inside. A rabbit scurries in front of them, but Damn Dog doesn't try to pursue it. Cory bypasses the security check-in station and uses the escalator that hasn't moved in years. The building is like something out of a scary movie where zombies roamed the earth and humans were the minorities. He half expects a hoard of them to come tumbling down the non-moving stairs of the escalator. Dim moonlight rains down through the skylights one story above. There aren't any dead bodies anywhere which leads Cory to believe that this place was where people had worked and had stopped showing up for said work soon after the first series of tsunamis. Most folks simply stopped reporting to their jobs once they realized that it was more important to stay home and defend their families and forage for food and supplies. A flock of barn swallows swoop on him and the dog. She barks once and tries to catch one in her jaws. Cory chuckles at her. Nothing surprises him anymore. He's seen all manner of wildlife in commercial buildings and homes since the fall. There are no clear boundaries for animals to understand where they should and shouldn't go.

"You're a real badass, aren't you?" he mocks. Damn Dog just replies with a sloppy, wet grin.

Once they are up on an elevated position on the second floor, Cory can spy down on the remains of the small neighborhood through an office window. He uses his binoculars. If he would've continued straight down that street, he and the dog would've come to a gated community less than a mile away. Gated would not exactly be the right word for it. There is a barricaded street where two men in military clothing stand guard with rifles. The area is cordoned off with high-tensile fencing like they use in the cattle pasture back at the farm. It's not really good for keeping anyone out, but those two guys with the guns look capable with them. Several lanterns that appear to be gas powered are at the top of the two primary entry fence posts. Questions start whirring through his mind.

His dog growls low in her throat and backs up two steps. The sound of something out in the hallway being accidentally bumped into alerts Cory that they are no longer alone. He crosses the room, skirts around a desk and a tipped over filing cabinet and listens near the door, his back to the wall.

A person crosses the threshold, and Cory pokes the tip of his rifle into the man's back.

"Freeze, fucker," he demands with open hostility. "How many are with you?"

"Nobody!" she says hastily. "It's just me!"

Cory yanks her hood down from her coat, revealing a full head of blonde hair pulled back into a ponytail.

"Hand me your weapon," he orders.

Cory is surprised when she gives over a simple dagger from her waist. "Turn around."

When she does, he gives her a quick pat down looking for more weapons. "What the hell are you doing running around the city at night with just a knife?"

She bites her upper lip and shrugs.

"Nobody's with you?" he asks and peeks out the door again.

"No, I told you," she answers. "I snuck out, ok? Shit! My dad's gonna kill me."

"Where did you sneak out from?" he asks of her. She can't be more than fifteen or sixteen. She's way too young to be trying to creep around a city by herself with nothing more than a knife.

She begs, "Please don't hurt me, mister."

"What?" he asks with incredulity. "I'm not going to hurt you. Where do you live? I'll make sure you get back home safe."

Without asking permission, she goes to the window and points. "See? Down there? That's my town. My whole family lives there."

"That's your town? How many people live there?"

"Oh, um, I think we have around seventy families now," she reveals. "What's your name?"

"Cory," he answers curtly.

"What's your last name, Cory?"

"Doesn't matter. We're not here to make friends. I'm taking you back," he states. Hopefully, those sentries don't decide to fill him full of holes. But he can't leave this kid out here unsafe and unprotected from potential jackasses who would hurt her. "Let's go," he barks with anger.

"I'm not really ready to go back…"

"Too fucking bad, kid," he says on a hiss. "No wonder your dad's gonna be pissed. He should be. This was a dumbass move. You could've been killed by someone."

She rolls her eyes at him. Cory would like to knock some sense into her but refrains since he'd like to return her unscathed to her family. Instead, he grasps her arm and tugs her behind him.

"Hey! You have a dog?" she asks excitedly.

"It's a guard dog. Don't try to pet her or she'll bite your hand off," he threatens.

Of course, she bends right over and rubs the dog's ears. Damn Dog wags her tail vigorously. Mutinous traitor.

"Let's go!" he tells her and pulls her arm again.

When they get closer to the guard post, Cory calls out to the sentries. "Hey! Don't shoot! I've got one of your people!"

Something dawns on him and he whispers, "What the hell is your name?"

"Kim. Kim Sanderson," the blonde replies with a sunny smile.

"Her name's Kim Sanderson!" Cory repeats her name to the guards while still keeping them both concealed around a corner a block away. He then shouts for their clarification, "I'm not gonna hurt her. I just want to return her safely to your group."

This kid is so dumb that she could've gotten her ass shot by her own guards. They call for them to come forward, so Cory moves with her in front of him.

"Hi, Uncle Joe!" she blurts to the guard on the left.

"Damn it, Kimmie!" Uncle Joe reprimands. "You got out again? How many damn times do we have to tell you not to go out alone? And at night again?"

Cory stands back, leery of the other men with guns. He's not putting his down. Uncle Joe extends a hand toward him, his rifle lowered.

"Thanks, man," he says. "We owe ya.' We really owe you."

Cory shakes the man's hand. "Nah, it's cool. I just didn't want anything to happen to her. It's not safe out there."

"No shit, right?" the other man says.

"Hey, Uncle Joe, can Cory come in and meet Mom and Dad and eat with us?"

"No thanks," he answers before her uncle can. "I've gotta get back."

"You live around here, too?" Joe asks of him.

"No, just passin' through," he replies.

"Well, at least let us get you some food or some provisions for bringing her home safe. It's the least we can do, man," Joe offers.

"Yeah, come on in for a rest," the other man offers. "At least grab a cup of coffee before you go. And my wife makes some damn good biscuits. Take a few with you for the road."

"Um…"

"Come on, Cory," Kim says and takes the sleeve of his coat between her fingers.

"Sure, but only for a minute. I do need to get going," he says unsurely. It's hard to trust people. Kind, giving people like these are so few and far between out there that he's skeptical and distrustful of everyone.

Twenty minutes later, he is well-ensconced within their small village and hearing more stories about people and their families than he cares to. Most of them are asleep since it's after midnight, but those who aren't come forward to talk. Everyone wants to know where he's been, what it's like elsewhere, and if it's better than it is here.

"We heard that an EMP went off over D.C. and that's what caused the power outages," one them says.

"I don't think so," Cory rebuts with confidence. If that was true, the men at the farm would've known this. "It was the tsunamis that took down the East Coast power. There wasn't an attack on U.S. soil, not yet at least."

"I can tell you for sure that there won't be any, either," one of the men answers. "I was Army National Guard when it happened. Those other countries out there are totally screwed. They couldn't attack anyone if they wanted to. The last report I heard before leaving South Carolina is that Russia had to shut down their nuclear program. They were pretty messed up from getting nuked themselves. They won't be a threat to anyone for probably damn near a hundred years if I was to guess. North Korea or China, either. They all lost a huge portion of their people, too. I heard they lost even more than we did. At least for us it was mostly coastal states. But those nukes took out major cities over there like Moscow and Beijing."

"We'd only just flown home the week before the first one struck," Uncle Joe replies. "We were coming from Germany. Stationed there. Think we were the last ones out. Good thing, too. It was way worse over there. The nukes were dumping fall-out all over Europe."

The other enlisted man says, "Right. We've got it way better than they do. At least we can grow food again. They won't be able to grow anything over there, not with the nukes and fall-out."

Kim's father says, "Well, inland they should do a little better, just like we have here. They'll eventually get on their feet. The interior of Europe should be fine. But someday it'll be a far different group of world super-powers."

"Hopefully we'll still be one of them," Uncle Joe says.

"We will be," her father emphasizes. "We always will be."

"How'd you get the gas up and running to power your lights?" Cory asks, changing the subject. He's not sure anyone will ever be a super-power again. This country and overseas countries are fully fucked. He's seen it firsthand.

"As a kid I grew up in Amish country," Kim's father replies. "All of our neighbors were Amish families, so I knew how they lived off the grid with propane lighting and appliances that don't need electricity. So when it hit, we made a quick trip up north into Holmes County and hit the hardware stores there. They sell gas appliances and lighting fixtures on account of the Amish not using electric lights."

"The natural gas lines still have gas pumping through them. I'm not sure how," the uncle explains, "but they do. It's not all that reliable, so we try to be really conservative with it. Haven't you seen anyone else with power or gas?"

Cory shakes his head. The others don't even try to hide their disappointment and surprise at hearing this.

"No, not really," Cory explains. "Some people are using propane for heat and gasoline to fuel generators. The government dropped a few big generators and crates of food by air that some areas were using, is what I heard. The National Guard moved into some of the big cities and distributed boxes of food and small generators, too, in the beginning. Won't matter, though. Still need fuel to make them work, so unless oil refineries get up and running again, we're still screwed. Unless coal mines open up and start delivering coal to power plants again, electric won't be fully restored, either. Some folks are using solar; others use wind."

They are all sitting or standing in the dining room of Kim's father. He had explained that this was his in-law's home and that he and his family were actually from the Cincinnati area before the fall. They'd come here to help his wife's mother. Unfortunately, his mother-in-law hadn't lasted long and had passed away shortly after they'd arrived. They hadn't felt like it was safe to try to make the trek back to their own home. It had become dangerous almost overnight in their own suburban neighborhood. Cory wonders if they know about the earthquake that had obviously hit Cincinnati hard enough to crack open the freeway in the downtown district. He doesn't tell them about it. They all have enough to worry about. Chances are that earthquake was from an aftershock or some other disturbance that had rocked the city.

Kim's younger sister clings onto her side and occasionally peeks at Cory. There are eight of them piled in discussing the shitty state of the world. Cory was fed a bowl of steaming hot bean soup whether he'd wanted it or not. He's pretty sure it had pork in it. At least that's what he hopes it was and not opossum or rat. Damn Dog had even begged a soup bone and is now sitting at Kim's feet chewing on her bone while the girl rubs at the dog's head. She explained to him that her other sister died last year of sickness that had swept through their small town with a fury. They'd lost almost a dozen people. They have no doctor in their precinct and only two nurses. One of the nurses said that she thought it was small pox. That seems so out of the realm of possibility that Cory almost didn't believe her. Then he remembered the pneumonic plague that had hit their farm. Nothing is impossible anymore.

"We work with another community just south of here," her father explains. "We got them up and running with gas, and they supply us with meat when we need it."

"That's good," he says with a nod. "Establishing trade with your neighbors is important."

"Yeah, we've been somewhat lucky," Uncle Joe observes. "We have had some problems from people out there. You run into any of that?"

Cory smiles. "Every damn day."

Kim's father says, "That's unfortunate. Were you in the military or something?"

He's indicating toward Cory's M16.

"Nah, I was still too young to join when it fell apart."

"You sure seem like you can take care of yourself pretty well," the uncle's friend says.

"My brother's ex-Special Forces, so he trained me. We have three men in our group that are Special Forces. They train everyone that wants to learn. We work with the people in our community, too. It's important that you know how to keep your neighborhood safe."

"That's smart," the uncle says. "Maybe we should start doing that, too. Whatcha' think, Merv?"

He's asking his military friend.

Merv nods and says, "Seems like a good enough idea to me. If we train the people over in Lewis Center, it could help to keep the scumbags out of our area. That's who we trade with, Lewis Center."

"That's good," Cory says. "Try to join in with other areas, too. Strength in numbers is a good policy now."

"No kidding," Merv says. "We had trouble with some nomad types passing through about a year ago. Man, they were some real ass-hats. They managed to get a couple of the women from the next town over and had 'em for a few days before we got to them. That was a real mess. Lost four men from our town, too. But we managed to kill most of them before they got away."

"Fewer assholes in the world helps everyone," Cory says to them.

"Right?" Uncle Joe asks rhetorically and bumps fists with Cory.

"Cory, we heard that Cleveland has power, like full power," Kim says with naïve excitement.

"You know anything about that?" Joe asks him.

Cory just shakes his head again. "I haven't heard that."

"They have a nuclear power plant up on Lake Erie, so some people passed through here last year and told us that there's power up there," the uncle provides.

"I don't know. Maybe," Cory answers noncommittally but doesn't believe this rumor. "I sure as hell wouldn't leave here to go out there to find out, though. It's safe here. This is safer than a lot of places I've been."

How the hell would they still be able to run a nuclear power plant without supplies being delivered and people trained in running a nuclear power plant still working there?

"Where's your place? I mean where is your community, your people?" her father asks.

"Pittsburgh," he lies easily. Nobody at the farm divulges its location. Ever. "Got family over that way. Just heading home."

"Do you guys have power, Cory?" her father asks.

"We use solar mostly," he divulges. "It's not a hundred percent reliable all the time, but it works."

"Solar? Oh man, we never thought of that. How's that work exactly?" Merv inquires before adjusting his rifle sling on his shoulder.

"I can draw you out the schematics for it if you've got a paper and pencil," he offers.

Ten minutes later he has the solar diagram drawn out and explained thoroughly. He's done this many times for people in their town and surrounding areas. They'll need to modify some things about their electricity and find the supplies to build them, but he is fairly confident they'll figure it out.

"So, Pittsburgh, huh? You're not far from home then," the uncle observes. "You're welcome to stay on here for a few days. Rest up and then keep going."

"No thanks," he rejects their hospitality. "Gotta keep moving. But thanks for the offer."

A few minutes later, he and his dog are jogging away. Kim's father and friends had forced him to take three jars of home-canned peaches, three apples, a small bag of beef jerky, and a takeaway jar of the bean soup. Plus, Kim's young sister handed him a cloth with four biscuits secreted away inside. She reminded him of Ari. He'd ruffled the hair on her blonde head. They'd invited him to come back again anytime. He'd politely accepted, even though he knows that he'll never take them up on it.

By the time he gets back to the rustic barn and his horse, Cory is exhausted. He'd gone looking for a fight tonight. He'd gone looking to kill more creeps. There are always plenty of creeps in every town. He hadn't expected to fall asleep in the hay with Damn Dog near his feet feeling like he'd made new friends. Tomorrow he'll push on away from this city of Columbus. Pittsburgh surely has lots of the creep types still lingering around terrorizing people that require his attention. He's so much better at the killing thing than the making friends thing. Friends just remind him of home, the last place on earth he wants to remember right now. He rubs the gold bracelet that used to belong to her between his thumb and forefinger before tucking it back into the neckline of his shirt where it dangles from the black leather cord.

Chapter Twenty-three
Sam

Grandpa calls out orders to everyone. Simon carries his sister to the shed, although she protests it. There is blood trickling and coagulating down the back of her neck near her braid. Apparently that man had hit her harder than Sam first thought. Everyone jumps into motion while Sam and Talia run to the shed to help set up. They put up the dividing screens and draw the draperies between each of the six areas. Sue is back and scrambling around with Derek, opening up the cots and covering them with sanitary, clean bedding. The lighting is turned on, and Sam starts moving stainless steel medical carts out from behind the storage shelves. Then she instructs Talia on what needs placed on each one. Talia, who the family has come to like very well, goes to the next aisle over and retrieves bandaging while Sam gathers hypodermics and sewing needles and thread. Grandpa has gone to the house to instruct Hannah and the others to boil pots of water for them. Sterilization of any and all medical tools will be essential in keeping the risk of infections down. She's not sure what types of injuries they'll be treating tonight, but she is trying to be prepared for anything. She swings around and nearly runs Simon down.

"Oh, sorry, Simon!" she mumbles as she stoops to retrieve her dropped cargo.

"That was my fault, Sam," he blurts quickly and bends to help her.

"How's Paige?" she inquires in a rush of worry for his sister.

"She's mostly shaken up," he relays. "Don't think she needs stitches. But she does have a minor concussion, I'd say. Doc said the same thing. Reagan's getting her bandaged up."

"She'll be ok," Sam acknowledges again, reaffirming it in his mind. She even squeezes his hand gently. He doesn't offer her an answer but gives a half-hearted attempt at a nod followed by a morose grin. His blue eyes are troubled.

Simon grimaces and touches the side of her face delicately with his fingertips only. "I need to clean this and…"

Kelly comes into the shed a moment later to announce that their allies are arriving and they've brought four injured men.

"No, I'll live. This is nothing. Don't worry about me. It's gonna be a long night," she says as she works quickly, trying to distract Simon from his woes over his sister.

Simon helps her stand again once they've picked up her fallen items. He's holding onto her elbow, although she certainly doesn't need assistance.

"Sam, I really should treat those scrapes before they come piling in here with the wounded," he says.

"I said I'm fine," she dismisses. "Let's just get ready."

He nods even more reluctantly this time and pauses a long moment before turning away and leaving her. When she emerges with her metal cart on rolling wheels, Sam can see the changes that have taken place in the shed. It no longer looks like an empty pole building with shelving. The cots are in place, separated by curtains. Medical carts stand at the ready near each bed. Canisters of oxygen, most of which contain very sparse amounts, wait by the beds. Grandpa and Reagan are suited up in sterile gowns, their stethoscopes hanging around their necks. Reagan helps her into a similar get-up as Simon is securing his own latex gloves and mask. They are as fastidious as they can be about germs and the spreading of them since they've already been touched by such deadly, potential plague-like infections on the farm. She catches Simon's eyes above the rim of his mask. He's wearing his eye-glasses that make him look even more like a young professor, which is the nickname that the men like to call him. He's still wearing camouflaged green and black war paint on his face which is a bizarre combination with his surgical gown. Sam smiles at him before she pulls up her own mask. Even though his mouth is covered, Sam can tell that he does not return her smile but scowls instead.

Kelly comes into the shed again and announces, "Power's cut to the house. We're good to go."

Grandpa replies, "Good. We're going to need all the power we can get out here tonight."

When situations get rough, they power down the electric to the house to conserve as much as they can for the shed. They could possibly need to use heart-rate monitors, the ultrasound machine or the electric ventilator, all of which pull a huge amount of wattage.

"I'll help her to the house, Simon," Kelly says.

He's referring to Paige, who is fully awake. Unfortunately, she still seems disoriented and groggy. And no wonder. She'd taken quite the clubbing from that thug.

"Thanks, Kelly," Simon returns.

They need the room in the shed for treating wounded men. Paige will be more comfortable in the house where she can rest. Sam's also quite sure that Kelly will take Paige to the music room where Hannah can tend to and mother her. Hannah mothers everyone, whether they require her tender ministrations or not.

Sam can read the worry still there in Simon's voice and in the crinkled corners of his eyes. Kelly gives up trying to slip his arm around Paige, so he swoops her up into his arms and carries her from the building. If she wasn't so tall, Sam is pretty sure that even she could carry Paige. She's still very thin, although she has observed Simon trying to practically force feed his sister at meal times. Maybe it's just her height that makes her seem skinnier, too.

An engine draws closer and cuts. Shouting men outside is the next thing she hears. Simon has set aside his worry for his sister. She can see it in the grave look in his eyes. He's ready to treat the wounded men. He's back to business as usual.

The first man through the door is Roy from town, being assisted and half-carried by Derek. He's a very nice man. He lives in section four in Pleasant View. His leg wound looks serious, and he's gritting his teeth against the pain. The bottom of his faded green pants looks like the one leg has been re-dyed to a dark crimson. Reagan immediately jumps in and starts questioning him on his blood type while indicating that John should place him in the first cot on the left.

The next man looks even worse, if that's at all possible. Grandpa handles this situation with Talia acting as his nurse. The man has taken a gunshot wound to his stomach. It doesn't look good at all. He's pale, lifeless and being carried by Condo Paul.

The third man walks through the door of his own accord and has been shot in the shoulder. Derek shows him to the farthest cot in the rear of the room. He's had some field medic training in his lifetime, so Derek will be able to help that man until one of the doctors is available.

The last man is brought in by Kelly, who carries him in an identical, gentle mode of transport that he'd used with Paige. His eyes convey all they need to know.

"Come, Sam," Simon says to her.

She nods firmly, and they begin on the man who is moaning in pain. When he places him carefully onto the cot, Sam tries not to notice that the front of Kelly's clothing is covered in dark red blotches that match the man's. Kelly backs away, staring at his hands, also covered in the young man's blood.

Talia shouts frantically, "Where's Gavin? Where is he?"

Sam can hear Reagan talking to her, "He's coming. Just help Doc and stay calm, ok?"

Reagan's speech must subdue Talia because she quiets again and doesn't say anything more. Sam is too busy with their own patient to fret about Gavin, or Talia's worrying over him.

"Left side. High power caliber," Kelly says to her and Simon, explaining their patient's wound.

Simon nods with no expression and gets to it. The man on their hospital bed can't be more than twenty-five years old. She doesn't recognize him from town.

"Get me a bp, Sam," he orders as he cuts away the man's clothing.

She does so and reports the very low blood pressure to Simon, who doesn't even flinch. They ascertain that he's been shot twice. The first was through his side from the front, which Kelly had reported. The second shot entered his back, high and near his left shoulder blade.

The next few minutes fly by in a blur as she and Simon work together on the young man. She prays for him as Simon demands calmly and orders Kelly and her to do whatever he requires. He finishes cutting away the man's clothing. Kelly tips him slightly onto his side so that Simon can view the wound more critically.

"Came out here," Simon observes the man's side. "Good."

"Blood type is O positive," Sam says after the man tells her to get into his wallet to check since he's not sure. Then he gives out a shout of pain as Simon rolls him onto his back again.

"I can't breathe, Doc," the man says to Simon.

"Just relax... Mr.?" Sam says.

"Andy. My name's Andy," he wheezes in return.

Sam can hear Reagan on the other side of the dividing curtain barking an order to Bertie Reynolds, who has come into the shed. Their neighbor has helped out on occasion at their clinic. It's difficult for her to get away since she has a toddler and no other women in her house to help her out with her daughter. The men in her house stay twenty-four-seven busy with their dairy farm.

Their patient's color starts turning to a bluish gray, and he does seem to be having difficulty taking in a full breath. She's never seen this before. Sometimes they treat gunshot wounds at their clinic, but this is a first treating four at the same time. One time she'd had to witness a stabbing victim's multiple, gory wounds. He'd been stabbed by a jealous neighbor who'd suspected him of sleeping with his wife. The town's justice system had taken care of his punishment.

That man's stab wounds and lacerations had been the worst thing she'd seen, until now. She's never seen this many severely wounded people all piled into one small room before. A child's earache or a pregnant mother is nothing compared to this.

Simon comes around the side of the bed at lightning speed and yanks Sam a few feet away. Their patient struggles to breathe and gasps for air.

"He's drowning in his own blood, Sam," he says tightly so that nobody else will hear. "Get me a hose and a bottle of water, or a clean bucket or container with some water. Pour half of it out. And when you come back, stand right beside me, ok?"

Sam answers with a simple, "Yes."

She rushes to the rear of the building again and fetches a clear plastic hose and water bottle back to him. He's at the head of the bed, and Kelly is now holding down the man's shoulders. Simon injects a quick shot of lidocaine into the man's pectoral muscle.

"Quick, honey, give me a scalpel," he says quietly to her.

Sam slaps a metal blade from the tray firmly into his latex-gloved hand. They are standing shoulder to shoulder. She has no idea what he's going to do with the scalpel, though. And then she does fully understand, but wishes she didn't at all understand what he is about to do.

Simon pushes the point of the scalpel into the young man's chest muscle and then much deeper.

A commotion at the other end of the shed alerts her that the second truck has arrived. Shouting adds to the overall calamity. Someone is apparently very seriously injured because she hears Reagan calling out fast demands to the men as the sound of a truck skidding to a stop and spraying gravel comes through the thin metal walls.

"Tube," Simon calls for harshly as if he's said it more than once.

"Sorry," she mumbles.

Sam slaps it into his palm in the same manner. A soft touch doesn't belong in an operating room, or a post-apocalyptic makeshift medical center. She's learned these procedures from Grandpa. She'd been much less aggressive when she'd first started her nursing training with him years ago. It had led to instruments being dropped or fumbled and deemed immediately out of commission because of contamination.

Simon pushes the plastic tubing into the man's chest as Kelly holds the poor guy's shoulders down with his strong hands. She watches Kelly's eyes slide away to focus on something else. This is the most gruesome procedure she's ever witnessed. She doesn't dare faint or vomit or even look away. Simon needs her help.

"Easy, Andy," Simon reassures. "You'll be able to breathe a lot better in a moment, sir. Try to relax."

His only answer is another soft moan of pain or fear or something beyond Sam's comprehension. His breathing is so weak and diluted with a bubbling, raspy purr.

"Sam, bottle!" Simon grinds out impatiently.

She quickly hands him the bottle of water. She watches as Simon lowers it near the floor and sticks the other end of the tube in.

"Now, Kelly," Simon orders. "Get him onto his side now!"

As soon as Kelly does so, a steady stream of blood begins pumping out of the tube and down into the bottle. Simon quickly replaces the bottle with a small bucket that she hands him. Andy takes a deeper breath finally. The pressure is subsiding from his lungs now that the blood has stopped filling them. She's so thankful that Simon is calm and cool under pressure.

Grandpa is at their side in the next second. He gravely shakes his head at Kelly's cocked-head, quizzical expression. Grandpa is letting them know that his patient didn't make it. He pulls on another pair of clean latex gloves as Sam steps out of his way.

"Thoracotomy?" he inquires of Simon.

"Yes, sir," Simon replies as he continues to work on Andy. "His lungs were filling with blood from the bullet wound."

"Good job, son," Grandpa praises and places a hand soothingly on Simon's shoulder. "Let's see what else we've got here."

He's always so calm. Sam doesn't know how he does it. His patient has passed and here he's helping them with another without missing a beat. It's also the middle of the night. Sam feels dead on her feet as if the adrenaline of the gunfight against those men has hit its crash-point. But Grandpa is wide awake, alert as ever. His calm strength gives her a surge of fortitude deep down in her gut.

"Is Gavin here?" Sam inquires because she can't stop being worried about her new friend. He's so sweet and kind.

"Just worry about what we're doing, Samantha," Grandpa corrects her.

"Yes, sir," she murmurs, feeling well put in her place.

"This is going to be difficult, Simon," he says. "We need to treat that other wound, but he's lying on that side."

"Yes, sir," Simon replies knowingly.

"Kelly, we're going to need you to lay him back just slightly and maybe prop him just a bit. We've got to get that side wound stitched and now. He's losing too much blood," he says very quietly.

"Yes, sir," Kelly answers.

He gives his reply with the respect that's always in his voice when addressing Grandpa, Sam's noticed.

"Does anyone have Andrew's blood type? He's likely going to need a donor," Grandpa asks of this patient.

He must know this man from town, but Sam doesn't remember ever meeting him.

"O positive, sir," Sam relays.

"That's good. We'll have a donor then," he acknowledges.

He and Simon work diligently on Andy's side wound, each inspecting and sewing stitches and inspecting some more.

"We're going to need an ultrasound on those lungs, Simon," Grandpa tells them.

"I thought so, sir," Simon agrees. "We need to know where that other bullet is and if his lungs are clear."

"That's right," Grandpa says with praise. "Good job."

Everything is a teachable moment to Grandpa. He's a huge believer, in biblical proportions, of furthering one's knowledge of medicine. They are always in learning mode. Not a day goes by that he doesn't work with Simon, teaching him new things, new techniques and passing on pearls of his medical wisdom. They've grown so close over the years.

Their fingers work swift and dexterously stitching the wounds.

"Cauterizer," Grandpa asks for.

"Yes, sir," Sam says as she places the wand in his hand.

Reagan's shout of anger interrupts them, "Damn it!"

Something is wrong over there. Sam's heart skips a beat and then begins pounding with fear.

"I need help!" she also calls out.

"Simon and Samantha, go now," Grandpa directs. "I've got this now. Kelly, stay here and assist."

"Yes, sir!" they all regurgitate like a well-trained army.

When they get to the next station over, John and Reagan are working on Gavin. Apparently John finally found him. Blood is everywhere. He's barely cognizant. She and Simon rip off their blood-soaked gloves and pull on fresh pairs so as not to spread blood-borne pathogens from patient to patient.

Reagan immediately gives an abridged summary of his injuries. "John said he was hit by a .9 mill round. I'd say hollow point from the amount of damage. We've got internal bleeding."

Gavin's wound is deep, to his mid-section, and still spilling copious amounts of blood out of it in a slick trickle down his side where it plops in red blobs onto the cot. Reagan is digging into the open wound, causing Gavin to cry out in pain.

"Hit him with morph, Simon," she orders. "Sam, clamp this."

She's indicating toward a bleeding artery with a pair of surgical scissors. Sam grabs a hemostatic clamp from the tray near Reagan's elbow and pinches the bleeder. They work a moment longer when Reagan declares that he's going to need surgery.

They are very ill-equipped for an actual surgery, the sterility of the room being the most lacking, but they have no choice in the matter.

"Run me an IV, Sam," Simon requests as he assists Reagan.

"Yes, sir," she answers and starts unfolding the tubing and bag of saline.

It takes her a moment to get the stick in his arm because he keeps writhing in pain, even though John is doing his best to hold him down. She tapes it down and starts the drip going at a steady rate. Reagan can administer a local anesthesia to block the pain and hopefully put him into a twilight state of being instead of fully awake. The overhead lights flicker, and that's when their real problems start.

Sam's eyes jump to John's. The lights flicker again and go out completely.

"Damn it, somebody get the genny running," Reagan shouts. "Sam, load that anesthesia. Two mill, tiny amounts at a time, kid."

John and Kelly sprint out the door to the rear of the shed. Sam can hear them rifling and shuffling around in the tiny, attached shed where the generator is kept as she sorts with a flashlight through the small refrigerator where pain medicine and anesthesia is stored. She searches for the right one. There are only a few bottles left of what they need, but Sam grabs the first one, Naropin.

Kelly and John are still creating quite a racket getting the generator going. They rarely use it, but the solar power is not built to supply the draw of machines like cardiac heart monitors, ultrasounds and cauterizing tools. The solar power can handle light bulbs, the hot water tanks in the house and minor appliances. Apparently spotlighting those men has drained their solar power.

Simon holds a weak flashlight so that Reagan can work. Sam shakes the tiny glass bottle and inserts a needle into the rubber stopper. She draws back enough to get the job done of numbing Gavin before Reagan digs around on his insides. Then she administers the dose into his IV. She hands another stick loaded with lidocaine to Reagan, who administers a dose to three different sites around the wound. Then she shoots him two more times inside of it. Sam and Simon hold flashlights for Reagan.

Her mentor swears under her breath a moment before the lighting comes back on. The low hum of the generator running at full blast is coming from the rear wall of the building. Reagan swears again, gaining Sam's attention.

"Simon, clamp," Reagan says.

"I see it," he answers and squeezes a bleeding section closed.

"Sam," is all he says to her.

She knows what he needs. She takes over holding the clamp tightly while he quickly sews the leaking artery closed.

Reagan works at a feverish pace on the other side of the small cot. She has managed to cauterize two areas and sew another. She's the fastest stitch maker in the family. Simon is much slower and more dedicated to precision than Reagan. She works on patients like she moves: fast. Reagan only knows one speed.

"We're losing him," she mutters to Simon.

Sam looks toward the heartbeat monitor, which has slowed considerably. The anesthesia may have done some of this, but he's lost too much blood. They don't keep a supply on hand like a hospital would have in the past. This isn't even a hospital. It's a pole barn shed with a cement floor out in the middle of nowhere on a farm. If Gavin needs blood, or any others, one of the family will have to donate. Then the monitor makes that tell-tale, solid beep, letting them know that it cannot detect a heartbeat anymore.

They begin CPR on Gavin. Sam performs chest compressions as Simon blows into the man's mouth. His heart has stopped, likely from blood loss and internal bleeding and damage. They continue to work on him while Reagan sews his internal wounds closed. Sam risks a peek and sees that most of the bleeders have been stitched and that blood no longer splatters onto the bedding. Unfortunately, Simon isn't able to get his heart started again. Reagan just about has his wound sewn shut. They work longer, even though it's been almost a full minute that he's stopped breathing. Reagan injects something through a syringe into Gavin's IV line. Sam believes it is likely adrenaline or something similar to stimulate his heart. She gently pushes Sam to the side and takes over the chest compressions.

"Oh my God," is being repeatedly whispered behind them.

Sam turns to look and is horrified that Talia is standing nearby watching her friend die. She quickly strips her gloves, goes to her and takes the other woman's hands into her own. Grandpa has now joined the melee. The three of them work diligently for another few minutes until Grandpa finally calls it. Talia collapses against her in a weak ball of tears and nerves. John comes over and escorts Sam's fragile new friend from the building. Reagan places both hands on the top of her head and holds them there in an act of frustration and helplessness. She is swearing prolifically and kicks the wall of the shed with the bottom of her red Converse clad foot. Simon is just standing there looking at his own hands and shaking his head in confusion.

Grandpa lays a hand on his arm. Then he pulls a sheet over the body and goes back to his other patient, Andy. Reagan joins him, but Simon goes to work on someone else needing medical care. Sam follows him, dons another pair of gloves and gets right into administering a pain-blocking shot so that Simon can stitch a man's leg wound closed. This time both of their hands shake slightly after the unsettling loss of Gavin, but they get the man's shoulder wound sewn and shut, sanitized and covered.

It is after four a.m. when they finish, remove Gavin's body for burial later when the sun rises, and sanitize the med shed. Simon's patient also dies. Andy's lungs filled with blood again, and Grandpa couldn't get the bullet removed.

The other man who'd been transported in the second truck had also passed, but at least it hadn't happened on the farm but on the ride there. The bodies will be taken to their families, if they have any, in town so that they can bury their loved ones where they would want them. The Reynolds brothers volunteer to do it. Five men have lost their lives tonight on a raid that was so well planned and for which they were prepared. It reminds Sam of how fragile life still is in this mad world. If the McClanes can be duped and overrun, everyone can be.

Mopping up and cleaning the shed, wiping all of the tainted surfaces, and replacing sullied bed linens has also taken a long time. They've all worked together, everyone but Kelly, who they'd sent inside to be with Hannah. Sue had come out to report that Hannie was out of her mind worrying about Kelly, even though they'd told her that he was fine. No wonder. She's been through so much. They all have.

Some of the injured men go home to their families, although Grandpa had offered them to stay in the med shed. Two men stay because they don't have much of a choice. The chance of their wounds infecting or having complications was too great for them to leave. Derek and Kelly take watch patrols for the remaining hours of the night. She highly doubts that John is going to go in and crash. They'll all be too edgy to find any sleep with what's left of this night. She has no idea what they will do with the dead bodies of the bad men, but Sam's also not sure she wants to know. One thing she is sure of is that they will never allow them to be buried on this farm.

Grandpa and Reagan will stay in the shed with the remaining patients. Reagan is angry and withdrawn. She takes the loss of patients hard and usually stays morose and removed from the family for a few days. John will be the only to bring her out of it. Everyone takes the time to scrub, grab fast showers and sanitize. Their hospital style surgical gowns will be boiled when the sun comes up.

Sam stands under the steaming hot water of the second-floor shower, letting the water soothe and relax her- if that is even possible. She weeps quietly so as not to alert anyone. Everyone is dealing with their own fair amount of stress right now. Too many lives were taken tonight. Some were friends, some were men from town who had families, and some were just lascivious people bent on doing horrible things to others. She would never wish them dead, though. But she's also smart enough to reason out the necessity of killing them or becoming their victims. She just wishes that they'd never found their farm and that she hadn't had to participate in their killings.

After rinsing her hair and tenderly washing her scrapes and scratches on her face, she gets out of the shower, trying to save as much hot water for everyone else that she can, especially since the power in the main house had been out for a few hours. She slips into her bedroom, trying her best to be as noiseless as possible. Pulling on clean clothing feels like a luxury. Sam grabs black sweatpants and an old, worn out baseball style, long-sleeved t-shirt that used to belong to her older brother. It helps her remember him. It provides comfort as if he is with her and embracing her in his strong, sure arms. It's no less painful remembering him, but she knows she must. Someday if she ever has children of her own and the country heals itself, she'd like to tell her children stories of her real family, the family that had been ripped away from her and murdered in their horse barn. However, in the wee hours of this ghoulish night, his shirt brings her comfort.

The sound of the shower running again lets her know that someone else is using the second-floor bathroom. She lights her hurricane lamp and flicks off the light switch. They do this most times in the evening to conserve solar power. There are simply too many people living on the farm to live in electricity excess as if it will simply be there forever. She works the towel on her damp hair, trying to remove the moisture. So that it doesn't soak her shirt, she pulls it into a ponytail when she's done. Whoever is using the shower, has finished and gone, likely John or Reagan.

She sits on her window ledge and looks out at the moon. In a few hours, the sun will rise on the horizon as if nothing dark and menacing had taken place only hours before. This has been a macabre night, indeed. So much death and morbidity have touched their family lately that it's hard not to feel swallowed whole by the darkness. She's glad that Paige is probably fast asleep somewhere. Tomorrow, hearing of her friend Gavin's death will be difficult.

A shadow moving near the horse barn catches her attention. Someone is standing there with their shoulder leaning against the wall. The slumped posture is that of someone who is filled with remorse and defeat. A reflection hits their eyeglasses from the moonlight. It's Simon. She must to go to him. She cannot allow her best friend to feel this way.

She wants to catch him before he heads out to his cabin where Paige will be staying most nights. Sam can understand. If her brother was still alive, she'd want to sleep out in the cabin with him, too. She grabs a hoodie and runs. When she gets to the barn, he's gone. However, she spots his lantern swinging as he walks between the horse and cattle barns on the path toward his cabin. Sam hadn't brought her own lantern, so it's difficult to catch him.

"Simon," she whispers in the near dark.

He immediately stops and turns toward her. They meet in the middle where Sam notices that his hair is still damp, too. He was probably the one in the shower. He and Cory don't have a full working shower in their cabin yet. It was on their to-do list before Cory left.

"What are you doing out here?" he asks. "You could've fallen. Let me take you back to the house, Sam. You're going to get sick with your hair wet like that."

She just shakes her head. "Are you all right?"

"Yeah, I'm..."

"Simon, talk to me," she interrupts and places a hand on his sinewy forearm. She tries not to flinch at his frown. He doesn't answer but stands there a moment and then regards the heavens. She knows he won't break his cool reserve to let his feelings loose and discuss them with her. "Come with me."

"Where?"

"Just come," she softly demands and takes his hand, leading him to the cattle barn's hay loft.

Sam climbs the stairs ahead of him while he holds the lantern. When they get to the top, she sets the lantern on an ancient, wooden trunk. The little kids in the family like to play up here a lot. She even spies a Barbie doll and a small stack of marbles laying near the trunk.

"Sit," she says and takes her own seat on a hay bale. He just stands there, so she tugs his hand until he sits beside her. "Is Paige in the cabin?"

He shakes his head and bites his lower lip. "No, she's still in Grandpa's old room."

Grandpa sleeps most nights in his office at the other end of the big house. She knows it's just too difficult sleeping in the room that he'd shared for decades with his wife. Sam can't even imagine the grief he must feel.

"Does she know?" Sam asks.

"No, she's sleeping," he returns. "Reagan gave her some painkiller for her headache. She's out."

"That's what I figured," Sam says with a nod.

He removes his glasses and rubs his eyes tiredly. Talia had taken it so hard, so they know that Paige will, too, that their friend and travel mate for so long is dead. Gavin is dead. Just thinking the words is painful.

"I don't know how I'm going to tell her, Sam," he confesses softly. "They were really close. She's going to be devastated."

"You just do," she says firmly, but quietly. "That's how you tell her. You just have to be honest and break it as soon as she awakens. It's not going to make it easier on her if you try to hide it."

He shakes his head but not because he disagrees. "It shouldn't have happened. John said that he found him back behind the cattle barn."

"How'd he get back there? He was supposed to be at the front of the house."

"He told John that he chased a man down that he saw sneak away from the pack. He was afraid the guy was gonna burn down the barns because he had a Molotov cocktail. He shot him, but the guy shot Gavin first. He tried to get back to the house but couldn't."

"Oh, that's so terrible. I feel so bad for him. He was out there hurt with nobody to help. He saved our barns. He did a very heroic thing."

"Yes, he did. But it shouldn't have happened. He shouldn't have been out there," Simon says on a scowl.

"It did, and somehow we just have to go on from here," she says, trying to soothe him. "We always do. We fight and we try to survive. That's what we do. That's all there is now, Simon. All we have is each other, and we have to hold on to that."

His eyes meet hers, and Sam tears up. She squeezes his hand.

"I'm sick of it!" he exclaims angrily.

This surprises Sam that he would become angry. He's so even-keeled and tempered. They even tease him sometimes for his mild-mannered ways.

"I'm sick of all of it. I'm sick of everyone dying," he rants with venom.

"We're all here, Simon. We're safe and…"

He interjects with a crude laugh of hypocrisy. "Safe? Are you kidding? My sister was almost killed tonight. Gavin *was* killed. We lost men. We could've lost this farm…"

"But we didn't…"

He stands and jerks his hand away from her. Sam follows him to the hay window where the moonlight spills in.

"We could've! Don't you get it?" he asks with acidity and swipes a hand through his unruly auburn hair. "People were killed. People from our own damn farm were killed…"

He never swears. She knows now how deeply he is troubled by tonight's events.

"It's not your fault, Simon," she tries and then rubs his arm, which causes him to yank back. "Is that what this is about? You think the men in the shed died because of you? Come on, Simon. That's not fair. You know how this works…"

"No! I mean, yes, I'm upset about that, but that's not all," he says as he turns to face her.

His bright blue eyes dance with agitation and excitement.

"Your sister?" she inquires. "She's going to be just fine, Simon. Don't worry so hard. You're going to make yourself sick over it. She's alive and that's all that matters."

"Damn it, Sam," he swears again. "No! That's not what I'm upset about. I was upset, sick even, when I saw from a distance that Paige was being held at gunpoint. But that's not what made me feel a violent rage, a helpless rage so white hot that I thought I was going to have a heart attack."

"The farm? Is that it? It's secure again, Simon," she implores and places a hand on his bare chest. He must've forgotten a clean shirt because he only wears a blue-jean jacket with nothing under it. "The farm is safe. Everyone is safe again."

"You!" he nearly shouts and then groans.

The only reason he doesn't shout his answer is because he partially says it through his gritted teeth in a seething rage.

Sam croaks out a confused, "What?"

Tears stream down her cheeks. Why is he angry with her? He places his hands on either side of her face, cradling gently. He scowls deeply as he gazes at her scratches. She doesn't dare confess that her tears are making them burn.

"Don't cry," he begs brokenly. "Damn it, don't cry. I didn't mean to yell."

She'd like to laugh. Reagan yells. Kelly yells. Cory downright bellows. But Simon doesn't yell. He's much too in control and refined for something so common.

"I don't understand," she says on a hiccup.

"Sam, I was worried about *you*," he admits softly. "Not the farm, not everyone on it, not even Paige as much. Just you. I was worried about you."

Sam flings herself against his bare chest and cries in earnest. She'd been just as distressed over him. Sometimes she feels like Simon is the only person she has left. She has the McClane family, but she and Simon have been through more than any of them could ever understand. The tragic events of their pasts have bonded them forever. He just stands there and strokes her damp head.

"I know, Simon," she admits. "Me, too. You're my best friend. You're the only family I have now."

He pulls back and frowns at her as if he's not quite sure of something.

"You have family..."

Sam stops him, "Not like you. You're all I have left, Simon."

He kisses her forehead gently, and they resume their hug. She feels him nodding against her, his chin to her forehead.

"Yes, I know," he says softly, the way he normally speaks.

"Stay up here with me tonight, Simon," she suggests and pulls him toward the messy hay piles. She pulls two dusty horse blankets from one of the trunks. "Please."

"I don't think that's a good idea," he says with a shake of his head to decline. "If anyone were to find out, they'd not like that,

Sam. The guys would not approve. Grandpa would definitely not approve."

"Nobody will know. Everyone's exhausted and already in bed or on patrols. I don't want to be alone," she returns with a sad smile.

"That's not a very appropriate thing to do, Sam," he says on a sad grimace.

"Just one night? Nobody will find out. It'll be just like we used to do," she reminds him of the times when they'd sneak off to sleep in the barns, just the two of them.

"We're not kids anymore, Sam," he berates and tightens the line of his mouth.

"Please?" she pleads and holds out her hand to him. "I'm afraid to be alone."

Simon nods reluctantly, and they lie in the hay together after he extinguishes the lantern. She rests her head on his shoulder, and he wraps an arm around her to keep her warm.

They talk for a short time longer until she is sure that she's made him feel a bit better. They talk until neither of them can stay awake. Sam falls asleep curled up against the one person who means more than anything in the world to her. He's the one person she can never lose. She knows that he thinks of her like a little sister, just like Cory does. But Sam has been in love with Simon since that day he'd tried to hide her away from the men and women who would and did mean her harm. He was a boy back then, but she'd seen such a nobility in him, such a deep-seated honor that she'd never seen in another human being. Now he is a man of even stronger conviction. And if someday he chooses to be with someone else, then she still hopes he'll always remain her best friend. He'll always be her knight in shining armor, the man who'd stolen her young heart and kept it, even if he never knows it.

Chapter Twenty-four
Simon

A few hours later after the sun has started to rise, Simon dislodges his arm out from underneath Sam's head. He covers her with his jacket and the blanket, grabs his holster and pistol and leaves. Simon doesn't want to be lying in the hay in the barn with her when she awakens all warm and fresh and sweet-smelling and tousled. He creeps down the stairs to the lower level. There is much to do and no time for lazing about in the hay with a dark-haired angel with fair skin and soft curves.

He jogs to his cabin, retrieves his work-boots and a t-shirt, an old one that he doesn't mind getting ruined. He isn't worried about the chill hanging in the air. There is a lot of back-breaking work awaiting him. When he returns to the barnyard, Kelly, Derek and John are already loading dead bodies into the enemies' pick-up trucks. Simon jumps right in to help.

"Get any intel on the group from the survivor?" Simon asks of John as he grabs a dead man's feet while John hefts his shoulders.

"Nope," John returns. "Not a thing. He said they were holed up in that Target, and he had no idea where the ones that got away would go next. Said they didn't have anywhere else to go."

Simon nods with the same frustration that John feels as they toss the body into the bed of the truck to join four others there. This is grisly work, but it must get done. These men will not be afforded a burial on the McClane farm.

"My sister awake yet?" he asks next.

"Not that I know of. I think we're the only ones up," John says. "Well, Doc's up, but he's the only one from the house up as far as I know. He's on the front porch smoking his pipe. I think he's upset about last night."

"That's understandable," Simon agrees with a nod. "It should've never happened. Man, we got played."

John's mouth sets in a tight line and he nods with anger. The men have obviously been working most of the night. Simon helps load the last ten bodies with John and Kelly's help. Then Kelly and Derek hop into the cab of the rusted red pick-up. Simon is left with the expensive, jazzed-up and flashy silver Dodge Ram. John comes over to the window, which is already rolled down.

"This truck didn't have the keys in the ignition. We're not picking their pockets to find them, either. Remember how to hot-wire one?" he asks.

"Yes, sir," Simon answers.

"Alrighty then. I'm taking Doc's truck. I'll follow you guys. We won't be bringing back anything of theirs other than the gas," he explains before jogging away.

Simon and Cory were taught everything that the Rangers know, including skills that are nefarious like hot-wiring cars, breaking into buildings, picking locks and such. Within a few minutes, he has the truck's engine roaring to life, and they are heading out on the oil well road in formation. They drive about five miles from the farm on one of the main roads and then back into the town where the Target raid had occurred. When the bodies are dumped, they siphon the gas and leave the vehicles on the side of the road. They travel home to the farm in Doc's pick-up truck, and Simon rides in the bed with Kelly.

"How'd they know where we were?" Simon asks. "How'd they find the farm?"

"Shithead said they found out from an old man in town. Beat him to death to get it out of him. We don't know who it was yet, but I'm sure that we will by the end of the day. You and John are going to town later. Gotta check in with the townspeople and Paul, make sure they did all right through the night."

Simon knows with absolute certainty that Shithead is the man who'd survived. He doesn't envy the methods that the Rangers would've employed to pry information from that prick. He is sorrier than he can even express that an older man in town gave his life in such a violent manner to these bastards, though. Whoever it was had certainly not deserved such abuse.

"Yes, sir," Simon answers. "You'll be staying at the farm?"

Kelly gives him a nod. "Yeah, Hannah can't take me being away again so soon. She's not doing so great."

Hearing this makes Simon feel like crap. All he can do is give Kelly a tight nod of understanding. Nobody likes the women to be in the doldrums, especially not fair Hannah. She's too delicate for this wretched, disgusting world.

When they get back to the farm, the men change their soiled shirts before being around the family or the people in town. None of the family needs to see blotches of other men's blood on their clothing. It certainly won't help the frightened people in town to see them in a poor state, either.

They meet in the kitchen, not bothering to sit as Sue shovels food onto their plates. The four of them eat a fast meal for the long day ahead of them. None of them have slept, but this was part of Simon's conditioning during the past four years of training. John and Kelly had pushed Cory and him to and way beyond their physical and mental limits, putting them through the same training they'd had in the Army. They called it "smoking" them. Simon used to joke that they were killing them, not smoking them. They'd known how far they could push them, though. Simon hadn't known at the time. Neither had Cory. Simon wasn't in good shape like Cory because he hadn't played high school sports. Simon had belonged to the chess club. They'd thought that they were literally going to die sometimes. When their arms were like rubber, John demanded another hundred push-ups. When their legs were like cement columns, Kelly ordered three more miles of running. When they were physically and mentally drained, Derek took them out and taught them how to hot-wire vehicles and how to go on no sleep for days on end. And finally after three days with no sleep, John had taken them to Clarksville in the Hummer and had left them with nothing but a compass and their rifles. Then he'd left. It was a terrifying moment for them both, but they'd made it. He and Cory made it out of the city alive but not without problems from a small group of creeps. Then they had managed to make it home in two days' time on foot. They'd hunted for their food. They'd scouted for and found water. They'd traversed the treacherous back country of Tennessee the whole twenty mile trek back to the farm where they'd been greeted with another hundred push-ups. The men had all three laughed at Simon and Cory's hardships many times and simply told them to "Ranger up." At first he hadn't understood the saying, but then Simon had finally got it. He understood why they pushed and demanded and then demanded more. It's what has made them the survivors they are today. He's thankful for what the men have turned him into, even though sometimes he doesn't like doing what he does to survive. He only wishes he'd known one tenth of it back when he'd first found Samantha hiding in a closet.

Reagan stumbles sleepily into the kitchen and says to her sister, "Kids still out?"

Her frizzy curls are standing on end, and she wears a black tank top and matching shorts. On one foot is a black sock. The other is missing, but she seems oblivious.

"Yes, thank goodness," Sue answers. "I'm letting everyone sleep in."

Simon is trying to shovel his biscuit smothered in sausage gravy into his face as fast as he can so that he and John can leave for town. Reagan plops into an island chair. Sue tries to place a plate of food in front of her, but Reagan simply grimaces, shakes her head and pushes it back.

"Babe, you should eat something. You know you lost some weight being sick. I don't think you've gained any of it back," John advises and lays a hand on the back of his wife's head.

"My stomach's sick from stress and not getting any sleep," she returns, takes his hand from her head and presses a kiss to the back of it. "I'm not sick. I'll eat later today."

John scowls but concedes to his wife's wishes, as he usually does. As Simon regards Reagan, he can tell that she doesn't feel well because she is pale, which is unlike Reagan's usual coloring.

"Think I'm gonna ride over later and check on Chet. That gunshot wound could infect. I just want to be cautious with it," she tells John with sad eyes.

"Ok, just take Kelly or Derek," he says, the lines near the corners of his eyes deepening with concern.

"Got it," she answers and shoots him a gentle smile.

Her husband pulls her forward by placing his hand to the back of her head. He presses a hard kiss to her forehead. Whatever unspoken communication they have, Simon isn't privy to it, but Reagan gives John a quick nod.

"We're gonna have to repair that porch," Derek says as Doc enters the kitchen.

"Yes, we can get right on that, Derek," Doc adds. "There should be plenty of wood around here or we can mill some trees and seal the fresh wood with some stain if need be."

Sam comes in the back door, her feet bare, her hair still with blades of straw and hay poking out of it, her cheeks pink from just waking.

"Hey, kid," Kelly greets her jovially. "Where you been?"

Sam's eyes dart to Simon, but she says, "Oh, just out for a walk… in the barn… you know, checking on the horses."

Kelly considers her answer with suspicious eyes but says, "Ok, just don't go out without your gun anymore. All right?"

"Yeah, sorry," she mumbles.

She comes over to Simon and stands right beside him, then wraps her arm around his back. Nobody even acknowledges it. This is the way Sam always behaves. She's always been his tiny shadow. Em had shadowed Cory, and Sam has always clung onto him. Sometimes when things get heavy like their current situation, she clings on literally.

"I'm off to check on Hannah, and then I'll come out to help, Derek," Kelly says to the room and Derek, in particular.

"Cool," Derek replies. "Take your time, brother. The work's not going anywhere. It never does. We have some burying to do. We'll work on that grave-site while you guys are gone. We'll wait for you to get back to hold a service."

When Kelly leaves the room, Derek asks his wife, "Hannie ok? It's not like her to sleep in."

"I checked on her already. She's just tired, scared, kind of traumatized, you know? Talia, too. She's still asleep downstairs with the kids," Sue answers.

Derek nods. Simon looks away. He feels an enormous amount of guilt over the attack on the farm. It's completely unjustified, but he feels it all the same.

"Let's roll," John says quietly to him.

He also seems like he wants to get out of the house, out of the kitchen and away from the tragedy that happened last night.

"I'll be right there," Simon tells John, who nods. "Gotta take care of something first. Gimme' five minutes?"

John nods and leaves.

Sam grabs his arm, "Wait! Where are you going?"

Simon lays a hand over hers, "I'll be back soon, Sam. Don't worry. I'm just going with John to check on the people in town. Stay close to the house, ok?"

She frowns hard before throwing her arms around his middle. Simon returns it but with much less passion.

"Be careful," she beseeches.

"We will. *You* be careful while I'm gone," he orders firmly. "No riding or going out in the woods. Remember, some of them got away. They could still be close. Stay near the house. Just help with the kids or something today."

When she pulls back and nods vigorously, Sam also looks up into his eyes. He lays a hand against her soft, unscraped cheek for just a moment. Simon swallows the lump of guilt in his throat he always feels around Sam. Today it has elevated to epic proportions. He steps quickly away and leaves the kitchen. He goes to the back of the house where Doc's bedroom is located and where his sister should still be.

He enters without knocking only to find his sister in the bathroom. Simon sits on the unmade, still warm bed to wait for her. A moment later she emerges, still rumpled from sleep and clearly exhausted. He's glad she is staying in the house. She's wearing the same dirty clothes from last night. Doc will probably check her as soon as she goes to the kitchen. Simon is worried about his sister's concussion and head injury.

"Hey," she says sleepily. "What's going on?"

Simon decides to adhere to Sam's advice and get straight to it.

"Sit," he orders softly and pats the bed. His sister does as he says. There are dark purple circles under her light blue eyes. Her red hair is a tangled bird's nest around her head. The white bandaging on the side of her head makes him cringe.

"I need to tell you something," he says and takes her hand. Her eyes jump nervously to his. "Your friend didn't make it, sis."

She inhales sharply and squirms on her bottom, "What? What do you mean? Gavin?"

Simon nods and proceeds to tell her what happened to her trusted companion. She cries, turns into a ball of mush in his arms. He knew she'd take it hard.

"I didn't want to leave without telling you," Simon acknowledges. "I wanted you to hear it from me and not someone in the family."

This doesn't seem to make a difference because she sobs quietly against him. A few minutes later a soft knocking at the door alerts them. Sam is standing there.

"Go, Simon," Sam offers. "I'll stay here with her."

"Go where?" Paige asks and squeezes his hand almost painfully.

"Just checking on the people in our town. I'll be back real soon, ok?" he says to his darling, red-nosed, puffy-eyed sister. She's a mess of tears and anguish.

Sam crosses the room and sits on Paige's other side. She gives Simon a nod. He feels reluctant to leave but knows he must. He lightly squeezes Paige's bony hand again, nods with appreciation to Sam and leaves.

He heads out of the kitchen, following John's path to the Hummer. He knows before he even gets there that this isn't just a check-on-the-townsfolk kind of run. A bullet-proof vest and weapons are waiting for him on his seat. He pulls it on and zips it, slaps down the Velcro patches. Then he jams a full mag into his rifle and fastens his holstered sidearm onto his hip. His K-Bar gets strapped to his ankle. Apparently John had placed all of their weapons on the seat. He's geared up and ready to go, too, as he climbs in behind the wheel. Simon consults his watch. It's not even seven a.m. yet.

As they pass their neighbors' farms and turn left onto the county road, Simon asks, "Got any ideas?"

"I don't know, man," John answers. "They could be just about anywhere, but most people don't go too far. They're gonna need provisions, food, weapons, supplies. They could have relatives nearby. Who knows? We'll head over to that town again. Then we'll come back to Pleasant View to question people, see if they heard or know anything."

"Yes, sir," Simon replies.

"We need to offer assistance with the man that was killed for information about the farm. It's only right we bury him if the townspeople haven't yet."

Simon says on a nod, "Right. I feel bad that happened."

"Everything ok with Sam?" John asks a few minutes later as he navigates the Hummer around an abandoned motor-home on the road.

"Yes, she's fine," he says, looking out his window.

"Was she pretty shook up?" John inquires.

"Yeah, yes, she was," Simon concurs and shifts uncomfortably in his seat.

"She's a tough kid. I think she took out a few of those punks last night," John says.

"I don't know. Probably. I didn't ask her," Simon responds without looking directly at John.

"Well, you two slept in the barn loft last night," John slides in slyly. "What were you doing if you weren't talking?"

Simon's head whips to the side to look at his friend and big brother.

"I…I…"

"Relax," John says with a chuckle. "I know you'd never do anything wrong by her, Simon. I was just messin' with you."

"Oh," Simon says on an expelled breath. "Sorry. I didn't want to stay out there, but she didn't want to be alone. She was upset."

John nods and says, "I'd be more surprised if she wasn't upset. It's cool. I was just giving you a hard time. Sam's close with you. It's understandable that she'd want to be with you and not anyone else. She relies on you."

"I know," Simon blurts and shakes his head. "I wish she wouldn't. Heck, look how last night went."

John regards him with a frown, "What's that supposed to mean?"

"It means she could've been killed. My sister could've, too. It's bad enough that I have to look after Paige, but not Sam, too. That's what it means. She'd do better to find another protector."

"I disagree, Simon," John tells him and pulls over to a curb.

John pulls out his .45 Kimber and checks the mag before jamming it back into its holster. Then he looks at Simon before turning off the Hummer.

"There's nothing wrong with you being Sam's protector," he punches Simon's shoulder. "You're the best man for the job, Simon. You've had all the training we could give you. Plus, Sam's a tough kid. She's good with a knife, and she's small and fast, too. She's also a good shot, but she's probably always gonna need someone to look after her. She's innocent and frail sometimes, too, which can be dangerous. She needs you to set her on the right path. You'll do fine by her. I reckon you always will."

Simon has to look away.

"We might have to work with your sister, though," he adds with a chuckle. "She needs some practice on tactical maneuvers and weapons."

Simon grins and turns back to John. "Yeah, I know. She's a fast runner, but not faster than a bullet. I'll start working with her soon, when we have some downtime."

John nods and gives him a smile. "Good shooting last night, by the way."

Simon doesn't want to accept his praise because it feels wrong to do so since people were killed on their team and in their town. He mumbles a quick, "Thanks."

John nods, pockets the keys, and they move out. John is an easy man to be around. He's a man's man. He's quiet when the situation calls for it. He's fatherly when Simon needs it. He's a friend to him all of the time.

Together they do a fast sweep of the small town surrounding the Target's direct vicinity. They work as a team for a few hours checking buildings, alleyways and houses. They come up with nothing. There are very few people even still living in Coopertown. This town has not fared as well as Pleasant View. There are no gated or fenced off areas, no armed guards to protect the citizens. It's a ghost town with the exception of the recently destroyed Target city. That's empty, too. John and he torch it after they ascertain that there is nobody in it and not much worth salvaging there. They spend another forty minutes out and then head back. There is much to do at the farm. They'll likely come out again tonight. Sometimes rats move around at night. They'll be easier to find in the dark scurrying around and inflicting pain on more people.

They bury Gavin; Doc says some kind words, as do Talia and Paige. The family is unusually quiet as they go about their chores and tasks. Nobody is even talking and chatting like normal. The cleaning up process is finished near dinner time, so Simon decides to do some reloading in the back of the med shed in the arsenal and wait to be called. He knows that a lot of ammo was expended last night and should be replaced as soon as possible.

Simon drags the padded stool over to the pine reloading bench made from salvaged wood and takes a seat. His rifle and shotgun also need to be cleaned, so he'll run a cleaning rod down the barrels of both and oil them down. The other men sometimes bring their weapons to him for cleaning, but today they will likely forego the cleaning until things settle down. He's only a few minutes into reloading shotgun shells, measuring out the correct grain count and setting the primers when Paige comes into the shed.

He pulls a stool over for his tall sister.

"Dr. McClane just checked me again," she states.

"Oh, good," he says.

"It's not necessary," she complains lightly. "I'm fine. I wasn't shot or anything. I just got nogged."

"Concussions are very serious, sis," he explains. "They are even more serious now that we don't have adequate medical care or a facility with a CAT scan. That bastard knocked you out cold."

Her brow furrows as she sits and changes the subject, "What are you doing?"

"Reloading ammo," Simon answers and starts again. "It's important to keep our ammo stocked as full as possible. We blew through quite a lot last night, so..."

"Yeah, this is really, really important. We need to help keep this place safe. I'll do whatever I can to help keep it safe. This is gonna be our home, right? Can I help you with this?" she asks.

Simon notices that her eyes are puffy and bloodshot from crying. There are still dark rings beneath them. She needs something to do to take her mind off of the loss of Gavin. She has finally showered and changed out of last night's soiled clothing. Her hair is pulled back into a tight bun at the base of her neck and is still damp. He also notices her change in attitude about leaving the farm or fleeing it when bad things happen. It sets his heart at ease that she is bonding to the McClane family and their farm. He has no desire to leave the farm, but he'd never let his sister leave it without him.

"Sure, you can help," he allows. "How 'bout you hand me that box of primers, and I'll show you how to load shotgun shells?"

"Hand you the what?"

Simon grins and proceeds to explain primers, the smokeless powder, the shells and the equipment. It takes a while, but she catches on and actually helps, even if she calls the shotgun shells 'bullet thingys.' He lets it slide. Now is not the time to correct her. She's just lost her friend. If hanging out with him in the reloading shed helps to relieve a little of her anxiety and take her mind off of the events of last night, then so be it.

They work for a few hours while chatting about anything but the previous evening or her friend's death before heading out and locking the door. On the way to the house for dinner with the family, Paige holds his hand in hers. If holding his sister's hand will make her feel just a smidgen better and offer her comfort, Simon's ok with that, too.

Chapter Twenty-five
Paige

"Would you like some help?" she asks Hannah, who is toiling away in the kitchen while the others try to find their own tasks to keep them busy until the men return for dinner later. Paige has spent part of her day in Simon's cabin cleaning and organizing it. She could tell that two young men had lived there for the last two years. It was either clean it or burn it.

Kelly and Simon are working on something out at the med shed, but Derek and John are gone and have been all day again. They are going in two-man teams searching for the men who'd gotten away. Reagan and Sam are in the horse barn, which, of course, is something of which Paige has no desire to be a part. Talia is at the neighbor's farm keeping company with Bertie and the captive but now freed woman who is living with the Reynolds family. Most of the children are downstairs playing for the time being or until it gets dark and they need to join the family on the first floor for dinner. They weren't allowed outside to play yesterday or today.

The men have worked diligently on cleaning up the farm after the attack last week. There were so many dead bodies to haul away. She asked her brother what they did with them, but he wouldn't answer. She'd plied it out of him, regardless. Simon told her that they'd taken the bodies back to that Target store and dumped them in front of the building. Then they'd attached a large wooden sign to a post near the bodies that warned passersby of the dangers of attacking the town of Pleasant View again. Paige had shivered when he recounted it. Then she'd gotten a lecture about not asking questions about things she couldn't handle. She'd felt like her father was giving her a talking down to instead of her little brother.

The Reynolds brothers took the dead townsmen back to their families to be buried. It must've been horrible for the people to see their dead husbands or fathers being brought home to them on the bed of a pick-up truck and not returning of their own accord.

As soon as Simon had come into Doc's bedroom to awaken her the morning after the attacks, she'd known. She'd known by the look in his distraught blue eyes that her friend was gone. Some things don't need fully explained. She'd cried hard over the loss of Gavin. She and Talia both had. He was their dearest friend, like a brother to them both. If this had happened a few years ago, they might both be dead by now. He'd been their protector of sorts and had gone on many runs without them to secure food and supplies that had kept them alive. His loss is felt greatly by Paige and Talia. They had even broken the news to Maddie. That hadn't gone well, either. She'd cried her little heart out over the loss of her buddy. They'd buried him next to Kelly's young sister on a hill that Simon told her will bloom early spring flowers.

"It's me Paige," she adds so that Hannah knows who has approached her in the kitchen. The other woman chuckles softly.

"I knew it was you," Hannah replies. "You don't have to announce yourself."

"Oh, sorry," Paige returns sheepishly. She doesn't feel as if she knows Hannah as well as Sam or Reagan yet. Even though Simon has told her many times how uplifting and joyful and full of light that Hannah is, Paige hasn't ever seen it. She does see a deep-seated melancholy in the lovely woman, though. Hannah is only a year or so older than her, but Paige believes that she looks a lot older than Hannah. Her life on the road the last few years have aged her, given her stress wrinkles around her eyes as if she is thirty years old and not twenty-two. If Hannah doesn't snap out of her depression, she'll be the next one with premature wrinkles.

"What do you have? I mean what did you just set on the counter?" Hannah asks her directly.

"My notebook? Oh, wow, you really do hear well. Simon said that not much gets by you," Paige blurts and then feels gauche.

Hannah just chuffs again. "I don't know about that. I feel like everything gets by me most of the time. I just heard you set something there. You carry it often, don't you?"

"Yes, I do actually," Paige admits with confusion. "What would you like me to do?"

"Crack those hard-boiled eggs over there into the bowl. We'll stock up on egg salad for tomorrow. It's the only thing I can think of to do with all these eggs. We're overrun with them. As the days grow longer with more daylight, the chickens go into full production. In the winter they slow down a lot," Hannah informs her and continues on without missing a beat or pausing. "It's just that every time I touch your arm, I feel you holding it. Is it a journal?"

Her brother has also warned her about this side of Hannah. She's intrusive, sometimes even nosy when she wants to know something and an unmatched general in the kitchen. But Paige doesn't mind. It's actually kind of nice to have people to talk to and a chore to do that she can actually manage without feeling like an idiot. It's been a long time since she's had this, other than having Talia and Gavin to talk to. But interaction with new people, friendly people, is a much-welcomed change. It's also a relief to not have to worry about somebody stealing her things. She'd had items stolen in the different FEMA camps and again on the road while traveling with other people. She swoops her hair into a fat ponytail to keep it back and gets to work.

"No, well…sort of," Paige explains. "I just think it's important to record the things I've seen, the things that have happened to me and others."

Hannah stops what she's doing and turns directly to her.

"That's funny that you do that," she says before pushing her long braid behind her. "Grandpa does the same thing."

"Really?" Paige asks. "That's cool."

"Yeah, he says that it's a written history or something like that. He even records the names and ages, birth dates, those sorts of things for our friends and family and acquaintances in town. He feels like you do, that it's important to have a written legacy."

"That's interesting," Paige acknowledges. "Mine are more about events and stories that I've witnessed or been a part of."

Hannah's toddler hides behind her leg. She's a timid, tiny thing but adorable as all get out. Mary favors Kelly with her dark hair, but she has a decidedly ornery streak. She has her daddy wrapped around her baby finger, too. Kelly is the kind of man that Paige would've avoided at all costs. He's literally huge and highly intimidating. She's a tall woman, but she likes that. She likes that she's as tall as most men. He can tower over her. She's never been fond of that. Now that she's gotten to know him better, though, he's rather sweet. His laugh is rich and hearty. He's still not her type, not that it would matter. He's completely devoted to his lovely wife. Paige respects that about him, about John and Derek, as well. It warms Paige's heart to see it, too. At least somebody in this world is happy. It's not that Kelly isn't good looking, even if he does look like a giant mountain man from Montana. It's just that she's always been attracted to the clean-cut, blonde, preppy kind of guy. A Wall Street trader would've been her type of guy, not some burly, large lumberjack. Likely this comes from the fact that her father was the clean-cut suit. Loafers and tweed jackets were always preferable to big and imposing or grungy with a beard. She'd always been a daddy's girl. He'd doted on her, and she'd basked in his praise and adoration.

"Up you go, Miss Mary," Hannah says to her daughter.

Then she bends to scoop her darling girl into her arms where she plies her with kisses before setting her on her bottom on the counter.

Barely any light comes through the plywood that covers the window space above the sink. The glass was shot by those men. The next morning they'd taken stock of their bullet-riddled home and immediately made plans for repair work including the porch which had been half scorched. They've worked diligently on the repair. It doesn't exactly match the intricate spindle work of the previous porch, but they've almost got it rebuilt. The men are also looking for replacement windows or sheets of glass if they can find them while they are out also searching for the escapees.

Paige continues to crack and peel the hard-boiled eggs on the stone surface of the counter and drop them into a big white ceramic bowl while Hannah mixes some different types of flours together. She still can't believe that people can eat like this after what she's been scraping by with for the past three years. What they wouldn't have given for some warm bread. One time they'd found a box of bread mix in an emptied out store and prepared it on their campfire. It was about one inch thick when they were done. They hadn't had a way to activate the yeast in a warm space for three hours because they were out in the middle of the woods. It was tough and chewy and coarse but had filled their stomachs for the night. It was like eating a brick. Most nights she'd gone to bed with a growling stomach to keep her company.

Most days Hannah and Sue whip up such miraculous concoctions like beef stews, vegetable soups, stuffed cabbages, roasts with root vegetables, baked chicken with potatoes and bacon pieces, pork roasts with home-canned sauerkraut and even pasta. The second week on the farm, the men had brought back fresh fish from wherever they'd gone ice fishing. That had tasted sublime along with the creamy roasted red pepper soup that Sue had made. The breads they make are heavy and dense and not like the bleached and refined bread that she'd been used to before the apocalypse. But they are nothing like the hard brick she and Talia had made on the fire that time. Hannah's breads are full of fiber and cracked wheat and are a lot heartier in texture. They keep her full, but that's actually a good feeling. She hasn't felt full very many times in her recent past. She and Gavin had carried two of the chickens with them when they'd left that farm where they'd wintered. Eventually they'd stopped laying eggs for some reason and after a few weeks of that, they'd become dinner. The meat had lasted them for a week.

"Are your friends in that journal?" Hannah asks.

"Yes," Paige answers softly, temporarily forgetting that awful, hard bread and the laughs they'd had over it when they'd lain awake out in those woods giggling for a rare change.

"How do you get the bread to rise? Do you still have packages of yeast or something?" she asks.

Hannah shakes her head, unknowingly swipes flour across her cheek with the back of her delicate hand and replies, "No, we've been out of yeast for quite some time. It's a recipe that is kept in a crock in the pantry. You don't add yeast every day. You just replace the dry ingredients cup for cup, teaspoon for teaspoon. It was a pioneer's recipe. Women on the wagon train couldn't make fresh rising bread every single day, so they used this recipe. The yeast is the same yeast that's been in there for a long time. It just has to be kept covered with a cheese cloth."

"Cool," Paige says with wonderment. "How'd you find that recipe?"

"My Grams had it passed down to her from her Grams," Hannah says on a sad sigh. "She was from New Orleans originally, so a lot of the recipes we make are from the Deep South. She grew up poor, so her mother and grandmother were good at making food go a long way."

"Sorry, Hannah," Paige apologizes for bringing up the woman that Hannah was close with and lost.

Hannah just looks in Paige's general direction and smiles gently. "It's all right. I miss her. I do. I'm not gonna lie. I miss Em, too. I know they're in a better place. Any place has to better than this."

Paige doesn't know how to respond to this. Simon says how optimistic Hannah is, but this is not optimism that Paige hears in her. She frowns hard and tries to think of another topic.

"Talia's from New Orleans, too," she offers.

"Oh, really?" Hannah asks with curiosity.

"Yes, her father played pro football for the Saints. Her parents got divorced when she was like ten or twelve or something. I'm not sure exactly. But she lived down there with him. It was later when her mother had a stroke and was placed in a home, but Talia stayed with her dad."

"What happened to him? Is he alive?"

Paige frowns. "I don't know. I don't think so. He was in London like our father. He was there to promote the NFL Europe something or other. London was nuked, so I'm sure that neither of them made it."

"That's a shame," Hannah admits. "It's not like they could catch a flight home even if they were still alive."

That certainly isn't optimistic. Paige frowns harder and swallows the lump in her throat. Thinking about her father hurts too much. The loss of her parents is the hardest thing she's endured.

"Is that in your journal, too?" Hannah inquires.

"Yes, I have everything and everyone I know in here. I don't want them to be forgotten."

"What about your boyfriend, the one from college?"

"Yes, he's in there, too," Paige answers and can't help but smile. Simon was certainly right about Hannah. When she wants to know something, she doesn't have much of a restraint button.

"Were you in love with him?"

Paige sighs long and wearily. "I guess. I don't know. I thought I was, but now I'm not so sure." She shakes her head with indecision.

"Why is that?"

"It's just hard to explain. Everything changed. There was never a time to even sit down and process all of it. It all happened so fast. One minute my friends and I were ordering a pizza and the next minute the world changed. I changed. I've changed so much that I don't even know if I'd recognize the girl I used to be."

"Yes, I suppose everyone has gone through some of that," Hannah agrees. "Of course not everyone's had it as bad as you and your group. Tell me about your life before."

Paige chuckles. She's more than tenacious. Hannah Alexander could've had her own television talk show. "I used to hang out with my friends, go to parties on and off campus, go to the movies with them. I used to really like to go out dancing. That was a lot of fun. I liked shopping with my girlfriends. I rode my bike everywhere, so I didn't need my car. I left it in Arizona at my parents' house. I'd just bike to school and everywhere I had to go. Not exactly the right mode for apocalyptic travel. But, heck, who knew that I should've taken my car to college because the world was going to fall apart?"

Hannah laughs softly and replies, "No, I suppose not. What were you studying?"

"Architecture. I always liked architecture and drawing and designing buildings," Paige replies but really isn't sure why she's disclosing so much about herself to this woman who, although nice, is still basically a stranger. "When I was twelve, my dad took me to Europe when he had to go there for work. He was a senator. I don't know if you knew that," Paige says and gets a nod from Hannah. Of course Simon probably already told them this. "I stayed with a nanny during the day while he worked, but then when he got home we went sightseeing. I think that's when the fascination with architecture started. He took me everywhere with him after that. It's amazing over there.... well, I mean it was amazing. I don't know what it looks like now."

"Your parents must've been so proud," Hannah praises.

She turns to the refrigerator and takes out a glass pitcher of milk. Hannah pours a cup for her daughter. Paige notices that she sticks her index finger a half inch into the top of the glass against the rim so that she can ascertain when it is full enough by the liquid touching the bottom of her slim, graceful finger. She's learned a lot about blind people by observing Hannah. Every little thing she's ever taken for granted like pouring a simple glass of milk has become something that she watches Hannah perform with concise and careful detail. Paige is in awe of the things she can do.

Hannah's praise is false, though. Paige swallows hard and goes back to her work. She forces the tears to halt their progress.

Mary hops down with her mother's help when Arianna and Jacob come into the room to fetch her. They've all been relegated to playing in the direct back yard and no further. They want her to play baseball. Paige has no idea what a toddler could possibly bring to a baseball game, but it is kind that they are including her.

"Yeah, I guess," she admits. "My mother and I didn't get along that great before I went to school. I could've gone to a closer school, but I wanted the distance from them. I felt like they were holding me down, restricting me and smothering me too much. I was a big idiot back then. I was so immature and stupid, and now I just have this giant dark cloud of regret that I carry. I just wish I could see her one last time. Tell her I'm sorry, you know?"

"She knows, Paige," Hannah proclaims so wisely.

Is she twenty-four or sixty-four? She's heard other family members, Simon included, speak of how insightful Hannah can be, but Paige hadn't expected this. The other woman reaches across the counter and takes her hand, giving it a reassuring squeeze before going back to mixing flour. Technically this is the first full one-on-one conversation they've had. Paige can't actually believe that she's even divulging this much about herself, either. She's not this open and communicative with the other members of the family. She just finally felt the other night during the battle that she even belongs with them.

"Your mom's probably the reason you made it here to Simon," Hannah adds as she turns her dough out onto the floured counter-top where she proceeds to knead it. "They watch over us. They have to. It's the only explanation I have for my husband coming home safely to me every time he leaves for something dangerous like the other night. My grandmother is watching over my Kelly."

Paige is so awestruck, so moved by what Hannah is saying that tears spring to her eyes. She's glad that Hannah can't see her childish reaction. She sure as hell never believed in something like what Hannah is describing. She's never even heard anyone talk so openly about their beliefs before.

"Maybe," Paige says and hates that her voice cracks. "I just hope someone's watching over the guys, I guess. It sounds like they'll need all the help they can get if they find those men again."

"I know," Hannah concurs. "But they'll be fine. It was only a few of them this time, not a whole battalion."

The way she says this makes Paige think that Hannah's also worried about the men, as if she is also trying to convince herself. Hannah's delicate features furrow into a dark scowl, and she has to look away from her.

Paige shakes her head, "I still can't believe my dorky, younger brother is out hunting down bad-guys every day and shooting people. You just have to know what Simon was like before all this. It's shocking for me to see him like this, so transformed. I mean, he's physically and mentally transformed."

"Oh, I know," Hannah says with a grin. "I knew him when he first came here, which was probably not a whole lot different than what he was like in Arizona. He was very shy, quiet even."

"You've got that part right," Paige agrees with a smile. "It's just weird. He looks like the poster boy for a join the Army billboard."

"Yeah, the guys were pretty hard on him and Cory," she says with a smile. "You haven't seen Cory yet. Just wait. He'll come home someday."

Paige notices the other woman's smile deepen when she speaks of this Cory kid. She seems to think he'll come home. He's probably dead somewhere. It's not safe out there to try to survive on your own. Paige probably wouldn't have made it ten minutes out there alone.

"I have heard about some of the training and the stuff the guys put them through. It's crazy. He was so tall and skinny the last time I saw him. Now he's wide, too," Paige says and actually laughs aloud.

"Yes, he is. That's good, though. He needs to be strong and tough. He'll always be able to take care of Sam that way. And you too, now," Hannah says.

"He's very different than he used to be in the way that he thinks, too," Paige says with a touch of sadness. "He's always on edge. Well, he's always on edge unless he's out in the woods picking berries or weeds. He's so tense and serious to the point of being *intense*."

"He's been through a lot," Hannah says. "He and Sam have both been through quite a lot. Sometimes the things that happen to us change us for the better, and something they just don't. They both decided not to allow their lives to be dictated by what happened."

"What did happen?" Paige asks. "He hasn't told me. He just said that he joined up with our aunt's group to get a ride back this way and that Sam was taken and that they did awful things. I know that John killed our cousin, but that's about it."

Hannah stops dicing celery, which she's moved on to and pauses. "I don't think I should say. Some of it, I don't even know. But it feels wrong to reveal another person's story without their knowledge."

"I don't know what happened, and I just want to help my kid brother... even if he is twice the size of me practically," she says with a chuckle.

Hannah smiles and goes back to the celery chopping, which makes Paige nervous that she'll slice off her finger.

"Your cousin, Bobby, was a vicious, evil person. I don't know what was wrong with him," Hannah says.

"He was always a punk, in and out of juvey, minor stuff mostly, but a real piece of sh...crap," Paige states.

"I think people like him saw the fall of society as their one-way ticket to total debauchery. I believe he raped Sam. Don't tell her or your brother, but that's what we all figure. She's never talked about it openly, and neither has your brother. But she has a lot of problems, and that group was very bad, all of them. I don't even want to think that any of the others raped her, too."

"Oh my God," Paige declares on a rush of air. "I had no idea. That's so sick. My poor brother. I can't imagine him having to stand by and let that happen."

"I don't think he did," Hannah says. "Reagan told me when the visitors were squatted on our property that Simon always looked beat up. You know, black eyes, bruises. She said when they first got here, he would hold his side a lot like he had broken ribs. He probably did. There were too many of them to fight, so he probably got beat up very badly by them. I don't know for sure what went on with those people, but I know it traumatized your brother and Samantha."

"Yes, I see," Paige says, her task before her on the counter completely forgotten.

"They found Sam in a house not far from our farm actually. They killed her whole family and took her, even though your brother tried to hide her. The men went and buried her family for her, all of her family including her parents, her brother and the twin toddlers."

"Oh my," Paige whispers. She feels sick to her stomach suddenly. A bead of sweat breaks out on her forehead and runs down. She whisks it away. She sways on her feet and grabs the counter for support.

"You know that Simon stabbed your cousin, right?" Hannah asks.

"What?" Paige asks on a sharp inhale.

"Don't tell anyone that I'm telling you this. He must not want you to know. But he did. Reagan told me. Your cousin and another really bad man in that group caught Simon, Sam and Cory out in the woods. They got away, but then Reagan and John were jumped. Cory killed the one man, Simon stabbed your cousin and then John shot him. You have no idea how bad that whole day was," Hannah says and turns away.

Paige thinks there is probably more to this story than she realizes by the way that Hannah reacts to the memories.

"I guess not," Paige allows. "I feel bad I wasn't there for him in Arizona. I should've gone home as soon as the nuclear war started overseas. I should've taken care of him. He would've never had to travel with Aunt Amber."

"You can't carry that guilt around with you the rest of your life, Paige," Hannah says. "You could've both been killed in Arizona. What happened to both of you was supposed to happen. But you're a young woman. You need to be happy. You just have to force yourself to find some sort of happiness in this world the way it is."

Paige smiles with a touch of melancholy and irony. Hannah talks to her like she's her mother or even grandmother.

"Guess I'll have to work on that," she says with a grin.

They don't revisit the topic of Sam and Simon's stay with the visitors, and Paige believes that they are both grateful to put it to rest.

"I'm glad you're here, Paige," Hannah says, her mismatched eyes meeting Paige's briefly before losing focus again. "He needed to have someone from his family here, especially since Cory left."

"Me, too," she admits. "Were they close?"

Hannah snorts delicately, "That doesn't even come close to describing them. They were like brothers, maybe even closer than most brothers. They are both orphans. They've been through a lot together. They are bonded like no two young men I've ever known. Well, other than John and Kelly. Those two are the same way. Maybe it's what you go through together that makes people so close. I don't know really, but Cory and Simon are... I mean, *were* inseparable."

Paige just nods.

"You know I can't see you nod or shake your head, Miss Paige," Hannah reprimands.

"Oh, sorry!" Paige apologizes for her imbecilic gaffe.

"It's fine," Hannah says on a smile. "It takes a while to get used to constantly verbally expressing oneself. You're forgiven."

Paige nods, smiles and then quickly corrects it with an awkward, "Thanks."

They work together on food preparation for tomorrow until it is time to prepare today's dinner. It seems never to end, the food preparation on the farm. Sue joins them and is carrying paper packages of frozen meat. Hannah announces that they'll be making cabbage hash. Paige has no idea what that is, but she's willing to help.

A short while later, the ground beef is cooked, drained, and the cabbage is frying with onions on the stove. Potatoes are frying in two other large skillets. Simon blasts through the back door, dripping wet and carrying an armload of dry firewood. Everyone is keeping a keen eye on the wood-burning stove in the basement and the fireplace in the music room. It's not quite warm enough outside yet to eliminate heat in the house altogether, especially not with the children sleeping in the basement bedrooms.

"Let me help!" Paige cries as she rushes toward her brother and takes a few of the split logs. They are exceedingly heavy, but she's not going to complain. He'd been carrying the whole load by himself. Her little brother isn't quite so little anymore.

"Thanks, sis," he mumbles.

"Any word yet?" Sue calls out to him from the stove.

"No, not yet, ma'am," Simon returns on a shake of his head. "Don't worry. They're fine."

"Right, don't worry," Paige says mockingly.

She follows her brother to the basement where they stack the wood against a stone foundation wall. Paige has already marveled at the century old, hand-hewn beams in this basement. The amount of labor that would've gone into the oak beams is mind boggling.

"Thanks for the help," Simon says.

He averts his eyes from her, which immediately puts Paige on alert.

"Hey, what is it?" she asks and touches his damp forearm.

"Nothing," he returns and pulls away.

"Simon," she says and stops following him toward the stairs. It works because he turns to face her. "Talk to me."

He starts arranging the glass jars of canned vegetables on a shelf to avoid looking at her. Paige positions herself between him and the shelf.

"What is it that's bothering you?" she asks quietly.

Simon shakes his head before answering, "I'm sorry about your friend."

"Honey, I know," she replies. "You already said that, Simon. You don't have to feel guilty. Sam talked to me, too. She explained what happened. Gavin was just in the wrong place at the wrong time."

"I know, but…"

"Look, he was my friend, my really good friend, but I'm not going to blame you for the rest of our lives for not saving his life or accuse you of being a bad doctor because you couldn't save him..."

"I'm not a doctor, Paige," he says on a sigh.

"You are practically a doctor, little brother," she corrects. "Reagan talked to me, too. It wasn't your fault. I'm not a naïve child, Simon. I know that none of it was your fault. He decided to go after that man. He wanted to help. Gav was like that. He couldn't have stayed here at the house if he saw someone was going to burn down the barns. He had to go. And he was shot. And likely his murderer was killed by one of you or he died from Gavin's shot."

"I'm sure he was. We didn't leave anyone alive over there," Simon confirms but looks away.

"Good," she says firmly. "Those assholes got what they deserved. Justice was dealt."

Simon nods solemnly. Paige pulls him in for a close hug. She almost starts crying again over Gavin. However, she manages to hold herself together, barely. She's not going to confess that she'd cried herself to sleep last night again in their cabin. He already feels guilty enough.

"I love you, Simon," she says quietly. "I know I never said it enough when we were dumbass kids. That would've been uncool, right? But I do, and I'm not gonna *not* say it from now on. I love you."

Simon grins, exposing his deep dimples. "Who's the dork now?"

She punches his arm.

"I love you, too, sis," Simon finally says.

Her little brother ruffles the hair on her head as if she is the younger sibling and he the older. It's as if their roles have been reversed. It's not a completely unwelcome feeling thinking of Simon watching over her. She feels safe for the first time in a long while.

They head back outside to the wood shed where they collect another wheelbarrow load.

She gets winded quickly and apologizes, "Sorry, Simon. I feel like you're working circles around me."

"You just got clubbed over the head last week," he says. "I was hoping it knocked some sense into you, but I think you're actually worse."

"Ha ha, are you trying to be a comedian?"

He chuckles and leads her by the shoulder to a massive chunk of log where he forces her to sit.

"Nobody expects you to haul firewood, sis," Simon explains with a soft smile and pulls the collar of her borrowed raincoat higher. "Just take it easy."

"I feel so useless around here most of the time," she tells him with embarrassment. It's true. She mostly just gets in everyone's ways.

"Nah, not useless. You shot some dudes the other night so I hear. Reagan said you did very well. Saved some lives by doing so. So I'd say not useless at all. We're gonna work on your training, though. Can't keep saving your skinny butt all the time when you get taken hostage," he jokes as he carries another armload to the wheelbarrow and motions for her to follow. "Come on."

She frowns and follows after him as he pushes the wheelbarrow which is weighted down with a heavy load of split wood through the rain and mud.

"Nobody thinks you're useless, Paige," he says with a slight grin. "Annoying maybe, but not useless."

"Hey!" she complains lightly at his jest. Her brother smiles at her. His smile could light up a room. His kind blue eyes twinkle with merriment. He's so devastatingly handsome and mature now, not at all like the gangly boy he used to be. Even his hands at the handles of the wheelbarrow are big and thick and strong, just like his wrists and arms. But Paige can still see hints of her nerdy, innocent brother there in his eyes. She hopes he never completely loses that part of himself.

"I want to check that laceration again and give you a quick exam before dinner, ok?" he asks.

They come to the side entrance that leads into the mudroom where everyone always stashes their wet gear and shoes.

"Reagan already checked me," she tells him as he holds the door for her. "Twice!"

Simon chuckles once and nods. "Yeah, that's not surprising."

"She was mad when she found out that the last man was leaving the shed this morning to go home to his family," Paige observes as they carry armload after armload of firewood to the music room.

"I figured she would be," he concludes. "She didn't think they were ready to go yet, but what could we do? They wanted to go home. We can't force them to stay. Once we get the practice in town going again, we can check them out there. I'm sure they'll be fine. Doc told them how to watch for signs of infection."

"She's kind of bossy," Paige says quietly as they go back outside to collect another armload each.

"Kind of?" Simon asks on an uproarious laugh.

Paige even laughs once. She hadn't been joking. For being a tiny thing, Reagan Harrison is extremely commanding of her surroundings and everyone within arm's reach. She's pretty cool, though. Paige actually likes her quite a lot, but she is bossy.

"You think she's bossy? Ask her husband sometime," Simon jokes. "He could tell you an earful, I'm sure."

Paige chuckles as they finish their work. Reagan walks into the mudroom as they are shutting the door again.

"What's so funny?" she asks.

Paige and Simon just look at each other and both mumble, "Nothing."

They get a queer look in return, but the little boss leaves the room without discovering that she was the source for which they'd taken a joyful moment, a rare moment of laughter. Neither of them is about to tell her anytime soon, either. They aren't complete lackwits, after all.

By the time they get washed up and Simon has checked her against her will, the men have returned.

They quickly take care of the outdoor chores and the animal feedings and milkings. Paige even helps milk the goats. She hasn't felt comfortable tackling a cow milking chore yet. They still scare the hell out of her. After they eat dinner, John announces that a meeting needs to take place.

They ready the children for bed. When that task is accomplished, the adults commune in the music room where there is enough space for everyone to sit. Talia opts out and goes to bed early. She's taking the loss of their friend very hard. Nobody questions or judges her. This family has seen enough of its own travesties to be compassionate and understanding of her grief.

There are rifles, pistols and shotguns littered about the room in case the farm comes under attack again. Paige hopes that doesn't ever happen again. She's not good at shooting guns, not unless the person is less than five feet from her. She'd made a few lucky shots that night, but she is under no false pretenses that she'll be the next Annie Oakley anytime soon. She'd even gotten her own dumb ass taken hostage.

"Did you find them?" Doc asks impatiently as he draws the double doors closed.

These doors are never closed. The room is always open and airy and full of light and usually the laughter of children. Nobody has felt much like laughing lately, not even the children. Her shared laugh with Simon was probably the first this home has seen in a week. She's never seen the doors closed to this room, but Herb must not want to take the chance that any of the children will come back up from their bedrooms in the basement and overhear their morbid conversation.

"We found one of them," John explains. "They got split up after they left here. He said some of them were getting out of the state; some were laying low. There are still four left. We'll find those ones if they're laying low."

"Yeah, right. Even if we have to hunt them down and go door to door and building to building," Kelly says. "They can't hide forever."

"Maybe we should just let them go now," Hannah suggests gently.

Her husband wraps an arm around her shoulders and gives them a reassuring squeeze.

"We can't do that, baby," he croons and kisses the top of her pale head. "They'll come back. They *will* come back here. Maybe not today or tomorrow, but someday they'll return. The next time we may not get so lucky."

Paige doesn't want them to let those creeps off the hook. Maddie could've been killed or left abandoned with the rest of the children. Hannah and the other two sisters would've been taken for sure. All of the women would've been raped, she has no doubt.

"I think we need to call a meeting in town," Derek says. "This can't happen again. Hell, it shouldn't have happened in the first place. Our town's security sucks."

"Right," John interrupts. "They need to set up a security detail. Nobody should be able to just drive in anymore. We need guards working details, especially when the clinic's open. If people want health-care, they gotta' contribute to the safety of the doctors providing it."

"Agreed," Sue says with resolve.

"We'll go in tomorrow, get with the leaders of the different sectors and call a meeting," Derek suggests. "I think they'll agree to it. We'll train whoever needs or wants to be trained. Then we'll make sure they're armed."

"We'll need to build some kind of barrier or fencing around the entire perimeter of the town where we have the sections established, beef it up extra good," Kelly says.

"Wish Cory was here for that," John laments. "He's good with engineering that kind of thing."

"Paige could probably help with that," Hannah offers up.

Everyone, including herself, turns to stare at Hannah.

"How's that?" Doc asks.

"Um, yeah, I could probably help," Paige offers. Everyone turns to look at her next, making her feel put on the spot. She's normally quiet during these kinds of meetings. That isn't going to happen with Hannah's declaration. She doesn't usually have anything to offer that she feels would be helpful. That was also before she felt like she actually belonged with these people. Now they are her family. Now she wants to contribute.

336

"Yeah?" John asks. "How can you help?"

"Well, I like architecture and structural building. I've studied it for a long time. That was my college major, too," she tells them. "I could look at what we have to work with and start drawing it out. I can work with just about anything to create a wall. We could use salvaged fencing, building materials, stone, whatever."

The men all look to one another. Paige figures they're about to burst out laughing at her. She braces for it, but it never comes. Slowly, one by one, they all nod.

"Sounds good to me," Derek says.

The other men nod and verbally agree.

Doc says, "That sounds great, young lady. We could get you set up on that first thing in the morning. The men can get you a supply list, and we'll let you draw it up."

Paige nods and can't help the smile that creeps onto her mouth. She feels proud of herself and useful for the first time since coming to this farm. It's a good feeling.

"Anyone find out yet who in town was harmed for not wanting to tell them about our farm?" Doc asks next.

"We found out who told them about the farm, sir," Kelly offers. "He is dead, too. They did beat him to death."

Her brother stands near the fireplace and has elected not to sit. He's restless and charged with stress energy. Paige can see the tension in his shoulders and his stance. He'd gone out in the wee hours of the night with Kelly on a mission of information gathering and scumbag stalking.

"Took us awhile to figure it out," Simon remarks. "Had to go house to house, but we found him."

Paige realizes that her brother hasn't told her of this.

"We buried him last night, sir," her brother tells Doc.

"Thank you for that," Herb McClane says and pinches the bridge of his nose.

"They tortured Mr. Lewis until he told them where we were located, and then they killed him," John relays. "Our friend spilled the beans on it today when we pressed him. Mr. Lewis also told them

337

that he thought we would probably be coming after them. That's how they knew to attack when we were gone. One of his neighbors found him yesterday morning. She came out to tell the guys last night when she saw Simon and Kelly doing patrols looking for him. Sorry it took us that many days to figure out who they got to."

"Ah, George Lewis," Herb says on a sad sigh. "He was a good man. He lived alone. I'm sure that's why they targeted him. Don't trouble yourself over not finding him sooner, son. We didn't have a name. You men did well."

"He was nearly unrecognizable, sir," Simon tells them. "He was older than you, I'd say. I think he held out as long as he could."

Paige watches as Samantha nudges closer to Simon, who wraps a comforting arm around her shoulders. He even whispers something in her ear which makes Sam grimace and nod. She's seemed depressed lately, too. Sam just has such a fragile aura about her. Paige can't imagine her suffering through traumatic abuse like rape, if that's what happened to her. She's so small and delicate, and she would've only been about fifteen if it happened four years ago. Paige looks away from her because that thought is making her nauseous.

"George must've been around eighty-two if I were to guess," Doc says with a melancholy hitch to his voice. "His wife passed on about a decade ago. His kids had all moved away. Thank you again for burying him, boys."

"Yes, sir," Kelly and Simon both echo.

"Did you get those women placed with homes?" Reagan asks, changing the subject.

She is referring to the women who'd been nothing more than slaves to the Target creeps. They'd found seventeen total. Some had hidden in the far recesses of the store to avoid being shot that night.

"Yes," Kelly answers. "Only three wanted to stay. Most of them wanted to go back to their own families. Some were from as far away as Nashville and Cincinnati."

"I pray they make it home safely to their families," Hannah says with a sad grimace.

"Well, we armed them with those assholes' guns and vehicles and got them some gas, so that ought to help," Derek says on a smirk.

John and he pound fists. Simon just chuckles and then bumps fists with Kelly. Sam immediately steps right back into the space against Simon's side. He immediately frowns but wraps a protective arm around her again. This young woman obviously only finds comfort and security from Paige's brother. The more Paige gets to know her brother again, the more she can understand why Sam feels this way.

Even Doc says fiercely, "Good. That's good. They need protection. Nobody deserves to be someone's victim. There's no place for that anymore. We need to start taking this country back from men like that. We need to fight for what's right. We need to restore order and stability and create a new society. We need to work with our neighbors, not against them. We need to build this America back up again."

"Hooah!" the three Rangers call out softly. Paige notices that Simon does so, as well. Her kid brother, the bookworm nerd, turned doctor herbalist, turned badass Ranger. What a world.

Chapter Twenty-six
Reagan

"Hey, sexy man," Reagan says as she slyly sneaks up behind her husband and wraps her arms around his trim waist. He smells of sweat and dirt. It's not unpleasant, not on John. He whips around and lifts her into his arms, into a tight bear hug.

"Don't start something you can't finish, woman," he threatens with an ornery grin.

"Who says I don't want to finish it?" she teases right before he plants a searing kiss to her mouth.

John sets her gently to her feet right in the middle of the crowded street. People from town are moving about, visiting with one another, helping to build fences, working on gardening projects and mostly getting out into the nicer weather. The men have been working day and night for the past two weeks with the team leaders of each city section to build walls around their small town that will encapsulate them and keep intruders out. Plans to take down sections of wall from their individual sectors to use on the big wall were made. The escapees had burned three homes in town to the ground upon their getaway from the McClane farm. Those families have been condensed into homes with others until abandoned homes can be opened. Many of the abandoned homes and buildings everywhere were ruined when water pipes froze and burst that first winter, so the men will also be working on helping with those projects, too.

She and Simon worked at the clinic today, offering what services they could to a growing number of patients. Three families had even traveled from Clarksville to receive treatment. Reagan isn't sure how the families heard about their clinic, but they are happy to offer medical care to those who come in peace. Some of these people haven't seen doctors or even a nurse in almost four years. The problem that they are starting to have is that some people need dental care. Their town dentist was killed very soon after the fall when druggies raided his practice. His widow and two children still reside in town with her brother who'd traveled from Texas to be with them. Reagan guesses that he was just as shocked as everyone else to find out that his brother-in-law was murdered.

Reagan presses another kiss to John's mouth, a kiss that holds promise. Unfortunately, her handsome husband pulls back which pisses her off. John is like her drug, addictive and all-consuming.

"I suppose this'll have to wait," he concedes with a frown. "We're almost done for the day, and your grandfather should be getting here soon. We're having another town meeting tonight at six."

"I see how you are," Reagan teases further. "Guess I'll just have to find a stand-in husband for when you're too busy for me."

She pivots on the ball of her Converse clad foot and receives a hard crack to her bottom. Reagan just laughs haughtily at her husband as she walks down the street back to their clinic. She spies over one shoulder to find him talking to Kelly. He's still staring at her, however. Just the sight of John standing there in a dirty, sweat-covered white t-shirt and his camo, olive drab pants sets her heart racing. To call John a sexy stud would be a serious understatement. He shoots her a grin filled with a hot secret that makes Reagan bite her lower lip and shake her head. She never dreamed she'd feel like this about someone. Neither did she ever think she'd feel so strongly about someone for as long as she has for John. A hundred years with him won't be enough.

"Reagan!" Paige calls out to her from her rickety work area.

The men set up her work space on a picnic table, some of which has rotted through from sitting outdoors for years and not having been treated with any type of weatherproofing sealant. They had commented on how sensible and practical her schematics of the exterior perimeter wall were drawn up. She's a good planner, engineer and architect. Her drawings and use of the materials they'd been able to salvage had put everything to its best use. John said he was impressed that, even though she's so young, Paige knew about the strength and functionality of each material like different metals and woods.

She joins Paige at the picnic table, "What's up?" she asks the other woman. There's a smudge of dirt on her freckled right check. Her pale blue eyes dance excitedly. She points to the diagram in front of her.

"I think if we use those big barn doors- you know, the ones that the guys said they could get from that huge abandoned dairy farm up off of route 41- that they would work perfectly. We could use those as the main gates. See here?" she says as she points with her pencil. "We can attach them to those two big telephone poles we got. We wouldn't have to cut them shorter, either. That's good. Tall is good."

"Sounds right to me," Reagan observes as she gazes down at the schematic drawing. Paige's handwriting is neat and concise, nothing like her own. Her drawings also look like they were done by a computer and not by hand. Reagan adds with a grin, "Fortress style."

Paige smiles brightly at her and nods. "Yes, that's what I was going for. Fortress. That's the most effective way of keeping people out. And we could use that fencing around the top of the sheet metal if we use these steel pipes."

She picks up a gray steel pipe about four feet long. The men found much bigger, longer sections of this piping material in a factory near Clarksville and had brought it back a few years ago. They'd figured that it would get used somewhere for something. That's the way they operate. They are always looking into the future, which is difficult for Reagan to conceptualize. They were right, though.

"And these clips here?" Paige asks and indicates toward some metal hooks. "Mr. Jones said we could use these."

Reagan knows that Mr. Jones used to own a fairly large home building construction company closer to Clarksville. Now he lives in their small town. He's already donated sheet metal and roofing supplies.

Reagan says, "That was generous of him."

Paige shrugs and chews the end of her pencil, "It's in his best interest. He lives in the perimeter precinct. If he wants the protection of the walls, then he needs to donate everything he can so that the men can get the walls built and finished before winter comes again."

Paige is definitely blunt when she wants to be. Reagan just grins.

"How many townspeople are helping on the build now?" Reagan asks.

"Thirty-three. One of the families here in sector two have relatives coming from Nashville, I guess. They said that they have three sons who will also be able to help. The dad of the family said that if they want to live here, then they need to come prepared to help. He's pretty cool. I think if we stay steady at it every day, we'll get it done before the end of fall. At least the immediate perimeter should get done or close to it and the areas farther out will be pushed into spring."

"Thank God," Reagan says. "We're safe out at the farm but not when we come to town. And the people here need a better sense of security. It'll help them to trust one another again and help to set up trade with outsiders in a more organized fashion."

"Exactly, this is a good thing we're doing," Paige says distractedly as she works out a particular piece of the drawing in front of her and then erases an area. "Here we can use the treated lumber that Kelly and Derek brought home the other day."

"All you need now is a castle moat," Reagan suggests lightly.

"Ha, yes, that would be helpful, wouldn't it?" she returns.

Simon joins them a moment later. Then Sam, who is never far from him at any time, trots over with her youthful energy, bright blue eyes and swinging, black ponytail. Paige ignores them and continues sketching. This has given her something valid and important to work on. Reagan knows the sense of purpose she'd needed. She had felt like Paige seemed out of place at the farm, like she didn't quite feel like she fit in with them. She's usually pretty easy to read. After the attack three weeks ago on the farm, she seems like she has bonded closer to the family. And even though Reagan wishes that it had never happened, she's glad that Simon's sister is cleaving to them. She was worried for a while there that Paige would wish to leave the farm and that she'd take her brother with her. That would've devastated the family. Simon is like their blood, and they've all lost too many family members already. To Reagan, he is like her nerdy younger brother.

"Your grandpa just arrived, Reagan," he announces. "He's with Mr. Oberholtz at the clinic. They are going over the bullet points that they want to cover during the meeting today so that it doesn't get too congested with conversation instead of planning. You know how these meetings sometimes go!"

"You're the only person I know that would use the words 'bullet points' after the end of the world, Simon," Paige jokes.

Reagan even chuckles at this one. Simon just blushes as Sam gives a grin.

"Whatever," he complains at his sister. "Sam and I finished cleaning the clinic and prepared it for next week's visit."

"Did you mark off your tasks on a bullet point check list?" Reagan teases. This gets a laugh from both of the other women.

"Yeah, yeah, you women," he spits hostilely. "I'm gonna go help the men. At least they make more sense and don't waste time with this sort of silliness!"

He stalks off to the laughter of the three of them, his wide shoulders drawn up in a tense posture.

"Aw, Simon, come back!" Paige calls out between guffaws.

He just waves his hand behind his back at them in irritation but doesn't turn around. He straightens his blue ball cap and keeps right on going. The women chuckle at him again.

"Now I feel bad," Sam says, trying to muffle her laugh.

"What?" Reagan asks. "Nah, don't feel bad. We can't let these men around here get bigger heads than they already have. It's good to knock them down a rung from time to time."

"Right, we don't want them getting cocky on us," Paige agrees on a smirk of arrogance. "Besides, he's easy to tease. Simon's always been that way. He's also always been way too serious."

Reagan glimpses a hint of the sassiness that Paige likely used to have. Her red hair is partially concealed by the blue bandana she has wrapped around her head and forehead. She sports either a blue or a red one most of the time. The sun catches some of her loose red strands causing them to shimmer like molten gold and liquid lava. The jeans she wears are at least three inches too short for her as they were borrowed from Hannah, and Paige is so much taller than all of the McClane women. If they could go on a run, Reagan's fairly sure they could find some women's sizes in tiny and tall somewhere in retail stores. Paige has unusually long legs for a girl. She walks around most of the time in flood pants. She'd probably be more comfortable in clothing that actually fit her tall, slim figure better.

Sam says, "I'm not so sure. It feels mean."

"Would you care if we were razzing Derek or John or is it just Simon getting flamed that bothers you?" Reagan probes with a grin.

"What?" Sam says and blushes pink. "Of course I would care if we were teasing the other men. Why wouldn't I?"

"Hm," Reagan murmurs.

"I'm… I'm going to help Grandpa," Sam stammers and rushes off.

If she's going to help Grandpa, Reagan would like to point out that she's going the wrong way. She just grins instead.

"What was that all about?" Paige asks.

Reagan's not a hundred percent sure she should share her observations with Simon's sister. She's not sure how she'll take it.

Paige looks up from her drawing and cocks an eyebrow.

"Sam's in love with Simon," she blurts. Damn, that wasn't exactly smooth. Leave it to her to blurt.

"Really?" Paige asks and looks around as if something or someone is going to confirm this for her. She repeats it as if she truly can't comprehend it, "*Really*? Are you sure?

"Uh, yeah," Reagan says. "I probably shouldn't have said that. I'm not good at being secretive. I'm a textbook blurter. So is Sue, in case you ever need to know that."

"Did she tell you that she has those kind of feelings for my brother?" Paige asks with a deep crease between her light reddish brown eyebrows.

"No, she'd never tell me something like that. I've just noticed. So has Sue and Hannie. If I'm being totally honest, I guess I should admit that it was really Sue who noticed first and then Hannie. They told me. I don't pick up on that kind of stuff very well most of the time."

"Wait, how would Hannah know something like that?"

Reagan laughs aloud, "You don't know Hannie very well yet, do you?"

Paige smiles and nods. "Yeah, I'm starting to figure that one out. Are you sure she's not just faking being blind?"

"I know," Reagan agrees with a smile. "She's like a damn Bassett hound when she wants to know something. She'll sniff it out if she has to."

"That's very true," Paige says with a nod. "She definitely gets information from me when she wants it."

A goat bleats near them in Mrs. Engle's front yard. It is quickly joined by two of its comrades in arms. It touches Reagan's funny bone that her once perfectly manicured yard with the white picket fence now contains six goats that she milks and trades for goods that she needs. Her daughter and grandchildren had moved in with her a few years ago from Missouri. Her daughter's husband had died of influenza, and she'd made the journey with her three kids. Since Mrs. Engle is in her sixties, it's a good thing that she has the extra help.

Reagan smirks. "No shit. You gotta watch Hannie. She'll fleece you for information, and you won't even see it coming."

Paige's blue eyes twinkle with merriment. She doesn't seem like a particularly happy person most of the time. This is a rare exchange for them. She's talked a few times with Reagan about her family and the friends she used to have, but those memories are always met with tears that quickly get shut down before she whisks herself away to take care of some chore or imaginary errand or to take care of Maddie.

"That's how she got Kelly," Reagan confesses. "She knocked him off his feet and he didn't even know what happened. Poor guy."

"You really think Sam is interested in my brother? I've never picked up on anything like that. He's very stoic around her, sometimes distant and kind of hard with her like he can't wait to get away from her. And Sam seems kind of shy around me. I don't think she'd confess something like that to me."

"No, she's not just interested in him, Paige. She's in love with him. Big difference. We don't live in a hook-up society anymore. Her feelings are real. Does that bother you that she has feelings for him?"

"I'm not sure how I feel about it," she admits. "The thing is, I'm just getting to know Simon again, you know? We were separated from each other during the most significant, life-changing event in history. And he's changed. And so have I. Good God, I don't even know who I am anymore. And he's so different, too. He's a man now. When I saw him last, he was a dorky fourteen-year-old kid who liked video games and studying and geek shit."

Reagan chuckles softly and says, "I don't know that he's changed all that much. He's just a geeky twenty-year-old."

Paige laughs and replies, "A geeky twenty-year-old who can apparently shoot very well!"

"Oh, yeah," Reagan concurs. "He's a crackshot, that kid. The guys talk about it all the time how good of a shot he is, even though he is a dork."

"Really? The guys talk about Simon? That's good. I'm glad he's had them to look after him and teach him."

Reagan smiles. "He's a good kid. Sam's a good kid, too."

"Yeah, she's great. I suppose with everything that's been happening and also trying to adjust to living on your farm that I missed it, this thing between Simon and Sam."

"It's no big deal," Reagan says. "They're both still young. I wouldn't get too excited about it. Simon sure as hell isn't about to act on it. Hell, Simon probably doesn't even know."

Paige nods, but her mouth tightens into a thin line as if she isn't happy to be hearing this tale of romance and young, budding love. Perhaps she is bitter toward that sentiment as Reagan had once been.

"Do you know if he feels the same?" she asks.

Paige readjusts her baggy brown t-shirt, also borrowed, and Reagan notices that she has a light sprinkling of freckles on her shoulder that match the ones on her nose and cheeks.

"I don't know. Well, I guess that's not really true," Reagan amends. She doesn't get to elaborate because Grandpa and Mr. Oberholtz join them a second later.

Three hours later they are all in the town hall, which used to house the mayor's office and the police force and the local court system. The building was only built about seven years ago, so other than the dust and cobwebs, it's still fairly new and holding together well without the benefit of maintenance. It has the largest meeting area in the criminal courtroom on the second floor, and the men and some of the townspeople have set up additional folding chairs they'd found in the basement.

Plans for finishing the wall are laid out on display, and plenty more volunteers come forward to offer their services to help on the build. The condo community, although not technically contained within the city limits or the new walls, is also present and being represented by Condo Paul.

John and Derek discuss a need for a twenty-four hour a day patrol and guard system on the wall and inside of it, as well. One of the former deputies has been sworn in as the new sheriff, done by a unanimous vote about a year ago. The town's former sheriff was murdered in his home while he slept at the beginning of the apocalypse. The people in the town thought that it was likely a grudge murder from someone he'd arrested in the past. They'd wanted Derek to fill the vacated position of the new sheriff, but the idea of going to town every day and being away from the farm hadn't appealed to him. The new sheriff and his new deputies will take on the city's patrols for the time being until men and women can be trained thoroughly. Some of these people used to be tax preparers, computer programmers and lawyers, soccer moms and homemakers, not gun-slinging guards and the security force of an entire town.

"The harvest season will be here before we know it. Our garden is already in," one of the men from an outlying farm states as he stands. "I can't manage the harvest on my own anymore, not since my boy died last year. I figured what with everyone needing food, I'd plant double this year to help out. But I'll need help come harvest time. I put in a field of corn and squash, too."

Grandpa jumps in to intervene, "Hank, everything will get worked out. We'll get you the help you need. It was a generous thing to do planting extra, to think of others like that. I'm sure that some of the people here could help in exchange for some food or crop, or meat if you can spare it."

Immediately two of the women and many more of the men in the room raise their hands. It's been this way for the past two years since they'd become more involved in their little community.

Mr. Jefferson, the town pharmacist, had helped bring in a field of corn last year by hand. He'd told Reagan a while back, when she'd treated his ten-year-old daughter for a cut that had required stitches, that his hands had blistered for weeks after that laborious task. He hadn't really been complaining. He'd said how grateful they were for the bushels of corn that they'd been able to can and eat throughout the last winter. Everyone is like this now. They work together and help the farmers in the surrounding areas in exchange for a share of the crop to keep their families alive. It's a barter and trade system that has worked successfully so far. Grandpa and Simon have also been working with him on compounding herbals.

The Reynolds and the Johnson families have even donated milk cows to a few people for trade items that they needed. Some of the men in town cut firewood for those who can't in exchange for things that they don't have like canned goods or dried meat or fruit leathers. Minus the lack of security, their town is starting to turn the corner for the better and Reagan is glad for it. For too long people had been afraid to even come out of their homes, out of hiding. They'd been distrustful of everyone, even each other. Hell, even Mrs. Crestwich, the former owner of the town's only bakery, has said that if things continue improving the way that they are, she may be able to re-open her old bakery again with the right power source by next year. Reagan's fairly certain that one's just a pipe dream. But everyone needs something to aim toward.

She's zoned out thinking about how good a doughnut would taste about now when an argument erupts. One of the men from the new neighborhood as they have labeled it, or sector five, is angry about something. The new neighborhood is over on the other side of town. John had told her that when he and Kelly had gone there one night looking for the parts for Grandpa's ultrasound machine they went to investigate gunshots near the stat care clinic. The neighborhood had still been under construction before the fall, which has now been mostly finished, or as finished as they could make six of the homes out there. Thus the name the new neighborhood. To call anything about it new is quite the exaggeration indeed. Most of the homes were finished using parts and supplies looted from abandoned homes and hardware stores from many different counties. There are thirteen families living in those six homes, but at least they have a source of water out there and can ban together to help one another.

"We want the same protection and take of the food as everyone else here!" Mr. Hernandez argues.

His first name is Jay, and Kelly sometimes calls him Jay the jackass. They've had disputes with him before. Reagan worries that her husband will stand up and shoot him on the spot. She's never too sure of what his reaction to things like this will be. She squeezes his hand. He looks over at her and rolls his eyes. Good, he's in a pleasant mood. His grin takes her breath away as usual.

"Mr. Hernandez," Grandpa starts, "you'll be offered the same food source availability in exchange for work. You know how the system works. You don't just get food."

"We don't always have as much time to offer. We've been workin' all spring trying to finish the next house. We've had to go on runs for supplies. We have to lug water from the lake over there. It's all time-consuming work!"

"Then you need to come up with some kind of new system, dude," Kelly says tightly. "We told you last fall to set up a wind turbine to power generate that water source. It's nobody's fault that you guys didn't get that done."

Jay the jackass glares angrily at Kelly but decides not to push his luck there. Everyone in the entire town fears Kelly. Reagan smirks. If they only knew that John was the one they should fear and not Kelly, they wouldn't walk around shrinking back from the big guy.

"We want the same protection from the wall," Jay rebuts.

"You know that's probably not going to happen, Mr. Hernandez," the new sheriff states. "We told you this before. We can't come that far with it before the bad winter weather hits again. It's just probably not going to happen. We'll have to start back up next spring."

"Oh, bullshit!" Jay argues.

His wife tugs at his shirttail, but he shirks her off.

"You'll be responsible for your own security for one more year, so start figuring it out," Kelly basically orders. "Set up patrols just like they're going to do here. Appoint guards. Work on gathering and training on weapons."

Reagan knows that he's probably getting impatient for this meeting to end so he can get home to Hannah and his Mary, the second love of his life and also his teeny shadow when he's home on the farm. That munchkin is never going to find a husband when she grows up someday. Her dad will always be her greatest hero. Also, he's likely never going to let her out of his sight long enough to even attract a member of the opposite sex. Reagan flinches from those funny thoughts because Jay the jackass is still railing.

"If the people would've started out in our sector instead of right here in the middle of the damn town, they could've finished ours first and then the town's wall in the spring."

Beside her, John stands. She's not about to tug at his shirt. Mr. Hernandez is always a pain in the ass. Reagan could care less how John handles this. She, too, would like to go home. Her back is tired from working all day at the clinic.

"Look, you all want free medical care?" John bellows at them.

Reagan almost cringes at his loud tone. He's not usually this quick to jump straight to anger, at least not at a town meeting. His handsome, fun-loving smile is gone. Some of the people from the town nod or shout out "yes" in response to his question.

"Then we shore up the walls around the town first. The clinic doesn't get protected, then we don't come back to work in it!" he blares.

Reagan can tell that he's tired. He's been working since dawn, first at the farm and then all day here in town building a massive, tall and thick wall. Unfortunately most of the people don't know that he's working double time. All of the men from their farm are for the time being while they work at the farm on their own planting and also come to town every day to work on the wall. They also don't know that the McClane Warriors are still searching every night for the last four men who'd gotten away. They are going on very few hours of sleep each night, and it's coming to a head for her dear husband.

"That clinic doesn't get enough protection," he continues on at a slightly lower decibel, slightly. "That's the reason it was attacked. You think I'm going to let my wife come here to work for free for all of you when she could come to harm? Or Doc? Come on, people! Who do you think is going to come here and offer free health-care services once we stop? That's right. Nobody! And with good reason, too. Nobody wants to work while they have to worry constantly about getting shot. That should've never happened in the first place.

This wall should've been built two years ago. We let our guards down, got complacent. That can never happen again."

Grandpa interrupts and lays a hand on John's shoulder since he's right next to him, "John's right, folks, the wall must be built around the direct vicinity of the town first and then continued outward later. The clinic must be protected at all costs. You are welcome, Jay, to move the families from your community into some of the empty homes here in town. We've offered that before, but you turned it down. But if you want the wall to continue all the way out to your neighborhood, then you'll either have to start that project yourself with your men or you'll have to wait until spring most likely."

Derek stands next and says, "Look, for some of you that haven't been touched yet by some of the sicknesses and diseases out there, you should consider yourselves lucky. One of our own doctors got sick just this last spring. We are taking huge risks to help everyone in this town, but if you don't want that help anymore then fine."

Immediately everyone turns on Jay Hernandez. They gripe and bitch at him until he becomes red in the face. Reagan doesn't know if it's from embarrassment or anger. She hopes it's not for the latter reason. He's already pissy enough to deal with most of the time. He's become somewhat of the leader of his district, even though that sort of anarchy away from the town was discouraged. Each district has a volunteer spokesperson like Condo Paul, who can represent the needs of their areas. But Jay behaves more like a dictator of his small district. They need to work together. Having ten different mayors and sheriffs would just complicate their growing community.

Grandpa quiets the room with a raise of his hand. The meeting wraps with every person in agreement of the new patrols, the wall, the security of the clinic and the exchange of working on the harvest season later in the summer for food. Everyone but Mr. Hernandez, of course, but nobody pays him any mind once again.

After the meeting, Condo Paul joins up with them to let Reagan and her grandfather know that Anita, one of the women at the condo village who is pregnant, says that she thinks she's getting closer. The widow that John and Derek had freed and saved from asshole creeps four years ago had married a nice man who'd sought refuge over there and had ended up becoming a very valuable member of their condo community. He was an ex-Navy Seal, an excellent strategist and planner who'd helped Paul fortify the hell out of that community. They'd taken the phrase gated community to a whole new level. Every condo on their small cul-de-sac is filled with families, and they all work together to make it thrive against all odds. They keep over six dozen chickens in the former pool house, around six or seven milk and beef cows, at last count, out on the golf course, and quite a few goats. They've managed to find eight abandoned and left for dead or turned loose horses over the years, as well. They'd turned a two acre patch of ground including the seventeenth hole into a healthy, robust garden. It still tickles Reagan's funny bone every time she goes over there and sees cows, horses and goats grazing on a former golf course. That is until she spies the armed guards that patrol it on foot. The women learned how to can, care of the McClane family, and their garden flourishes each season. Paul's miniature community is a kick-ass fortress, and he's become the McClanes number one ally against outside enemies. Reagan is glad that she and John helped Paul and his family in that hospital four years ago. He's a good man who only wants to keep his family alive.

Grandpa reassures him that one of them will be available for Anita's birth and that he should just call on the radio when she's ready. They part on their usual handshake. It's hard to believe that she and John had met him when Paul and his family had been on the run from murderers and thieves in the hospital in Clarksville. He'd been defenseless, was shot and bleeding and afraid for the lives of his family. Now he is a survivor and warrior like the Rangers.

They ride home to the farm in the SUV, which Kelly had repaired the other day. Something about a fuel line or pump or some other thing that Reagan could care less about. Gasoline is becoming more difficult to find and salvage. Trips to town will soon have to become modified by other means of transportation if they don't source more fuel somewhere. Every time she thinks things could get really bad, though, the men seem to put their heads together and come up with a plan.

They stop to pick up Talia and Maddie on the way home from their visit with the Reynolds. Reagan slides over and takes Maddie onto her lap as Paige scoots to the middle so that Talia can get in beside her. Talia is grinning ear to ear, her cheeks flushed against her mocha, smooth skin.

"Have a nice visit?" Paige asks slyly once they are moving again.

Reagan wonders at the playful tone in Paige's voice.

"Shh," Talia says.

Reagan spies Talia poke Paige in the ribs gently with her elbow.

"What's going on?" Reagan asks. "What'd I miss?"

"I don't think Talia's been visiting the Reynolds for *Bertie's* company if you know what I mean," Paige teases her friend, getting a scowl from Talia.

"Oh really?" Reagan asks. She wishes she could tell John, but he's in the truck behind them. Kelly is driving their SUV, and Grandpa rides shotgun as usual. But Simon and John are following them in the truck. Sam is also with John and Simon, of course. Those two rarely separate.

"Stop!" Talia hisses with feigned anger.

"So, Chet Reynolds, huh?" Kelly asks from the driver's seat.

"Oh my gosh!" Talia cries out with embarrassment.

Reagan and Kelly both laugh. She's not at all surprised that he's figured it out before her. Some of Hannah's intuition must have rubbed off on him over the years.

"Chet's a good man, Talia," Grandpa acknowledges, furthering Talia's humiliation.

"Oh no," Talia says as she covers her face with her hands.

"Get used to it," Reagan jokes. "Nothing's private in this family!"

"You could do worse," Kelly adds.

"Worse what?" Maddie inquires.

Everyone laughs as they pull into the gravel drive next to the house. Maddie forgets her question as she bounds over Reagan and out the door. She Charlie-horses Reagan's leg in the process. The other kids, Jacob included, greet her with calls and cheers before they all take off for the swing-set. A grin touches Reagan's mouth as she watches her son Jacob climb like a monkey all over the fort part of the swing-set. He's a crazy maniac who knows no fear. She and John have decided not to tell him about his real parents until he's an adult. This world is tough enough without finding out that you're an orphan of it and its cruelty. Besides, he actually looks a tad like John with his light hair and eyes, and his mischief-making personality.

The rest of their group join them, all wanting to know what all the joking and razzing of Talia is about. Even Hannah and Sue have come onto the back porch. It takes a nanosecond for Hannie to figure it out. Damn Bassett hound sister.

All she elicits over this newly-discovered relationship news is a sad smile that doesn't touch her different-colored eyes before calling for the children to come inside to wash up. Reagan wraps an arm around her shoulders and leads her back inside where she is instantly met with the smell of wonderful home-cooking.

"Good grief, Hannie," she exclaims as some of the others join them. "What the heck did you make?"

"Nothing special really," she replies demurely. "Sue and I just made chicken and dumplings."

"Well, that smells fantastic, little sister," Reagan tells her as she uses the kitchen sink to wash her hands. A timer sounds near the stove. "Need me to get that, whatever it is?"

"Sure," Hannah says. "I just threw some vegetables into the oven to roast since the garden's going well, and we should try to use up the vegetables from the winter storage."

"Mm, these smell good, too," Reagan says when she opens the oven door. "I see Kelly got the gas going again."

"Of course, does that actually surprise you?" Hannah asks with a smile.

Reagan knows that he doesn't like Hannah to have to cook on the fireplace or the wood-burning stoves in the basement. He still coddles her, but everyone gave up trying to make him stop. It was just easier than facing the wrath of his sneer.

"Not really, sis," Reagan concedes. "Mm, rosemary. That's what smells so good in these."

"Yep, that's about the last of it until the greenhouse herbs go in the ground," her sister tells her.

"I hope the strawberries do well this year, or at least better than last year," Reagan says. Last year, they'd been eaten by deer and wildlife, and the family hadn't been able to save many of the plants from attack. "We could make a few of Grams's strawberry pies."

As soon as Reagan says it, she regrets it. Her sister's face immediately falls, and she turns away busying herself with another task. Sometimes even bringing up Grams's name causes Hannah to fall back into a depression.

"Sorry, Hannie," Reagan apologizes, even though Grams was her grandmother, too. Everyone knows that she and Hannah were closest, but there was never a jealousy over it. Hannah had been the youngest when they'd all moved to the farm, and she'd never left it like Sue and Reagan had.

"You don't have to help," Hannah says. "You worked all day at the clinic. You must be tired."

"I'm fine. Don't worry about me. I'm super tough, remember?" Reagan jests.

"Uh huh, I'll take your word for it," Hannah jokes. "I seem to recall just a short time ago when you almost croaked on us from a little old flu bug."

"That was harsh!" Reagan teases. Hannah has always been able to make her smile. She makes everyone smile. Reagan just wishes she'd do it more often again.

"Hey, baby," Kelly's deep voice interrupts them.

Reagan notices that all her sister offers Kelly is a sad half smile. It brings down Reagan's playful mood almost immediately. Nobody likes Hannah to feel bad. She's always been the family's core of lightness and joy. She's been this downtrodden for so long that

Reagan worries about her constantly. They all do. Losing Em had put the finishing touch on Hannah's deep-seated depression.

Dinner wraps up later; John plays music on the guitar for the kids at Ari's insistent demands. The children dance and twirl, mostly the girls, while the boys play with their cars and Army guys with the click-clack attached feet.

Later as they lie in bed, Reagan cuddled next to John in the attic after they've made love, she tells him how worried she is about Hannah. She's told him many, many times how worried she is about her darling sister.

"She'll come around, honey," he tries at appeasing her.

This is his usual answer, but tonight it feels forced. Her husband rubs at her scalp soothingly and then down into the curve of her back lightly. He kisses her full on the mouth when she looks up at him.

"I don't know, John," she says on a sigh. "I feel like…"

A tiny voice interrupts from the doorway, "Mama?"

Jacob has come into their room. Thank goodness she'd pulled on John's t-shirt. Reagan sits up and turns on the bedside wall sconce. "What is it, sweetie?"

"My ear hurts," he complains.

Reagan makes eye contact with John, who gives her a quick grin. He knows her so well.

"Want some help?" he offers, laying a hand on her arm.

Reagan kisses his hand and says, "No way. I've got him. You need some sleep if you're leaving at four again."

John nods and pulls her over for a kiss before resting back again, folding his arm behind his head. His unruly blonde hair has lightened quite a lot with the early summer sun hitting it. His tanned arm muscles seem to beckon her. She hides her grin. If he knows what she's thinking, he may not let her leave for the whole night.

"Ok, buddy," she says to her son as she swings out of bed and pulls on sweatpants. "Come on, let's get you downstairs where Mama can take a look."

She scoops her small boy into her arms, kisses John on the cheek and leaves their room. Jacob buries his face in her neck and clings on as they go downstairs. His skin feels warm with fever.

Her medical bag awaits her near the back door in the kitchen where she can grab it quickly and be gone if need be. She places Jacob on his bottom on the island and fishes out her otoscope. Jacob does indeed have some redness inside his ear canal. He's running a very low-grade fever. Hopefully, a hot wash cloth will draw out the pain and ease his discomfort enough without going as far as needing to take antibiotics. They are nearly out of medical grade antibiotics. A minimal dosage of fever reducer should help, too. They don't have much of that left, either. Having this many children on the farm means that they've used up almost all of those simple supplies.

"Stay right there, sweetie," she tells him. "Mama will be right back."

He nods and places his chubby palm against his ear.

"It hurts," he complains.

Reagan smiles sadly at him, kisses his smooth, warm forehead and nods. "I know, kiddo. Stay here, 'kay? We'll get ya' fixed right up."

Reagan goes down the hall, intent on fetching a washcloth from the linen closet, when she hears Kelly speaking quietly to Hannah. His tone causes her to inch closer to their room, where the door stands open. Her brother-in-law is kneeling in front of Hannah, who is sitting on their bed.

"…I can't do this, baby," he says. "You gotta come back to me, Hannah, to all of us. We need you. Mary needs you and so do the other children."

Hannah is crying softly. It breaks Reagan's heart. She knows what he's talking to her sister about. It's the same thing she was just discussing with John upstairs.

"I'm sorry, Kelly," Hannah says weakly.

"You don't have to be sorry, baby. But we need you to come back to us. You're the one person everyone in this family relies on for nurturing and love. It's what you do. It's what we've come to lean on you for."

"It's just too hard, Kelly," she says brokenly and sniffs.

Kelly sighs long and loud and rests his head in Hannah's lap.

"Come back to us, Hannah," he pleads again.

Jacob calls her from the kitchen, breaking her trance of spying on her sister and brother-in-law. She snatches a rag from the linen closet and hurries back to her son. After giving him a dose of fever reducer, Reagan carries him to the front room where she'll stay the night on the sofa with him. First she takes up position in a rocking chair next to the dying fire. After about an hour of heating and re-heating the rag and holding it pressed to his soft ear and rocking him soothingly, Jacob finally falls asleep again. His fever breaks a short time later, but she'll not risk him going back to bed where she can't monitor him. She simply tucks him in on the sofa and slides in behind him where she can cradle him to her.

Worrying about her baby, even though he's almost five, has prevented her from finding sleep. As she lies awake most of the night, she has time to reflect on Kelly and Hannah's conversation that she'd overheard. He, too, knows that her sister has to snap out of this, to move on from her grief that is literally causing her to waste away mentally and physically. She's going to be the next one to become ill. Reagan could never bear it if she lost one of her sisters. Perhaps she could just stay home more instead of going to town to the clinic or when the men work on the wall. She could spend more time with Hannah, help her out more, too. A frown mars her features. She's not even sure that would work. Her sister is in the deep bowels of depression and has been there since Em's death. Perhaps if Cory came home, she'd feel better. Hannie's crazy about him. Perhaps that would do the trick, if he'd just bring his ass home.

Chapter Twenty-seven
Sam

Sam chuckles and moves closer to Paige in the garden, who is about as clueless at weeding as she is about milking cows and riding horses.

"No, Paige," Sam corrects her. "You're pulling carrots. Silly, we need to put those back in. See?" she asks and points to the feathery fronds of the carrot tops. "These aren't weeds."

Paige frowns, unknowingly rubs dirt on her forehead from the back of her soiled glove and says, "Shit. Sorry. That one really did look like a weed. We used to boil down stuff like this to eat."

This isn't the first time Paige has pulled vegetables thinking they were weeds.

"I'm glad you're here, glad you aren't out there anymore," Sam acknowledges about her new friend. "Even if you do like pulling out our baby vegetables."

Paige laughs at herself and nods.

"Me, too. I'm glad I'm here," Paige says and lays a hand over hers in the dirt.

Sam still feels like Paige holds back from sharing her thoughts and feelings, but she's coming along. Sam understands that it must be difficult to trust people after what she has been through.

"Well, the horses might get mad if we kill all the carrots before they get a chance to grow," Sam says with a chuckle. "I try to sneak a few every once in a while to them. Unless Hannah happens to be around. Then I don't even attempt it. She'd get mad for sure since she likes to put them in stews and sauces."

Paige finally smiles, but Sam can tell that she still feels bad about pulling weeds that weren't weeds. She touches her arm and offers a lopsided grin.

"Don't worry about it," Sam appeases her new friend.

They've all been busy tending the garden while the men work in shifts on the wall in town. They are making fast progress, but it's still a huge undertaking surrounding an entire small town with a wall system. Some days Paige goes into town with them, but on others she'll stay behind to help on the farm.

She tells Paige, "Just wait till canning season starts. It gets downright crazy around here. The kitchen gets like two hundred degrees it seems like. Sue and Hannah do a lot of the canning outside to help."

"Really?" Paige asks as she picks actual weeds this time.

"Oh yeah," Sam says. "They do almost all of the tomatoes in the cauldron and old canner over a fire in the back yard. Everything gets canned. Plus we make applesauce as long as the orchard doesn't get infested with worms. And peaches, too, those are great for canning. Sue always makes sure that some kind of fruit gets canned to help ensure the kids stay healthy all winter. If we didn't can the vegetables and even the fruits, we'd never make it."

"Yeah, I guess not with so many people living here," Paige concurs as she swipes loose tendrils of red waves behind her ear. "There were many times on the road that I wished for an apple or a peach or even some broccoli, which I hate."

Sam chuckles and nods. "I don't mind broccoli, but I'm not too fond of the spinach. I wish we didn't plant it at all. But Sue makes a pretty good dish with it where she stuffs it inside pieces of chicken with herbs and our goat cheese. That's not too bad. Any other way that it actually tastes like spinach makes me wanna' hurl."

"Yeah, I think I remember having that dish once since I came here," Paige says. "It was good. Heck, everything they make is good."

"What kinds of things did you like to eat before… you know, *before*?" Sam asks.

"Um, well, I was a vegan. So I didn't eat dairy or meat. My diet was a lot different. But my mom used to make a really good veggie lasagna for me," Paige answers.

Sam doesn't miss the flicker of sadness that passes over her features like a gloomy, gray cloud on a sunny day. She sketched a picture of Paige the other day when she'd found her asleep in the hammock in the side yard near Grams's rose garden. She hasn't had the courage to show Paige yet. Maybe she'll just show it to Simon instead.

"That sounds good. You should tell the girls. They'll probably make it for you. They can make just about anything," Sam offers, trying to make her feel better.

"Yeah, maybe," Paige mumbles.

Sam knows that talking about her mother is difficult for Paige, so she doesn't push. Some day if Paige comes to her to talk, then she'll be there for her. Until she's ready, though, just coercing her into it will feel forced and disingenuous. She figures a change in subject matter will help.

"We were thinking about playing music tonight," she says as she wipes a bead of sweat from her forehead. The sun is high and hot. It must be nearly two in the afternoon already. They've been in the garden for nearly three hours already. They planted two more rows of vegetable seeds to stagger the crop harvest. Her back is starting to feel kinked. "Do you play an instrument? Or do you sing? I notice you never get involved."

Paige just furrows her brow and shakes her head before answering, "No, do you want me to attract wild cats for miles away?"

Sam laughs good-naturedly and says, "No instruments, either?"

She gets another shake of Paige's head in answer. Simon's sister is wearing a pair of his faded, threadbare cut-off blue-jean shorts that hang off her very slim hips, secured by one of his brown leather belts. Paige also has on a borrowed t-shirt that she's knotted at her slim waist to keep it out of her way. Sam is fairly sure it's one of Cory's tees since it has a picture of a 1940's era pin-up girl perched on the front of an old airplane, but it hardly matters since he's not around to make use of it. Everyone on the farm tries to share and offer up clothing and supplies to Paige and Talia since they came to the farm with one small bag of belongings, most of which weren't really even usable anymore. They'd given her group a tub of clothing for Maddie to use, as well since the tiny tyke only had two outfits that they'd been forced to rotate on her. Unfortunately, not one of the women wear the same size shoes as Paige. She's so much taller and leaner than the women, too, which doesn't make for ideal swaps. They just do their best, and she never complains.

"I like the way you play the violin, though," Paige offers. "It's really lovely, Sam. You have quite a talent there."

She gives a shrug and says, "I don't know. My mother thought it was important to learn a musical instrument. She grew up playing the cello. My older brother played the drums. That wasn't popular in our house!"

"Ha, I bet!"

Her new friend's laugh is very raucous when she actually allows herself to laugh.

"No, my dad would come home from work, and my brother and his friends would be in the garage banging away at their instruments. He even thought he might like to be a rock star, but my dad wouldn't have gone for that. He wanted him to take over when he retired."

"What did your dad do for a living? Simon said you guys had a really nice house and… well," Paige stammers.

"Oh, yeah, I suppose we did. I didn't think of it like that. It was just the house I lived in, where I grew up, where I used to have silly slumber parties with my girlfriends from the riding academy where I took lessons."

Sam loses her train of thought for a moment, thinking of her friends, so young like her, so full of hopes and dreams, all ridiculously childish dreams given the current circumstances of the world. They used to stay up late after horse shows and talk and giggle and fantasize. Sam had been hoping to gain a scholarship from riding in the show-jumping and cross-country circuit and eventually making it onto the US Olympic team for the three day eventing. Her mother had even taken her to meet two of the coaches for the team, and they'd been impressed with her stats. They'd told her mother that with her tenacity and passion that she should be a shoe-in someday. Her father had bought her a national level show-jumping gelding from Germany and had shipped him all the way to their home. He was a big, muscular handsome bay at sixteen and one hands. His name was in German, so she just always called him Brutus since the guttural sounds of his native language were too complicated for her to master. He seemed to like it, too, because he used to nicker and call out to her when she went anywhere near the barn and said his name. The show-jumping circuit season was just about to start back up when the world fell apart. She and her best friend were both involved in show-jumping and dressage. They were excited to get back into the swing of things which meant trailering the horses all over the country, meeting up with long lost friends from the circuit, and competing for ribbons and points toward that elusive scholarship offer. Sometimes her mother would take her, sometimes her father and sometimes her friend's parents. It seems like a whole other life, her old life. Thinking about it seems surreal, as if she is remembering a movie she'd watched and can just barely make out the characters' faces instead of what it really was which is her own story. It doesn't seem like her life or that she was ever a part of it. The life that she has as a McClane seems like the only one she knows. That other girl died a long time ago, along with her hopes and dreams of being an Olympian. When she glances up, Paige is staring at her before quickly looking away.

"What? What did you ask? Oh, yes, my father," Sam says with embarrassment. "Um, he owned a real-estate development company, townhouses, office buildings, commercial real-estate mostly. I know he wanted my brother to go to college and take over when he got closer to retirement."

Paige nods and says, "I'm sorry, Sam. About your family, I mean. That must've been…"

It's Sam's turn to frown and look away. She turns back with a smile and announces, "Let's take a break, shall we? My back is getting sore. I think we got quite a lot done today."

"Sounds great," Paige agrees unsurely.

They carry their buckets full of weeds and dump them in the compost pile near the hog barn. Paige tries to make small talk with her, but it's hard to concentrate fully on her words. Sam chooses to ignore the fact that her hands shake. Forgetting the past, which is what she mostly attempts to do, is so much easier than remembering it. The place in her heart where her family used to reside sometimes feels so empty as if it will swallow her whole. Remembering any part of that old life is difficult and painful. Remembering what happened to her directly after she'd lost her whole family is entirely unbearable.

"I think I'm going to take a walk," she tells Paige.

"Oh, um, is that ok? I mean the guys are gone, and they say we're not supposed to leave the farm when they are," Paige says protectively.

Sam smiles gently and says, "I'll be fine. I'm not going more than a few feet beyond the barns. Don't worry."

Simon's lovely sister with the pale blue eyes and striking red hair nods nervously and looks around as if she is trying to find someone to halt her.

"It's fine. I do it all the time. Besides, they aren't all gone, just some of them," Sam reassures her before turning to go.

She heads past the hog barn, climbs over the horse fence and strides into the forest. Jogging about a hundred feet into the dense woods, Sam finally rests against a massive oak. The roots of the ancient tree spread far and wide, its huge top providing a reprieve from the June heat. There she gasps for breath. This time is harder for some reason than others. It's just too painful to breathe around. The feeling of loss has come over her hard and fast this time. Normally she's prepared for it. A long, rainy day brings it on sometimes, reminding her of the day and the mood of the weather when her family had been taken from her. She hadn't expected Paige's simple question about her father's profession to bring forth this much anxiety and so many bad memories.

It's not Paige's fault. Sam just needs to pull her crap together before she goes back to the house. Everyone has their own problems. Nobody needs to be brought down by her negativity. They are all still reeling from the loss of Em and then Gavin and some of the townspeople during the Target creeps' raid. Talia is still distressed over the loss of her friend, especially. And poor Hannah just seems to keep getting knocked down emotionally because she doesn't process loss well at all. When these relapses come on, Sam tries her best to hide it from everyone.

Her chest feels constricted, the walls of her lungs closing in on her and making it difficult to draw a full breath. Sometimes this is followed by flashing lights in her peripheral vision, nausea and a lovely, intense migraine. She reaches her hand out to lean against the rough bark. She aches for her mother's soft and gentle touch, to be held by her again and told that everything will be ok. She aches for the comforting, encouraging words of Grams. She'd been so helpful and thoughtful with Sam when she'd first come to be unofficially adopted by the McClanes. It's just one more perforation in her broken heart, the loss of Grams.

Sam slumps to the ground at the base of the tree, mindful of the poison ivy that is growing only a few feet away. She leans her head back against the trunk, closes her eyes and reminisces a moment about her mother.

She had dark hair like her, nearly black. Her mother was youthful and fun. They'd play duets together, she on her violin, her mother on her lovely cello. She told Sam that when she was a young woman she'd been offered a scholarship to Juilliard but had turned it down in favor of staying in Tennessee to marry Sam's father. Her mother's parents, Sam's grandparents who'd been killed in a car accident while on vacation in California when she was still quite young, had been furious. At the time of the story telling, Sam hadn't been able to comprehend giving up something so huge. She could never have given up a riding scholarship for any boy. But, then again, she'd only been thirteen or fourteen when her mother had told her. She had no idea what love was back then, nor did she care to find out. Her life had been all about riding or music, right up until it all fell apart. There wasn't much room for anything else. Boys weren't even a thought.

When her mother had gotten pregnant with the twins, they'd all rejoiced. But Sam knows that it wasn't a planned pregnancy. Her mother was forty-one years old. Nonetheless, she'd gone through with the pregnancy and given birth to Sam's younger brother and sister. They'd been perfect, too. Well, perfect unless one counted middle of the night feedings and bizarre sleep patterns that woke everyone up for the first full year. But Sam had been crazy about them, had shown them off to all her friends and bragged them up constantly. They were stinking adorable rugrats. She helped her mom as much as she could, too because she knew how much they wore her out. They were only two years old when they were murdered by Simon and Paige's Aunt Amber's group of insane criminals. Her older brother had been seventeen, two years older than she was at the time.

They hadn't been particularly close since he mostly thought of her as a pest, but she still loved him just the same. They had their fair share of sibling rivalry, arguments over pointless things, relentless teasing from him, and the typical "stay out of my room" moments. He favored their father with sandy brown hair and matching eyes. He was very good-looking, always charming some girl in school. She used to jeer him relentlessly about jumping from one girl to the next and that he was going to run out of date prospects in their school. He usually just noogied the top of her head for her. And he absolutely hated the horses. He went to most of her shows just to be supportive, but he didn't ride, not ever. Sam knows that her parents had probably forced him to go since he likely would've preferred to hang out with his friends. But he'd gone, nonetheless. He'd been thrown from a mare when he was young and had never mounted up again. In his defense, he had broken his collar bone. He rooted her on, though, and also picked up girls while hanging around the barns by bragging about his band.

Sam doesn't even realize that she's crying until she has to sniff.

One time her mom and dad were preparing dinner and had asked her to fetch her brother from the garage where he was pounding away on his drums. Her baby siblings were also in the kitchen. Her tiny, two-year-old sister was in a baby saucer entertaining herself with the gadgets and gizmos and light-up mechanisms attached to the chair. Her baby brother was busy banging on the cupboard doors and tearing items out of drawers and throwing them on the floor at their father's feet. After she'd called her big brother, she'd returned to the kitchen to find her parents laughing. She'd caught them in the middle of talking about her brother and his noisy, nerve-rattling drums. Her father had said that perhaps they shouldn't encourage any more musical instruments, especially for the new babies. Sam distinctly remembers her father leaning his hip against the granite counter munching on red pepper strips her mother was slicing at the island. She was making beef stir fry that night, a family favorite. Her father was wearing dirty blue-jeans and a cotton button down shirt because he'd just come from a construction site. Dirt and dust still clung to his forearms, the front of his shirt, and even in his hair. Some days he came home spic and span clean in a dark suit which meant he worked at the office on a deal or had met with clients, but other days when he visited the job site, he came home filthy. He was very hands-on according to her mother, although Sam really hadn't been able to comprehend that saying at the time. If her father was alive today, he'd have plenty to be hands-on about on the McClane farm and on the building of the town wall. That day her mother's shiny, dark hair was pulled back into its usual bun at the base of her slim neck, and she wore her ever present workout clothing of yoga pants and a zip-up jacket. She enjoyed walking five miles every day with one of the other moms in their development. Their neighborhood was more like small, five to seven acre mini-farms, nothing like the McClane farm.

    Sometimes her mother would go to town and take various exercise classes at a local gym, which has since been totally ransacked and then burned to the ground after the apocalypse for some reason. She was always such a health nut. Once she'd even dragged Sam to something called a spinning class. It hadn't made sense to her. Riding a bicycle but not going anywhere seemed pointless.

It's still hard for Sam to believe that her mom got so sick after the apocalypse. Her mother's cough and fever had been worsening with each passing day. Sam had volunteered to stay home and take care of the chores which were mostly fixing food and feeding the horses. The twins were asleep in their cribs, and she was to keep an eye on them while her brother, father and mother went to find medicine. That morning she'd wanted to clean her parents' room, to rid their bed of fever-soaked sheets that she planned to hand-wash in their tub while they were gone. She was in the middle of that when the group arrived. She heard the big, noisy RV's pull into their circular drive. She'd checked to make sure the twins were still asleep and had locked their door from the inside. Then she'd hidden in her closet. Simon had found her. He told her to stay hidden.

Their neighborhood had not been impacted yet with the violence that seemed to have spread nationwide on the television reports. She'd locked the front doors. But sometimes when she thinks back on it, she is pretty sure that she hadn't locked the back door after coming in from feeding the horses that day. She hadn't had a gun like she's worn on a constant basis since coming to the McClane farm. Her mother had hated guns, hadn't wanted one in their house. It may not have helped anyway. Sam knows that she would've been severely outnumbered by Amber's group.

Her parents and brother were only going about three miles from their home. Her dad and brother went out almost every morning to find water and haul it back to the house. That morning had seemed like any other when they left to forage, only that time they were looking for meds. Her mother was worried that the twins would get her sickness, so she wanted to have more of a stock-up of antibiotics or even some children's fever reducer or decongestant. It should've been safe. It had quickly turned so horribly wrong.

"Hey!" Simon yells angrily.

Sam jumps out of her skin and presses her back to the tree. Simon stalks purposefully toward her, smashing through thickets and summer overgrowth like a raging bull.

"What the hell are you doing, Sam?" he barks. "You know you aren't supposed to be out here by yourself."

He snatches her to her feet by pulling her arm. It doesn't hurt, but it does anger her just slightly. Apparently Paige has ratted her out because she was worried about her. Sometimes she'd just like a few hours alone, but it's hard to get any on a farm literally full of adults and children.

"Stop! I don't need your help, Simon," she says with irritation tinging her voice. She doesn't like to raise her voice at anyone, especially Simon. Sam looks up at him.

"Oh crap," he mumbles. "Are you crying, Sam?"

"No," she lies badly and pulls free of his grasp. "Let me be, Simon."

"Wait," he says.

Simon lunges for her when she turns to leave but misses. Sam stumbles over an unseen log, her tears blurring her vision. She swipes the back of her hand over her damp cheeks while keeping her head low and marching on.

"Sam, wait," he repeats. "Wait a damn minute. What's wrong?"

She doesn't answer but waves her hand over her shoulder at him, dismissing him. Sam picks up the pace when she clears the woods. He tries to help her over the fence, but she shrugs off his hand.

Once she hits the pasture, she says over her shoulder, "Just leave me alone, Simon. Everything's fine. Sorry I went that far into the woods. I won't do it again."

"But wait a minute. What's going on? Why are you crying?"

She doesn't answer but speeds up until she is switching between jogging and walking. A glance over her shoulder lets her know that he's stopped following her and is standing near the cow barn staring at her. He's wringing his hat in his hands with clear frustration.

She ditches her dirty shoes on the back porch. Upon entering the kitchen, she finds Hannah and Reagan hard at work. They are making cheese, which is a long and malodorous process.

"Sam, just in the nick of time!" Reagan jokes.

She's at the stove while Hannah resides at the island working.

"Gimme' a hand?" Reagan asks.

They haven't noticed her distressed state or the dampness on her cheeks. Good. She doesn't want them to, either.

She plasters on a happy face and replies in a tremulous voice, "Sure. Let me just scrub up first."

They work for the next few hours on making the cheese, which is generally a multi-step process, one that they all know by heart. Today's project is cow's milk cheese instead of the softer goat's milk type. She knew this was coming because the milk has been souring and scalded twice in the last few days. Reagan and Sue have been baby-sitting it, skimming the loose liquid on top and putting it in the chicken scraps bowl. There are still many steps to go.

"Grab the cheese knife out of the pantry for me," Reagan requests.

Sam finishes drying her damp hands on a cotton kitchen towel and moves quickly to the pantry.

Hannah is already preparing the wooden molds. Sam grabs the long sharp knife and meets up with Reagan, who has also moved to the island. The cultures were already added, so they are ready to separate the whey, which Hannah will use to improve the texture of her baked goods. Any that is not used will be fed to the chickens. Hannah's baked goods are sublime on any given day, but adding the whey makes them transcendent. It's one of the benefits of cheese making in Sam's opinion. Hannah could put the best French pastry chefs to shame. Of course, France probably isn't even functioning on the same level as the McClane farm. There were mixed reports at the beginning of whether or not France had been nuked. She prays they were not.

Sam hands the long knife to Reagan, who pierces the semi-solid mixture in the heavy pot all the way to the bottom. This lets them know they are ready to begin straining.

"Whatcha' been up to, kiddo?" Reagan inquires.

Sam doesn't understand why everyone calls her kiddo. She'd like to remind them that she's an adult, but for some reason they all still look at her like she's a child.

She lies, "Nothing, just working in the garden with Paige."

"Yeah? Paige came in a while ago to wash up and go help Simon. What have you been up to since then?" Hannah boldly questions.

Sam pokes her finger into the soft, creamy solid mass. Liquid whey immediately fills the small hole where her finger had been.

"We're good to go," Reagan announces.

"Nothing really," Sam lies again. "Just went for a walk."

"Everything ok?" Reagan asks and makes eye contact.

Her frizzy curls are escaping her ponytail. Reagan's intelligent green eyes see her too clearly. Sam looks down quickly and nods.

"If you want to talk, you know where I live," Reagan jokes and bumps her shoulder into hers.

Sam affords her a pained grin and says, "Just thinking about my family again."

"I figured," she returns.

Sam's not sure why Reagan isn't in town working at the clinic. They've been busy lately with injuries from so many men working on the wall. This is not the kind of work that she usually does. Sam, Hannah and Sue usually make the cheese. Sometimes Simon and Cory help if they aren't doing other laborious tasks outdoors.

"I'm fine," Sam lies again. She gets a look from Reagan that lets her know that this falsehood isn't going to be believed.

Reagan places the knife on the counter and lays a hand to Sam's cheek. This is a comforting gesture that Reagan would'nt have been able to offer anyone a few years ago. Sam can relate to Reagan's mental blocks. She has the same problems, but not in an all-out aversion to touch.

"Careful, kiddo," she warns softly.

Sam nods shakily and answers, "I know."

"The colanders are ready, girls," Hannah says.

She has spread the gauzy cloth over two wide, steel colanders stretched tight and secured over two buckets. This process will go slowly until all of the liquid whey has drained completely, and all that remains are the cheese curds. Then the curds will be placed into the molds, packed down, salted and covered. They'll have one of the men carry the heavy molds to the new section of the basement where it is cool and dry and dark. It will take a few weeks of tending and turning the molds until this particular cheese is ready. Sometimes they'll make mozzarella, which is ready to eat immediately as it is a soft cheese. Other times they'll make goat cheese which requires a lot of stirring over a hot pot. It is very back-breaking and tiring work but tastes great when Sue adds fresh herbs from her garden. They like to serve goat cheese for the family to spread over Hannah's warm bread from the oven. They already have three wheels of cheddar aging in the cellar, some of which they'll trade in town with other families for items they might need.

When they are finished, Sam excuses herself. She wants to get away from Reagan and her prying, knowing eyes. The sisters let her know to come down in a few hours for dinner. She grabs an apple off the counter before going to her bedroom for some alone time and to get a grip on her feelings. Working and talking with Hannah and Reagan had been helpful, but her mood is still dark. She knows before she gets to her room what is coming. Making a straight line dash to her desk, she takes out her art supplies, which are severely dwindling. Her hands, fingers and mind take over in such vigorous fervor that she can't stop.

"Sam?" Huntley asks from the door.

His voice startles Sam. The sun has disappeared from her window view. She's lost time again. This frequently happens when she draws. She swings around in her seat, observing her intruder with surprised eyes. He's such a sweet boy, also an orphan like her, also a former slave to Amber's group, and also taken in by the McClane family. He is becoming so handsome. His tanned, Native American skin a dark reddish brown contrast against the light hazel of his pretty eyes and black hair. Although he'd probably have a fit if she called his eyes pretty to his face. He's too proud for that kind of girl-talk. It's hard for her to believe that he's almost fourteen. They have been through some horrible things together. First he'd been incessantly, physically abused by his bastard father, Frank, from the visitors' group. Then he'd lost his twin brother Garrett to the pneumonic plague. Finally, the Rangers had killed his father, although she isn't really supposed to know that part. Nobody ever told Huntley, either, but he's too smart not to know. Surely he does. She'd overheard the men talking of it one day soon after the visitors had "left." She knew from the gun shots that they hadn't all just left of their own accord. Plus she'd watched Cory kill one man and John kill the other out in the forest. John had killed that evil Bobby, and for that reason alone she'll always be grateful to him. But for everything that Huntley's been through, he is a good kid. He sometimes suffers like she does from certain dark spells in his mood and behavior mostly because he lost his twin brother. Grandpa tries to spend a lot of time with him, teaching him how to work on projects like the tractors and equipment and reading books.

His light eyes regard her warily.

"What is it, Huntley?" she asks.

"Hannah said to come up and get you. Dinner's almost ready," he tells her.

"Thanks, bud. I'll be down in just a minute," she says.

"What are you doing?" he inquires shyly.

She smiles gently at him, "Just sketching some. I'll be down soon, 'kay?"

He nods and leaves quietly. Wow, she really has lost time.

Huntley is usually with his cohorts in crime, Justin and Arianna. Those three run the farm like feral children, getting into everything, climbing trees, running through the barns, shooting BB guns, playing tag, and hide and seek. The younger ones, Isaac and Jacob usually have to stay behind since they are both only four and five years old and much too slow to keep up with the cool kids. They have to stay in the immediate front or back yards or the swing-set. Sometimes the older kids take pity and hang out for a while with them, but most of the time those three are gone from morning until dusk.

She turns back to her current drawing and tries to finish it before needing to wash up for dinner. Another noise at her door lets her know that Huntley is back.

"I said I'll be down in a minute, bud," she says over her shoulder without turning around.

"That's a new one," a deep voice says. Simon adds, "You've never called me 'bud' before."

Sam spins in her seat to find him closing in on her and smiling. She rubs at an itch on her cheek and frowns.

"I thought you were Huntley," she acknowledges. "I know dinner's almost ready. I'll be along in a sec."

"I didn't come up to tell you that dinner is ready," he says, standing at her shoulder. "I came up to see how you were doing. You were upset earlier."

"Fine. I'm fine," she replies.

Sam tries to place a blank sheet furtively over her sketch. Simon places his hand over hers, though.

"What's this?" Simon asks.

His eyes meet hers, and he knows. She can see it. Simon pulls the sheet of heavy weight sketch paper free and regards it pensively. His mouth turns down as his eyes slide to hers again.

"Sam," he says with disappointment.

She starts picking her thumbnail.

"Sorry," she apologizes as Simon squats onto his haunches beside her.

"Honey, you can't do this. We've been over it many times. This is a wrong turn for you, Sam. Don't do this to yourself again," he says gently and places his hand on her knee.

Sam swallows hard past the lump in her throat. She takes the drawing from him and places it back on her desk. She also tries not to think about his long, tanned fingers squeezing her knee.

"I know," she answers in a squeak.

"Sam, look at me, honey," he orders softly.

She drags her gaze to his. Simon gathers her hands into his and gives them a squeeze. He takes a linen handkerchief from her desk and wipes at her cheek where she must've smudged charcoal.

"Don't do this again, Sam," he orders more firmly.

He picks up the drawing again and holds it between them, forcing her gaze to drop down upon it as he speaks in soft tones, his usual tone. Sam wills herself to look at it again. The somber shadows and harsh lines, the melancholy feeling that exudes from it is like the dark hand of the grim reaper himself coming from the paper. The picture depicts a hallway that is shadowy and foreboding, no end and no beginning. In the center of the corridor is a young girl sitting directly in the middle of the floor, her knees drawn to her chest, her arms wrapped around them. The hue is black and gray charcoal monotones. The tips of her fingers carry the remnants of blending those dark colors to such blurry, muted tones. This is the style of art she succumbs to when she is in the bowels of depression, when the depression is so profound and has such a tight hold on her that she can't breathe around it like she'd felt earlier at the tree in the woods. Everything that is on her mind, all of the negativity and anxiety of bad memories come straight from her subconscious down into her fingertips. It is like the darkness takes over, takes hold, and she is helpless to stop it.

"I'm sorry," she replies softly, refusing to meet his gaze.

Simon very slowly and carefully folds her drawing and tucks it away into his jeans pocket.

"I won't tell anyone, all right?" he says reassuringly.

Sam nods because it is all she can manage. Sometimes on this precipice Simon is the only one who can talk her down, usually the only one who can because she doesn't share it with anyone else. He'd discovered her issues with depression and lapses into it shortly after they'd been taken in by the McClane family. She'd been in the barn sitting on a bale of hay toward the back wall and drawing something just as sinister as what she's sketched this afternoon. It was a picture of her slaughtered horses, shot and killed by the men who'd taken her. They were dead in their stalls, locked there that morning by her. If she hadn't locked them up, perhaps they wouldn't have been killed. They had probably made a fuss and lot of racket when Frank's group had taken her family out there to be executed. Horses sense danger. They sense evil. They know when to be wary of people. She often wished that she'd had that same intuition back then. Simon had caught her in the middle of drawing her murdered, shot to death horses who were unable to escape because of her.

Tears are plopping onto her bare legs, just landing there and adding to her overall embarrassment at being caught by Simon. She hates upsetting him like this. He has more important things to do with his time than to be bothered by her encroaching bout of depression.

"Don't cry, honey," he pleads.

Sam raises her eyes to meet his. There is a painful recognition there in his gaze. They both know why she is so upset. Neither of them wants to recognize it, though. It is too painful to reconcile, to admit, to share.

"Come here, Sam," he says.

Simon pulls her gently to him and stands. There he hugs her close while she weeps against the front of his soiled shirt. He and Derek have been finishing rebuilding the porch where the Target men had caught it on fire the night of the attack. When she pulls back, Sam can see that she has turned some of the grime and dirt on his shirt to a richer, muddier appearance.

"I'm sorry, Simon," she apologizes again, shaking her head. "I just got... messed up again."

"I know. It's ok, honey," he says comfortingly. "You don't have to apologize to *me*."

Sam just attempts a grin and looks at her feet. His hands are on either side of her face the next instant, and he forces her to look up at him. His thumbs wipe at her wet cheeks. Simon shakes his head at her.

"No more, all right? You have to control it. Use your music. Talk to me. Go for a walk with me, but don't do this. Don't let it pull you in, honey. Don't let it drag you down," he says.

Sam notices a wrinkle between his brows. A lock of his auburn hair has fallen over his forehead in a boyish manner. She nods again and sniffs.

""Kay," she accords and attempts a lop-sided smile.

Simon pulls her toward him, places a brotherly kiss to her forehead, lingers there a moment and steps away. His eyes are haunted and darker than just a second ago. He gives a quick puff of breath through his nose as if he is confused suddenly and leaves her room.

Sam stands there another moment before hiding the other four drawings in a drawer, which were under her sketch pad. There was no sense in revealing those equally macabre spectacles to her best friend. She uses the upstairs bathroom to clean her face, brush her hair and straighten herself away before plastering a sunny smile on her face and going down to dinner with her beloved family.

Chapter Twenty-eight
Simon

Two weeks have gone by since he'd caught Samantha trying to lapse into severe depression again and had hopefully stifled it. As far as he knows Reagan is the only other person on the farm aware of Sam's issues, and Simon fully believes that she recognized it in Sam because of what she, too, had gone through. He doesn't know the entirety of Reagan's story, but he knows it was horrific. He's also seen glimpses of her physical scars, as well as, her emotional aversion to touch, which has improved exponentially.

Tomorrow is technically the fourth of July, although he doubts they'll be lighting off any fireworks, nor do they have any with which to celebrate. He just hopes they don't have to light off any other types of explosives. The heat today at the wall build had been excruciating. They'd had to take three men to the clinic to be treated for heat exhaustion by Reagan, the only doctor on duty. Plywood still covers the front windows of the clinic, which doesn't help to cool the building in any way. It is almost unbearably hot in the clinic. Another man had been severely injured when a telephone pole had been cut with a chainsaw and landed on his leg. He'd admitted to not paying attention to what the other men were doing. Reagan had declared deep tissue bruising along with a slight, hairline fracture of his tibia. A woman was burned accidentally while assisting her husband on welding two particularly important steel support braces on the exterior of the wall. Simon had needed to scrub up to assist Reagan on that one. Her burns were second and third degree and will need to be carefully monitored for infection as time goes on. Luckily for her, the burn had only encapsulated her right forearm and nowhere else.

Now he's relaxing a moment before hitting the shower. Sam sits on his left. Paige is on his right. And they are all sitting on the top board of the cow pasture fence where those beasts graze lazily in the last, fading light of dusk. Dinner is over, chores completed, and the rest of the evening he plans to devote to study. He's in the middle of studying a book on human microbiology. Tomorrow if the weather is good, they plan on cutting hay, but tonight he'll study.

He wants to find new ways, unconventional methods to prevent and cure disease through herbal treatment. Reagan had lent the microbiology book to him, so there are notes scribbled, pages bent over, yellow highlighting marks and general messy disorder to try to weed through. He's been wondering lately if a mixture of oil of oregano combined with stinging nettle will cure a severe case of lung ailment like pneumonia or even influenza. Unfortunately before the apocalypse, doctors hadn't really put much stock in herbal remedies. If only they'd listened to instinct and not pharmaceutical sales reps, people might know more now about surviving since those drug companies are gone.

They'd talked to a group of people who'd passed through town a few years ago, friends of the Johnson family, about what they'd seen out on the road. They'd told Doc about a new form of money called drug bartering. Supposedly people had located a few drug manufacturing plants and had commandeered everything that was left. They would then trade off useful drugs, anything from heart medicines, aspirin, high blood pressure meds, to antibiotics and more. One such manufacturing facility had been located in New Jersey and raided by jack-booted thugs, another in Indiana. If the people had nothing to trade, then the drugs were withheld, and the peddlers would move on to the next established camp or town. Simon would like to get his hands on those kinds of people, people who would hold out giving medicine to the sick. Or snipe them from afar and not sully his hands on the likes of that type of scum.

"Now that's a sunset," Paige observes beside him.

He'd been too lost in thought, angry about jerks who treat others badly for their own gain. He nods absent-mindedly to his sister, observes the streaks of orange and pinks and fiery reds in the sky. Some areas look like his sister's hair. Good grief. He's starting to look at colors like Sam and her little artist brain.

"Yes, it is," Sam chirps up. "I like watching it fall behind those old, tall pines."

Her artist brain never shuts off. Her black ponytail is missing, and her hair hangs long and loose, halfway down her back like black silk. It's still damp from her shower but mostly dry. Her light blue tank top fits loosely, revealing her pink bra strap on her slim shoulder. Pale, muscular legs stick out below the hem of her black shorts. She doesn't seem to tan. She does burn easily, though, which is something he's always warning her about taking extra precautions to prevent. She usually laughs at him. Her skin always looks so smooth and creamy, like freshly squeezed goat milk. Simon frowns. Goat milk? What the hell? He makes a note never to say that out loud. She'll just laugh at him again.

"Right?" she asks, hitting Simon with those piercing blue eyes of hers.

"Yeah, sure," he answers, although he has absolutely no idea to what he's agreeing. Hopefully it wasn't something he was agreeing to do for or with them that he wouldn't enjoy.

"It feels like a moment of grace sitting here with you guys," Paige says solemnly and tilts her head back to take in the last rays of the sun. "I think this is the first sunset I've actually sat and watched and felt true peace in years."

Simon takes her hand into his and gives it a reassuring squeeze.

"We're glad you're here, Paige," Sam offers kindly. "You're one of us now."

He's not sure how his independent sister is going to feel about Sam's comment.

She replies, "Yeah, I guess I am, aren't I? I'm not leaving unless Simon does."

"I'm wherever you are, sis," Simon tells her. "We're a team in this together. I won't ever let us get separated again."

"And Sam?" Paige asks.

Simon almost flinches at the boldness of his sister's question and the serious intent of her stare. He also questions the motivation behind it.

"Yes, Sam, too. I won't let you get separated from us, either, Sam," he says and looks directly at Sam. Unaware or uncaring of social etiquette boundaries, Sam just lies her head against his shoulder.

"I know, Simon," she answers directly. "You'll keep all three of us safe."

The weight of her words feels like cement blocks on his shoulders, but he's happy to carry them, honored to do so. These two women are solely his responsibility. Samantha is an orphan, and Paige is his sister. They need him. He doesn't take this job lightly.

He also feels this way about Huntley, the other orphan in their group, but he's darn near capable of taking care of himself. He's a fairly good shot already. He runs around the farm with a bb gun and plinks at everything. Then he shoots real guns with Derek and Derek's oldest son, Justin, as well.

Simon feels the same about the whole entire McClane family, but they each have protectors or husbands or just each other to look out for them. Sam and Paige need his protection. They have no one. Sam is small and fragile. His sister is not so on either account, but she has no idea how to fight or shoot or use a knife. Her one ability is her speed at fleeing on foot. But he knows well enough that she can't run from every single situation that life throws at her. Soon he plans on starting her on basic combat training to enhance her skills. They've just been so busy since the planting season started. The garden's planted, the hay is ready to cut for the second time, and the building of the wall has commenced and is a time-consuming, slow process. If anything were to happen to him, to take him from his sister, he needs to know that she could take care of herself.

The last rays disappear behind the tall hills surrounding the south side of the farm. Paige sighs contentedly.

"Guess I should go get a shower, clean some of the grub from myself," she says with a laugh.

"Go ahead, Paige," Sam says cordially. "It's a lot of dirty work we do around here. It always feels good to get clean before bed."

"I'm just thankful for a shower."

"What'd you and your group do before you came here?" Sam asks with curiosity.

Simon glances out of the corner of his eyes at Sam. She's chewing a long, thin blade of grass. Her small, dark mouth puckering as she nibbles it.

"We'd find water when we could and store it in jugs. Then we'd try to heat some on a fire or on the rare occasion on a stove that actually worked. Then we'd pour it into whatever we could find and use that to scrub up. It was pretty primitive, to say the least. When there wasn't a whole lot of water to go around, we did community sharing of that wash water between the four of us. You do *not* want to go last, let me tell you."

They all laugh as Paige climbs down the rails of the fence.

"It was more important to make sure we had drinking water, so we tried to limit washing to once a week unless there was a creek or lake or pond nearby," she adds.

Simon doesn't laugh at this. Neither does Sam. His sister's harrowing journey just to make it to the farm is like nothing that he'd ever experienced or even heard of before.

"Alright! I'm off," she announces. "I'll meet you at the cabin later, 'kay?"

He gives his sister a grin before she leaves, her long legs sprinting for the house. He's so glad she's here with him now. Simon frowns as he remembers Cory. He's sure that Cory would like his sister, too. They'd probably get along great. They are actually a lot alike. Simon misses his friend greatly and worries that he's never coming home.

"We should head in, too," he says to Sam a few minutes later. He hops down lithely, reaches up for Sam.

"Get out of the way," she retorts. "I can jump down, too."

"You could sprain your ankle. You really shouldn't do stuff like that, ya' know," he tells her with a grim expression.

"Simon," Sam says dramatically.

He just jerks his arms in front of him with impatience, letting her know to take the help. She gives him a snarky, little lopsided grimace. He can't help it. He returns it with a big grin. She places her hands on his shoulders and allows him to help her.

"You know I jump off the horses without your help, sir," she remarks.

"I know," he says with a frown. "You really shouldn't do that, either."

Sam actually laughs up at him. She's definitely not laughing with him because he's not laughing at all. She's laughing at him as if he's being ridiculous. Her insolence is slightly irritating.

"You're being rather dramatic, don't ya' think?" she asks.

She hasn't stepped back, and neither has he. Her hands are still at his shoulders. He is hyper aware of her standing so close, so he backs up quickly.

"And you are being purposely defiant, young lady," he reprimands and gets laughed at again.

"Young lady? Really? You're so silly," she mocks arrogantly.

Sam doesn't say anything else but walks around him and toward the house. He is left following her, which is not a good idea. Her shorts are too short. He'd like to tell her this, too, but doesn't need any more of her impertinence tonight.

Reagan blasts out the back door before they even get to the house.

"Hey!" she yells at them. "You and Grandpa gotta go, so get your ass in here and clean up!"

He regards Sam before they both jog the rest of the way to the house. They ditch their shoes quickly and go in.

"What's going on?" he asks of Reagan.

"Anita's labor started a few hours ago. Just got off the radio with Paul," she answers.

"Oh, ok. Yes, fine. I'll grab a five minute shower first. Be right back," he stammers. Condo Paul has a radio and so does Roy in town in case they come under attack.

For some reason, he can hear Reagan and Sam chuckling as he ascends the stairs at lightning speed to the second floor. Less than ten minutes later, he has showered and is wearing clean duds and ready to go. There is a big meeting taking place in the kitchen.

"Change of plans," Reagan tells him quietly as he comes to stand next to her.

Paige has also joined them with damp hair but clean clothing. Most of the time, she showers downstairs in the bathroom attached to the bedroom where she and Talia used to stay.

"What's going on? Aren't we leaving?" he asks and notices that nearly everyone with the exception of the children are in the kitchen. Doc is conversing with John and Kelly.

Reagan answers, "You're taking Sam and your sister. I'm going with Grandpa. You guys will drop us off in town on your way to the condo community. We'll radio Kelly when we're ready for him to come back to town and pick us back up."

"Why? I don't understand," Simon admits.

"There's a problem in town," Reagan says. "The new sheriff called on the radio and said that there was a small explosion, nothing set on purpose, just some guys screwing around with shit they shouldn't have been. Anyway, two of them are pretty fucked up. A few others aren't as bad, but the sheriff said there are six men and one woman who are burned. So, Grandpa and I will need to get there immediately. Guess they're burned pretty badly. Multiple severe burn victims in one day. No wonder doctors are skinny. Peeling off layers of charred flesh is fucking gross."

"But I've never delivered a baby by myself," he says nervously, ignoring Reagan's colorful language. "I've only assisted."

"Yeah, but you've assisted probably a few dozen times. You're ready," she says. "Trust me, I'd rather trade you places and not have to treat the burn victims, but from what the sheriff said, it's a bad scene in town. We gotta' go."

Doc comes over and lays a hand to his back to offer comfort and support and probably an ounce of his strength.

"You'll be fine, son," Doc says. "She's had a normal pregnancy so far. No problems. No complications. She'll be fine and so will you. You'll have Samantha for help, Kelly as your guard and your sister."

He looks at Paige. His sister doesn't look too thrilled about this arrangement. Her eyes widen, she grimace and shakes her head ever so subtly at Simon. Doc takes him to the hallway where they won't be overheard.

"Your sister needs this. She needs to get over her squeamishness, Simon. She has to start helping more in the clinic. We need all the hands we can get. She'll be fine, too. She's a smart girl," Doc explains his decision.

"Yes, sir," Simon answers. There isn't much else he can say. Doc has the final say in how things are handled, and if he thinks Simon can deliver this baby into the world without his assistance, then he can. "I'll do my best. I won't make any mistakes, sir."

"I know that, son," Doc acknowledges. "That's why I'm sending you."

Simon feels that one all the way through to his marrow. Doc's confidence in him gives his fatigued body a surge of energy, his harrowed mind a boost of empowerment.

When they are all in the SUV and moving at a very fast pace, John driving, Doc tells Simon that he'd personally packed his medical bag. He'd put everything Simon could possibly need to deliver Anita's baby safely. There is even local anesthesia in there for an emergency cesarean section. Simon prays it doesn't come to that.

"Yes, sir," Simon answers solidly. Their group breaks into a planning conversation while he mulls over the coming evening.

Sam sits next to him in the rear while everyone else sits in the middle and front. He's nervous. He doesn't feel ready for this, but it's going to happen. Life has a way of doing that. It moves forward with or without a person and whether or not they are ready and have given it permission.

"You can do it," Samantha says quietly.

Her small hand covers his, and Simon takes a huge amount of reassurance from her faith in him. He looks down at her upturned face so full of trust and hope and unabashed support of him.

He gives her a short nod and says, "Thanks, Sam. Thanks for having faith in me."

"It's not faith, Simon," she corrects, regarding him through her thick black lashes. "You *can* do it. You don't need me to tell you."

Simon bites the inside of his cheek and drags his gaze away from her. The innocence permeates from her, draws him in like she does every time he's around her. He's never brought up the kiss she'd bestowed upon him in the side yard before he'd gone on the Target raid. She hadn't brought it up again, either, so Simon just figures it was a fluke and that she didn't mean it the way that he took it. Sam always calls him her best friend, so she obviously doesn't have romantic feelings for him. But sometimes when she looks up into his eyes, Simon thinks there is something more than kinship there in her blue gaze. When he permits himself, which isn't often, Simon can still remember the way her soft lips had felt against his own and the sweet smell of her skin that teased his nostrils. This is exactly why he doesn't allow himself to think too long about Sam's kiss that he'd mistaken for something else. She's a huge distraction. How the heck could Sam even think of him in a romantic way? He'd failed her on every level possible. He's just thankful that she can even think of him as a friend, let alone her best friend.

Sam holds his hand all the way to town where they drop Doc and Reagan in front of the medical center, along with John, who will guard it. There are men from town waiting. Some women linger and are crying. Some of the men are armed, the new town militia. There are people milling around, townspeople worried about the burn victims. Kelly jumps in the driver's seat and speeds them along to the condo village. His sister has climbed over the seat and rides next to Kelly. They talk quietly in the front. Kelly says something that makes his sister laugh loud and obnoxiously. Kelly is probably trying to take her mind off of the task that awaits her. Simon and Sam have agreed to stay in the back without verbally communicating it.

The moments tick by as each mile passes way too quickly. They pull up to the gates of the condo community, met by Paul and offered entrance by him and his teenage son. They are whisked along to the condo where Anita and her husband and children reside. Armed guards are walking their patrol route along their own fence of which Paul had overseen the construction. It had taken them nearly two years to complete. Simon knows it will take just as long to complete the much larger one in town. Their system is effective, though, and no one discourages the decisions they make within their small community because they are thriving, which is more than most can say these days.

They disembark from the Suburban and file into the spacious condo. Paul and Kelly stand outside, near the front where Kelly will stay until it is time for them to leave again. It doesn't take long to find Anita. Her cries of agony can be heard from the foyer. Her husband, the ex-Navy Seal, meets them in the hallway and leads the three of them to the first-floor master bedroom.

"Oh, Simon!" Anita calls out to him from the bed. "Thank God! I thought I was bringing this baby into the world on my own. Or with his help."

She points to her husband as if she finds him offensive. He hangs his head in shame. Such is the way on the day of a baby's birth. Most women can't stand the sight of their husbands as if it is their fault they are in the situation to begin with, and nobody argues because all men value their lives and their testicles.

"Everything will be just fine, Anita," Simon tells her in a calm voice, much calmer than he feels, as he squeezes her hand. "We're here to help you."

He's heard Doc say similar things before, so he takes a cue from history and tries the same approach. It works because she passes a barely there smile to him.

"Let us just scrub up and get ready, all right?" he says.

They use the master bath to clean up. Water in the condo community works, although the system is not always reliable or steady, and the pressure sure isn't strong. They'd hand dug wells, four to be exact, that feed the twelve homes. The pumps and water storage tanks run on wind turbines and solar attached to the roofs of each condo. Paul is planning on digging at least three more wells. Their families are expanding every year with people finding them and taking shelter there.

They wash their hands while trying to stay calm. His sister is nervous. He can tell.

"Girls, why don't you prepare the room and collect the things we'll need?" Simon orders softly as they enter her room again.

This is something that he and Sam would do together, but since he's the lead doctor tonight, it's up to him to ask for the items they'll need and take a leadership role. It's not a misogynistic move on his part. Doc and Reagan expect him to take the lead. His sister also needs some busy work to keep her mind occupied.

Sam has always acted as a nurse in their practice and has never wanted to go any further than just that. She doesn't prefer to get in the trenches other than in an assistant's role. She is sublimely talented with keeping patients calm and distracted from their woes. She's a people person through and through. Simon's not so much. Reagan is great with people, too. As long as they don't mind her being direct to the point of being rude or using a whole lot of inappropriate swearing and sarcasm. So she is basically horrible with people.

"Anita, I'm going to check you now, ok?" he asks permission as he closes in on her bed. He pulls on short latex gloves and positions himself beside her hip.

"Yes, Simon. That's fine. Just get this kid out of my body!" she says on a long groan.

Her contractions are strong and forceful already. After he ascertains that she is only dilated to about a four, Simon tells her that it would be preferable if she rose from the bed and walked some. It will help her labor to move along and progress instead of slow down or stop.

"Stay here and I'll get your husband," he offers.

"No, wait, Simon. I want you to help me. He's a wreck. This is his first kid, you know. Let me just walk with you for a while."

"Sure, Anita. That'll be just fine," he says complacently. This tactic is something he's also learned from Doc. Appease the pregnant woman at all costs. Promise whatever they request, even if it is ridiculous. They won't remember it in a few hours. It also helps to ensure one's personal safety and to get out of the birthing room alive. "Let me just run out and let him know what's going on, that you're doing fine."

Simon finds Kelly with Anita's husband on the front lawn razzing each other about whether or not Rangers or Frog men are better. He recognizes that Kelly is trying to take her husband's mind off of the situation at hand. Simon knows that Kelly and John were a part of an elite unit called Delta, but not everyone in the family knows. Frog men was a nickname for Navy Seals. There is always a lot of good-natured taunting that goes on between the Rangers on the farm and the Seal in the condo community.

It takes just a second to allay her husband's fears and return to Anita, who he helps rise from her bed. He, Sam and Paige take turns walking with her. The room has been set up by him and Sam, and prepped for an emergency should one arise. Anita already has other children, but she'd delivered those pregnancies by cesarean section. They are staying across the street with Selena and her family. Derek, John and Reagan had found the two women, Selena and Anita and their children, alone and being brutalized by the same types of men who'd inhabited the Target store. He's so glad that they are safe and healthy with the help of the Rangers and Paul, who John had sent along with his family to secure the condo village.

Doc says that it's been quite a few years since Anita's last C-section and that she should be able to deliver naturally. He had even checked her just a few days ago and declared that the baby is presenting head first, which is good since he or she is not in the breech position which would make things considerably more dangerous and complicated.

His sister is a ball of nerves, which Simon tries his best to quiet and also instill a sense of serenity in her. She's never been witness to a live birth. She told him that she'd been forced to watch a video of it in high school, one of those P.S.A. type documentaries to discourage teen pregnancy. He knows how badly she handled the situation at the clinic the day it had been shot up. She hasn't been back there as a nursing volunteer since. She works on the wall build or out in the reception room of the clinic or stays at the farm with Hannah to help out there. She's squeamish to the ninth degree. She'll have to get over it tonight. New life waits for no man or squeamish young woman.

Shortly after three a.m. Simon declares that Anita is ready to begin pushing. She declares that she is more than ready. She is fully dilated and in incredible pain.

"We're going to the bathroom for just a moment, Anita," he tells her. "We'll all three be right back in. Let us get scrubbed in. We want the environment to be as sterile as possible for you and the baby."

"Do whatever you need to catch this kid, Simon!" Anita says on an uncomfortable moan.

Paige's hands shake as she pulls on her surgical gown in the master bathroom. Sam ties it for her; then his sister returns the favor. Simon turns his back, and Samantha ties his and pulls his face mask strings to the back, securing them as well. Next, she assists him with his gloves. Paige's hands tremble still as she tugs on her own rubber gloves.

Simon places his hands over hers and says, "It's going to be fine. Just take a breath. Relax. Remember who's really in charge here, sis."

Paige asks in all seriousness, "You?"

Simon smiles gently and shakes his head.

"Let's pray like Grandpa always does," Sam suggests smartly.

Simon nods and leads them in a quick prayer, surrendering up their hands and talent into His. If God wills this child into the world, then it will be by His grace alone. Simon and his two helpers are only the vessels of His work tonight.

His sister's hands still just slightly in his, which helps to in turn motivate Simon. They collectively return to the bedroom.

Anita's bedding has been replaced with recycled, yet sterilized sheets from the farm, all other bedding removed. Plastic sheeting and buckets are near Simon's feet below the end of her bed. Sam sits near her head, assisting Anita with leaning forward since they don't have an actual adjustable hospital bed. Her husband waits outside the bedroom door as per Anita's request. His sister stands beside him near Anita's spread legs.

His tools have been sterilized in boiling water, and he wears a pair of fresh latex gloves. The baby is crowning. Simon knows he should feel more nerves than he does, but his only concern is for the safety of his patient. It is important to stay cool and collected. Keeping Anita and his assistants calm is more important than him losing his crap and freaking out. He tells himself that women have been doing this since the beginning of time, literally and that he is only here in a helping capacity.

She pushes for about an hour. It seems as if she's running out of steam. Sam takes her blood pressure periodically since they don't have any electronic monitoring equipment to use with their patient. Sam gives him a thumbs up to let Simon know that her blood pressure is normal. Periodically, Anita curses. A few times she even curses at them. Nobody remarks on it, though. They just keep reassuring her that she's doing great and continue encouraging her with soothing words. It's rather understandable in his opinion to use foul language. He'd be ready to use his rifle on someone if he were in her place.

The baby seems as if it will fit through the birth canal without Anita needing an episiotomy performed. Doc said that many times in the past doctors would rush the situation instead of letting the birth happen naturally. Then they would end up cutting the woman. It just meant a longer, more difficult recovery for the woman. He said to be patient and allow the labor and pushing to progress naturally with each contraction. Don't hurry her. Let her work at her body's own pace.

At nearly four thirty in the morning after Kelly has retrieved Doc and Reagan from town because their work is finished, Simon safely delivers baby girl Amelia into the world. Her mother cries. Sam cries. Paige cries. Even Reagan sniffs hard a few times before carrying the baby girl away to be cleaned. Doc had allowed him to proceed without his assistance. He'd stood back and observed Simon. His unwavering trust in Simon had boosted his confidence a bit. After Anita expels the afterbirth with Simon's aid, she rests back on a bed of clean pillows and bedding.

Reagan returns with the new baby all swaddled and warm and delivers her to her father's outstretched arms. The Navy Seal has finally been permitted entrance by Anita into their bedroom. His eyes are full of unashamed tears. He sits on the bed next to his wife where he strokes her brow in between placing kisses on his daughter's downy forehead. Reagan also helps Simon get Anita cleaned, wiped down and cloths pressed against her which they'd explained to her husband will need changed every few hours until the heavy bleeding lets up.

Simon excuses himself a few moments later where he joins Sam and Paige in the bathroom again to scrub and remove their gowns. Childbirth is somewhat of a messy affair requiring a lot of rags, clean linens and hot water. Their soiled gowns and anything else they've brought from the farm such as cotton rags are placed in a plastic bag that will be taken home to be laundered and scalded. Sterility is more important now than ever before. Disease and sickness can spread so easily from the lack of sanitary work conditions. He read once in one of Doc's medical books about Baron Joseph Lister, the first surgeon to promote the idea of a sterilized surgical suite and sanitary surgery to prevent post-surgical infection. The thing that Simon found surprising about the article was the fact that it took someone an epiphany to even think that sanitary conditions were outside of the box in the first place.

"I can't believe I just witnessed that," Paige remarks beside him at the sink.

"Me, either," Sam says. "I've seen quite a few births in the last few years, but they never fail to lift my heart. What a little miracle she is."

He's quite sure that Doc is giving her a comprehensive new baby examination. He'll probably even notate a newborn APGAR score on her chart, which Simon has no doubt that Doc has started. Simon grins in the mirror above the double sink at the two women. They are both bright-eyed and uplifted. Sam's color is high, her cheeks a pale pink.

"You were great, Simon," Paige remarks. "You're an amazing doctor. That was just.... crazy."

He corrects her like he always does anyone else who says this, "I'm not a doctor, sis. She did all the work. I was just there in case of an emergency."

Paige chuckles, "Uh, yeah right. I was down there beside you, bro. I saw. You were doing a lot more than just standing there."

He changes the subject, "You did great, too. You were helpful. And you didn't puke or pass out this time, so that's an improvement."

Paige slugs his shoulder playfully, and he smiles.

A short while later they are comfortably ensconced in the SUV, John at the wheel again. It's been a long night. Rising in a few hours for chores will be difficult, plus, they will need to come back to town to check the burn victims, one of whom had died according to Reagan, and to the condo village to check on Anita and the new baby.

"Today was a good day," Sam whispers beside him.

Simon grins down at her and takes her hand. She falls asleep against his shoulder on the ride home. He kisses the top of her head and inhales the heady, sweet scent of her dark hair. A good day.

Chapter Twenty-nine
Paige

"That's perfect, Mr. Harrison," Paige says to John as he shows her some new padlocks they've found on a scouting run. They'd actually taken Talia since they have been working with her on improving her tactical maneuvering. She confided to Paige later that day that she doesn't want to go out anymore. She likes the safety of the farm better than looking over her shoulder, and she's content to stay there. She's just done being afraid. Paige, however, had teased her friend that she enjoys hanging out on Chet Reynolds's farm even more than the McClane's.

"What?" John asks. "Who's Mr. Harrison? Don't call me that. Geez. What am I, an old man?"

His brother, Derek, laughs beside him, too. They are standing near the new gates to the town.

John jabs at his brother and says, "He's the old man, not me."

"Our dad's name was Mr. Harrison. We're just Derek and John, Paige," Derek tells her. "You keep trying to call us that, but we're not going to answer to it."

"Sorry, I just…"

John lays a hand on her shoulder, "It's cool, kid. Anyway, I got this new padlock for the front gate. Those slider gates from the dairy farm are great, but we need to be able to secure them closed."

"Right, I agree," Paige says nervously. "We should lock the town down at dusk and have sentries posted."

"Yeah, we've been talking with one of the guys here in town who's been working on the construction of the wall. Jason's his name. He had some good ideas, and we added to them," John tells her.

"We're thinking of building a platform with an overhead shelter that is higher than the tallest section of the fencing," Derek says.

This piques Paige's interest. She looks to John to explain further.

"During the Vietnam War, there were sentry posts like this used at the American fire bases," he explains patiently. "We surround them with sandbags to help protect them from hostile fire. We should also build them in a few other areas around town at the fence, too. Find some places where we can get a good view. Can't be too careful."

"That's a really good idea," she concurs. "It would keep the guards out of the weather but also let them see who might be trying to approach the fence, especially at night. The sandbags will help, too. That's smart."

Sue walks over to them with containers of water. They all take a cup and ladle some out. July in Tennessee feels like the surface of Mars. The humidity is through the roof. Paige wishes that she'd have taken the time to braid her hair this morning before leaving the cabin. It's just hanging down to the middle of her back and causing her to sweat. She's wearing a pair of Reagan's shorts, which actually fit since they aren't full-length jeans. They fit her waist but come off as some sort of attempt at being sexy since they are pretty short on her. She can't help the fact that her legs are much longer than Reagan's. Hell, everyone's taller than Reagan. Back at the cabin, she'd grabbed a plain white t-shirt from her box of clothing that Simon had foraged for her from an empty house a few towns over when she'd first come to stay on the farm. She doesn't like to dwell on where the owners of that house could be today. They are likely dead somewhere. Her navy blue, satin bra is probably showing through her t-shirt, but she doesn't have much of a choice since she only owns two and the other is in the dirty clothing pile in the cabin. She also wears her only pair of shoes, which are black leather ankle boots.

"Hey, guys," Sue greets them. "What's going on?"

"Just scheming, planning and more scheming," her husband answers. "The usual."

Derek pulls her close and kisses her cheek.

"Gross, Derek," she complains. "You're all sweaty and dirty!"

"Since when does that stop us?" he teases. "How do you think we got three kids?"

Sue blushes and steps away from him. Paige just grins. The other day Sue had cut the men's hair in the backyard. They are all freshly groomed with shorter locks, but Derek had his wife buzz his off micro-short. He seems to be a man of strict, military discipline. Paige assumes it is likely because of his long service in the Army. Even Simon's unruly waves are shorter. Paige only wishes she'd lined up and had Sue lob off about a good ten inches of her own hair. It was strange because Herb McClane had seemed particularly sad when he'd observed from the back porch swing his granddaughter cutting everyone's hair. Paige meant to ask Simon about it, but so many things are always going on that she simply forgot.

"Why don't you go and scout out a few places that those watch towers could go?" John asks her.

"Oh, sure," Paige replies, delighted that he would have so much faith in her to do a good job of it. "I'll go right now."

"Good idea," Derek says. "We'll need to be able to get them built in place before winter sets in. It'll make it easier to keep an eye on the town."

"No problem," Paige says. "I'm on it."

"I'll walk with you," Sue offers. "I brought a basket of food for the single man that was burned. I know he doesn't have anyone to help him."

"That's really nice," Paige praises as they leave the men. "Simon and Dr. McClane were supposed to be heading over to check on them after they visited with Anita again."

"They're back from Anita's," Sue clarifies for her. "I went with them to see the new baby. She is so cute. Good grief. I think my baby-making hormones amped up just looking at her."

Paige laughs aloud and is joined by Sue as they walk down the sidewalk in the secure section of town. They both still wear a pistol on their hips. And it still feels highly strange on Paige's.

"I don't know about the baby hormones thing, but she is really adorable," Paige acknowledges.

"Makes me wish I could have more," Sue pines as she swipes a loose tendril of mahogany hair back into her ponytail.

"Yeah, I heard that you can't have any more kids. Sorry about that," Paige says.

"It's ok," she says with a nod. "I've got three great ones, so I'm lucky. And they're healthy, so that's kind of all that matters now, isn't it?"

"Yeah, no kidding," Paige says.

Sue bumps her elbow against Paige's arm and says, "I'll just wait for you to have kids and then I can play with them and not have to get up in the middle of the night for feedings."

"What?" Paige exclaims. "Not me, no way."

"Never?"

Paige furrows her brow and thinks a moment before answering, "I don't know. I used to think I wanted that. You know, the house, the 2.2 kids, the dog and a big back yard."

"You can still have children. We've got plenty of dogs on the farm. And you've got a lot more than a yard there, too. You'd have a few hundred acres instead of a yard," Sue jokes, causing Paige to laugh again.

"Things are just different now," Paige says after a moment.

"I know about your boyfriend from college that was killed," Sue allows.

Everyone in the McClane family, of which she is now a part, seems to know everything about each other. Her family was more reserved when she was growing up, dignified, proper, sometimes even cool and distant. They were expected to behave a certain way because of her father's job. Even in the middle of a world-wide apocalypse, the McClane family seems to find joy and laughter and even love. No wonder Simon loves them all so much.

"Yeah, he was. But I don't really even know how serious that would've become. I mostly moved in with him and my friends because I knew I didn't want to live on campus. He was fun. I was young and independent for the first time. It wasn't like it was the greatest love story of all time."

They stop at the burned man's small home on a side road, and Sue drops him off a basket of homemade baked goods and two jars of soup. He is more thankful than Paige would've thought. Part of his face and a section of his right forearm are covered in bandages. He has fared better than some of the others who were burned a few days ago.

When they finish with him, Sue starts right back up where they left off as Paige walks along the completed fence sections looking for a good spot for sentry posts.

"So you don't think you'll ever get married or have kids now, is that it?" she asks.

Paige scoffs as she examines an area where people from town are working, "I doubt it. I mean it's not like there are a lot of single guys to choose from out on the McClane farm. You know, unless I'm gonna count my own brother."

Sue laughs and says, "Well, you certainly have enough admirers when we come to town."

Paige whips her head to the side to look at Sue, "What?"

Sue grins slyly and indicates toward a group of men taking a break on the build. "Seems like there's a few of your fan boys now."

Paige peeks over her shoulder. Two men immediately turn their heads as if they are embarrassed to be caught staring at her, but a third continues to stare openly. Unfortunately, he also rises from where he and his buddies are sitting on a stack of lumber and walks toward her.

The slim, young man extends his hand and says, "Hi, you're Paige, right?"

Paige shakes his hand and says, "Yep, that's me."

"I'm Jason," he answers with a grin. "John and Derek were talking to me about building some guard posts."

He has light blonde hair and brown eyes and is about her height because she is looking directly into his eyes. He's also rather handsome. He's also not interested in her as Sue had incorrectly guessed. He simply wants to discuss the wall.

"Um, yeah. That's a good idea," she replies and tries to hide her disappointment. Good grief. She's obviously a hell of a lot lonelier than she'd thought.

"I have a drawing over here if you'd like to check it out," he offers, indicating a card table someone has set up in the middle of the street. "I know how you like your architectural drawings."

His comment gains her attention, and Paige's eyes dart to his. He's teasing her, exposing his dimples on his clean shaven face.

"I'll catch up with you later, Paige," Sue says to her. "Make sure you're back at the truck by five. That gives you about an hour."

"Oh, ok, got it," Paige answers.

"I'll make sure she gets there, Sue," Jason says.

Paige regards him with open astonishment. She hardly needs him to walk her back to the clinic at five o'clock. Sue just laughs, agrees to it and leaves. Paige is feeling set up all of a sudden. Is Sue Harrison trying to play matchmaker? She tries not to groan, even if Jason is good-looking.

She walks with Jason over to the table where he has laid out his own drawing which is more of a rough sketch. She gets the general concept behind his idea and suggests some improvements like a longer roof overhang and a slightly higher platform elevation.

"How do you know Sue? I mean it seems like you know her," Paige asks.

"I went to school here in town with the McClane girls," he tells her.

There is a sophisticated finesse about Jason. His hair looks like it was professionally highlighted in a salon, but Paige knows it's from working outside, likely on this wall all summer.

"Oh?" she prompts for more information.

"Yes, Sue was older than me. Reagan's closer to my age, but little Einstein bumped ahead and went to college, leaving the rest of us dummies behind," he jokes.

Paige affords a lop-sided grin.

"And you?" she asks, genuinely curious now. "Did you go to college?"

"I did. I went to Yale," he answers proudly and then frowns.

"Really?" she asks with surprise. He looks like a grungy construction worker covered in dirt and wearing work-boots. "What was your major?"

"Economics," he tells her. "I worked for a law firm over in Nashville. I know, that's kind of a strange place to end up. But I handled all of the accounting for them and their clients. Their clients were corporations, so…"

"How did you end up back here?"

"My uncle's the vet."

"Oh," Paige says. She knows the veterinarian is an alcoholic and has been through his share of woes since the apocalypse hit. He literally has nobody anymore.

"Yeah," he agrees with her knowingly. "My folks were on vacation in France when it all started, so they're gone. I lived over closer to Nashville, so I moved back here when it all started. I figured I could help my uncle and his family, but I was too late. Now I just live a few houses down from him in my folk's old house and try to keep an eye out for him."

"I'm sorry," Paige says as they start walking around the fence perimeter looking for more ideal spots for guard towers.

"It's ok," Jason offers. "Guess everyone's got a story like that now, right?"

She just nods but doesn't start spewing her own sad tale. She's just not comfortable with that kind of disclosure a half an hour after meeting someone. He seems very comfortable, though, with himself and her and their time alone away from other people. Paige knows that Sue never would've arranged for their meeting if he was an untrustworthy person.

"So you and your brother, Dr. Simon, live out on the McClane farm, huh?" he presses.

He is tenacious, she'll give him that much.

"Yep, me and my doctor brother," she says with a smile thinking about Simon. Apparently everyone in town considers him to be on the same level as Dr. McClane, although that would anger Simon.

"That's cool," he says. "I haven't seen you around, though, until recently."

"I just arrived here a few months ago," she tells him. "With my friends. I came with some other people."

"Good. We can always use more people to build up our town's population again and grow it. Not too many of us twenty-somethings left."

"How old are you?" she asks, not that it really matters.

"Twenty-nine," he answers.

This surprises Paige. She wouldn't have guessed that he is seven years older than her.

They walk a little further, Paige making notations on a small notepad about good locations. He continues to tell her about growing up in this small town, something of which she is unfamiliar having grown up in a big city. Then he tells her some stories about going to Yale. She can see hints of his former self when he speaks with a fondness and a touch of sadness for his alma mater.

She consults her watch, noticing that it's almost time to head back. She's sweaty and grimy and probably completely unattractive in her borrowed clothing, old boots, and dust. It's a long walk from where they've ended up, which is close to the end of the built wall where no protection is offered. It's really not safe to be out this far, and she notices that Jason doesn't have a gun of his own unless it's hidden underneath his clothing. They turn direction and good to his word, Jason walks her all the way back to the clinic which will force him to walk home to his dead parents' house over a mile away. He doesn't seem to mind. He's also openly flirting with her. Paige isn't a juvenile thirteen-year-old girl. She's an adult woman who's had relationships, good and bad, and knows when a man is flirting. She fiddles nervously with the thin strips of leather she has tied on her wrist.

Her brother is standing near the truck, tapping his toe and glaring at her as they approach.

"Well, thanks for walking me back. I told you that you didn't have to. That was kind of far," Paige tells him.

"Maybe I like the company," he suggests lightly and catches her eye.

"Ok, thanks again," she offers cordially.

Jason snatches her hand and says, "I hope to see you again, Paige."

This time there is no doubt in her mind that he is interested in her.

"Oh, um, sure," she mumbles.

When she glances toward Simon, his eyes have widened, and he's stalking toward them. Oh great! Another confrontation like when he'd barked at the single dad to get lost when she'd first come to the farm. She turns to Jason, interrupts whatever he is about to say and blurts another quick, "Thanks. It was nice meeting you!"

Then she pivots and walks quickly to her brother who resembles a muscular bull. He's just missing the steam coming out of the nostrils.

"Who was that jerk?" he demands angrily.

"Simon!" Paige admonishes. "That's unfair. Be nice."

He doesn't answer but raises an eyebrow waiting.

"He's the vet's nephew. His name is Jason, and he is a very nice man," she explains, although she has no idea why she'd need to explain herself or her actions talking to someone to her younger brother.

Her brother snatches her arm, glares over her head and leads her to the truck where they climb into the bed with the other family members. Sue is also sitting there next to her husband. She has a rotten grin on her pretty face. Paige just mouths the word, "thanks" to the other woman who chuckles. Paige returns it with a light grin. Her brother, on the other hand, is fuming.

They arrive at the farm after dropping Wayne Reynolds and Zach Johnson at their respective farms. Her brother hops down and offers assistance to her and Sue. When Paige tries to walk toward the house, he pulls her back.

"Who the hell was that?" he asks again.

"Simon, chill!" she says vehemently. "I told you already. He's just some guy that lives in town."

Derek comes over to them and says, "It's cool, bro. Jason seems all right."

Simon doesn't look like he's about to let it drop or let her out of his sight again in town.

"He looked weasely," Simon declares angrily.

John comes around the other side of the truck and laughs before saying, "Jason's an ok guy. He tries to help out his uncle. Tries to help *us* keep him sober long enough to do his job so that he can help the farmers with their livestock. Jason's a pretty good guy. Used to be some kind of lawyer or something in Nashville."

"Accountant," Paige corrects. The men look at her. "He worked for lawyers. Look, Simon, I'm an adult damn woman. I'll talk to whomever I please."

She stomps off but glances over her shoulder to find the men trying to talk some sense into her protective brother. As soon as she enters the back door to the kitchen, Hannah asks her to find Sam. She always seems to be missing, off somewhere drawing or playing with the horses.

"Sure thing," she returns.

"I think she's in the horse barn," Reagan says as she comes into the room with her son. "I'd start there."

"Yes, ma'am," Paige replies and goes right back out the door she'd just come in.

She is glad to see that the men have dispersed, her brother included. Striding right up to the barn door, she almost interrupts Simon and Sam in a heated discussion which she decides to eavesdrop on instead. People on this farm seem to believe that Sam has feelings for her brother. Either she's just missed it, or they're wrong, this might be her opportunity to find out for herself.

"Simon, your sister is plenty old enough to choose someone to spend time with or marry or whatever," Sam is lecturing.

Marry? What the hell? She'd walked a mile with Jason and now they are getting married? Paige frowns hard. Granted, he's an attractive man, but marriage? Get real.

"We don't even know him!" Simon hisses angrily.

"I've been around him quite a few times. He comes out with his uncle sometimes to neighbors' dairy farms to help with their cattle. You are kind of a control freak, Simon," Sam says on a haughty laugh.

Simon actually growls. Paige's young, innocent, sweet brother just growled menacingly at his supposed friend. She hears Sam laugh at him with insolence.

"I am not a control freak," he argues. "Paige is my responsibility. So are you, young lady, so don't go getting any ideas from her."

"I don't take orders from you, Simon," Sam says intolerantly, yet very quietly and with more calm than Paige could've mustered. "I'll do as I like, thank you very much, sir. And if I want to start dating a boy in town, then I will."

"Excuse me?" Simon seethes in the most hysterical tone Paige has ever heard.

She decides she'd better intervene before her brother completely loses his shit. She clears her voice loudly and strolls down the middle aisle of the barn.

"Hey, Sam," she yells out as if she wasn't just listening to them. "They're calling us all in for dinner."

"I'll be right there, Paige," the smaller woman returns kindly. "I'm almost done. One last mare to check on."

She's obviously been at home with Kelly and Reagan taking care of the chores while the rest of them were in town working.

Paige's brother glares at her, narrows his eyes suspiciously and takes his leave. She decides to help Samantha, although she really doesn't know anything about the horses, especially not pregnant or sick ones which would be the only reason any of them would be stabled.

"Can I help?" she asks the delicate- or not so delicate in light of the conversation Paige has just overheard- woman with the pitch black hair.

Sam glances over her shoulder and nods with uncertainty. Paige is glad that she came out to fetch her. There is also strife between the two of them, and she wishes to correct it.

"Hand me that can of grain?" Sam requests.

"Sure," Paige says through the stall door, locates the can half full with grain and opens the door. "Here ya' go."

"Come on in," Sam offers.

"Hm, I don't know," Paige says with a grimace.

The horse inside the stall is huge, pregnant and due any day. It looks uncharacteristically angry in Paige's opinion as if it would like to bite or kick her and probably will.

"She's a sweetie," Sam lies. "Come on."

This time she holds out her hand to Paige, which makes Paige feel like the world's biggest wimp. She takes Sam's hand and inches into the stall. It immediately feels a lot smaller and more cramped as she presses as hard as she can into the stall wall.

The horse makes a weird noise which in turn causes Paige to jump.

"She just wants her food," Sam probably lies again. "Here, Paige, place it in this corner feeder for her."

"How... how do I get over there?" Paige asks because Sam has squeezed past the giant horse and left her.

She comes back and takes her hand again. Sam tugs her along after her and helps her pour the can of crushed corn and oats into her corner trough.

"See? Not so hard. She wouldn't hurt you," Sam lies once again in Paige's opinion. "None of them would do it on purpose. Usually when people get hurt from horses, it's their own fault."

"By using that reasoning alone and the fact that I know zero plus zero about these giant beasts, then I'll probably be killed by one," Paige admits with large eyes.

Sam laughs gaily. Her laugh is light and feminine. She's been nothing but kind to Paige since she'd arrived, and Paige had betrayed her.

"Hey, I wanted to say I'm sorry," she tells her.

"It's ok, just give her some attention and she'll love you. They all will. Pet her here along her neck or scratch her chest like this," Sam instructs.

She takes Paige's hand and lays it against the huge mare's neck.

"No, I didn't mean I'm sorry about the horses. We're never going to be friends. I like them but just for looking at them in the pasture, not being up this close to them. I was saying that I'm sorry to you."

Sam looks directly up at her, pinning Paige with her bright blue eyes.

"I kind of ratted you out the other day to Simon when you went into the woods," Paige confesses.

"I know," Sam says quietly.

"I'm sorry. It's just that you were gone for kind of a long time, and I got worried," Paige explains. "I didn't chase him down immediately and tell him. I waited for you to come back, but it seemed like it was taking a long time."

Sam lays her hand on Paige's, still on the horse's neck. "I forgive you. I wasn't mad. I knew it was you. Nobody else knew I went out there."

"I just didn't want you to be angry with me. You've been so nice to me since I got here, and you're close with my brother. I just want us to be friends," Paige offers.

"Me, too," Sam says and hugs her.

It surprises Paige that the younger woman is so completely open and honest with her. Sam is a rare treat. Simon would be lucky if this young woman was in love with him. She's a good person with a big heart. Her heart is probably the biggest thing on her. She only

408

comes as high as Paige's chest when she hugs her. Perhaps she's needed a friend closer to her own age, too.

    They walk back to the house together for dinner, and Sam loops her arm through hers. Paige just smiles. Twenty yards from the house, she can hear the calamity of dinner coming together inside of the kitchen as everyone gathers. The smells of something fantastic cooking is permeating into the back yard as the children race ahead of them. It feels good to have a true friend in Sam, a group of people to call her new family, and a safe place to finally live.

Chapter Thirty
Cory

He's been moving, hunting, foraging and traveling for almost seven months, and it's almost the end of August. The heat is still sweltering. He's hunted wild game, some of which he's never come up against before, like a feral pig. He's also been killing for that same amount of time. He's hunted men, some beasts of which he has never come up against before. Didn't matter. He'd selectively hunted and killed those societal fiends, as well.

Fall is once again on the horizon, and the weather has improved considerably. It seemed as if it had rained for the last thirty days straight. He'd taken shelter in numerous different places. He and his crew of motley animals have been to Pittsburgh, where he'd stopped at the Three Rivers Stadium, the home of his dad's favorite football team, the Pittsburgh Steelers. They used to be the shit. They'd won eleven Super Bowls before the apocalypse changed everything and people started eating pig skin instead of making footballs out of it. He'd let Jet graze on the once-coveted turf on the field and had snagged two footballs from the locker room to take back to the kids at the farm someday. He'd even found some medical supplies in the sports medicine center off of the training room. They'd stayed in the stadium a few days where Cory was able to root out and get rid of some perverts. A small cluster of creeps had holed up in a restaurant in the downtown district. He'd taken them out easily enough and returned the two teenage girls that they'd kept captive to their parents. He'd sat at the top edge of the abandoned football stadium and sniped a truck full of jackasses who were trying to run down a family in a Volvo station-wagon on its last leg. It had almost been too easy. They probably had no idea where the shots were even coming from. The Angel of Death had rained down judgment and thunder upon them. Then he'd smoked his last cigarette and watched the roaring three rivers, which had overtaken the banks years before, flow and speed along, filled with debris and non-native materials like lumber, parts of cars, a water wheel, chunks of cement, and even a turbine motor. He hadn't seen any dead bodies, but he'd still boiled the water from that river for an extra long period of time that night before he'd drunk it. Then he'd zig-zagged northwest.

Cleveland had proven fruitless, to say the least. He'd stayed about a week there and had fished out of Lake Erie on a small rowboat that he'd found in the middle of the street in the downtown arts district and had commandeered. He'd toured an old barge and had marveled at the sheer size of it and the strange fact that it was still anchored near the Science Center. He'd stayed two nights in the State Theater, had even led his horse right through the front double doors. They were greeted by two does and a buck in the entranceway where snacks were sold. They'd sprinted away further into the theater, and he hadn't seen them again. Cory had led his stallion up the grand, red-carpeted staircase to a massive, marble-floored foyer where guests would have mingled before the show. Then he and the horse had gone right onto the main stage where they'd camped out. Jet hardly spooks at anything anymore. He's about as dead-broke trained as one horse could be. He doesn't have much a choice.

A dirty and yellowing poster for The Phantom of the Opera had been plastered proudly in the lobby and out front near the ticket booth. Apparently that was the last Broadway play on tour that had been running at the State Theater. It was a lavish, ornamental building with carvings and plaster molding from a century before. The lack of maintenance on her was showing, though. Mold was growing on the curtains for the stage area and on the plush, velvet seating in the audience. Dirt and dust balls bigger than the ones in the horse barn at the farm clung to every corner. He'd even found some outdated candy bars, some packages of peanuts and a case of blue Gatorade. He'd consumed all of it without a second thought to the expiration dates. He'd raided the bar, but someone had beat him to it. All he'd found was some fruity drink mixes for chic cocktails. He'd passed on those.

As he traveled from one big city to the next, Cory could see that the smaller towns and rural neighborhoods had fared so much better than the large metropolises. Not many signs of life had been found in Cleveland, Columbus or Pittsburgh. They had been ghost towns. The less populated boroughs were starting to ban together to keep the trouble out of their neighborhoods, though. He'd seen many dead bodies, dead from what looked like starvation or illness, in the homes in the big cities. In Cleveland, he'd gone into three different high rise condominiums that had once overlooked the lake or the skyline of the city only to discover more dead bodies. He'd found a few useful supplies but absolutely no food. He'd resorted to hunting. Once he'd traveled out of the city limits into the more rural communities, he'd found small bands of people forming or maintaining their tiny networks. It was one of the few encouraging things he's seen since leaving the farm. Most of what he's seen has left him with a bad taste in his mouth. A lot of what he's seen has turned him into a murderous madman. His thirst for blood lust is somewhat settling down, but he's not done yet. He feels like he's contributed a lot to help the help*less* in the country.

And today he's stopping in Ravenna, Ohio. There's an old Army ammunition post supposedly there. He's about to find out. It closed years ago according to the information he'd found in a book about Ohio. He passed the sign for Ravenna Arsenal a ways back. According to the map, this place should be huge. He's not really thinking he'll find anything useful but is mostly looking to spend a few days undisturbed before moving on. No armed guards work at the checkpoint. He passes a helicopter on his left, displayed on a small hill and surrounded by decorative brick. Poison ivy vines curl and twine from the ground and have almost encompassed it. They even wrap around the rotors and twist and wind around inside of the cabin of the Cobra gunship, nearly engulfing it. The Huey near it is being overtaken with moss and foliage, as well.

Cory hops down from his stallion and walks beside him just in case anyone is around. Better to not be an open target sitting high on a horse. The area is silent as a mausoleum as the sun beats down upon them. Damn Dog follows cautiously behind him. She's turned out to be an all right dog, but he would still rather she'd go away. Luckily she's quiet and stays alert when he's not.

He scans the area, taking note of the chain-link fencing surrounding the complex that has been caved in by multiple cars, a pick-up truck and one school bus. Had civilians tried to take over or invade this base? Had they just been that desperate for aid? Why would they have come to a closed munitions storage facility? It was not an active duty base to begin with. They wouldn't have had supplies, would they? Derek had heard from some Army friends who had passed through and stopped at the farm a few years ago that some military bases like Fort Knox were being run by the men who'd been stationed here. He's not sure why anyone would've wanted this abandoned place, though. Of course, it would've been one hell of a good fighting position. It's about as secure as any fortress could be. Maybe they left the city to seek a place of security for their families. He'll probably never know, nor does he care. He's only sacking out here for a few days until he moves on again, so he's glad that nobody is occupying the place.

Long, thin grasses grow up through the cracks of the blacktopped lane. To his left is a wide open field where over a dozen deer graze idly in between three tanks. With the absence of humans roaming around shooting them, the deer and most other wildlife has multiplied with great ease. In July, he'd spotted a mountain lion in Pennsylvania. He's not sure if those were native of that area before the apocalypse, but he doubts it. He's seen black bear and three grizzlies, more deer than he can count and even a small cluster of buffalo or bison; he's not sure which they were. He can only assume that they were domesticated livestock that had either been released into the wild or had broken free of their fencing if left abandoned. It's like living in America circa the 1700's.

On his right is row after row of cement bunkers built half into the ground. There are literally hundreds of them. Apparently the Army had a shit ton of ammunitions to store at one time. His stomach growls loudly, causing Damn Dog to mewl softly before he gives her a look to let her know to zip it. He's wondering if there's anything left in the armory or any food supplies left in the kitchens. Highly doubtful, but it's worth a shot.

Jet startles and prances in place with agitation. Cory tightens his grip on the horse's bridle. The stallion has spotted something even before Cory. He urges the horse closer to a tall stone wall which seems to have encased some sort of courtyard on the other side. His dog's hackles rise. It's still early afternoon. The sun is high, but the air carries the tinge of ozone as if a storm is brewing yet again. The leaves on the maples and oaks occasionally flip over as winds dance through the tree line to his left.

Cory removes his binoculars from his pocket and scans more carefully. He'd vetted this place from quite a distance away on a nearby hilltop. He hadn't seen anything, no signs of life, but he could be wrong. With the bunkers and buildings, he could have easily missed movement. He's been wrong before. It had cost him the most important person in his life. There are dozens of buildings on this base, all of which could contain someone or many, many people.

He'd come through Aurora, Ohio, a few days ago where he'd snagged some high-quality duds from an outlet shopping center there. Now he wears Ralph Lauren blue-jeans, Nike gym shoes and some other designer label t-shirt. He could give a shit about fashion labels, but at least the items were all clean- after he'd shaken four years of dust out of them. He'd taken three other pairs of jeans, a pair of khakis and a half dozen tees. He'd burned his old clothing that was filled with holes and more mileage than he could count. Then he'd shot a small buck and butchered him. He and his dog had eaten well that night and the next. He'd found flour mix for hot pretzels in the small cafeteria at the outlet mall. That hadn't gone well. He'd eaten one of those mess concoctions this morning, but it had tasted like shit. It wasn't like anything that the women on the farm create. He knows almost nothing about cooking, other than skinning, cleaning and cooking meat on an open fire. After he'd come through that small burg, he'd just hung low in the wooded area around the arsenal watching for movement. He hadn't seen any, until now.

Nothing happens for a few minutes, but then he spots two small children running from one building to another. The building they disappear into looks big enough to store planes or helicopters or tanks, tanks like the one that sits motionless on the lawn to his right. A moment later a woman comes out of the first building and begins hanging clothing on a long line stretched from one telephone pole to another. A second woman and then another join her with more wet clothing. They talk animatedly, even laugh a few times. They seem peaceful and friendly enough, but they could be here against their wills. He can't allow that.

Cory decides that a flanking maneuver will be better for further observation. He crosses the road. He needs to find a place to conceal Jet so that the big stallion doesn't give them both away. He moves quietly, sticking to the grassy areas in preference to the blacktop which would cause the horse's hooves to clip-clop loudly. He finds the perfect spot behind a tall building, perhaps a barracks of some kind, and ties the horse to a pole there. He takes a second to pat his thick neck reassuringly before leaving.

Moving furtively and using the buildings for cover, he jogs down a long alleyway of sorts and comes in behind the building where the women were working. When he spies inside through a back door, he can see people sitting around, talking, and working together cooking food. Mostly they seem like older people and the women from the clothes line and the children who were playing outdoors. Are the men out hunting, foraging, or worse?

"Can I help you?" comes a woman's soft voice from his left.

He hadn't seen her before. She's standing outside near the corner of the building as if she's just rounded it and come upon him. Cory instinctively swings his rifle her way. She squelches a scream and immediately puts her hands up in surrender, dropping her basket of wet clothing.

"Please, don't shoot," she pleads. "I'm not armed, sir. Please. I have a little boy."

"What's going on here? Where are the men?" he asks in a harsh tone.

"What men? The soldiers? I don't know. They probably…"

"No, not the soldiers. This place hasn't had soldiers here for years. Your men, the men with your group, where are they?" he asks. The blonde with the fair skin seems confused.

"I don't know what you mean," she says. "The only men that are with us are in there."

She points toward the door opening where Cory still has his foot in the jam, preventing it from shutting all the way.

"Are you being held against your will?" he asks as his gaze skirts around the area watching out for problems.

"What?" she asks with confusion. "No, we're here together because we want to be. We work together to survive. This is our little home… for now."

"No husbands? No boyfriends?" he probes. This seems strange. Most of the groups he's run into have men with them.

"No, most of us are either widows or just never married," the blonde says. "My husband was in New York City when the first round of tsunamis hit. He's gone. All of us have lost people. We're kind of a band of misfits. I have a sister in there and an aunt and uncle, but there aren't any young men."

"Are any of you armed?" he asks, not wanting to take a surprise shot to the back.

"We have a few guns, but we're not very accurate with them," she clarifies. "Look, I'm not gonna lie. We're barely managing. Please don't rob us, sir. We're farming the ground here as best as we can, but we're not farmers. We figured with the buildings and the little bit of ground, we'd be able to stay here for the season at least. So that's what we've done. We're going to start harvesting the gardens soon. We've started breeding some chickens we found at a farm up the road. And we're surviving. We're just surviving."

She has walked closer and is now within ten feet of Cory. She's a tad on the short side and thin. Her cropped pants hang on her hips. Her legs are skinny. But she's pretty enough. Her brown eyes regard him cautiously as if she's afraid of him. And no wonder. He hasn't shaved since he left home, which has left him with a scraggly beard. His hair is now lower than his shoulder line. He could use a good clean-up in the form of soap and running water. The last time he'd bathed was three days ago in a creek, but he hadn't had soap to do the job well because his bar from the farm was completely depleted.

"Do you hunt? Do you people know how to hunt for wild game?"

She shakes her head in answer. Cory just nods. Well shit. He's actually starting to feel sorry for her. Not knowing how to hunt would just about guarantee a person's death in this day and age.

"What do you do for food?"

"There's food here on this base!" she tells him so trustingly. "It's canned goods mostly, but it works. And we know how to butcher the chickens. We have a steady supply of eggs, too. And when the garden's in we'll have fresh produce again soon."

"How can this place have food? It's been abandoned and shut down for years."

"Josephine is from around this area," she explains. "She's one of the older ladies here. She said that after the fall, the military came through and set up here for about three months. They must've left stuff when they pulled out. She said they all poured out of here in a hurry. Not sure where they were going, but they've never come back."

"When did you guys set up here?"

"Before winter set in last fall. We thought we'd be safe here 'cuz it looks so abandoned. Didn't think anyone would come all the way back here to check it out."

Cory nods his head and looks around at the desolate, lonely buildings and unkempt grounds of this formerly secluded military establishment. It's kind of fucking depressing actually. Proud men, brave men like his brother probably once roamed these grounds.

She adds, "You're the first person who's come back here. I'm Jackie."

She's extending her hand as if he isn't still pointing his M16 at her. It's amazing she's made it this far. She's rather trusting since he likely resembles a well-dressed yuppy caveman and is pointing a loaded weapon at her. Cory sets the safety and slings the rifle behind his shoulder before he extends his hand.

"Cory," he returns and gets a big smile from her.

"Do you want to meet everyone else?" she asks.

"I was just gonna rest up here for a few days before I move out again," he tells her. "I'm not staying now. I'm gonna take off."

"Wait! No way. You gotta at least stay the night," she says amiably. "You can stay as long as you like. Maybe you can help us with a few things before you leave, Cory?"

Cory frowns and gives a long, exasperated sigh. "Like what?"

"Well, we found an abandoned truck with a full tank of gas, but it won't start," she adds with a sly grin. "There's another one, too. Uncle Steve said that it's called a Deuce and a quarter."

Cory frowns harder. He doesn't correct her mistake about the truck's name.

"It's pretty big, though. We don't need anything like that! The other truck's more like a big pick-up. We were thinking we could run to the nearest town to pick up some supplies we need," she says and quickly adds, "if there's anything left to take, that is."

"I just came from there," he says and looks over his shoulder to ascertain that none of Jackie's friends are about to club him over the head. Two little kids are hovering around the other corner of the building. The girl giggles and waves. Cory scowls. "There's a pharmacy. I snagged some drugs if you need any medicine. Wasn't much left. The grocery store's been wiped out. The outlet mall is still filled with some items that you might need." He also still has a full sack of medical supplies from the zoos of Pittsburgh, Cleveland and Columbus, but Cory is hoping to take those home to the farm someday.

"Hm, that's too bad about the pharmacy, but we're ok for food. It would be nice to not have to eat canned meat, but we're doing ok. One of the kids has asthma, though, and we're down to his last two inhalers. Plus, we were thinking of some gardening tools. We found shovels here on the base but couldn't find anything else for gardening. And some kind of pesticide. The bugs have been getting at our tomatoes."

"I can show you how to make some pesticide. It's pretty simple really," he offers, although he's not sure why he's even doing so. His first thought when he'd seen the shelter full of old people, women and kids was to get the hell out of here and hit the road again. And now this single mom with the doe eyes is suckering him into staying on and working.

"Oh my goodness! That would be amazing. We don't know anything about that stuff. We're all from big cities," she explains and steps even closer. "I lived in Cleveland. Some of the others are from there. Some are from Pittsburgh and Toledo. Maeve and her husband were from Buffalo. They traveled to a town near here to her daughter's place, but they were gone."

"It's a miracle you've survived this long," he mutters irritably and allows the door to the building to close again.

The two children have crept closer and are joined by three more who have sneaked up behind Jackie. A tugging on his shirttail gains his attention.

"Is that your big huge horse behind that building over there, mister?" one of the youngest girls asks.

She has two dark brown pigtails that bounce around when she speaks. She reminds him of Ari back at the farm when she was younger. He frowns hard at her, though. He thought he'd hidden the stallion better than that. Of course, these kids probably run and play on this base at their leisure.

"Yeah, you didn't bother him, did you?" he demands harshly.

"I petted him. He's really pretty," she adds without fear of him.

"Don't mess with my horse," he orders her but gets a giggle for an answer. She has a lisp when she speaks and a devilish set of dimples in her cherubic cheeks. She can't be more than five or six. Jet is not an overly friendly horse. He's downright territorial back at the farm, especially around his mares. Apparently he and his horse have a soft spot for ruffians with pigtails.

"You're really scruffy," she says in a tiny voice. "You look like a great big hairy gorilla."

"Hope, cut it out," Jackie corrects the girl. "Honey, that's rude. His name is Cory, and he's going to be staying here a few days and helping us."

"Uh, wait a minute," he interjects.

"Come on in," Jackie orders as she brushes past him. "I'll introduce you to the rest of our group. They'll be happy to see someone like you is going to be sticking around for a while to help us."

"Yes!" Hope shouts and jumps up and down. "And I wanna' ride on your horse, too!"

Good grief. It truly is nothing short of a miracle that these people have made it this long. They are way too trusting, gullible, and much too friendly for their own good.

By later in the evening, Cory knows everyone in their small camp, which turns out to be seventeen adults, seven children and a cat. He'd been welcomed in with open arms as if he'd just been some long lost old friend of the family. A few of the women had even heated hot water for him to wash in one of the former barracks bathrooms. He'd cleaned up his beard, as well, trimming it a bit shorter and scraping some down from his cheeks. It's not likely to get repeated anytime soon. They each had a story to tell him about their real families, their losses and how they'd all come to be together as a new family. Damn Dog ditches him and sleeps next to Hope. Some watch dog.

420

Chapter Thirty-one
Simon

It is almost dawn. The sun will soon be peeking above the tree line on the horizon. They are near Clarksville, not far from home, but far enough away to make Simon nervous. They got a lead from a farmer between their town and Clarksville about three men traveling through their area who were robbing people while they slept. The farmer had fired a round from his shotgun at those men which seemed to work since they hadn't tried to return to his farm. His story had turned Simon's stomach because the man had been close to Doc's age and because they believe those men were the Target creeps. He had no idea what sort of people he was shooting at.

Now they are stalking on foot, hopefully closing in on the men who've evaded their grasp so far. A bead of sweat trickles down his back. He is with Kelly, and Wayne Reynolds is partnered with John and Condo Paul. Simon wishes that Cory was also with them. They certainly don't need five men to take out four, but they also don't know if the men who'd escaped have come to Clarksville to join up with others from their group that the family had not known about or have just recruited new jerks to their band of bastards. They've been tracking the last four men nearly the entire summer. He has no idea if there are still four or if they are down to three. He understands implicitly the importance of finding those rats. But he's also pragmatic enough to realize that they might not ever do so.

They've gathered enough intel on them to know their names, where they are all from- which is Clarksville and Nashville- and their potential hideouts. Simon just doesn't like being away from the farm and leaving them in possible danger. They only make these trips twice a week now because of the fuel shortage and the looming harvest. Plus, it's exhausting since they are working long hard hours finishing the wall in town and keeping the farm going.

Simon sighs, which earns him a chuff from Kelly.

"You gonna make it, Professor?" Kelly jokes.

They are positioned in the doorway of a former office building still under construction that is about seven stories tall. The dirt site around the building is muddy from the rain that hit a few days ago and deluged the area. The humidity is jacked up, causing Simon and the others to sweat profusely with all the gear they are wearing, even though the sun hasn't even risen yet. John and the others are across the street going through an old warehouse. They've been fed information that the quad of dicks is holed up there. John's team has been gone for more than fifteen minutes. Simon doesn't think they are going to find anything. There would've been shooting by now.

"Yeah, I'm cool," Simon says as he adjusts his helmet. "Just anxious to get back to the farm."

"They're ok, bro," he says quietly. "Don't worry about them."

Simon nods but doesn't really feel any better. Kelly adjusts his weight to his other foot and shifts his rifle in front of him. He's always so calm. Unless, of course, Hannah is in danger. Simon had never seen him more frazzled than the night that the farm came under attack and they were rushing through the city to get back to it. He was near frantic. Simon felt the exact same thing. All of the men did. Now he just wants to find these jerks and finish it.

"Derek and Doc are holding down the fort," Kelly mollifies him. "Chet said he'd come over, too, but I think they'll be fine. We've got the oil well road blocked now. It's cool."

"Yeah, Chet's been busy. No wonder he doesn't want to come over," Simon razzes playfully as they continue to wait.

Kelly chuffs softly again. "At least he stole your sister's friend away and not your sister."

Simon grins. "Lucky for him."

"Yeah, something tells me if Paige had wanted to move in over there and not Talia, then you might not have been so approving."

"Ya' think?" Simon jokes. Talia had moved into the Reynolds farmhouse with Chet and his family about six weeks ago. They are planning their wedding. It was fast, but nobody judged them for it. The current state of the world has taken away slow courtships and coy dating. They want to start their life as soon as possible. "Chet's cool, but I don't think I'm gonna be too excited to let Paige out of my sight for a long time to come."

"I don't blame you, little brother," Kelly says and bumps his fist to Simon's.

Paige has been hanging out more and more with Jason in town when they go there to work on the wall. The other day, Simon left her at the farm without even waking her or saying goodbye before they left for the build. She doesn't need to be consorting with men in town. It's just bound to end up being a problem for him.

Neither he nor Kelly brings up Em or the fact that Kelly will never give her away some day at her own wedding. He really never talks about her at all. None of the family does. It's simply too painful. They do discuss Cory a lot, however. They worry that he's even still alive, or that he might be injured or sick somewhere out there. Everyone is hoping he comes home before winter arrives again. Simon knows his friend better than any of them. He knows that Cory isn't hurt or sick. He's surviving the only way he knows how. He's going to wreak havoc on the evil in this world, the evil that took the most important person in his life away from him. When he's finished, he'll come home someday. Simon's sure of it.

"Comin' back," John's voice comes over their ear pieces.

A few minutes later and they are piled into the station wagon and driving back to the farm.

"They're gone," John explains once they are moving along on back roads safely. "Someone or a few someones were staying there."

"Think they were our guys?" Kelly asks.

"Could be," John answers. "It's very likely. But they're gone now."

"The intel on this lead was pretty good," Simon adds. Kelly and John nod.

"We'll try again in a few days," Kelly says. "We have too much to do at the farm and in town right now."

When they arrive at the farm after Paul drops them off there, the sun is just rising, promising a real scorcher. They shed their gear in the armory and get ready for the morning's chores. Derek, Sam, and Reagan are already out in the barns, and he finds out that Paige is checking on the hogs. Simon discovers her near a pen full of piglets with their mother.

"Hey, sis," he says, startling her. "Sorry."

Paige rushes to him and embraces him tightly. "I was worried about you."

"I'm still in one piece, Paige," he berates her softly while rubbing her back. When he pulls away, she's scowling hard at him. "We're working the search in bigger parties now, so there's really no danger at all."

She pulls back and glares at him. He gives a one-shouldered shrug.

"Yeah right," she argues.

"Checkin' on the babies, huh?" he asks, distracting her. It works, and they both turn to observe the piglets again. There are seven of the little porkers. "Don't get too attached if you know what I mean."

She chuckles once before replying, "Right. These are future slabs of smoked bacon. They're just so cute. Hard to believe they're going to get so big and fat and... stinky!"

"No kidding, right?" Samantha says, alerting them both to her presence behind them. "I heard you guys got back. I just wanted to make sure you were ok, Simon."

She walks straight up to Simon and reaches her hand out to him. He shoves his into the pocket of his jeans. She gives a sad little frown and drops her hand back down. It makes him feel bad. It makes him feel worse than he already does about Samantha on any given day.

"Yep, all my limbs are still intact," he repeats sourly. It's bad enough having an overly protective sister, but Sam also hen-pecks him.

"That's good!" she replies happily, her bright eyes dancing.

Paige sighs loudly and frowns as she watches the piglets again from a bale of straw. Simon scoops a can of crushed corn mixed with oats out of a metal feed storage container. He sprinkles it into the sow's trough.

"What's wrong, Paige?" Sam asks.

Simon's gaze darts to his sister's. Is something wrong with her? What had he missed? What doesn't he miss is probably a better question when it comes to the women on the farm?

"I'm just mulling some things over," she confesses to Sam.

"Like what?" Samantha asks, her kind blue eyes sincere.

Paige looks at him before speaking, "Talia came over yesterday afternoon to talk. We both have been having the same feelings about Maddie."

"What do you mean? What about Maddie?" Simon inquires after his sister's young charge as he fills a bucket full of water for the mother pig.

"Well, would it be better if Maddie lived over at the Reynolds' place? I mean Talia is going to marry Chet soon, so would it be better if Maddie was living with them full-time? Her life has been so confusing and unstable already. I just wonder if she'd be better off if she lived with Talia and Chet instead of here with me."

"What does she want? Have either of you talked with her or explained to her what's happening?" Simon asks. Sam has climbed to the top of the enclosure's fence and is sitting on the rail. Her knee is inches from his face. The dark green color of her t-shirt somehow makes her blue eyes bluer. There is dried dirt on her pants near her knee. He'd like to rub it away so that she doesn't have to walk around in soiled clothing for a change. Instead, he takes a step back.

"No, no. We haven't told her. She just thinks Talia is staying over there for a few days to help them out. She's been asking me constantly about when she's coming back, though. I don't know what to do."

"Poor little Maddie," Sam laments and lays her hand gently on the top of Paige's head.

"I think it'll be good for her that Talia is getting married. It will lend stability to her life," Simon tells them.

"I think so, too, Simon," Paige agrees. "I think she needs to live over there with them, but it's going to be so hard letting her go."

"She's just a few miles away," Sam offers lightly. "You can go over whenever you want. And when Maddie gets older, she can walk or ride a horse over here whenever she wants to see you."

Simon looks up at her where she perches on the railing and can't help but grin. Even though she has been so scarred, so damaged by her traumatizing past, she still doesn't like it when others are upset. She looks down at him and smiles before bumping her leg against his shoulder.

"Right, Simon?" she asks him to confirm her idea.

"Yeah, sure," he mumbles and has to tear his gaze away from her angelic face. Whatever she's been working on this morning while he was gone chasing dirtbags has left her filthy. Her hands are covered in dirt, her shirt matches, and there's a smudge of dirt or dried mud on her fair cheek. Probably the horses. She gets as dirty as they do, and they roll around the pasture in it.

Paige nods sadly and says, "I know it's not far, but it *feels* far. I've been with her every day of her life since she was a baby."

"She's still young enough, Paige, that she might come to think of Chet as her father and not just some stranger," Simon tries to encourage.

His sister grimaces and nods with reluctance.

"You can always try it for a short trial period of sorts and see if it works out," Sam suggests jovially.

Simon knows that she's reading the regret in his sister's voice and trying to make her feel better. It's just what she does. She hates it when anyone is sad. Sometimes, however, she is the one who drops into that well. And more unfortunately still is the fact that he is usually the only one she'll turn to for help getting back out again.

Simon suggests, "Let's head out. We've got work to do."

Paige climbs off of her bale and strides ahead of them. Sam swings her leg over the top of the fence as if she plans on just jumping down from it. Simon holds his arms up to her.

"Really?" she inquires with sass.

"Why do you insist on doing stupid stunts that could twist your ankles?" he asks in return.

"You're so silly," she admonishes and takes his help.

It's almost too much lifting her down, feeling her small waist in his hands and the rush of her scent that comes when her ponytail hits him in the face. She may be covered in grime, but Samantha always smells clean and sweet. Simon turns abruptly and stalks away.

"That's true, I guess, Sam," Paige concedes as they leave the hog barn. "If it doesn't work out, we could always make a new arrangement."

"I think it will work out, sis," Simon says to offer a realistic point of view. "And it will be good for Maddie. She'll have a mom and a dad, but then she'll have all of us as her aunts and uncles, too. The Reynolds are a good group of people. They'll take as good of care of her as we would. I promise."

His sister loops her arm through his and rests her head against his shoulder. She's probably getting his sweat on her freckled cheek, but she doesn't seem to mind.

Reagan calls out for help with one of the mares in the pasture. Sam doesn't even miss a beat, naturally.

"Catch you guys later," Sam says with a big smile of white teeth.

She trots over to the pasture and nimbly climbs the fence, landing on her feet gracefully on the other side. He and Paige continue to walk together toward the milking parlor where they'll work on the goats and the one cow who is producing milk.

"How do you feel about her?" Paige asks a moment later as she leads her goat out of its stall.

"Maddie? I'm crazy about her. Everyone is…"

"Oh my God, Simon!" Paige says on a raucous laugh. "Not Maddie. Of course I know you like my little Maddie. Why wouldn't you? I'm talking about Sam. How do you feel about Sam?"

He stops dead in his tracks. Simon doesn't answer right away but places his stool near the Jersey's udders.

"What do you mean?"

"Don't play coy with me, little brother," Paige demands rudely.

He'd like to squirt her with milk. She's poking her nose into business that isn't any of her affair. He chooses to ignore her instead. It doesn't work.

"So?" she prods. "How do you feel about Sam? She's very pretty."

"I think of her the same way I think about you," he tells her firmly and continues on with his task.

"Hm, I don't know about that," she argues. "She's a really good artist. She showed me some drawings she did the other day of one of the horses. It looked like a freagin' photograph. She has an incredible eye for detail. Oh, and did I mention how pretty she is? And sweet and kind and generous? She's a real sweetie, Simon."

"Don't be annoying," he says testily. This time she does drop it, which is nothing short of a miracle. They work on their respective milkings in blessed silence. The only sounds are the occasional moo of the cows outside, or cluck of a chicken, or the crow of the roosters.

The family mascot and dog, Molly, comes into the barn and plunks herself down at his feet. He notices that her left eye is runny as if perhaps she has a cold. It could be an allergy. Maybe she's run into a stick in the forest and poked it. Dogs get into trouble like that from time to time.

His thoughts about the dog are interrupted by his obtrusive sister, "I think you're lying, Simon."

She's standing next to him with her pail of goat milk. They try to reserve the goat milk for the children since it has a higher nutrient value. They use whatever the children don't drink to make cheese, usually about once a month. His mother used to like goat cheese rolled in roasted walnuts for dipping crudités in.

"What are you talking about now?" he asks irritably.

"The same thing, ya' dork," she teases.

Simon fails to find the humor. He scowls up at her from his milking stool. She bumps her knee against his shoulder.

"Cut it out," he chides. "I'm trying to work."

"Ohhh, you are so serious, aren't you?" she jokes. "Or is it that you just don't want to talk about this particular subject?"

"Go away," he grinds out through his gritted teeth. He's not ready to discuss his feelings for Sam with his nosy sister or anyone else for that matter. He's not ready to deal with his feelings for Sam even in his own head. They are feelings that are inappropriate and unwelcome.

She doesn't leave but pulls her stool closer and sets her pail in the stainless steel sink behind them.

"How does she feel about you? Do you know?" she presses.

Simon frowns, shakes his head with irritation and says, "Like a big brother. As it *should* be."

His sister is quiet for an unusually long time until he finally looks up at her to find Paige staring thoughtfully at him as if she is considering what he's said and doesn't quite believe it.

"Drop it," Simon warns.

"Hey, I'm just teasing," she says in a softer tone. "I just care about you, little brother."

"I know," he mumbles.

She pets the cow's flank. In return, Paige gets a flick of the cow's tail to her face. Simon chuckles. His sister gives him a fiery glare. He chuckles again.

"Pet the dog, ya' dork," he teases, using her own lingo on her. "Cows don't exactly like being petted."

"Shut up," she murmurs in jest. "This farming shit isn't exactly my thing."

"You'll catch on," he says. "Besides, even if it never works out for you to be Farmer Paige, you have proven yourself in town with drawing up those schematics for the wall. Everyone has their own talents. Don't worry about the farming. You help… a little."

She punches his shoulder playfully.

"You're just not used to it. Trust me, I wasn't used to it when I first came here, either. I had a lot to learn, and it didn't happen overnight."

"I feel like a stupid idiot most of the time, like I'm just getting in everyone's ways," she admits on a frown.

"I know. I was like that, too, at first. Mirroring Cory help me out a lot, though. He was here before me so he pretty much had it all down pat by the time I came along. He's a natural at this farming stuff," he explains patiently.

"Well, I need this Cory kid to show me the ropes," she complains.

Simon chuckles. His sister always refers to Cory as a kid. If she only saw him, she'd stop that immediately.

"Yeah, well we'd all like him to come home and show you the ropes because that would mean he was home," Simon complains about his friend. He misses Cory greatly but also understands his need to stay away. "He's a great rider, too. I mean I like riding, but I'm not as good with the horses as Cory and Sam. She was into horses before the… well, you know."

"Oh really? She's never mentioned that," Paige says with surprise.

"She doesn't talk about her life before," he mumbles.

"I know. She clams up if I ask about it. Hannah said her family was killed?" Paige asks for confirmation.

"Yeah, they didn't live far from here," he explains. He can't help the tension from entering into his voice. "She used to do what's called show jumping. You know, city slicker, on horses?"

"Funny," Paige chides and shoots him a scowl. "Are any of those horses out there hers?"

"No, they were shot, too," he recalls the grisly scene in her fancy small barn.

"Aunt Amber's group?" she asks, even though she probably already knows.

Simon just gives her a nod and makes eye contact for a brief moment. "Everyone's been through something bad, I suppose. Cory especially. That's why he's not here."

"I can't believe he just up and took off," Paige says with confusion. "Who would want to be alone now?"

"It's not so much about the being alone stuff, sis," he explains. "He had some things he had to work out. You know how you felt when your friends and boyfriend were killed at the beginning?" Simon gets a simple nod. "Well, multiply that by about a thousand. He feels responsible for his sister's death. You can't understand unless you knew them, saw them together. She was his shadow for the last four years. She hung on his every word. She hero-worshipped Cory. He's a really good person. You'd like him a lot. I do."

"I'm sorry, Simon," she replies, trying to comfort him.

"Me, too," he says. "But I think he'll come home someday."

"That's good," she observes. "I think Kelly would like that, too. Reagan said that the family really misses him, especially Hannah. I guess she really likes Cory."

"Yeah, he's great. Everyone likes him. He's a good guy, fiercely loyal to the family, and has a really high morality that has no room for gray areas."

"There are a lot of gray areas out there right now. A lot of people are having to do things they never thought they would or could do just to survive," Paige says.

"Not with Cory. There's right. There's wrong. No gray areas. He can be pretty intense sometimes, but he's still a great guy," Simon tells her.

His sister smiles grimly and says, "Simon, honey, he could be dead. You need to think about that...."

Simon smirks. "You don't know Cory like I do."

Paige drops it but continues with, "What I went through with my friends was nothing compared to what this Cory kid has. It was nothing like losing my sister. Or in our case, you."

"Yeah, we got lucky," he says. It sounds strange, but they were lucky. They are still alive, and they've found each other. He's never going to let Paige out of his sight again. He can't.

"As lucky as we could be, I guess," she agrees sadly.

His sister unties his cow, and they turn her out together. Then they collect their buckets and start toward the back of the house.

Sue is ahead of them carrying a basket of eggs. The children are running and playing a game of tag. Reagan is walking toward the horse barn. Sam passes them with a wave of her slim hand as she rides bareback toward the horse barn on one of the geldings. Her bottom is going to be covered with gray dirt, too. She doesn't even have a bridle on the horse, but a lead-line wrapped around its neck. He really doesn't like it when she takes chances like that. The horse could dart or startle, and she could be unseated. He's only ever seen that happen once before. They'd been come upon in the woods by those creep visitors. His degenerate cousin, Bobby, had waved his hands frantically at them, causing Sam to fall from her frightened horse. He'd done it on purpose so that he and the other man could overtake them, use them as bait to get at the family. She'd been hurt by that fall but only superficially. Bobby had hurt her more than that one time. He'd hurt and abused and damaged her for life. That bastard cousin of his, whom he'd stabbed in the back and John had shot and killed, is the reason that she sinks into that well of despair from time to time.

And this is the reason that Simon sometimes has a hard time reconciling his feelings about Samantha. He'd failed to protect her from the demons within his group. He hadn't known they were that evil, but he'd known they were bad. He'll never be able to forgive himself for not saving her from them.

Paige breaks his train of thought again, causing him to shake his head to clear it of such morose feelings.

"So how do you feel about her, Simon?" she asks him in a quiet, serious tone this time.

Simon doesn't even pause. And maybe it's because he'd just been thinking of the shared, dark past that he and Sam have together. Or maybe it's because he truly feels this way. But he states very clearly and soberly, "I'll do whatever it takes to keep her safe. I'll kill anyone who ever even thinks of touching her."

He leaves his sister standing there, mouth agape, pale blue eyes bulging in shock and staring at him as if he is a madman. Perhaps he is where Samantha is concerned.

Chapter Thirty-two
Cory

"Watch the gut bag," Cory instructs the small group of people around him. He has a dead deer, dead by his shot, hanging in a maple tree on a low branch. He slices carefully through the tough inner skin of the deer's carcass.

"Eww, this is so disgusting," Jackie responds on a horrified grimace. "I think I'm going to throw up."

She turns away, and Cory tries not to laugh at her. This is important for her group's survival. He's not going to be with them forever. They need to learn how to hunt. Two of the older men step forward to help him after saying that they'd gutted a few deer when they were younger. He hands his knife to Clint, a gray-haired older man with gnarled, crooked fingers.

"You need to learn how to do this, Jackie," he says to her after he leads her a few feet away from the group.

"I know, Cory, but this… this is… ugh," she says with a shiver, curling her top lip in disgust.

He'd rub her back to soothe her, but his hands are covered in deer blood. He just shakes his head at her instead. Jackie offers him a sly grin. Then she puckers her lower lip with a pouty sexiness.

They've been sleeping together since the third night he'd come to the closed armory. The group is housed in just the one building where two old Army jeeps are located. They don't separate and go into their own buildings, although there are certainly enough places where they could be on their own. They'd moved mattresses from the barracks to the cement floor of the building. Cory moved another one for himself when it became clear that he couldn't leave as fast as he'd hoped since he felt obligated to help them. Sticking together is a good idea for this group. They aren't exactly brilliant in the security department.

And on that third night Jackie had led him to a building much farther away than the one in which they all live. She'd set her lantern down near a makeshift cot on the floor complete with a blanket and pillow. Then she'd removed her top. Cory hadn't needed a whole lot of encouragement. She's an attractive woman, and they were both unattached and unmarried. For her, it was more about the comfort and filling the void of a man's touch. For Cory, it was simply physical. They sneak away most nights and return before everyone rises in the morning.

Tonight he's planning on going on a run for supplies. At least that's what he told her and the others. If he finds supplies, that's fine. Mostly he needs to get away for a short time by himself. He may leave for a few days. Possibly he may not come back. He's not sure. He doesn't really want to stick around the armory with them, become attached to any of them or stay longer than necessary. Unfortunately, he also doesn't want to leave them unprotected and vulnerable. They were extremely lucky so far that nobody had traveled onto the deserted armory property who would mean them harm. Very lucky, indeed.

Some of them have lost family and friends already. Cory certainly doesn't want the rest of them to become victims to lawless bastards, too. They are good people who need protection and training. A *lot* of training.

The first week he'd settled in at the armory he'd broken into the semi-underground bunkers. Almost all of them were empty, but there were three on the far outskirts of the base, that once he'd used bolt cutters and a pry-bar to open, had contained cans full of ammo. It was mostly 7.62, 9 mill, .45 and .223 rounds. Perfect for him but not for the group as they only have two shotguns and a .22 pistol. He's still not sure how they have managed to stay alive.

"That's it, just cut along the hide right here," Cory instructs again. "Good, Marvin. And then we'll start cutting the meat."

Another of the men has come forward to help. Cory would like some of the women to learn this, too. They may not always have the men to help them. He'd taken Jackie and two other women and the only able-bodied man hunting with him this morning before dawn. Sometimes the hunt is difficult and time-consuming. But if a person knows what they're doing, it's like shooting fish in a barrel, as Derek had once phrased it. Two days ago, he'd taken the same hunting party, and they'd shot two turkeys. Jackie's friend, Steph, had shot one, and the man, Didier, had shot the other. The remaining men are literally too old and out of shape for traipsing through the forest hunting wildlife. The women and Didier, who isn't much younger than the other old men, need to hunt to enable their survival. Those chickens aren't going to keep them fed forever. Jackie had told him that they'd been to various FEMA camps at the beginning, but that those hadn't lasted long.

When they have the deer completely cleaned, the meat stripped away, some bones thrown to Damn Dog and the crazy ass cat that lives at the armory with them, they gather for lunch. The women in the building have started lunch with rice, onions, garlic and chunks of deer meat that were delivered to them earlier. They have an open fire pit with a black kettle suspended over it on a steel bar for cooking. One of the other women has cut up vegetables from the garden and has spread them out on a platter. Most of their meals are vegetarian. Cory has not been impressed, to say the least.

"I'll be back tomorrow night or the night after," he says later to Jackie privately. He has pulled her to the far end of the building outside. Clouds have covered the sun, predicting a storm on the horizon. He doesn't care. He's been traveling for months in the elements. A little rain won't hurt him now. He needs to get away from the group for a few days. Cory packs his sack with a few carrots and potatoes and some of the cooked deer meat wrapped in a cloth.

Jackie frowns as he knew she would, "Really? Two days? Can't you just go for a day and come back tonight or in the morning?"

"No, we need some supplies," he lies easily. "I'll be back when I can."

"Be careful," she yields.

Then Jackie moves in and hugs him, presses a soft kiss to his closed mouth and steps back. He doesn't want her feelings to become too serious for him. He may have to leave in a few days, if not tonight, for good.

"Yep," he replies and leaves her. He mounts Jet, whistles to Damn Dog, who immediately trots forward to him.

They leave going southwest toward an area he's already been. There is a small college near Ravenna that he'd like to investigate. He remembers studying about it in government class about a shooting that happened there many decades before. There may actually be some supplies over there, but who really knows anymore? Kent State University should be a few miles from the armory, and he hopes to make it there by nightfall.

A few hours later as the sun is getting low, he arrives at the college. This place doesn't look to have survived any better than Reagan's college. A few of the buildings have been burned, the black charcoal still staining what's left of the brick structures. He sticks to the perimeter near the surrounding forestry before going in. It doesn't appear as if anyone is living on campus and probably haven't since the fall.

He dismounts and leaves the horse in a congested copse of trees where it can graze. He circles the buildings with the dog, coming around to what looks like some sort of student center or possibly a cafeteria. He's not sure. He never went to college. He toured a few, didn't get too excited about the idea of it. He'd wanted to enlist like his brother, but that had been stripped away from him. The back door is locked, but with a few kicks, it swings inward. He brushes his unkempt, long hair back from his face and moves forward. The interior of the building is shadowy and dark in places where the waning light from the windows does not reach. Scanning the area, he discovers that he has come into a student lounge area. Sofas are dispersed here and there. Tables and chairs are set up for the students to intermingle and study. Rows of single chair desks are in a long line against the far wall where computers are stationed. He moves quickly through the massive and long room and comes to a set of swinging double doors. He listens a moment before pushing one open.

The lighting in the adjacent hallway is much better because of the long row of windows. Some of them have been busted out, broken with chairs and one with a table which is still suspended half in and half out of the broken frame. He scans left and right, and then heads right. He ends up in the cafeteria next where he doesn't find much. A few canned goods lying on the kitchen floor get stowed away in his pack. Then he swings the M16 around front again and moves out. He jogs to save the last vestiges of daylight so that he's not forced to move around in the pitch dark. From time to time, a ping or ding or pop will echo through the long hallways, but he doesn't run into anyone.

When it becomes nearly dark, he leaves the main buildings and heads into the dormitories. The sights and smells that greet him there are not so pleasant. The building has been ransacked. There are two dead women, likely students by the appearance of their dust-covered clothing, lying prone and decomposed near the elevator. According to the elevator floor indicator, there are six levels in this building. Damn Dog growls low in her throat as the hair on her neck comes up. Cory swings left then right and creeps along the wall silently. The dog is on his heels.

Finally, he hears whatever the dog had. There is a rustling in an area off to their right in the far distance. A few moments later a person who resembles a caricature of a former homeless man appears around the corner.

Cory calls out, startling the other man, "Stop there! Don't move!"

The man, a man that he now realizes, is an old man who walks in a semi-stooped over position, instantly juts his arms skyward in complacent surrender.

"Don't shoot, sir," he pleads.

Cory closes in on him and immediately lowers his rifle. This man isn't a threat to anyone. He must be over eighty years old, his black skin covered in dark moles, his unkempt, curly hair completely white. His flannel shirt is holey. The pants he wears look as nice as his shirt. Cory's not even sure why he's wearing such hot clothing in the summertime, but perhaps it's all he has.

"You with others?" Cory prods.

"Nope, not me," the man replies cheerily and smiles, revealing a lot of missing teeth. "I'm a loner. Been a loner my whole life. Married a woman once, but that didn't work out."

Cory furrows his brow at this man.

"She up'd and run off with my cousin. That's ok, though. They deserved each other," he says with a crooked smile. "Left our boy with me to raise. And that was fine with me. Better than being raised by her."

Cory has no idea why this old man is telling him his life story. He has no interest in this.

"So I moved out to the woods into my pappy's hunting lodge and didn't ever come back out. Raised my boy out there. Worked for me. I come to town 'bout once a month or so for supplies. Town's kinda' changed a bit, but…"

"Where were you going in town?" Cory interrupts.

"Oh, I just come here every now and again," the old codger starts slowly.

Slowly seems to be his only speed. Cory is impatient to be done with him.

"What for?"

"I got a still, you know, for makin' hooch," he discloses behind his cupped hand as if he's worried someone will overhear him.

"Hooch? What the hell's hooch?" Cory asks.

"You ain't never had hooch?" he asks.

Cory shakes his head, peers over his left shoulder just once to ascertain they are still alone, and then turns back to the man.

"It's moonshine, son," the hooch maker says. "It'll put some hair on your chest."

Cory glances around, walks forward and checks the area while replying, "You obviously haven't seen my chest."

Hooch maker chuckles bawdily.

"I'm done here," the other man says. "Wanna' come back to my place in the woods? I've got a batch waitin' for us there."

"No thanks," Cory says with a grimace and makes eye contact with the man. He has cloudy brown eyes as if cataracts have taken over. "I'm not sticking around. Just moving through."

"Yeah, that's smart. That's real smart, young man," hooch maker says. "Not safe out there no more for stickin' around and settin' down roots. There's some real crazies out there."

Cory would like to say that there are crazies in here, too, but he holds his tongue. He tries to be courteous toward his elders. His dad had raised him to respect his elders, but this guy is a little off.

"Yeah, be careful," Cory tells him as he keeps moving farther into the building and then out the back door. The dog and the old man are right behind him.

"You remind me a little of my boy," the hooch maker says.

"Yeah?" Cory asks but doesn't really care. He kicks in the back door of the next building. He's found the main cafeteria.

"Yessiree," he confirms. "He was a big kid like you. Strong as a bull, too."

Cory would like to tell him to shut his yap so that they don't take a bullet from anyone who might be on this campus. His dog trots ahead of him, obviously not feeling any possible fear or trepidation of separating from him. The old man just keeps shuffling along and jawing Cory's ear off. He rolls his eyes as he tries to sweep the area quietly.

"Hey, young man," the hooch maker says as he taps Cory's shoulder." Ain't nobody here. Ain't nobody been here for years, son."

"How do you know that?"

"'Cuz this is where I come to get my stuff," he says as they go into the kitchen. "See? This is where I come once a month now. Not the town, that place dried up a long time ago. But nobody comes here no more, so I can sneak right in and take what I need."

"Like what?"

The old man pushes open a door in the kitchen and says, "Anything I need. See, kid?"

Cory is astonished at the amount of canned goods and bags of dried foods like beans and sacks of rice that are still in the pantry of the college's kitchen. Why hadn't people thought to come here to raid for goods? Well, anyone other than the hooch maker. He also ponders why rodents haven't destroyed and eaten the food in the sacks. Apparently they've snacked on enough dead bodies to forego a meal of beans.

He nods slowly and tosses some ideas around in his mind. It doesn't take long to come to a conclusion. There are two options in this scenario, but he's not completely lost his sense of humanity. He's not going to take any of this, nor is he going to tell the armory group about this place. Someday people will think to come back onto this campus to search for food or shelter. Until then he'll leave this stash to the old hooch maker. They have enough food with the garden and hunting to last a while. He's not too worried about it for now.

"Come on, kid," the other man says. "I'll make us some dinner out at my cabin. You can stay there for a few days if you like."

"Where's your son you were talking about? Is he out there?"

"You ain't too trustin' of people, are ya'?" he asks with a devilish grin and adds canned meat and another can of potatoes to his threadbare sack. "My boy was like that, too. Nah, he ain't out at the cabin. Nope, he joined the Marines and got himself killed over there in Syria nigh on seven years ago."

When the hooch maker's eyes meet his own, Cory can see that the loss of this man's son still haunts him today. Kelly and John were also in Syria, but his brother never talks about it.

"Sorry," Cory apologizes.

"It's alright, kid," he says. "Come out and keep me company. Tell me what's been going on in the world. I ain't got no radio or television or nothin' fancy out there. Just me and my goats is all."

Cory has absolutely no desire to hang out with this guy for the evening, but he feels bad that he's alone and has been for years. He's probably not even aware of how the fall of the country happened if he has no outside communication with people. Plus he's just packed about thirty pounds of crap from the kitchen into his sack. The least Cory can do is carry the damn thing for him.

"You want any more of this shit?" Cory asks before he leaves the room.

The old man shakes his head, so they head out. Cory attaches the man's bag to his saddle and leads it instead of riding the stallion. They travel through the woods for about an hour until they come to a ravine where the hooch maker's tiny cabin is located. It's a ramshackle structure, to say the least. Cory will not spend the night. He'd already decided that, but he will keep the man company for a few hours because he seems lonely, at least long enough to explain the current events of their nation.

Upon entering the shack, Cory is greeted by the smell of something cooking that stirs his stomach into wakefulness. There is a cast iron pot on top of a wood-burning stove. The old man wasn't lying. There wasn't a soul in sight and hadn't been for the whole trek to the cabin.

They eat at a small table in the one room shack while Cory enlightens the other man on what happened in the world. Then he introduces Cory to his first sip of homemade moonshine, which burns his mouth, his throat and all the way to his gut. He's surely gonna piss fire after drinking this shit. They sit on the front porch with a single lantern glowing on the floorboards between them while sipping at the hooch.

"Got a girl, kid?"

They have not exchanged names. The older man is wise enough to realize that Cory won't be staying and that names are not necessary for an evening of companionship.

"No, none for me," Cory tells him before taking another sip. Damn. This is going to give him rot-gut. He's surprised that the hooch maker is still alive after drinking this for who knows how many years.

"Really? A good looking kid like you and no girl?"

"Nope, not lookin' for one, either," Cory admits.

"Gotta have a family," the hooch maker says. "You have to have kids so that you can pass down your legacy."

"I don't think in the current state of things that there'd be too much legacy to pass down."

"You pass down your story, who you are, who your family was," hooch maker says.

Cory thinks on this for a few moments. His legacy isn't too commendable lately. What would he tell his kids? That he spent eight months killing creeps to keep people safe from them? That he was hell bent on ridding the earth of them so that his sister didn't die in vain? The legacy that he'd pass on to future generations would be something twisted and dark, full of gory and macabre tales. Since he'd taken his first life, that of the man named Levon with the visitors' group, he's never looked back. In his mind, it was a justified killing. Every murder he's committed since then has also been justified. He has shot and killed men. He killed a woman, too. She was the evil, fucking aunt of Simon's who was going to stab his brother in the back. She got what she deserved. He's shot men, stabbed them to death, killed one with a piece of lumber when he'd dropped his rifle when he was ambushed and grabbed a broken two-by-four nearby. Cory doesn't think these are the kinds of stories one should pass on to his children. So far in his life, he has no other stories to pass on to anyone.

He takes another sip, feeling the effects of the liquor starting to work in his system. It's not such a bad feeling tonight. He doesn't want to think about his family.

"I never had much of a family, just my boy. But you've got family. I can tell," the man assumes.

"Humpf," Cory grunts.

"You better hold onto 'em," the man tells him.

It almost sounds like an order, but when Cory looks at him, his face is complacent again and smooth- minus the million wrinkles. They sit another few minutes in the dark before Cory decides to take off for the night. The man insists that he take three mason jars of moonshine with him, even says that he could use it for cleaning a wound if he needed to. Cory leaves the fresh vegetables from the garden at the armory on the man's table without him seeing. The hooch maker could use them more than him. Cory also leaves the wrapped, cooked deer meat there, as well.

    He rides back to the college, sacks out in the library on a couch. Jet and Damn Dog join him in the building, not on his sofa. He thinks they'd both like to, but there's really no room for a mangy German shepherd and an eight hundred pound stallion.

    Sleep won't come to him, even with the liquor in his system and the room slightly spinning. He rubs at Em's gold bracelet twined around the leather cord at his neck and thinks about the hooch maker's words. He's made a decision tonight. It's time to go home.

Chapter Thirty-three
Sam

"Grandpa! Grandpa!" Sam calls at the top of her lungs from his study.

She sprints down the hall, through the kitchen- startling Hannah and Sue- and jumps off the back porch. Grandpa and Simon were supposed to be herb hunting in the forest.

She was dusting his bookshelves when the radio, which usually never plays anything but the constant hum of static, actually started broadcasting a message.

"What's going on?" Reagan asks as she pulls her gelding to a halt.

Jacob rides happily behind her, and John rides beside her on his own horse. It's still relatively early in the day, not yet even noon, and they'd gone on a patrol. Derek also jogs over to hear the news.

"The radio!" Sam blurts but keeps on running. "Go listen to the radio!"

She doesn't even bother to stop and explain. They'll figure it out as soon as they get to the house. She spies Simon and Grandpa coming toward her, rounding the corner near the hog barn. She waves like a crazy woman, her ponytail bobbing around. They pick up the pace, realizing her urgency.

"Grandpa, there's a radio broadcast!" she says excitedly while also trying to catch her breath.

"Calm down, Samantha," Grandpa instructs. "Take your time, honey."

Sam takes a deep breath and says, "There's a broadcast looping over and over again on your radio. It just started a few minutes ago."

Grandpa looks for the briefest of seconds to Simon before the three of them walk briskly, or as briskly as he can walk, toward the house again. When they get to his study, everyone except for the children is crammed in there listening intently.

"…again God Bless America and…"

Derek interrupts, "This is the end of it. Just wait, it restarts, Herb. It isn't coming in too great."

Grandpa is wiping his sweaty forehead with a handkerchief as he takes a seat behind his desk and adjusts the volume to be a little louder.

"This is a message for the citizens of the United States of America. This is your President, Ezra Hofstetter…"

"That's the Vice, not the actual President," John interjects.

"Something must've happened to the President," Derek adds.

"Shh!" Sue demands.

"…there have been many changes in our government and our country since the tragic events that destroyed our coastlines and infrastructure. From what information we have been able to gather during the last four years, we are doing better than most other nations." Static interrupts the transmission, and it becomes sketchy. "…are going to need to work together to re-establish our country back to its former glory…men and women in our country with military experience or who are active-duty ….set up as temporary…"

"What the fuck?" Reagan yells. "What is he saying? Do they want you guys to come back? No way!"

Grandpa holds up his hand and says, "Let's hear the rest, dear."

"…Iowa and Oklahoma. In 2033, our country came under direct…."

This is all they get, no matter how fast Grandpa and Derek adjust and readjust the controls of the old radio.

"What's going on?" Sue asks with apprehension. "What do you think is happening? The feed wasn't any better when I came in here."

"Yeah, are they wanting the men to return to active duty status and report in somewhere? Is that what he was trying to say?" Reagan asks angrily.

"I'm not sure," Derek answers. "Kind of sounded like it. I don't know."

"Wonder what happened to the President? That guy was the Vice President," John remarks.

"He probably died," Reagan remarks coolly. Some of the family regard her as if she is being insensitive. "What? I'm just saying that he's probably dead. I mean, would it really be all that surprising? If he survived the initial catastrophes, then he could've died from disease."

"They have a bunker out in Wyoming or Colorado in a mountain, a massive structure meant to withstand anything and meant for living in for fifty years if they need to. I would've thought they would've taken him there immediately," Kelly says.

Hannah inches closer to him and leans into his side. He immediately wraps an arm around her shoulders and kisses the top of her head. Sam knows that she must be worried that someone will take Kelly away from her.

"Do you think they want us to report in somewhere?" John asks his brother.

"I don't know. That wasn't a very clear broadcast," Derek says.

"If the government's getting back on its feet, then that would be a good thing, right?" Sam asks.

Grandpa frowns and says, "Possibly, Samantha. But we don't really know for certain what's happened. Perhaps there was a coup, and the old President was overthrown. Perhaps this man is running the military or what's left of it and has turned them against the administration. We just don't know."

"Right, and if they want to take the men from the farm to go out on more peace-keeping fool's errands then that's total bullshit," Reagan states with venom.

John tries to comfort her, but she still scowls and pulls back.

"It'll be ok, babe," he says. "Either way, we'll figure it out."

"No, John, we won't! I don't want you to leave the farm. If they want military men, then they're going to want to take Simon and Cory, too. Well, just Simon now, but make no mistake that they'll want anyone with military experience to rebuild an army," Reagan argues.

Sam can tell by her eyes that Reagan is frightened. Paige mirrors the same look as soon as her brother's name is mentioned. The idea of Simon having to leave the farm makes Sam feel downright nauseous. She bites her thumbnail.

"What did he mean in 2033? What was that about?" Simon asks, changing the topic slightly.

"I heard that part before I came out," Sam offers up. Everyone turns to stare at her. "He was saying that there was a deadly virus that attacked the country. I guess it spread worldwide, too. It wiped out millions more. I don't remember what he called it. Sorry."

"That's fine, Samantha," Grandpa says gently.

Reagan asks, "Think it was the pneumonic plague?"

Grandpa shakes his head once, "I don't know. Could be. Could be something else."

Sam adds, "No, it wasn't that. It was some other thing."

"That would've been two years into it," Kelly says.

"Right, but there have been so many diseases that have spread. Remember a few years ago when we thought we were seeing a derivative of cholera at the clinic?" Simon asks.

"Right, Simon," Grandpa praises. "We just don't know unless this plays again."

"Maybe it'll play again like once a day or something," Sue suggests.

"Perhaps," Grandpa says. "Why don't we just go about our work, everyone? I'll stay in here and fiddle with this a while longer."

"Yes, sir," Derek and John echo one another.

"Simon, take Sam and maybe Paige with you to the woods to finish for me," Grandpa orders.

"Yes, sir," Simon mimics the other men.

"We'll get back to our canning," Sue says, taking Hannah by the arm.

Everyone disperses, leaving Grandpa to his peace and quiet and tinkering. Sam hopes they never get the radio broadcast to come in again. She also doesn't like what was being suggested by the new sitting President. Simon leads her and Paige to the area in the forest where he and Grandpa had left off.

They are less than a mile from home, but it feels completely desolate because of the tranquil noises of the forest. Birds chirp and flutter their tiny wings and screech to one another. The wind kicks around leaves on the trees, passing secretive whispers through their proud branches. The sound of the nearby creek gurgling lends the woods a romantic and calm atmosphere. She'd rather be riding through the forest than walking, though. His sister seems to have no problem with the exhausting hike. Paige is very athletic and has a great stamina. She even told Sam that she used to go to an indoor rock climbing facility in her college town. Sam, on the other hand, likes sitting and sketching nature, not hiking it.

"Here, Sam," Simon says as he offers her his hand.

He's acting as if she needs his help just to get down a small hill. Simon has been behaving unusually overly protective lately for some reason. Sam has reasoned it out that it is likely stemming from the attack on the farm.

"Thanks," she returns as she accepts his offer of help. "For being the middle of September, it's awfully hot."

His hand wraps around hers and then is at her elbow. Simon has long lean fingers and a very sure grip. Her skin looks so pale against his. For redheads, he and his sister are very tan. Of course, the tan that Paige sports is probably why she has splatters of freckles on her cheeks, her chest and shoulders. She's moved up ahead of them quite a distance.

"No kidding. Be careful. That's poison ivy," he points to a vine on a fallen log.

Sam just smiles at him. "I know, silly."

Simon readjusts his khaki messenger bag on his shoulder. By the end of their afternoon of foraging, he'll have filled that bag with so many different herbs, roots, plants and flowers that it will be bulging. On his other shoulder is a hunting rifle. Sam didn't feel the need for a gun today, but Simon had insisted on strapping a gun belt onto her waist and placing a .38 revolver in it. Paige is also wearing a pistol on her hip.

He squats and turns the leaf of a plant over, examining its underside. Then he rises again and declares, "Not ready yet."

"Did you guys come up with any new leads the other night?" Sam asks, then hands him a twig of wild thyme that she's located.

He shakes his head, "No, and I'm starting to think we aren't going to find these guys. They could be laying low somewhere. They could've left the state for all we know. The trail's run cold."

"Maybe it just wasn't meant to be then," she offers, trying to put a more positive spin on it. She doesn't really mind if they kill those remaining men who'd gotten away that night, but she minds every time the men leave the farm in the middle of the night to track them down. She holds up a plant she's picked, "What about this?"

"No, that's just a weed, Sam," he says with a frown. "And it may not be 'meant to be' like you said, but a lot of things in this life aren't meant to be and they still sure as heck happen."

"I know," she agrees.

"See here, honey?" he asks and pulls her closer by tugging at her hand. "This is wild oregano."

Sam squats beside him and plunks down onto her knees, oblivious of the dirt and ferns staining her bare knees. Her much smaller sack lands on the ground beside her. The white t-shirt she wears has a logo for the soft drink brand Mountain Dew on the front of it. It's at least one size too small, but she's behind on doing her laundry. There is also a dirt smudge on the hem. It doesn't take long each day for all of them to get filthy. It also doesn't take long for her feelings for Simon to bubble to the surface every day.

She's barely paying any attention to what he's saying about this herb. She could really care less anyway. He'll probably use it to compound some wretched tasting tea or something equally bad tasting. Sam looks at the long line of his smoothly shaven jaw bone. The thick arch of his brow gets studied next, followed by his wide, chiseled mouth. She runs her finger along his jaw line, startling him and causing Simon to stop talking about herbs.

"What... did I have a bug there?" he asks her.

Sam smiles widely and replies with a simple, "No."

"Why... why did you do that?" he asks.

She also notices that he'd like to get away from her. He looks ready to sprint, balancing on his haunches that way.

"I don't know. I just wanted to," Sam admits honestly. Simon's eyes dart around as if he's not sure how to respond to her.

"Um... well... don't do that, Sam," he finally says.

"Why not?" Sam asks, and before he can answer she hits him with another idea. "I'd like to sketch you. You have great bone structure, Simon."

"Oh, um... ok, thanks," he replies nervously.

"I think I'm going to," she tells him pluckily and opens her sack, pulling out the small sketch pad she has tucked away in there along with her small tin of art pencils.

"Hey, we're supposed to be out here getting medicinal herbs," he scolds.

There isn't really any true anger or discipline in his voice. His eyes dance playfully, the blue color mimicking the water of the ocean depths.

"You pick. I'll draw," she demands saucily. She gets a full-blown smile this time, his white teeth bright against his skin. "It takes longer for you to tell me that I've picked more weeds than for you to just pick the right stuff in the first place."

"Sam, come on. Draw something worthwhile at least. Not me," he pleads as he goes back to picking. "Draw some herbs or some of our finds so that we can document them."

"Quit irritating me," she quips and gets a smug look in return.

Ignoring him completely, Sam sits cross-legged right there on the forest floor and begins her drawing. In no time at all she has Simon's face sketched out and shaded in. The vantage point is from an upward side angle, focusing on his strong jawline. In the back of her mind, she is vaguely aware that Paige comes over from time to time to inquire after an herb or berry that she's picked. Sam uses her fingertip to blend in a particular area. This isn't her first sketch of Simon. It's just the first one he knows about.

She startles when he takes a knee beside her. Sam looks around with confusion, "Where's Paige?"

"She went over that hill over there to keep looking for hawthorn root for me. I sent her on a mission."

Sam smiles at him and says, "That's a hard one to find, Simon. You should've sent her to look for something easier."

"She was driving me crazy," he says with a conspiratorial grin. "Every ten seconds she brings over goldenrod or ferns or stuff I don't actually need right now."

Sam laughs, "That's not very nice, Simon."

He grins and replies, "I know. Ready to go to another area?"

"Sure," she says.

He stands and holds out a hand to her which she takes. Simon tugs her easily to her feet where she dusts off the backs of her legs and bottom, trying to remove sticks, leaves and mostly dirt. For some weird reason, Simon averts his eyes and blushes.

"Finish your picture?" he asks. "What did you end up drawing?"

He's fastening his bag and then picks up his rifle from where it had been resting against a tree. Sam is standing on a slight grade that makes her almost as tall as him.

"Wanna' see?" she asks and turns her drawing pad toward him.

He frowns hard. His mouth forms a tight, disappointed line as he scratches at the stubble on his chin. That wasn't the response she thought she'd get from him.

"Do...do you hate it?" she asks nervously.

He shakes his head slightly and tries to turn away from her, but Sam grabs his arm.

"Simon?"

"No, I don't hate it, Sam," he says, looking down at her hand on his arm. "But I don't think you've drawn me in an accurate way."

"What do you mean?" Sam inquires. "I drew you exactly the way you look, Simon."

She feels a bit affronted by his criticism. Art is hard enough to share with others without being criticized and judged harshly.

"No, you didn't, Sam," he argues softly, his usual tone. "You drew me with some kind of Greek god or superhero face. This isn't what I look like at all."

Sam snatches her drawing back angrily.

"That's not true!" she spits with accusation at him. She also removes her hand from his sinewy forearm.

"You should just stick to drawing angels and horses or something," he insults with a swipe of his hand through his auburn hair, which needs to be trimmed again already.

Sam isn't about to tell him that he just smudged his forehead with dirt.

"I don't need you to tell me what to draw, Simon," she says with fire. Then she levels him with a glare. "You should stick to herbs and plants and…and ignoring me all the time like you do nowadays!"

"What? I don't…"

She wags her finger in front of his face. "Yes, you do! Don't even try to deny that one, mister. You ignore me. You avoid me. You never want to hang out with me anymore."

"We're not kids anymore, Sam," Simon says lamely. "I can't hang out with you all day and sleep in the barn or run around here with you. I'm an adult now. I have responsibilities…."

"Oh, bullshit," she swears, using one of Reagan's favorite curses. Simon's sister also sometimes swears, although Sam knows that he doesn't like it. His dark blue eyes grow huge.

453

"Hey!" he says more loudly. "Don't talk like that. That's crude talk. You don't need to use that kind of language, young lady."

"So? You're not my boss, Simon. You're also not my big brother, either. You're supposed to be my friend."

"I know I'm not your brother or your boss. You don't have to tell me that. *I* know."

His tone is pained as if he harbors some deep secret.

"Forget it," she says, turns away and tears the picture out of her portfolio. She tosses it to the ground. "I'm going back to the house."

"Wait. Don't go, Sam," he says.

Simon snags her arm, which halts her at once. He's a lot bigger and stronger than she is, so the task is not difficult for him. Sam is not fond of new men being around her and is generally distrustful of most men. She hadn't taken too well to Gavin at first, but he'd ended up being a nice person. She trusts the men on the farm, but that's about it. Her past does not allow for youthful naivety when it comes to men. But she'd trust her life to Simon. She knows he'd never hurt her, except for, perhaps, her feelings as he has done so now.

Sam swings around to face him. She liked it better when they were eye to eye. Now she has to look up at him.

"You're very rude today. I don't want to be around you," she retorts in a huff.

"I'm sorry," Simon apologizes. "Don't be angry."

"How can I not be angry? You've insulted me, Simon!"

"I just didn't like that picture. I don't look like that, not at all."

"Yes, you do. I don't understand. It's a mirror image of you, Simon. What are you talking about?" Sam pleads. He hangs his head slightly, refusing to look at her.

"Don't build me up to be something I'm not, ok?" he asks in a desperate plea. "I'm not anything worth drawing in such a manner."

"What?" Sam asks with a frown. "You are to me."

"Don't say that, Samantha," he says.

He uses her full name when he's being superior or condescending, and he knows how much she hates that. If Grandpa wants to call her Samantha, then that's fine with her. He never uses anyone's nicknames. But Simon knows she doesn't like it when he tries to lord over her like he's so much older and wiser. He's only a year and a half older than her for goodness sake.

"You're my hero, Simon," she confesses softly. Sam lays her hand against his cheek where there is a fine stubble coming in. Sometimes in the winter he doesn't shave at all and grows a short red beard. She doesn't like the beard. It hides too much of his beautiful face and fine bone structure.

"No, I'm not," he says and turns away. "I think we both know that's not true at all."

Sam, not one to be put off by him, walks in front of Simon, which stops his retreat. How can he feel that way?

"You are," she insists.

"Don't say stuff like that. You know what I mean," he says more forcefully.

"I don't care. I still think of you as my hero, even if you refuse to think of yourself that way," Sam admits and places a hand against his chest to prevent him from going around her.

Simon grabs her shoulders and gives them an irritated squeeze. He doesn't hurt her, but Sam knows that he's becoming frustrated.

"Just stop talking like that. Stop drawing pictures of me like that. Don't ever call me your hero again, ok? We both know that I'm not. If I was any sort of hero, that… stuff never would've happened to you."

Sam flinches. She doesn't mean to, but it happens. She doesn't really like to think back to that time with the visitors.

"You did everything you could, Simon," she says softly and refuses to meet his gaze. She studies his worn out work-boots instead. He doesn't say anything more. A second later she feels him pull her in where she rests her head against his warm chest. She raises her eyes to meet his finally. "You're still my hero."

455

He smirks angrily, shakes his head and places his hot palm to her left cheek. His expression reads so much barely concealed emotion that Sam cannot tell what he's thinking.

"Sam," he whispers.

His eyes are sad and confused when they meet hers. Simon's thumb strokes over her cheekbone. She doesn't dare say what she's thinking. She's content to stand there for all eternity waiting for him to talk to her if need be. He opens his mouth to speak but shuts it again much to her disappointment.

Then he says, "You mean so much to me, but I don't want you to look up to me like that."

"Too late," she remarks with a bit of sass. "I already do and I always have."

Simon scowls. He slides his hand into the hair at the base of her neck and pulls her forehead to forehead with him. The breath of his soft sigh brushes against her nose and mouth.

"What am I supposed to do with you?" he asks rhetorically.

Sam's insides turn to mush at the husky timbre of his voice. A lock of his hair falls forward and rests against her cheek.

Paige calls loudly as she comes over the crest of the hill, "I found this bush and it had some pretty big blooms on it!"

Simon jumps away from her and lets his hand fall to his side. He goes into instant calm and in control mode. This is how he normally acts, and it completely aggravates Sam. He walks straight over to his sister and takes the plant from Paige's slim fingers all while not making eye contact with Sam.

"You have a lot there, sis," he says.

There is just the slightest touch of unsteadiness in his voice, a wavering hesitancy that he doesn't usually display. He takes the two huge bundles of plants from Paige. It isn't hawthorn, but it is apparently something he can use.

"Good find," he remarks.

Sam doesn't miss the look on Paige's face. She's looking at them both, back and forth between them suspiciously. Simon begins stuffing the leafy foliage into his bag, which is overflowing. He still won't look at her.

"I found more than that up over that ridge," Paige tells them.

Her clothing is dirty and dusty. She looks sweaty as if she's been working hard while Sam sat drawing and then arguing with Simon. It makes her feel guilty.

"I'm going to take this back and get started. We can call it a day," Simon tells them.

"Wait, I want to go back up there and get some more," Paige argues.

"This is plenty for now," Simon concludes.

"All right, fine, Mr. Bossy Pants," his sister jokes, earning her a frown of disapproval from Simon.

They walk together, talking about the family, the progress on the wall and the harvest that will start soon. Simon is distracted and not looking at her as they come down a short hill. She catches him tucking the discarded picture of himself into the front pocket of his satchel. She hides her grin from him.

Sam tilts her head back, soaking in the warm sun. It's not going to last forever, unfortunately. Soon the wet season will once again be upon them and then winter. There is so much to be done before then.

Simon's sister brings up the radio feed, "Do you think they are going to draft all able-bodied young men like you, Simon?"

He shakes his and says, "No, it's hard telling what they want. I don't see how they could enforce something like that since we're not exactly a fully functioning country anymore."

"It might help, though," Paige says. "If the military men out there come together, maybe they'd be able to get the power restored or water treatment plants back up and running."

"They wouldn't call the military in for that, sis," he informs her.

"Why not? What do you mean?" Paige asks.

"They'd use the men and women who worked for those places to restore power and water. If they are calling in the military, then they need a military for something."

Sam narrows her eyes and looks away.

457

"What do you think, Sam?" Paige asks her next.

Simon's sister has her hair in a loose braid that is untangling. Her khaki shorts were borrowed from Sue, and her brown tank top came from the tub of clothing the men recently found in a house in Sam's old neighborhood. She's so earthy and pretty. They've become such fast friends that she hopes Paige never leaves the farm or gets separated from them.

"Me?" Sam inquires. "Um, I don't know. Maybe they just need help building something."

They both look at her strangely and continue talking without asking her opinion again. Good. Let them think she doesn't know what she is talking about. Sam has no intention of telling either of them the entire message she'd heard on the radio. She's never telling anyone on the farm the entire message and why the new government really wants former enlisted personnel to show up and report in to the three new centralized military bases. She'll never tell them because the men, her new family members and adopted brothers, may decide to listen to the President's dictate and leave the farm. Later tonight when everyone goes to bed, she plans to sneak downstairs into Grandpa's office and sabotage that damn radio so it never works again.

Epilogue
Herb McClane

Not able to sleep as usual, Herb rises right before the men leave on a search mission. He plods through his dark house to the kitchen in his pajamas and house slippers, careful not to make noise and disturb the children.

"'Morning, Herb," Kelly greets him. "Did I wake you? I was trying to sneak out."

"No, no, Kelly," he answers the big man. "I couldn't sleep. Thought I'd brew some coffee. Want a thermos to take with you?"

"Is it the stuff we brought back a few weeks ago from Nashville?"

Herb turns on the lowest wattage light over the kitchen sink and fills the glass carafe with water from the tap. "Yes, it's all we have. Ran out of the good stuff."

"Think I'll have to take a hard pass on that one, Doc," Kelly jokes as he pulls on his Army issue boots and grins.

"It'll clean out your guts. That's for sure," Herb jokes as he scoops the grinds and pours them into his Bunn coffee maker.

"No thanks, I'm good. I like my guts the way they are, sir. On the inside," the other man jokes.

A moment later, Simon comes through the back door.

"Good morning, Simon," Herb acknowledges the young man.

"Oh, hey, good morning, sir," Simon says, clearly surprised to find Herb up in the middle of the night. He says to Kelly, "Think it's gonna rain."

"Should we call off the mission?" Kelly asks with a smirk as he finishes lacing his boots.

Simon's gaze jumps to Kelly's and he quickly amends his weather report with, "No, sir. Not at all. I'm ready when you are."

"Good thing, Professor," Kelly tells him.

Herb knows that Kelly was just giving Simon a hard time, but the young man is so serious and doesn't take well to sarcasm.

Kelly adds, "Gonna need you up high this morning. Got your rifle?"

"Yes, sir," Simon answers as if he's still in basic training and Kelly is his commanding officer. "Where are we headed?"

"Nashville again. Gonna go a little further this time. Heard some chatter that maybe their leader made his escape and went over that way."

"Sounds good to me," Simon replies as he packs .308 ammo into his rifle magazine.

"Your sis awake out at the cabin?" Kelly inquires after Paige.

Simon answers, "No, thank God. If she was awake, she'd be nagging me not to go."

Kelly chuckles softly, "Probably right about that. She's a firecracker, that one."

Simon snorts and says, "No kidding. Our mom used to say it was from her hair color. I don't know about that. I've got the same hair. I think it's just a woman thing."

"You're smarter than you look, Professor," Kelly jabs playfully.

"Not when it comes to women. All I know is to stay as far away from the ones on this farm as I can," Simon says on a chuckle of his own.

"Well, I'm an old dinosaur and I still don't understand them most of the time. So good luck," Herb joins in.

Kelly chuckles and grabs a carafe of milk from the fridge, pouring himself a glass before they leave.

"Don't forget your sacks," Herb tells them.

"Right," Kelly says and snatches his brown bag from the counter containing food that Hannah has packed them. "Don't wanna' piss off the wife."

"Smart man," Herb replies. "You'll do well to take notes from this man, Simon."

Simon blushes and grins uncomfortably before replying, "Don't think I need to worry about that, sir."

"Oh, you will someday, bro," Kelly teases.

The coffee starts percolating, the smell teasing Herb's senses in a comforting manner. Kelly reaches under the ceramic lid of the cake saver and snags a few of Hannah's shortbread cookies.

"Tell Hannah I had a healthy breakfast," he says with a wicked smile.

Simon takes a proffered travel mug of coffee from Herb, although he usually prefers tea. Herb figures the caffeine is good for him, will help him be more alert and on edge for whatever they will walk into this morning.

Herb replies to Kelly's request for conspiring with him, "Don't get me involved. She probably, *asleep*, knows you are eating poorly."

Kelly actually looks nervous and hesitates for a moment before stuffing the rest of the thick cookie into his mouth. "I'll take that risk."

Samantha comes into the kitchen, half asleep and still fresh faced and pretty as ever. She's wearing gray sweatpants and a black t-shirt that comes to her knees.

"Good morning, Miss Samantha," Herb greets her.

"Sam, what are you doing up so early?" Simon asks with worry creeping into his voice. "Are you ok?"

Herb smiles gently. Sam's self-appointed guardian looks distraught at her being awake in the middle of the night.

"What's going on? I just came down for some milk," she says and then looks at her feet.

"We're heading out," Simon answers her.

"Couldn't sleep, kiddo?" Kelly asks.

"I was… worried you were down here eating the rest of the cookies," she razzes Kelly, who ruffles her already tousled hair with a grin before stealing another cookie. "Where? Where are you guys going?"

Herb notes that Samantha does not attempt to pour herself milk or reach for the cookies.

"Not far," Simon says, calming her fears. "We'll be back in a few hours for morning chores."

Samantha crosses the kitchen and slides her slim arms around Simon's trim waist. He is the only one in the family with whom she behaves in this manner. He'd thought perhaps they should correct her when she does things like that, but his Maryanne had told him that it was fine. These two kids have been through the trenches of hell and back together. Who are they to dictate how they should behave?

The little waif says, "Be careful, Simon."

Simon reacts as he normally does where Samantha is concerned. He frowns and sets her away from him with a grimace.

"We will," he answers stoically. "You should go back to bed. You need your rest. We have a long day ahead of us. Clinic day, remember?"

She nods and turns away from him. She waves to Kelly before leaving. Herb worries about her. He's seen her fall into moods that she tries to hide from the rest of the family. He is certainly not a clinical psychologist, although at times he wishes he was if for no other reason than to help his own family. Samantha has never spoken to anyone in the family that he is aware of about her past. Maryanne never told him that she spoke to her about it other than that she missed her family. Time doesn't heal all wounds. He knows this to be true. But sometimes if you're lucky with the passage of time the wounds can be skim-coated over with a thin plaster of loving hearts, kind hands and good memories.

Kelly was right. The coffee tastes like tar. He'll take his mug to the front porch in a short while and watch the sun rise like he used to with his Maryanne. Sometimes Hannah joins him now, but he knows how difficult the past year has been on his tender Hannah. Herb just hopes the devotion and love of her daughter and Kelly will help to break the spell of gloom that life has cast upon her with the loss of her grandmother and then Emma.

"We're good to go," Kelly says, breaking Herb's train of thought. "See you in a few hours, Herb."

He nods and gives them a salute, "Watch your backs out there, boys."

"Derek's outside on patrols while John sleeps, so you're covered," Kelly tells him as he goes out the back door.

"Ok, Kelly. We'll be just fine. Don't worry about us here," Herb tells him to allay his fears. He knows how much Kelly worries about Hannah and little Mary. He gets a firm nod from the big man before he and Simon leave.

Herb turns off the light in the kitchen and carries his mug back toward his office where he sleeps most nights on the leather sofa there. He's been working on compounding a new antibiotic. With their supplies being depleted every week, he needs to work harder on making penicillin and antibiotics from scratch.

As he turns the corner in the dark house, he catches the slim shadow of Samantha tiptoeing from his study. She sprints across the hall and up the long staircase that leads back to her room. Her behavior in the kitchen and now this piques his curiosity. What was she doing in his office? Why had she lied in the kitchen about wanting milk in the middle of the night only to not pour herself a glass?

Once he is in his office, Herb closes the door and turns on a low wattage light on his desk where he places his mug of strong coffee. He looks around the familiar room. Nothing seems out of sorts, misplaced or missing. Her behavior was peculiar, though.

He opens a window to let in a breeze, sits behind his desk and gets to work, forgetting Samantha and her odd nocturnal roaming. After making notes for a short while, Herb finally realizes what's wrong. The constant humming static of the radio behind him on the shelf has ceased. The silence and absence of the white noise have triggered the answer to his question. She'd come in for the radio.

Herb swivels in his office chair, rolling over to the back shelf. He turns on the old radio again, not wanting to miss that report from the President if it should run more clearly on a repeated loop. But nothing happens. No sound emits from the speakers, not even static. Upon further inspection, Herb finds the cut wires behind the square box. She'd come into his office and cut the wires to the radio. Why would she do such a thing? He sits back and lights his pipe.

Whatever Samantha had heard before the rest of them had arrived in the office has caused her to react in an uncharacteristically deceitful manner. His first instinct is to confront her later when she wakes for the day at her normal time. Then, after more thought and consideration, Herb sips at his coffee sludge as he stares at the broken radio. He should've added some cream to his tar coffee. Maryanne would've thought to do so. He hadn't realized until she'd passed just how much he'd come to rely on her for little things like that.

Perhaps young Samantha has done them all a favor. Perhaps whatever she'd heard had been so detrimental that she's trying to protect them.

After a while, Herb goes back to his studies, making notes, studying the compounding of herbs and purposely not thinking about the radio and what would've caused her to do such a thing. He turns back to the radio, lifts it from its shelf. There is now a clean spot with no dust in the unmistakable shape of the obviously missing radio. Herb places it in a cupboard where it won't be seen again. He re-lights his pipe, hums a ditty that his Maryanne used to favor and resumes his research.

Character Sheet:

The McClane Family

- Herb McClane, "Doc" to his patients and grandfather to the kids

- Maryanne McClane, Doc's wife and grandmother to the kids

- Sue (McClane) Harrison, married to Derek and the oldest of the three granddaughters

- Reagan (McClane) Harrison, married to John and the middle child of the granddaughters

- Hannah (McClane) Alexander, married to Kelly, and the youngest of the three granddaughters, also she is blind

- John Harrison, Special Forces, married to Reagan and brother to Derek
- Derek Harrison, Special Forces and highest ranking soldier on the farm, older brother of John and married to Sue
- Kelly Alexander, Special Forces, married to Hannah

Kids on the farm:
-Mary Alexander, 2-year-old daughter of Kelly and Hannah
-Sue and Derek's kids: Justin, Arianna, Isaac
-Jacob Harrison, adopted son of John and Reagan
-Huntley, orphan taken in by the McClane family who lost his twin brother to sickness

- Simon Murphy, orphan teen taken in by the McClane family
- Samantha Patterson, "Sam," orphan taken in by the McClane family when she was 15
- Paige Murphy, sister of Simon who makes first appearance in book 4

Paige's travel mates: Gavin, Talia Jones and Maddie (little girl)

Reynolds Family, neighbors and allies to the McClanes
- Wayne, oldest brother and patriarch of his family
- Chet, Wayne's younger brother, unmarried
- Bertie, wife of Wayne and has a daughter named Sarah

Johnson Family, neighbors and allies to the McClanes
- Ryan, father and grandfather to his clan, Doc's age
- Zach, son of Ryan, middle-aged, has children and a wife
- Evie, daughter of Ryan, widowed

Made in the USA
Middletown, DE
26 July 2015